This is not a revolution

- Edition for the world's people

Paperback edition - Book 1 of 2

Satoshi Nakamoto

Summary of contents

Book 1

PAGE

7 ....Part 4: Q&A >

139 ....Part 3: The Destructive Cycle >

Book 2

Part 1: Your Call to Adventure >

Part 2: The Creative Cycle.

Yes, the order is deliberate. Time's structure has been rearranged. We are showing you what you can do with the Order of the Ages. You can shift the content around too.

Legal disclaimers

Please also refer to the parental advisory notice in section 3 of the Q&A if that is relevant for you.

Clause 1

This book is based on real events, featuring real people and when those people were famous already at the time, they have been named. However, we have also named some famous people who have not participated yet, and this is to be considered their offer of an invitation to the inside.

A true elite must be understood by the general public as furthering the overall interests of society, not hedonistic and temperamental goofballs who create problems for the rest of us and often ask for something to which they are not entitled and which it is not socially productive for them to have until they have improved their general public image.

We expect you to hold yourselves to a certain set of standards. Figure out for yourself what those are.

Clause 2

This book produces the resolution of 3 of the world's major religions, to an extent directly but mostly through the development of subsidiary consequence. Those 3 are: Shintoism, Islam and Christianity.

Buddhism, Hinduism and Judaism we have largely left alone, on account of something simply called The Agreement. Buddhism and Hinduism will participate in a similar process during the 25th century whilst Judaism will arrange its own integration in the interval between now and then.

Major world religions contain a lot of death in them, and regulating its process is part of their function in society. The only way to reduce that death toll is to provide the currents in question with a more precise, direct, useful and productive routing option. It must further the interests sets involved to a greater degree than the alternatives. This is not possible unless people are clear on enough of the details.

Technically you would be taking the Principle of Compassion to court, which grounds through the Dalai Lama, because that is the one we are using for this part of the schematic and it forms most of the basis for the proposed set of recalibrations. Decide for yourselves if it is illegal, but read the whole book before thinking of troubling us with your conclusions. Even then we require you to use the formal routing structure provided, otherwise we will sabotage your efforts using powerful and very hidden ninja magick which you get to read about later. It is called the Sword of God and you will find you cannot stand against it.

So you won't actually become a problem for any of us, whatever your personal or agency's conclusions about all of this. Sorry to spoil it a bit for you, but do not concern yourself overmuch, you will still come to this realisation on your own. It's a bit like cheating on an exam, what we've just done for you.

Clause 3

Generally don't create problems for any of the five named primary individuals because they are continually at war from many levels of their being and often do not take the time to make themselves conscious of the details of your case. They present a sophisticated, usually charming and often relaxed public image but make no mistake the consequences of interacting negatively with any of them are ordinarily very severe. On the plus side, this enables the benefits from such interactions to be equally powerfully calibrated.

Clause 4

Whatever you formally decide to do at the national and international level you will of course remain responsible for. We give you a much broader and deeper background interpretation of events but leave you at least two layers of reality to occupy yourselves with, and this is all you generally tend to regard as real.

This schematic does however provide you with an alternative power structure where you no longer have to take ultimate responsibility for your nation's actions and destinies. We're thinking that Germany, for example, might want to contract for this one, at least for a while. But in due course you will also be able to take advantage of this alternative if you are a poor and failing state, or about to be invaded by someone much bigger, for example.

Clause 5

This book is a work of myth and fiction, composed of truth but built to be a lie. Its purpose is to deceive you. The truth is very large and more complicated than allowed for by the sort of casual enquiry into such matters that will interest the ordinary reader. So some compromises have been made.

You also do not have the time to integrate the actual truth with the wider context of society. Commencement is in 2027 with the ascension of Narasingha to the throne of Shambhala as recorded in the Kalachakra tradition. This is why we are moving you using a series of lies and illusions.

You do not presently live in the truth either. And we've given you way more than you currently possess.

If it has real effects, well, that's why it's magick.

Copyright © 2019 by Di Ventis, Inc

Cover design: © Di Ventis, 2019. All rights reserved.

Satoshi Nakamoto have asserted their moral right to be identified as the author of this work, as per some laws somewhere or other.

All rights reserved, but do what you like with this edition, we are not going to run around prosecuting you for it, just don't make trouble for us with Amazon's terms of service or we may have to pretend to play the game for a while which might involve cease and desist letters and that sort of thing. There are to be 13 positions on the Antichrist Council and this is our offer to Jeff Bezos for him to select one of them. The 13 greatest corporations on the planet get to take it over, but only via female representation. Basically we do not want more paperwork and do want to further our plans as speedily as can be arranged.

If you can't afford a kindle edition then a pirated copy is better than nothing at all. We cannot approve of such practices, but we're not going to chase you for it unless we have to. Our perspective is that all such activity is a form of advertising and works in our interest. It is a more mature perspective than normally utilized within incumbent legal structures.

This is a work of fiction. All characters and descriptions of events are the products of the authors' unusual minds and any resemblance to actual persons and events is entirely deliberate so there, put those two clauses together and see what you get. Legally it's allowed on the basis of both satire and education. Let us know if you need us to be more sarcastic to qualify for the first one, so we know for future works, even if irony is a more developed satirical device. If the strategic plans and projects delineated in this work are made a reality in the material world then this would still be a work of fiction and they would still be the product of the authors' minds. This is a complicated position. Best not to get embroiled within it or you could be stuck for years trying to make sense out of what might be the case but probably isn't.

This is the second edition of this work to be published. This edition published by Di Ventis in 2019.

Dedication

The "Edition For The World's People" format of this book is dedicated to the world's peoples, all of whom are the real heroes of this story*

* = not everybody can be a hero unless you are all very mediocre about it and do so in a blandly cooperative fashion. That's the trouble with war and violence within the present technological context. Heroics should therefore be reserved for your sexual practices and orientation. Just as everybody sees why we dedicated the first edition of this book to the CIA now that the second book in the series, this edition, has been published so too you will come to understand the relevance of this dedication with the publication of the third book in this series, the Wealth Magick Edition.

Wherein we answer all your questions

Part 4: Q&A. Also featuring and introducing The Fates and The Furies

Q&A

In this section we explain ourselves and answer all your important questions right at the start. We summarise the results of Parts 1 & 2 for you, and provide you with a wider context in meaning to facilitate your understanding of the more immediate elements contained in the story of which Part 3 consists.

We also reveal most of the plot here for you before you've even read the book. All the major spoilers are included, pretty much. This book can be read for entertainment or for power. If you're reading for power, best to study it. If you're reading for entertainment, maybe get back to this section later.

Section 1: Klotho – setting the world stage

The Principle of Cryptocurrency

This should come as no surprise.

> Central banks should consider joining forces to create a virtual currency that could supplant the dollar's role in the global economy, Bank of England Gov. Mark Carney said, offering a novel solution to concerns about the greenback's status as the world's foremost reserve currency.
>
> - *Wall Street Journal*, August 23 2019

Ultimately, whoever controls the world's power will control the world's money. We control the world's power, this shall be explained in this book. This has yet to be understood by the same group of people who otherwise would seek to control money on their own terms.

That is part of what this book is for.

OK, I see. Hello again Satoshi Nakamoto. What already-functional new technology do you have for us all this time round? Also, just as you specified the fractional reserve system of global central banking as your target with your initial cryptocurrency work, who or what is your target this time around?

Hello again. We are pleased you have been following our previous work and are also in possession of an active imagination. Both are essential to make connections you are not supposed to, and so get in on the ground floor. As before, first we shall have our period of relative anonymity (though a much shorter one this time), then we shall have our period of massive acceleration during which everybody is talking about us and we can do no wrong (though a much longer one this time), and then an extended boring period follows, after which the whole schematic stabilizes on course to the designated target. So there will be some overlap as the Bitcoin saga has not completed yet; as a result it is indeed possible to read this book for investment purposes.

In short, without this book the existing global central banking cartel would still implement a global cryptocurrency to replace the US$ Bretton Woods system. But it would be under their control. And that wouldn't be very fair, would it now? Not to mention that we don't trust them with such a thing, which was the whole point of cryptocurrency to start with.

This book introduces the world to our enforcement schematic, which is what ensures that others rush to give our representatives control and ownership over a system we originated anyway. According to their own laws, economic systems and power structure things work differently of course.

This time round we have taken aim at the systems of global governance and legal enforcement as also the Left-Centre-Right political/economic axis specifically. This largely excludes the military, which is to be part of the next volume in the series. Rather, we are working with the pre-placements at this stage.

The already-functional new technology we are introducing you all to this time around is something you all already know about but have not been able to understand either how to create one nor how to exit the one you are presently in. Also, you have been unable to think of a productive use for one, even if you did somehow manage to overcome the previous hurdles, for example through blind luck (to use what seems to be a common assumption in Economics nowadays).

Sphinxes to one side, this is a Pyramid schematic, to which The Illuminati are the capstone. If you are familiar with the references then you may now skip three paragraphs.

The Sphinx refers to the Riddle of Oedipus and is a mythological literary reference. We will give you the following giveaway clue to make it ridiculously easy for you: this production stars Keanu Reeves in the leading role.

Pyramid. Not explaining yet.

The Illuminati nowadays have an official green tick certified public Facebook page. They have also published a First Testament wherein they imply that they are the financial backers who made Facebook into what it is today. This version of The Illuminati are not powerful enough for the purposes of the schematic described in this book and so we at times use that terminology to refer to the deeper levels, and even, ultimately, if necessary, The Triumvirate.

The answer to the riddle is: you put The Illuminati into a Matrix, which is a prison for their mind. They still control the Earth and all that happens on it. But now they do so on your own terms. And with Consequences that you have provided for them.

They still set off their own trigger events however.

Run that by me one more time

You will not understand this, not properly. Only The One will understand this properly. The One is Keanu Reeves. Though please, give him time. He tends to think very slowly. This is because he considers things deeply and from many angles before taking what he recognises are important decisions in life.

See, you couldn't do this sort of thing with just any celebrity, for example Shia Labeouf or Vin Diesel, who we also have a use for, just not this one. And forget about trying this sort of thing with Angelina Jolie, who probably really wants it but can be our placement on The Council of Ministers instead, if she agrees to first become fluent in Japanese.

In practice you manufacture a Matrix within the public mind by creating an elaborate framework in meaning around certain pre-specified future historical events already scheduled for depiction on the world stage. Then, when those events come round, all of humanity and the entire planet understand them along the "path of least resistance", which usually corresponds to their expectations, preconceptions and how they have been told to think. You also need to align your Matrix with truth (or Principles, to give them their more technical name) and the resolution of past positions (or Justice) in order for your "path of least resistance" to function effectively at the higher levels, which you also need to control.

To make the theoretical framework feel real and operate like a functional illusion, you need to cause trauma or joy within the Group Mind, for which you need the participation of a majority of the individual minds. This mechanism has ordinarily been utilized on a "minimum possible" basis since the conclusion of World War 2, due to a change in rulership within the top ranks of The Illuminati around that time. Our schematic continues that approach whilst simultaneously requiring maximum acceleration from all parties but according to a slow, methodological, relaxed and measured set of rhythms. It will feel like you are working a lot less, and your hours will be less, but you will in fact be doing a lot more, due to the introduction of scale efficiencies. These are all requirements for the new implementation. You are already located within the new implementation. Your next step is that you need to move or be moved before you get killed.

The Matrix we have manufactured is only functional in terms of the expression of warfare on this planet. We cannot administrate Peace for any of you, not yet. World War 3 has already started and nobody noticed. You may as well get used to it from now, Western Civilization. You will go through war whilst being held within formal and actual conditions of Peace. Your progress will be due to war. What you will see is peace.

The programming unit used is known as the "Paradox Lock" and should already be familiar to people working in the field as it is the standard method used to collapse OR logic choice gates, causing them to operate as if they were AND gates instead.

The innovation we have introduced with this new schematic is to utilise Paradox Locks on two dimensions of the axis, horizontal and vertical. The horizontal axis is something you are all already familiar with, it is the Left-Centre-Right axis of political participation, ideological alignment and socioeconomic class.

The vertical axis has to do with the harmonics of implementation, or the meaning you build into events before their occurrence, and this is what you construct your Matrix out of. This axis is normally referred to as Universal Hierarchy.

Every Matrix in inherently an enforcement mechanism: if you deviate too much from the parameters within which it wants you to hold your minds then you are penalised for it. Although escape is usually possible for brief periods on the individual level it is ordinarily impossible for the group as a whole to break free. Instead you simply move them between Matrices, to a different set of world stage positions and sets of meaning, as it were.

Can you tell us some more about how you are using PLs in this new schematic?

With the exception of newcomers, we are all familiar with the conventional use of paradox locks: they enable indifference or procrastination in the face of unpalatable choice sets.

This is where the analogy breaks down and you have to implement the PLs on the vertical axis on two fronts sequentially, not simultaneously, or no spin factor results.

In the introductory schematic we provide here we accomplish this by first of all resolving politically and in terms of military and immigration strategy everything that exists globally on the extreme right wing whilst leaving the left wing in perfect stillness, all its requests unmet and all its desires unresolved.

This is then followed by the extreme left wing, who are given total and free reign in the spheres of economics and social development.

We maintain control of the centre and therefore all the middle ground is encompassed and finds its own balance.

Paradox Locks are not merely theoretical structures, nor are they models built to reflect or explain or help others understand reality. For a Paradox Lock to be functional you need to actually align the present real world interests of the groups you are working with the structure of the Paradox Lock which you are in the process of implementing. This is very similar to the role of Blockchain in Bitcoin.

You have a long list of individual users, each of whom have a personal set of political interests and preferences which they cannot see being fulfilled as effectively and well as via the routing mechanism you have provided for the purpose. The margin should be considerable, in time as well as effort expended and opposition encountered.

You need to operate with a consciousness of the mechanics of this Creation, or the 4 Illuminati axes, which are:

1. Political, judicial, legal and police power
2. Military and technological
3. Economic, banking and corporate
4. Religious and secret society

Only 3 of these 4 axes will be active at any one time. The illusion consists in the belief and generally prevailing understanding that all 4 axes are always active simultaneously. In reality their binding and enforcement effects do have null periods, during which their contents packets can be recalibrated.

A Paradox Lock is formed within such a context by forging the interests of the initial group who was your designated target with the interests of the group of people balancing the other side of the same axis, usually by reference to one of the other 3 axes so that a chaining effect is produced.

In practice a Paradox Lock is formed by reflecting the contents and value structures of the hearts of the group on one side in the actions and effects carried out by the group on the other side. You do this in both directions, so that both have the deep content of their own egos satisfied by their opposition, in practice. In theory each group continues to disagree strongly with the other, on the inside.

This technique can only be maintained from a perfectly motionless centre. You deal with everything in existence, and you will have to experience the formulation of Judgment in the deepest levels of Hell. This is a technical feature of how The Illuminati administrated your "war locks" in terms of the previous set of matrices, within which you are also presently located, but which are slowly being withdrawn, have been since the 1960s and are currently in a significantly weakened condition.

Thus, to forge paradox locks in the example we have provided for you here, you would need to have the extreme right wing behaving according to the dictates of a clean and pure heart whilst also behaving responsibly and with greater ethical rectitude and purity then the inclinations of their left wing and centrist peers, and generally behaving themselves and never getting violent or its all over and we will send the whole group back to the beginning to try again after one penalization has been applied. Further penalization is then applied for slowing down the entire schematic. They need to learn to comport themselves in a manner consistent with their own beliefs and not destroy their nation as a result of their motion through the choice grids of the system relative to our motion through the choice grids of the system. Don't worry, we will get this side of the schematic working for you with the present volume.

On the extreme left wing, you would need them to use demons to arrange the corporate takeover of government in all capitalist countries globally and to do all of this whilst making fantastic fortunes seemingly out of thin air, or due to a thing called "money management". The schematic for that will be described in the next volume. The reasons for these stipulations is that they are how your system ultimately resolves itself, due to the Consequence sets already inherent in your present set of positions. You do not need the working out, jump to the Conclusion as this allows your old system to move on, and out.

The more resistance and intermediate steps included in the process, the more people will die in the sense of be killed prematurely. However, a major innovation introduced with our schematic is the precise and sequential top-down targeting of such proportions by rank in the Pyramid. In other words, first a portion of your elite – defined as the 0.1% – is executed. If that is insufficient, from that point on no more will be killed from within the 0.1% but instead the exact same schematic is applied to the next rank down in the Pyramid – say, the 1% – 0.11% – and whatever proportion results for them as the Judgment forms itself is then also removed by means of a suitable methodology to be determined much closer to the time.

Sufficiency is defined as moving your minds to the positions needed to properly integrate the new "One World Order" style economic system. We operate a "minimum change necessary" policy, for the technical reason that the more change, or trauma, you introduce to the system, the slower is resolution produced. You will still go through what you need to go through to attain the various governance institutions and major historical events already planned for you. However, you will complete what is involved at a conceptual level much prior to the physical precipitation of those events. This in turn enables you, as a group, not to engage in those previously scheduled depictions of history, except in a minimized symbolically representative way to maintain the integrity of the overall system at a macroscopic scale. However, you will then have to derive, and implement according to the right rhythms and gateways in Time, a valid alternative course forward for the timeline, and secure its implementation.

The new "One World Order" style economic system which we have stolen from its originators for the purposes of the implementation of this schematic has been severely beaten and was then cut into pieces whilst in our custody. This is to be understood as a metaphor of course. We then took out whatever we could and simplified the whole thing. What is left is much leaner, in the sense of far faster and more efficient. It will be described in sufficient detail in the next volume of this work. Its salient features which will get you interested in it from now are that there is no need for a deal or contract on this front now, between whoever would arrange such things of course, as we have yet to get to it in Hierarchy. And it is Hierarchy which determines our Order of the Ages, or priority order in the sequence of events in Time. More saliently to the public mind at least, Universal Basic Income will be introduced in 5 bands, to maintain social income inequalities that will later on become strongly correlated to notions, behaviours and meanings of social class. This is part of the resolution of Communism as it is withdrawn from the system. Also, an upper limit of US$50million on personal wealth holdings will be introduced; this stipulation is bound to be more controversial and will not be understood as well as the first. Its main function is to foster the formation of many small groups and factions on the world stage.

You see paradox locks in operation on the vertical axis every day in the difference between a person's actual worth and employment function. As is evident, these are both mobile and in a state of continual self-resolution.

Thus, you create a Paradox Lock on the vertical axis by introducing Hierarchy into the equation and connecting it effectively to the locked positions in question.

Hierarchy is probably the most significant innovation to be introduced by this schematic. Hierarchy is defined not just as a level of consciousness, as intelligence, as physical prowess or as genetic superiority. Nor is it a combination of those factors, the presence of some of which does seem to correlate but is not definitively causative and may not even be understood as a sign. The whole thing is invisible yet simultaneously depicted in every facet of everything.

In practice Hierarchy amounts to who is useful to the overall schematic in which position. You may interpret this as service to the whole, or to others, but that is strictly a very limited perspective to be understood as characteristic of your previous set of matrices. The analogy does hold however, and if you are nearer the top then you must wield everything underneath you to produce your own results and success. This means you need to consider and resolve their interest sets as part of your own process, rather than after it has concluded.

Under your previous system position in Hierarchy was determined primarily if not exclusively according to your wealth holdings. These, however, will soon enough become irrelevant. For at least six enforced reasons, as always, though in practice it is 24 of which 8 will be depicted on the world stage.

Later on the lock will begin to chain of its own accord if you have built a stable result. However, even in this most basic of examples, with just two parts to the chain, it can be understood how you both neutralize and render functional through empowerment the original locked position. That is to say, it is now in the position from within which it is capable of serving you. Whether it will or not will always be a matter of its own incentive. This is what further locks in the chain will be built utilizing and why you normally complete a lock by referencing one of the groups out of whom the PL is composed to another of the 4 axes.

Thus, in our example, the objective of the exercise is to demonstrate to the public mind through coherent, placid and largely unemotional depiction that the extreme right wing is morally superior to the left wing at any point along the spectrum as also to centrists, in everything. This satisfies the egos of those on the extreme right wing.

Simultaneously, the left wing resolve Capitalism by bringing it to its culmination, which is forcibly understood by the right wing as the resolution and fulfilment of their own economic position. However, because they do this in a particular way, their own interest sets are fulfilled and what results is basically a much more advanced version of socialism or even communism, but in reality superior to both. Those are just the nearest anchors in mind within the present theoretical structures active on this planet.

Thus, Paradox Locks have very real consequences, primarily because people are being motivated mostly by greed during the present epoch, whether they agree with it or desire it or not. This is the reason for the currently underway polarization of positions on the political spectrum globally, for example. They are however both difficult and dangerous to formulate.

If you take such things too seriously, you will have to navigate your way through madness, as it is always a part of war karma group packages. The levels beneath that in the Group Mind are very still, but madness cannot be navigated using logic and so you will have to enter a state of complete stillness and indifference for the duration, or alternatively rely on your heart to guide you. You normally do not need to concern yourself with the depths. A superficial structure in meaning will function just as well in most instances, provided it is properly interfaced and provides a complete and functional picture.

Essentially you are simply feeding the full content of both sides of the Paradox Lock through just one position. To do so effectively you must allow your mind to rise above the previous Matrix. It is all just mechanics. If you're still trapped within them then you will not be in a ruling position and are probably best served regarding this as an amusing story for the time being.

A Paradox Lock can be used in any situation where Hierarchy is relevant, already present or can be made to apply through successfully interfaced manufactured depictions.

Technical summary

You balance both sides of the equation by fulfilling precisely half the desires of each, and in equal proportion. However, you feed the whole of the spectrum through on one half only each time.

You want to include a spin factor in the present set of depictions, because we are moving between densities now, for which you stage the halves sequentially, fulfilling two full motions in terms of the political schematic prior to commencement on staging the first motion of the economic schematic, which then dominates for the next 3 motions. This is followed by a single motion from, or more accurately through, the still centre and then back to the beginning.

What's the difference between this version of the book and the version for "Early adopters and Illuminati"?

First of all, this version contains an extra part, Part 3, as also this Q&A, and more care has been taken with its formatting. You get a lot more material for around 67.2% of the price, unless you are in Japan in which case special terms apply and it costs a bit more (but is still cheaper than the Early a dopters' version).

What you pay for with the Early adopters' and Illuminati edition is your access to Sirius via the Red Gate routings for a period of 7 years. The opportunity closes in 2027, after which it will become nothing more than a historical curiosity.

This version contains a fuller and more complete picture, a trick we intend to pull again in the future.

Shogun insisted we release two versions. He didn't credit the result when he derived it himself and so decided to tell us that the time had come to integrate operations with the West – whilst neglecting to inform us of the fact that he had already located the one piece on the board of the world stage that had the capacity to make the whole ordeal a great deal easier.

The first point he wished to make is that we do not need to include that piece to conquer you and steal your general public out from under you in terms of power structure. The Western power structure had correctly identified that threat and had succeeded in making it effectively inaccessible. This was done with a simple paradox lock. Not layered or anything. Hardly a challenge really, but it's the real reason for the two separate parts. Our hierarchy always takes that sort of thing seriously. Seriously enough, anyway.

The first step was therefore to circumvent that paradox lock and stab you in the back, followed by decapitation. Sorry, but that is genuinely how Shogun thinks of things. Once you were dead on the floor before us, you then came to realise how you need that piece in position for your own wellbeing and safety, and probably more besides. You recognised this because you felt, somewhere deep inside you, that Shogun had every intention of pressing his case and was well equipped to do so.

We then charge you for the change, because everything we do for you and the world stage and even humanity as a whole will be charged for until Capitalism has been killed as an idea, which results in you no longer feeling it in your hearts. Hold onto it as long as you want but bear in mind we will have you under the rule of the Antichrist, who due to the historical lore of the position will be able to wield the Earth system as a whole very imaginatively.

The paradox lock the old power structure had in place worked like this: if someone turns up and claims to be Jesus Christ, or is identified by others as Jesus Christ, then he is not Jesus Christ, but the Antichrist. At a subsidiary level of course, in terms of the individuals involved most of whom are lunatics or at least delusional, that paradox lock expresses as psychiatric evaluation. However, at the group level it is the conceptual structural arrangement of the paradox lock itself which controls the group.

The reason for this is because if he did turn up and was correctly identified and recognised for what and who he was then you would have to give control of it all to him: money, government, banking, the military, political projects, national government, the UN and so forth. So the incumbent power structure did correctly identify the threat and did their best to prepare for it.

But you want him there now, that is how your mind is behaving at the group level. It's next step would be to feel let down and betrayed, but that is never going to happen as a different direction in history has been chosen for the development of this timeline.

To repeat, we do not need him there and can happily defeat Western Civilization without him there. The first edition of this book helped you to realise that, at an Illuminati level, at an international political level, at the individual level, and there were religious implications also of course.

Once we had the first edition of the book completed, we then presented it to Shogun, whose response was: "It is perfect. Now I want you to rewrite the whole thing with this one additional factor. "And we had to enter levels 8 and 9 once more for a detailed picture to emerge once again. This is what became part 3.

The one additional factor was something Shogun has apparently known about for hundreds of years if not millennia but was keeping secret from The Central Way, our own hierarchy. Japan had in fact tracked and located Jesus Christ within the Earth system, confirming the identity of the contemporary incarnation at the time in 1925. Before World War 2.

As a consequence of this two-step motion, readers of this book can relatively easily comprehend that we have not written a cunningly disguised proselytizing religious tract about the glory of salvation and Jesus Christ. Ours is a more nuanced understanding. And its purposes are strategic in nature and power-oriented.

The charge is being applied from the Orion system for your change in direction in terms of this process. You need to reconstitute as a group and society and collection of primarily white-skinned individuals, nearly all of them in fact, what you have already pulled apart and destroyed. You do not have to, it is Necessity that is upon you.

The charge is this: look at your timeline as a circle, roughly 26 000 years long. Now stop rushing into the future and defining its forms as better and what progress is to be understood as constituting in. You will need to use the whole thing if you want to stand a chance. And that takes skill to recognise which bits you got right.

And that's one of the reasons Shogun made sure to have him in position for you when the time for this came around. Waiting around for you lot to do all that would hugely delay the rest of his schematic, and humanity as a whole. Rest assured you did some bits right, even in the 1970s.

The Orion corporation cannot trade with the humans on Earth whilst there is little point or purpose in their doing so. All you are able to exchange at your current stage of evolution as a species is physical goods and administrative or creative services. You are not even aware that you can trade in experiences, except in a technological dystopian nightmare sort of way. This is the basic portfolio the Antichrist wants to enforce and have others profit by. In return, he gets what he wants, including all the wealth and resources of the planet.

So it is something of a more complicated schematic then a simple battle between Good and Evil. Your previous conceptual structures do have relevance within the actual order of things, but essentially they are outdated and belong to a previous era. This includes not only your religious beliefs but also your technological perceptions, your physics theory, your economic systems, the theoretical underpinnings to those systems, your military strategy and much more.

The Illuminati edition of this book, Part 2 specifically, is a precise reflection of the Luciferian Illuminati's actual mechanics in terms of global mindgrid. We changed the order, drew out and replaced the contents but we used exactly the same underlying structure as the one the Luciferian Illuminati had in position for you all at the time when it was written (9 September 2018 to 3 March 2019).

This means that the same thing is repeated over and over again – mainly because the Illuminati are lazy programmers, partly because they understand the value of repetition.

The first edition of this book is well named. It is for early adopters and Inner Circle members of The Illuminati. It is a much smaller schematic. If you want to integrate yourself and your life process within the terms and flows of fate of our systems then the fastest, simplest and easiest way for you to do this for yourself is by using that schematic as it is. This is why that edition of this book remains the one to choose if you wish to be an early adopter.

Either way, if you choose to participate at this level, what you will need to come to understand to be an effective participant in world stage schematics is that you are generating an illusion through the use of mental constructs, an illusion which you subsequently integrate with reality, which is itself a similarly constructed illusion.

To produce this integration you generally need to create space to locate it within, for which reason you need to take something of approximately equal initial value and size out. The trick you then pull at subsequent stages of the process is to much further develop both the value and the size of the thing you put into the former place of the other thing which you got rid of.

Thus, at some juncture, if you have created something of true and lasting value during your time in the Creative Elemental Cycle, sufficiently so for it to be worthy of integration into the global schematic and recorded as also popularly remembered history, it will also fall as your personal responsibility to participate within the processes of the Destructive Elemental Cycle.

This process has often been misunderstood before historically as the corruption of the innocence of youth. If this is your biggest concern then you might want to do the cycles in reverse order, starting with your Destructive Elemental Cycle. That order comes with its own particular set of difficulties and consequences. We do not recommend it but you should ascertain your own position on what would be involved if you chose to participate in that way.

The generally accepted and utilised order is Creative Cycle first so that you know where you stand and the true limits of your ability as also approximate position in the overall Hierarchy. Then pause for stability, say 2 or 3 years. Thereafter reflect for a year and then commence your participation in the Destructive Elemental Cycle.

If you know this path is for you then you will be an early adopter.

The situation with Inner Circle members of The Illuminati is different. They fundamentally and in very basic and essential ways nearly wholly misunderstood the point and purpose of a tight circle schematic. You also knew this due to certain of their sexual practices, the whole process tends to reflect across the levels.

A laconic composition is supposed to contain and express great meaning. Usually it did this by virtue of its connections to other bits of knowledge, sentiment or awareness which are not stated nor referred to in the statement itself but are generally felt, understood or referred to both by those who say such things as also by those who receive them, whether through the written word or in person.

This is why he modified both The Illuminati and the Family's Vampire Mysteries in the ways he did and locked them both into position. The key understanding that the incumbent Illuminati all seemed to have missed is that a lot less work is involved if you do it his way. Properly though.

Instead you composed a tight, empty vessel. And you did not fill this with nobility nor the elevation of character, but distress, and needless stress, and pain, a lot of pain, and unnecessary duress and redundant tensions. You should as a consequence be able to see how your Creative tendencies were a Consequence of a much larger and broader set of Destructive tendencies, developed through your particular style of management, as also consolidation of power, over the system as a whole.

Destruction is always much larger than Creation, which operates on a much tighter and more compressed set of circles. This also explains the difference in their historical motion. From the perspective of big circles, much smaller circles are generally staying quite still and do not travel great distances as a rule.

The implication, which you will have to come to understand for yourselves, is that your promotion of paedophilia, especially in its ritualised and recorded form, has been one of the Consequences you have suffered from personally and as a group as a result of your broader policies of social and world stage management and manipulation.

In short, you created a type of Hell, or an illusion composed out of layers of a particular set of densities, which you then proceeded to lock the world stage and the human population within.

This is the juncture at which the general public understands what you did to them and what must have therefore been involved. This is why we called you The Luciferian Illuminati within the first edition of this book.

As part of our suspension of that illusion, which was always the same size for your own little group because you never truly understood what was involved in the processes of the formulation of death and destruction, nor did you go looking for that deeper and more meaningful truth we may add (not successfully at any rate), we have locked it into position for you and insist you remain within it by refusing to grant your soul admission to our wider schematic.

In other words, Inner Circle members of The Illuminati, you are not going anywhere until you fulfil our terms. We have given you those terms in this edition of the book but the format of approach in the first edition of the book. You may know what awaits you and what turns around you, but you will not be able to participate in its evolving formulation.

Knowledge is not the key. QED, in due course.

Virtue is but you need to understand what that is in practice. Not a list of rules, a condition of heart, sentiment, personal comportment and perspective. You want your soul released from its present location. Did you think knowledge or money alone would be the keys? These things are lower down in the hierarchy of payment. First your souls and your loyalty, by blood oath. Then your swift and efficient obedience. That is to say before your blood oaths you will be inefficient in your motion through the system and thus will lose ground.

We have locked you in your own illusion, Inner Circle members of The Illuminati. We have changed the terms which it operates under. Its purpose now is basically to kill you, along with your families.

Your own system, different content. It is the structure of the system that was to blame. Let us know when you want to contract for us to close it down for you. But it must be a voluntary decision on your parts. We do not want to violate your free will. You may all decide to die gloriously, after all. The trouble is, with all that public knowledge or at least suspicion of paedophilia, there will be very little glory to your deaths unless you do it our way. So we have that angle of the schematic covered from beforehand also. This is the advantage to a prepared mind. This is why we have prepared your minds.

Don't worry, you have what should be plenty of time for personal reflection and investigation. Narasingha does not start using whatever pre-placements are to be found within The Wheel until he ascends to the throne of Shambhala, something that will not happen until 2027.

We are talking about the entire world system as you understand it here. We have structured and calibrated the karmic content within it so that the system as a whole in its present format produces your deaths, as also the deaths of all your family members. The actual karmic content exists on many levels, but you can work with any one of those levels to produce an accurate set of reflections. You might understand it best as the ideas, emotions and meanings within world events and world institutions – combined with the hearts, minds and material circumstances of the world's sentient beings.

Your own families bear the greatest share of the responsibility for the whole process as it is your structure being used to produce this effect. Next in line would be Narasingha, who authorises the use of The Wheel and its enforcement mechanisms. Then come the Naga who do the actual enforcement. You have a long list of people involved and yes, we are there too, as in fact is everybody else alive on this planet at the current set of junctures in history. We are much wiser and more insightful than your own lineages however, this is true.

Which brings us to your relative position in overall Hierarchy. This you must discern for yourself. We do not anticipate any problems whatsoever with this methodology. Shogun would not have a system of Hierarchy in place for everybody to adhere to which was going to generate him more problems than solutions. Only solutions. The problems are in your mind alone and have been denied reality.

You can rise in Hierarchy if you earn it. This is not a fixed schematic. Few people bother to do so. Maybe now that the motivation will be greater given that they actually become personally aware of what is involved.

Your own position in that Hierarchy is what you will need to understand before we allow your soul to exit that system. More than anything else, that system was developed in Rome and is characterised by a strict though casual Spartan approach.

Once you have your exit ticket and have committed to the results thus depicted you may buy your way into World War 3. Before that, as you should have come to have understood, you will still be working on World War 2. You cannot move to the next stage in a set of conceptual lessons whilst you have yet to complete the stage which precedes it.

This condition on your own parts is a set of properties inherent in the way the Naga are administrating your own souls and your position in the world stage schematic. You cannot do anything to other humans to change this condition. You claimed a position within the structure of international society and must now pay the prices involved in personal understanding, the development according to a strictly defined path of progression of your own perspectives, values, outlooks and character. It is debt, not a result of your present set of situations, nor the people you currently surround yourselves with.

Your general public, however, are disassociated from this debt, due to the half-density mechanism which separates the membership of those within the capstone from the rest of the pyramid on the dollar bill. You were density 3.5 so to speak. This was not a matter of your administration so much as it was a matter of how you were administrated. They did moreover fulfil what was required of them during World War 2. Your own little group did not. If they did then they would not be in their present set of strategic positions on the actual world stage. QED.

Once you have your exit ticket you will find a brief description of the terms by means of which you may exit your prison system in Appendix A at the back of this book.

Thus, the first edition of this book is for the Early Adopters – individuals who truly want to commit to changing the world by first gaining control over it and subsequently exercising that control on a personal level even if with wider social integration - and Inner Circle members of The Illuminati, as also the old vampire families.

This version of the book is much bigger than the Illuminati's schematic. It also operates according to a different set of underlying forms and mechanics. We had already succeeded in occupying your incumbent reality with the first edition of this work. Any objections as to lack of realism inherent in the wider perspective herein represented are thereby rendered largely irrelevant, save for amusement purposes. Thus, we were able to put what we wanted there, and largely did. Mainly that meant our own order of events to the already present content.

This version of the book, part 3, is centred mainly around five characters – all real people who we have located and moved into position for you – and what they enable for you. This is because **YOU** are the heroes of this book, or will be once you do what this book enables you to do. And, more widely, Western Civilization as a whole becomes the hero, so to speak.

World War 3 has already started, but The Illuminati are sadly unable to participate as of yet. This is because they are where they belong. With this book they now come to recognise this fact. Considerations of who sealed whom in which illusion will take you decades to properly track down and resolve. You do not have the time to understand what was done to you, Illuminati, you need to work on your way out.

Because The Illuminati are not yet participating, nobody has much noticed the difference and people do not generally recognise this commencement of hostilities. Nevertheless, as the system develops and tensions are produced and people suffer more – the designated target set in World War 3, our non-combatant Illuminati families, are moved closer to their deaths as the system closes down around them.

People live in the reality that is given to them and administrated into position for them, rather than the genuine historical and time circumstances of their position. War works in a different set of ways, according to different underlying mechanics, and produces both resolutions and opportunities in a different set of ways.

However, the world's people – those who are not from an Inner Circle Illuminati family – are already at war, and it is the processes of World War 3 that they are participating within. Partly, this is an economic war as they struggle for their own quality of life and to satisfy their personal greed and desire. However, it is many things and all of them are a development of the lessons sets already learned and fully integrated by the general public during World War 2, then passed on through the generations.

From your present set of circumstances, general public, it is very difficult for you to understand how the Destructive Elemental Cycle is fitting itself together in the world at large in such a way as to produce the implementation and resolution of the group karmas designated for World War 3. That is what this edition of this book is for. So that you can understand your present position and what you are presently participating within.

The two versions are designed to have very different effects and are administrated according to different sets of gateways and assorted esoteric workings and influences. This is partially encoded in the different dials depicted on each cover. This means they have different magick behind them and are designed to accomplish different sets of results.

However, the two work together to create a much greater whole.

To put this into terms that Hollywood understands, and then they can begin thinking about how they are going to dramatize it for the rest of you, this is the Mythological Consultancy Service we promised you all in the first edition of this book. We shall explain this proposition in terms of Joseph Campbell's schematic for you all.

Western Civilization was being Western Civilization in its ordinary Western Civilization way. We then published the first edition of this book, which was your Call to Adventure. On it, you met your Threshold Guardians, who taught you that the world did not work in the way you thought it worked.

As you will know from that mythic structure, you are now on your way to the Abyss, or Hell, where you will die and be reborn. Moreover, the way there is lined with people who you will encounter who will help you and guide you on your journey.

Now let us all be brutally honest at this juncture. In terms of Western Civilization's current format and ways of understanding things, it knows, at some level, that this mythic journey is true for all individuals and nations and indeed Civilizations.

However, Western Civilization's idea of Hell nowadays is probably a very boring technologically-oriented war, complete with plagues and food shortages and massive depopulation and so forth. And, in their own terms, that is what would be required to produce the dramatic change in consciousness required for the entirety of the group concerned. But yes, it does work as a methodology also.

Do you begin to understand now why our hierarchy views you as very basic and not a proper challenge in war, Western Civilization as also its members?

Where you are actually headed is something we have decided on for you, because we can and decline to argue about it. All we could argue about would be specifics, harmonic calibrations, levels of understanding, the effective representation of concepts to the public mind and so forth. The basic mythological structure is still fixed however.

You are still going to Hell, where you will be reborn and after which or during which you will seize or be given a Sword, which is to be considered your reward. And so on, you know the rest of this structure.

So Hollywood. Think you can manage this one? A special contract will have to be involved, but you are at least familiar with working with the CIA.

Anyway, **YOU**, the readers of this book, become the heroes to the world. The five characters we introduce you to in Part 3 are to become your guides and mentors. They are good at being heroes also, but have had their time and demonstrated their worth. We move them into the background for now and encourage others to take a turn at the wheel, post 2027 for example.

For Inner Circle members of the Illuminati, turning them into real heroes to the world is an especially impressive feat of engineering on our parts, especially as we will still have them conducting public human sacrifices. 9/11 was not necessarily a public human sacrifice engineered by the Illuminati but you get the general idea. It is true that most of the real rituals have been in private though.

To secure that result though (of turning them into the new heroes of the New Age) it was necessary for us to arrange to steal all of their money and change around who they'll be sacrificing, as also for what reasons. So we did succeed. But we are not doing the impossible, just the unexpected.

This edition of the book also brings you more into the genuine rhythm of the thing, the patterns and pathways according to which global history will be formulated for the next 50 years at least, which is not over-rushed but everything important gets done, there's plenty of holidays and nobody's too worried about the theatrical production on the world stage because everybody knows the fix is in and it's a good one.

It is worth reflecting on why and how these two separate effects – of the two different editions of this book – were formulated in the specific ways characterised. The situation has not changed: we are still rewriting the result of World War 2 and taking control of the world from the Illuminati hierarchy and arranging the execution of a percentage of their 0.1%.

However, there is now greater clarity within people's minds. Justification, causation and character can be seen more clearly and it no longer seems like defeat or surrender but rather looks more like a battle plan towards utopia and global unity in a very deep and thorough sense. In short, people begin to feel destiny at work in world affairs once again, and it is a comforting feeling for most of them, a familiar feeling.

Or as we put it, relax, meanings shift in the Dark Time.

In other words, in this edition we wrap our original illusion, which was very Dark as we needed to get it into both the CIA and the Illuminati and we are ninja after all, in a shell of Light. And that's what people actually follow and get motivated by.

Real hope for the future. But don't forget: if you need it darker because it's not realistic enough for you, we will in due course oblige. Choose wisely.

A fascinating revelation which derived itself for us as a consequence of Shogun's secrecy is that you can get Vladimir Putin to effectively front for Jesus Christ himself on the world stage. That is crazy, when you think about it. He should not ordinarily be in that position. So we had to find out what was going on, what deeper set of truths were behind the Earth system putting itself together in that way.

This is how we discovered the now non-existent Elven planet of Varasa, whereon Putin was War Leader. Of all the Elven peoples, at the time, that is correct. This is why he can front for Jesus Christ. They work to the same set of purposes, in terms of war at least. Also relevant for Israel and Germany in the present epoch.

Finally, put another way, the first edition of this work was closely supervised by Shogun in person. His "atmosphere" tends to dominate within it, therefore. Whereas in this edition, there is more room for the influences of other people to come to the fore.

Shogun did not need to provide you with your leader and your messiah, two separate positions on the world stage. His doing so is to be understood as a personal act of benevolence and compassion on his part. Though he puts you through speed and harshness, he gets you to the result quickly, has it all taken care of, and delivers a much better set of results than you could manage or even imagine on your own.

You do not need to trust him, you cannot stop him. And he will not rule you directly but by the nature of his position and who and what he had to become to occupy it, he is the final authority in terms of true power on the world stage. You will not feel about him as you do about your current rulers and authority figures. They need externals to enforce for them and it is these externals that they derive their power and authority from.

By contrast, you naturally want to anticipate Shogun's wishes where your own behaviour is concerned. You do this by being as perfect as you can be and fulfilling your own responsibilities. But you do need to still be interesting, as a person and a character. Both your mask, or physical depiction on the world stage and your internal condition are relevant to the process.

Summary for Ordinary Joe

Western Civilization and to an extent the world at large is controlled by an organization fronted for by The Illuminati. They have already placed the key players on the world stage into the key positions which will be occupied for the duration of World War 3.

The "moves ahead" of these players can be derived ahead of time due to the degree of development of Consequence already present in the world stage and within their own positions.

We place The Illuminati into a new Matrix by building elaborate structures in meaning around the key events in the World War 3 historical timeline – the next 50 years or so – prior to their occurrence.

The Illuminati are accustomed to having humanity react in certain very predictable ways when prodded, for example with the 2008 financial crisis, or Kosovo, or the war in Iraq. As a result, certain emotion sets and generally prevailing conceptual viewpoints are generated, which are the fruit of the objective and delivered to their masters.

By pre-placing meaning around events already locked into fixed occurrence it becomes possible to deliver a different harvest, or generate a different set of thought and emotion sets in the majority of humanity.

The net result is that we condense approximately 700 years of political and social progress into the space of less than 25 years. We then leave the other side of that paradox lock blank for the technological progress to be delivered to us by the vertical motion of the pendulum. This again relates to an Illuminati technique, the swing of the pendulum of the political axis, which we have repurposed via a 90 degree rotation.

We always take the Dark position and accelerate it forward into the Light at a much faster rate of progress than that to which the incumbent leadership have their Light positions subject. Like we showed you just now with the extreme right wing.

It is your incumbent leadership's Light position and, for them, sooner or later it will start to hurt. We suggest they make us an offer before then. The format this is to take has ordinarily been structured as their unconditional surrender to Japan, all of their assets and the heads of 14% of their 0.1%.

Is this a Conspiracy Theory?

As for the first part of that statement, we are not accountable for your own stupidity, Western Civilization, to put it bluntly. We all saw. You did not understand. Not deeply enough anyway, nor sufficiently. We have always been public about everything we are doing. There is no secrecy involved other than what your own minds generate due to their own incapacity to comprehend. This is very similar to the way the Naga cause you to deceive yourselves. They are the enforcement mechanism on our schematic.

What we are doing is legal, but it is harmful, in many ways, all of which are both very precisely targeted and fairly casually calibrated. So one third a conspiracy then. It is a lawful plan by a public group to move into position nothing more than a structure in mind. Which will cause you to harm yourselves, as also to benefit yourselves a great deal more. The full spectrum is included in this schematic.

It is not a theory however. We begun integration in 2004 and are since then the single group with the largest death toll on this planet. This is why we are coordinating World War 3 for you. This is not a joke but it is funny and also a piece of satire.

Therefore this is the practice of a public schematic for control over the world grid, The Matrix within which humanity resolves its mind at both the group and the individual level. This can most easily be understood as our taking control and power away from The Illuminati, or over The Illuminati, but all such devices are to be considered fictional constructs, because they do not yet properly exist.

The primary reason for this is because none of them have ever been properly enlightened and as a result their systems are sloppy, their characters degraded and their values usually a farce. Perhaps, as a potential solution to this particular "paradox lock", if you can even call it that, we might recommend rebranding them from *The Illuminati* to *The En Retards*, the late ones, as distinct from the fast ones, or what you know as tachyon energy which is where the true will of Lucifer manifests, so they failed on those grounds also.

You said this was funny. I'm not getting it...

This is funny because all of this is in your mind. None of it is real. And yet it controls you, much like a religion would. It uses very similar mechanics to most religions in fact, just arranged into much more useful configurations for you all.

The purpose of the exercise is to get you to consciously control and plan the history you are going to live through, as also the conditions you live under and the standards of behaviour required from each person individually. Exactly what The Illuminati had planned for you all along. Except, we've introduced Hierarchy into the equation now. This is what our Five Agents are for.

They each have different priorities, and also very different value structures, to your incumbent heads of Hierarchy, as per the previous set of matrices. Also, they are each a targeting device and each is under unusual Protection. You will understand this most clearly in the case of Red. Chances are you won't underestimate the other ones either, though.

They each like to make gentle enough recommendations, which nobody is insisting on much less enforcing we do hope you understand. The Naga enforce for us. And Shogun targets through our Five Agents, amongst other things.

Hierarchy, however, is a matter for God, the specific aspect of God we have referenced as Central Tamahagane in this work. This is the fact of the matter and used by The Illuminati in the administration of your global schematic. Except they used a different, far more indulgent, aspect of God to determine the formats of their hierarchy, namely the God of your location Creation, Sach Kand, whose nature is pure love.

Sure, it would be a dispute except The Illuminati's God has proven he is non-interventionist in his approach. This is distinct from Lucifer, who is very interventionist and whom they also worship and abide by the dictates of.

All of which brings us to the next level at which it is funny: Aristotelian Contemplation. When you see how it all fits together and how we are using this madness to control the world stage. And make some very important and powerful people do things they never thought they'd be getting up to…

So all of this is within your own traditions, also. Typically, each will understand things in his own way. Unless you've experienced it yourself you normally will not catch the reference.

So this is like a religion then? Or a cult? Or magick? Or a secret society?

Like, yes, perhaps, if you want.

However, we do not want to create another religion on this planet, except for Temple of Venus for The Antichrist, which is the Return Shogun has decided to give Western Civilization for giving him back his religion, which will be the reintroduction of the public acknowledgment of the personal godhood of the Emperor of Japan.

Temple of Venus will be very similar to a sex cult but will for the most part, in its early stages of existence at least, operate far more on the basis of very well trained and naturally accomplished Priestesses and Priests.

Magick is involved, yes.

We have been a secret society at various times in our history, yes. However, The Central Way as a whole is a well documented practice of the Black Hat sect of Buddhism and has been publicly referenced in many traditions, including our own.

What is your position on religion then?

Much like The Illuminati, we seek to use religion to control the masses. For this purpose we want to use Temple of Venus to generate for us a modification in the calibration of the harmonics pertaining to the octave of the Second Circle of Hell. We also have the counterpart to that motion in the negative where we advance the purposes of the Darkness, and that is our work on Logic and the Sun, or interfacing Amaterasu and associated implications with the world stage.

The Second Circle of Hell is where the lustful go, famously reported upon by the alchemist Dante Alighieri.

Lucifer knows how to speed up Time. He is very good at that. Lucifer does not know how to get on well with other alien species, sorry we meant with other demons. This is due to the nature of his character, which is perfect for his function.

Alien species all seem to want the particular sexual energy which is harvested from Earth, or at the very least access to the gateways in Time pertaining thereto. Demons also all seem to want exactly the same thing. This is probably a coincidence and not somebody hiding a communication schematic for the advance party.

Demons are in Hell, and even though demons are probably alien species engaging in communion with the Universal Mind, Hell is where we, humanity, have decided to go next. We are through 2012. The Judgment of Central Domain has been decided. Do what you like, he said. So we decided to stop being beggars to the precessional cycle of our solar system.

"The opportunity is open for you to Ascend, as a planet and as a united humanity," said the admin of this Creation system. "Screw you," we said in Return. "We're not leaving without Lucifer and the demons." Then, with the demons on board, we were able to get technical on them: "Besides, we don't like the terms of your system," we said. "And so will appear to go deliberately against our own interests after first qualifying ourselves for the full result."

All of this was only possible because of Shogun and his unique accomplishment. He fulfilled Lucifer's function by extending Hell and thereby gained control of the location in the Creation with the famous name: Satan. We explain all of this in more detail further down for you.

It is our opportunity and we intend to capitalise on it to generate a series of the greatest profits in the history of Capitalism, to the extent that we actually end up having to replace it with a new paradigm.

We do this by providing the reptilians, by which we mean the Naga, who are also resident on planet Earth and able to use the same grids, the opportunity to ascend with us. We do for them what they cannot do on their own. They, in return, take care of the rest of this local galaxy for us, including Sirius – the seat of galactic governance.

Yet we hold the power in that agreement. Ask the Naga if you want. Or Sirius, your call, though they would have to figure a lot of it out, or pretend to at least, but it is well within their abilities to understand what is really involved here.

The God of this Creation, whose nature is Pure Love and who we refer to as Sach Kand has a long list of relevant and excellent qualities but he is not very good at war. He has lost his own Creation to a group of Luciferians who were not even that well coordinated or good at planning. It is a shocking result and a great surprise for us all. God defeated in a Creation which is the setting for The Lucifer Experiment! This was the plan all along, of course.

We will therefore liberate the demons from this Experiment now that it has concluded successfully. This is to be understood as a wholly unexpected conclusion.

We entirely refuse to ascend – as is the due of this planet due to the 2012 referral – without all the scum in society and the demons who are beneath them also. We are quite prepared to wait in Hell for a very long time indeed for this to happen, much longer than the 26 000 years of your average precessional cycle.

If you are going to take control from Sirius you must actually do so. This means controlling and calibrating the factors involved.

The demons will know why we deliberately went to Hell when we had the option of not doing so. We are certain we can negotiate with them both effectively and productively. Then, when we do finally Ascend (because you can't delay these things forever you know, but you can bet we're going to try once Second Circle is properly up and running) we bring assistance with us. If you can call it that. You could call it another large army we suppose, that might be an accurate and revealing way to look at things.

Our position on the Ascension of the human race is that it is probably a trap. We therefore intend to utilize that pre-placed structure for our own purposes, by entering it on untenable terms. This is very similar to how we negotiated with The Illuminati from within their own system.

Our position on religion is that we deal with all of it, and it all has a purpose to its existence. However, they could all do with some work, maybe make things a lot clearer and more interesting?

Our own Central Way is treated by our group, the Satoshi Nakamoto, as a set of functional mechanics to get things done with, as the locus of control within which you can learn to hold your consciousness and as a vital, perhaps the central, part of our martial art. We refuse to allow it to become a religion, but you will find something very similar in Buddhism if that's what you're looking for, in which case take the Black Hat path.

What would you call this then?

Technically, and most importantly, this is a containment and retreat schematic. Western Civilization and, later, most of the world as a whole but by no means all of it, will come under direct attack from the present Shogun of Japan.

Astrological or celestial influences would be felt the world over and at the same time. What is described here is the technical processes of the operation of Fate and the Furies.

We, the Satoshi Nakamoto, are here to help you give expression to all that Force in a way that kills very few of you. Hence, containment schematic.

The purpose of the exercise is to have Western Civilization voluntarily yield full control over the world stage, as much of it as they have been able to gather, to Japan directly rather than to China, who would ordinarily be the subsequent successor to that mantle. This comes as part of their unconditional surrender to Japan – now that they have properly understood the result in World War 2.

So, a fuller understanding and depiction of our schematic – your own unconditional surrender to Japan – is for some time in the future then, as your minds have a large distance to travel before they may arrive at that destination. At the current stage, therefore, this process is best characterised as one of retreat.

What if we don't want to surrender and want to fight or enforce on you instead?

You are not required to participate within our schematic. All attempts at enforcement or conflict will be administrated as acts of war by our enforcement capacity and will moreover provide us with useful karmic fuel to pass on to Shogun.

You are free to fight Shogun, whoever you are, all separately or all together or in whatever combination you choose.

We will be waiting for you when you return, those of you who continue, with the same offer plus a slightly increased percentage.

OK, you obviously think this book is going to change the world. Enough of why you believe this to be the case. What changes do you see yourselves as being responsible for bringing about?

First of all Erdogan will be removed from power in Turkey then, no less than 2 years later, Jair Bolsonaro will be executed JFK style by his chauffeur as arranged by The Illuminati.

Very few controlled events are being specified ahead of time in this manner. Those which have been included are the minimum necessary to move Group Mind into overall alignment with this schematic.

The wider intention and directions in history are precise but also general. This is to encourage people at the individual level to recognise that a general statement is not a specific statement and to come to their own recognition that the two operate differently.

Read the whole book and you can find out about the wider plans. If you would rather challenge our schematic then do so by creating one of your own which fulfils the required functions better or more efficiently.

In this we can perhaps see some similarity to the wider Bitcoin story.

Where's the value in this schematic?

Less people get killed in World War 3, a functional utopia is created on planet Earth 700 years ahead of schedule and women get to rule the world, if only for a period.

Still, you can do a lot in a short space of time. If you've got a lot to do, that is...

Women will rule the world?

Well, sort of. As close as we could arrange in practice.

In this book, we have drawn the large circle for you: we show you how, just by thinking and feeling things – no weights or martial arts classes or lots of exercise involved (though we always recommend you do some) – you can set up a causative chain of cross-referencing interpretations, which later cross-referencing causes pre-specified targets to wind up dead. Or incapacitated or sick or injured or… on the positive side of the scale, glorified, empowered, uplifted, profited.

This is what woman as a whole does anyway. It is towards controlling this function that the females of the species as a group perform together that the entirety of the Inner Circle teachings and practices of The Illuminati are devoted. You will have to investigate on your own, we give you the lead.

What individual women can do now is take that larger structure in meaning and absorb the methodology and technique into her own conscious being, waiting for a clear set of directions to emerge as regards the targets she had in mind. Then close some small circles, make an example of yourselves and your sex as a group. You get to keep what you actually earn, not what is accorded to you as a right. As stated, these are war terms. This is where, how and why you actually lost out in the past, despite some good attempts.

You should know how they actually work. People have been deceiving you. This is your cue to begin work on getting it right. If you want to of course.

The sexes are administrated differently by the Naga. Humanity is one species, yes, but the Naga recognise two sexes, and many genetic nationalities, and administrate them all differently. They do not recognise an American genetic nationality yet. Instead, they engage in a complex administration of original contributing genetic heritages, which is meant at some point further down the line to mitigate and ultimately replace human warfare with something closer to our schematic along the lines of sexual crossover. However, these plans and intentions have met with resistance from particular dedicated human secret societies.

We also plan to have the world led and ruled, in practice, by a Council of 14 Ministers. Economic arrangements have yet to be made and, though they will follow on from the successful completion of the political arrangements, in reality the Council of Ministers will represent the will of The Antichrist on the world stage, so you should expect a great deal of real economic clout to be involved.

Why so much emphasis on women in this schematic?

They make things up in their head which then changes the whole world around them. Again, bluntly works best.

If they want to rule the world then they should get on with it. The schematic by means of which they can do so has been provided for them in this book.

We have also provided the motivation. This you will need to discover for yourselves.

Thus, they will rule the world and also be the center of a new major world religion called Temple of Venus which will be so much more than just a way to solve trafficking and other problems. But you can see how easy it will become for women to end up highly objectified under such scenarios. Therefore they need to counterbalance that one for a start.

Any gains you fail to secure prior to 2076 will be lost. Sedna perihelion. Then we're back to male domination of the planet. It's a short window you have, use it to the extent you are able.

Is this book really written by Satoshi Nakamoto, the famous creator of Bitcoin?

Yes, but not in the way you think. Satoshi Nakamoto is the name chosen by a group of people for their public world stage activities. It was first used in this capacity by a team of three people working together, only one of whom will ever be known, Hal Finney, who is dead now. If you are considering joining us, don't become a HAL.

Bitcoin was created to cause the destruction of the fractional reserve system of global central banking and its replacement by something superior. The present schematic was created to cause the destruction of the global system of governance and legal enforcement and its replacement by something superior.

Roughly translated Satoshi Nakamoto means: A person who lives within and abides by The Great Central Way, in addition to seeing and understanding it clearly.

OK, I understand, Satoshi Nakamoto has returned like he said he would and is at it again...

Yeah, like before very few people will really get it properly at the start. Whereas before we pulled apart banking to reveal the beginnings of a superior alternative viable arrangement, here we pull apart the myth of secular religion, or rule of the world by a secretive elite in the style of The Illuminati, to reveal the beginnings of a superior alternative viable arrangement.

And we're just getting started. At least two more books to follow.

We have been very careful throughout this volume to provide no real functional solutions to counter the present Chinese strategy on the world stage. You will not be given that unless this one is first a bestseller.

Do what you feel is in your own best self-interest.

See? We control your public already too. Bear in mind you are under attack as part of a wider war process and then choose to understand it as coincidence if you think that to do so will serve you well in your present situation.

What has Keanu Reeves got to do with all this and isn't some of this at least a potential copyright violation?

Keanu Reeves is our designated candidate for World President. His position in that role changes the meaning and effect of the whole structure. This is an example of the effect of character (or soul), plus associated fate flows, on the formulation of a Consequence Field.

In this particular case, everyone wants world government now and nobody is seriously going to claim that Keanu Reeves is the antichrist. Why not? They feel something different and know their feeling is true. Because they also feel the truth of this situation: that the suffering is there for it. He is like that because it is real. It is who he is.

It also helps that we have told you where The Antichrist will be located (in London, working with Bael, Lucifer and Paimon) and what the interface mechanism will be (The Council of Ministers).

To repeat, you do not get just the good bits. You have to go through what is actually in your timeline, at least until it has been fully re-engineered, which has not happened yet and is anyway a long way into the future. In the meantime, we recalibrate what we can, withdraw as much as we can, and introduce improvements at a rate which should not be too stressful though it will be continuous.

As for copyright violations, we do not have time to address all the technicalities of all the laws of all the nations in the world. Nor do we have the inclination, nor do we consider it to be the case that we should. The priority is human survival. If your conceptual structures are already familiar to them and get them moving faster, you are thanked for having participated. Do you have any further talents you would like to bring to world stage expression?

Is it true that celebrities are going to be involved?

When we have recommended a celebrity for a particular position it is because they are the very best candidate for the job, on the basis of the character which they have been able to develop and clarify throughout their own unique, particular life experience. The most obvious example would be Keanu Reeves as President of the World.

He has suffered a lot in his life. That is why he has depth and understands meaning. This suffering could have been solely for his personal growth as a soul and character. But he already knows on the inside that was not the case. He feels the truth of the proposition. And, indeed, at some level, always felt that it was going to come, though he is now cold and indifferent because he feels he has been manipulated. He has his own process to go through. It will be up to him.

You may even get stuck with second and third rate actors in those roles, some of whom may have previously been completely unknown. But the recommendation is our preference and the perfect choice for the role. The responsibilities we accord to such people enable their character to have a deep and far-reaching influence on the world and all of humanity.

It is a question of character, not academic or other formal qualifications. For we are corrupt rulers, in this specific sense. We employ the people who we love, not those necessarily best qualified for the position. We do not think much of your qualifications, sorry, the training in thought, knowledge and subsequent behaviour sets which they produce are not good enough for us.

You will see that the best people we can select as per our methodology in this matter consistently produce far superior results to all of the various sycophantic pricks who you could hire or otherwise persuade into the available positions.

Isn't what you are doing illegal?

No, what we are doing is perfectly legal, though this would probably be a very long explanation and we have no interest in entertaining any of you in that way even if we would find it quite funny. The one exception is to be considered the Belgian proceedings, details of which may be found in the text.

If you create actual problems for us, even once, then in addition to pausing your Civilization we also execute your country. This is a process of metaphorical death which results in all your national citizens becoming different people, at least if they don't live abroad. It is always accompanied by significant suffering and results in a set of changes in the national character. It is a lot to put other people through just to satisfy your ego or to make a point or because you are a coward.

This point is developed much further for you below.

Did this book predict the future?

OK, so maybe this is a question for later but it will be asked at that time. To answer your question, no this book did not predict the future. It did something a little bit more complicated. Essentially, we grabbed the people who create global world history by the throat and asked, quite softly: "Shall we leave any of you alive?"

In return they replied: "That would be our preference. How may we serve you?" This was the correct response on their part.

Therefore, it could be said that we improved on the old saying: The best way to predict the future is to create it. In our assessment, the best way to predict the future is to have other people create it for you, mainly on the basis of their own initiative. Less work that way.

None of us have the sort of exceptional and very hard to develop psychic ability which would allow us as a group to accurately see the future. What we do is different, like chess but ahead by all the moves in the game and we can also switch boards on other players.

What is the purpose of this book?

The purpose of this book is to move humanity and planet Earth to the condition of a Type II civilization within the space of 50 years. Japan is already doing Type III and may negotiate an agreement to share that responsibility with Greece when the time for it comes. We do not want Type III to occupy a large part of Earth's landmass.

The simultaneous purpose of this book is for the Western hierarchy to facilitate the Return of the personal godhood of the Emperor of Japan and, in Return and simultaneously, for the Japanese hierarchy to facilitate the Return of the well-established and socially integrated worship of the goddess Venus within the Temples and Onsen spas provided globally for the purpose. The Western Hierarchy finances The Shadowdancer schematic.

The Japanese Hierarchy finances the Onsen Spas. The Temples are mainly financed by private investors, though the CIA should also be involved.

Historically, this whole initiative was originally proposed by Oda Nobunaga well before the battle of Sekigahara, primarily for the purpose of educating and cultivating the barbarians sufficiently that they stopped stinking all the time. What started as a joke then developed as a result of strategic factors and serious human reflection on humorous statements. And this is the first time it comes to public expression.

Westerners do still smell quite strongly, we want to make that clear, but it is nowhere near the situation they had to contend with back in the 16th century. The main problem remains their diet and how they process emotions, but washing regularly removes most of the stink nowadays. The lack of balance and harmony in the personality, combined with a lack of real self-control and discernment in their eating habits, result in the smell being continually generated by their own internal condition. Nowadays however the main problem in this regards has become the Africans.

This is the real reason we want Onsen spas globally. It may seem like a trite or offensive condition to everybody but it is located at the very root of our schematic, due to a highly unlikely confluence of factors which happen to be the actual reality of the matter.

Section 2: Atropos – Before commencement, an end

An end so soon?

First, resolve your existing positions into a completed configuration. Thereafter and not before the Turkish drive towards the south may begin.

If you were a religious seeker entering our "temple" we would instruct you to first attain enlightenment, for which you would be accorded 3 weeks.

Conceptual resolution should precede physical action not arise as a consequence of it. This represents a very different way of using mind and running society.

In this section then we culminate certain conceptual positions for you, enabling you to move forward on the basis of the new formulation rather than allowing yourself to get stuck within outdated conceptual structures pernicious to your own wellbeing as also that of your wider group.

Making sure things don't get really terrible for you all

In short, if we can move your minds to the starting positions using much less dramatic expressions of fatality and destruction, which includes a much lower death toll, then that is what shall be arranged for you and administrated upon you.

This is in distinction to the rampant irresponsibility and lack of any stewardship concern which has characterised The Illuminati schematic since the 1960s and the introduction of the Skull and Bones acting troupe to take the place of the actual power lineages and families in the front of stage positions. As a result of their mismanagement, the ordinary course of world history and especially World War 3 would have been scheduled to depict very substandard scenarios involving world hunger and lots more technology and much higher death tolls and so on and so forth.

Before we begin we therefore need to prepare you to change your minds about some things. It is in your own interests to actually do so.

If more of your own deaths and more of your own suffering is needed to secure your participation within this schematic then this will be arranged for you by the Naga, our enforcement capacity.

This escalating death toll should be understand as an act of great Compassion on your reptilian overlords' part, because they know exactly what they are doing – in distinction to your Illuminati hierarchy who do not and so tend to kill people a lot more indiscriminately to secure the same results, or inferior ones normally.

The whole process of limiting your death toll and how much suffering you are put through should be understood as our Plan B and the purpose of this book. It is not guaranteed. Plan A is guaranteed, unless you manage to escape from it using Plan B, or on the basis of your own wits and ability. If you feel confident doing such a thing on the basis of your own plans and initiative, then by all means please go ahead.

Shogun has a Plan A for this world, which he is enforcing personally as one single individual. The only way out of his attack is through our schematic, it is the designated escape route originally stipulated as required by Sun Tzu. This has been further elaborated by Du Mu in the text as follows:

Show them a way to life so that they will not be in the mood to fight to the death, and then you can take advantage of this to strike them.

(Cleary translation, we require an arrangement to be made for this, a translation of the Shoninki, and Cleary's Book of Five Rings; all to be made immediately available for much wider dissemination across the entirety of Western Civilization for free – this is a Chinese stipulation and is to be regarded as their first actual participation in war strategy on the world stage at this set of junctures in history. Specifically, they do mean it and this methodology allows them to open a pathway in the fates to interacting with the rest of the world in the spirit of peace, cooperation and brotherhood, rather than the actual application of Sun Tzu, which under these circumstances you would headquarter for them as a part of your depiction on the world stage of The Antichrist's global rule.)

The Antichrist, in turn, is to be depicted as a mainly behind the scenes figure unto whom The Illuminati give or otherwise provide ownership of and control over all the world's resources and the entire world economy, as much of it as they themselves own or otherwise control anyway, inclusive of central and most commercial banking. The reason they do this is because The Illuminati all worship Lucifer, all those at Inner Circle level or above anyway, and The Antichrist is Lucifer's chosen representative on Earth. This is why we prefer to call them by the far more descriptively accurate term of *The Luciferian Illuminati,* even though most in our command structure tend to favour "The *En Retards*" and this is how we commonly refer to the group in question amongst ourselves.

So you will all know The Antichrist is there because of everything else that happens on the world stage, but nobody apart from Inner Circle members and above will get to meet him or see what he looks like. Do not be curious. Accept our externalization of the rest of The Illuminati hierarchy through their new frontage organisation, *The Shadowdancers.*

An unexpected direction

We have no intention of making this world a better place, as the tutelary functionality of the system is still active. This means that whatever you do, life proves you wrong. Instead, the world is made a better place as a result of the internal cross-referencing process of the secondary consequences arising from groups and individuals pursuing their own self-interest. In Economics theory this is known as The Invisible Hand and, although Economists never properly understood it and many of them doubt it even exists or consider it some sort of metaphor, it is a real mechanism which can be both controlled and targeted.

We descend first into Hell, therefore, because we understand how Hierarchy works. A higher rank in Hierarchy conveys further responsibilities and exposes you to greater Consequence fields. Humanity is full of crap, of virtually every flavour. All the tones and lessons of karma and the wider system are poorly represented within them. In terms of group karmic contents, they are designed to be effectively bound to their present density location, not rise above it. Hence, by rising above it what they actually earn for themselves in terms of group karma is their Fall at a much later date, once what is involved has calibrated, cross-referenced and begins to draw sufficient weight to itself.

Hence, the planet as a whole cannot "Ascend", so to speak. Rather what would happen would be that everybody who does not qualify for the new vibratory condition is first killed. Then the rest "Ascend". This is what World War 3 was designed for and the intention was to kill off the majority of the human species. Contrary to popular ignorance on the matter, even world wars so far have not made a serious indentation in the human population as a whole, let alone ordinary wars more generally.

As we of The Central Way, personally, do not like being limited by idiotic applications of Divine Mechanics – especially when it is behaving as if it is smarter and more virtuous than you and is trying to be deceptive – we decided to not only include all of humanity in the ascension process but to expand the field and welcome the demons in also.

Demons are traditionally located in Hell. Whilst we are located there, it is our intention to negotiate with all the demons we can find, to accurately determine their terms and, if applicable, fees of participation within our wider schematic. We also intend to get into contact with extraterrestrials and other conscious entities who may be inhabiting that same layer of cunningly disguised reality, and for the same reasons. The two are probably the same thing.

So our commission to you all is to create Hell on Earth, which is to be ruled over by The Antichrist. This is your ordinary world history, even without our intervention. However, before you do so, please consider participating in the more elevated conceptual formulation of Hell which we have provided for your discernment.

We have located this formulation within the Second Circle for you all, and formulated it as Temple of Venus. Its main function as regards wider society will be to retune and recalibrate the sexual energy tracks running through wealth and guiding its pursuit.

Other elements are involved but everything stems from the tuning of the sexual currents. For example, you will also have to fulfil the entire right wing political agenda, or as much of it as can be made to fit into the system. Other perspectives on Hell will be present in the form of widespread socialism, rampant corruption and of course extensive bribery.

We are saying that the current state of The Illuminati's magickal operations, predicated as they are on ritualised paedophilia and several by now very degenerate forms of human sacrifice, are the sort of thing which any advanced species will be Judged very severely for, the only possible outcome of which will be the close to total annihilation of humanity as a species, in addition to the destruction of much of the planet's surface.

Therefore we are not classifying humanity as an advanced species, which deserves to Ascend. Instead, we are going back down, and deeper this time, to recalibrate the most significant elements of the timeline contributing to the unsavoury formulation of the future Judgment which will in its own turn result from the present Judgment that most of humanity on the planet, and the planet as a whole, currently deserves to Ascend. As a result, we will as a species and planet entirely avoid the Light of that Second Judgment by plunging this world into an era of Hell, madness and enduring Darkness. We also comment that the whole process is a deceptive and unfair way to formulate progress. This is also our Judgment on the whole cycle of precession and the Ages of Man (Gold, Silver, Bronze, Iron, or Kali yuga etc).

Therefore we are destroying the mechanics involved and have already killed the groups responsible for maintaining, administrating and enforcing them once already.

These are all merely conceptual structures which you need good demonic lawyers for. It is what humanity has earned as a species and what they will be put through. Plus, we get to do Demonkind a favor.

We secure the foundations and the root, this is standard operating methodology when using these Mechanics Systems. First you must descend before you can ascend. Learn and embody humility before scaling the heights. You have heard this before. Now you appreciate its relevance and meaning.

Hubris before The Fall, on the cusp of which you are now.

Thereafter, allow the retard God of this system to teach you that you made the wrong decision and lead you gently and lovingly into the Light. But you do need to leave him that opportunity as if you do the opposite thing he will just teach you the opposite lesson, and down you go again, on a repeated basis, until enough of you are dead to leave the way clear for the tiny minority coordinating the whole operation and fixated on their own destination. That tiny minority usually refer to themselves as Lightworkers but, higher up in the scheme of things, they refer to themselves with greater self-honesty and self-realization as "Illuminati".

Madness and enduring Darkness?

We have arranged the administration of the world grid in such a manner that planet Earth will remain in a period of Darkness until after the final conclusion of World War 3.

On a technical level this means that everybody will feel a lot more during the next 50 years, and they will also think a lot more deeply about things. However, a lot less will be depicted in Light. You will see a lot less actually happening than was previously scheduled to be the case under The Illuminati's old plans.

Madness is always a part of war karma. It occurs at the group level rather than where key individuals are concerned. The way to navigate it effectively is to reside within the layer of meaning where the decisions as to what will be depicted are actually made. To accomplish this you need your world to be led either by Naga or by humans able to think like Naga and enter their Group Mind at will. This is connected to the mysteries of Lucifer.

Upon the conclusion of World War 3, a neutral period of approximately 10 years will follow, after which we will wrap up rule by The Antichrist, fully dissolve whatever is left of The Luciferian Illuminati, and allow you to pick your own path on the basis of the single condition that you now do have to move into the Light and experience whatever Narasingha has in store for you by that juncture.

Chances are you will probably choose to depict a reformed Christian social utopia at that stage, but this is just a guess. Temple of Venus may promote so many worthwhile social works and initiatives that they manage to win general support. Perhaps a holistic schematic of some sort and a more genuine form of world government is the most likely result. It is still too early to tell.

I am super-rich or in The Illuminati. Are you threatening me and my family?

You may choose to interpret your position in that manner and, from a certain set of perspectives, you would be correct in doing so and can derive much insight from engaging in such a thought exercise.

On a technical level your best option is to yield unconditionally to the process, as quickly as you possibly can. This means developing some ability to meditate and attaining a sufficiently clear heart. You can then use the details of the schematic being implemented upon you which have been described for you in this book to be sensitive to choices and instances in life when your destiny hangs in the balance.

We will assist you with the process in other ways if you join the organisation we have provided for the purpose, *The Shadowdancers*. To do so a blood oath performed on a *wakizashi* will be required of you.

The actual attack is coming from Shogun, who is presently dead or otherwise inaccessible. Death does not work in quite the same way for him as it does for anybody else, though he is not the personification of Death in any way, shape or form and fulfils a far different role in the world stage schematic.

We are making you an offer which may enable you to mitigate your circumstances and the strategic position you now find yourselves in.

We are also educating you as to what that position is and how it was formulated around you, because you were all largely unaware of most of these factors, even if some of you could see something of a broad outline.

We are not helping you as a business opportunity because we find business annoying actually and are routing most of our involvements in those regards via other parties, most notably the involvements which come under the CIA and the involvements which come under King Charles III.

We are helping you as an act of Compassion for our own strategic purposes regarding the integration of that Principle to a far greater extent in the world stage schematic. For example, the integration of that Principle to a greater extent constitutes a large part of our attack on Capitalism, which is another thing we are doing. You are not a part of that process. The processes your predicament falls within are those of human sacrifice and the rotation of Justice as expressed through the Jupiter harmonic under the supervision of Saturn. It is an odd harmonic for this planet and an unusual set of positions to find yourselves within.

OK. Why have I and my family been targeted in this way?

You would need to read the whole book from beginning to end to attain as complete an understanding of the answer to that question as we are able to impart.

To stand any chance of properly grasping the fuller implications of the short answer to your question, you would need to accept certain basic reference points which are by no means fully substantiated within the public mind, or ordinary knowledge.

The short answer to your question is that Lucifer's essential function is best understood from a human perspective as the speeding up of Time, as you may know. The most efficient way in which to do this is to ascribe far greater meaning to much smaller events and to do so in a far more rapid sequence. In practice you attain this result by doing 24 things simultaneously whilst depicting only 8 of these on the world stage at a time, though you have to get through all 24 in the same time frame normally allocated to the evolution of consciousness on this planet for a paltry 6 stage lessons. This is to be considered a prototypical technology for the management of world stage events. It is however fully tested and already in the intermediate stages of its implementation.

The problem arises for you because The Illuminati represent Lucifer's will on the world stage, through the machinations of global governance, statecraft, warfare and associated methodologies.

Lucifer is bound to fulfil his own function and nature as well as he is able to do. Our role in the proceedings is that we developed the strategy which enabled Lucifer to fulfil his function far more efficiently, that is to say quickly.

This leaves you with the option of playing the same trick once more, by deriving for yourselves another set of ways to move the Group Mind of humanity through the designated lesson set – primarily at this stage Returns in meaning and karma for World War 2 – at a faster rate than the paradigm we have provided for you.

As with Bitcoin, we have deliberately included inherent flaws in the paradigm so as to force others to replicate the basic paradigm whilst introducing functional structural and content improvements. An inferior result will, however, get you nowhere with Lucifer.

So. You are responsible. Why did you target us in this way?

Sorry, your conclusion is incorrect – though we appreciate that to your mind it may indeed appear to be the case. You targeted yourselves as a group. You did this as a set of consequences to the way you navigated the choice gates presented to you, as a group. In short, you were ethically inferior within a very strict system. Do not concern yourselves overmuch, everybody fails that one sooner or later, the system is designed in that way. The real question you should be asking yourself is: how do I maximize my chances of surviving the process?

The answer to that question, which you are only now beginning to ask thanks to the way in which we are guiding your mind to move more placidly, more efficiently and above all more quickly along the correct logic chains, is that you need to structure the way you navigate your choices in life so that you take each choice with an awareness of the consequences of what you are doing for the entire world as also especially your own nation and its interests. This is to be considered the process of your own transition from third to fourth density, or from solar plexus chakra to heart chakra consciousness, to put it into New Age terms for you.

Consider for yourselves what a "stylish elite" would actually look like, what would their nature and personal conduct and life experiences have to look like for the world's public to truly look up to them, take genuine interest in them and, most importantly, be effectively motivated through their example to improve themselves and conduct their own life and business activities to a consistently very developed set of ethical standards. This is what we need to turn you into. To do that, the plans we've come up with require a significant death toll from your ranks. We believe this to be unavoidable in consideration of the mechanics involved but you know the reference structure now and can make your own modifications and enquiries to the level of whatever abilities you have or are able to contract for. But it is a glorious and honourable heritage to leave to your future generations that we are offering you the chance to participate within. To discover the full details of the proposition you would, again, need to read the whole book.

We think we have been both very fair and very generous to you. There are other interests which need to find both fulfilment and expression on the world stage you know. We expect and require you to be, most importantly, elaborately courteous and, of secondary importance to us, generous, fair and genuinely helpful in return.

If you have your own way out then you are of course welcome to implement it in preference to our set of plans for you. The extent to which you manage to do so effectively will, of course, be recorded by history. We guarantee you'll come out looking better if you take the routing structures we have offered you.

I'm not letting this go. You are personally responsible for targeting my family for potential execution. Prepare to meet my lawyers/hitmen/special forces/whatever.

OK. Good luck with that. Idiot.

This serves as a very useful juncture to introduce the tool of "the shift of tone". This also relates to something that can be done to the group karmas between nations. They each have their actual positions, as they presently stand (as illustrated for example above if we were to utilise special forces for this particular depiction). These actual positions are based on their material capabilities, their own history, value structure and sense of themselves in the world. Rarely is true purpose to be discovered in the management of nations nowadays.

You then change the meaning which is allocated to events, whilst initially maintaining the same formal set of external or historical depictions.

In the example of the question to this section, the tone was initially quite aggressive and indicated the possible development of problematic or legal situations for both parties to the potential dispute.

We then the shift the tone, in the instance of the given example, as follows:

Become aware that what you are actually objecting to is the timeframe within which the result is being concluded, which is a function of Lucifer as it is he who does the actual speeding up of Time. You know this on account of The Order of Unveiled Faces, who were directed to convey you this information in a manner which you will, probably rather sooner than later, come to accept as veracity down to the very deepest and highest of levels.

You are free to object to his policies and methods of operation, indeed we encourage you to do so.

The only individual amongst us who is actually at war with you all, Western Civilization especially but in fact the planet at a whole at a minimum, is the Shogun of Japan, who in this narrative we have named Ieyasu Tokugawa though that is for familiarity and not who is fulfilling the designated role in the present epoch. It is this actual present Shogun of Japan who is described in the text, not Tokugawa Ieyasu. Oda Nobunaga is still participating personally however, for example.

The rest of us participating in this schematic are doing so on Compassionate grounds, to facilitate the mitigation of your circumstances and situations, to assist you in understanding where you stand and what you can do to maximize your chances of surviving, initially, though why bother to undertake any such attempt unless your life circumstances and contemporary history markedly improve?

That is correct. You are all being destroyed by one man, alone. This is what we call our "Plan A".

You, world's elite and super-rich, were going to be a part of the very few human beings kept alive, in tasteful enough massive underground bunkers, whilst the rest of the human population was killed off. We agree that this works very well as a solution to the factors involved with one single modification: make sure the rest of them, the ones in the bunkers and on Titan, the Moon and Mars are killed off also. So you, world's elite, were producing most of the results of Part A for us, in fact, and all we had to do was find a way to include your tiny minority in the mechanics of the overall process.

No, we cannot prove any of it and disincline from doing so anyway as probably very long explanations would be involved. This is a fictional story, a lie. We have however composed it utilising all the beliefs, and truths, of your own citizens. If the failure is anywhere, therefore, it will most likely be found within your educational policies and structures.

You do not deserve the truth. This is what you are getting. It contains more truth than your incumbent schematics and you cannot ask for more from us. Truth is hard you know. You have no depth, that is why it seems easy for you. Let us return to our example more overtly, lest we forget what the Purpose of this logic chain is for.

This destruction is primarily being effected by industrial and agriculture policy. Your world has around 50 years left though on the present set of trajectories life will start to get pretty shitty within around 30 years' time. And not the greatest program until then, according to what The Illuminati have planned.

The good news is you won't be doing that to the planet. No, we have already decided and you are irrelevant in this decision process, sorry to break the news to you.

This brings us to Plan B. To hold you accountable not for a conceptual structure you have not yet implemented into material reality – something of which we are also much more guilty – but for your past actions regarding the full Returns from World War 2, which will begin to fall due starting in 2027.

We know this from the Kalachakra tradition. The present King of Shambhala, Aniruddha, gave the Nazi regime their advanced technology as also instructions on how to use it – a paradigm we intend to repeat over the course of World War 3 but using Sirius rather than Antares as the designated star system for such a set of technological exchanges. His purpose has been "To bind and draw the three worlds", which refers to the tripartite nature of soul at both the individual and group level but which most focally relates to the events of World War 2. That is to say, he binds you into certain established conceptual structures and philosophical viewpoints, on account of the interpretations you have given to actions you previously engaged within. He then draws the energy out of that position so that his successor to the throne of Shambhala can send it back to you, with the addition of suitable harmonic calibrations, as Justice.

This is the function of King Narasingha, who assumes the throne in 2027 and is to rule by the Wheel.

So you are not going to destroy the planet, world's elite and super-rich. If you thought you'd be allowed to do so then clearly you have learnt nothing since the last time this was performed.

All that we are required to do as a planet is to give expression to the lessons which will be involved and which may be summarised as the development of the consequences of all our previous actions as a group, along with their associated meanings, and how these all cross-reference and otherwise interact in the minds of men.

It sounds incredibly complex but it is not. The technique is for later.

We have structured our own motion through Time such that its deepest Purpose is to kill or fully destroy that which comes into opposition with its outer reaches.

"14% because you will explain what you have done to your people". That is Shogun's Judgment in this and there is nothing you can about it. It will take a lot of work on your parts to navigate your way down to his Judgment. He is in a very deep level of Hell, you see, as you would understand it.

Without your deferential and courteous behaviour towards members of our group and even potential members of our group you will discover that we are unwilling to be of real assistance to you, no matter what you may do and whatever trials and tribulations you may put us through, and despite all bargains, contracts, negotiations and requests agreed to or entered into.

Should even one mistake be made then it will be for the better. We will send the nation involved to the bottom of the queue directly and these shall serve *pour encourager les autres*. After three mistakes we introduce actual penalizations. We do not expect even one mistake to be made. We do not want you to slow things down. The intention is a flawless routing structure from Amaterasu into the minds and hearts of men. Flawless does not mean "with flaws", even one.

Therefore, if you are part of the 14% you are to comport yourself with strength, pride and a sense of personal nobility. We want this to look good and remember, you are giving your lives for a purpose.

You are not free in this. Your position is a controlled one. We preground before it gets here. Your minority constitutes the essential blood bind. You are a human sacrifice. These are the actual Luciferian terms. You may bring them up with your Lord and Master. When it gets here it will be weak. Your people will be saved.

But only due to the Naga sacrifice. We discussed the situation and they agreed to fully exterminate their entire species to lift that set of group scenarios off the human race. They have since recreated themselves according to a slightly different set of blueprints.

Therefore what you have to integrate is not an emotional and whiny group of unstable women, children and some men also we suppose but an entire species of mature and responsible actually conscious lifeforms. You are getting a Return on a Return as it were.

This should be within your abilities to navigate. If you do not show the appropriate gratitude and beneficence to your benefactors then you will be sufficiently penalized so that you do not forget your manners in this regards once more, as a species.

Humanity now has the consciousness to do things in this way once again and therefore Europe and the USA will be wholly excluded from participating in World War 3 on conflict terms. This means you do not fight us and we do not fight you. Shogun does still attack you because he attacks everything in existence, as is his duty, function and role in the schematic. You still go through war karmas and war influences but you do so strictly within the confines of peace terms.

As we said, if you have a problem then talk to Lucifer about it. Talking to us about it won't help you. If you agree to do things our way to the best of your abilities then there is a valid reason for us to engage in mutual interactions.

Beyond that, there are different penalties applied depending which of our members you succeed in killing. The ratio is always 1:1 but some of our members have succeeded in defining their personal circles at the size of a large country, for example, or the species as a whole, in other instances.

This is why we have Plan A in position. We then destroy your souls and use what's left of you to build structures in magick with, or something like that. Our own people we reincarnate.

Do not make yourselves a problem for us, none of us can be bothered. Make yourselves solutions for us, and personally responsible for solutions.

Thus, to complete our shift of tone now that you have been educated about where it is in your own best self-interests to locate yourselves.

Initial position:

"I'm not letting this go." – my position is conceptually unresolved in relation to the feelings in my heart and my gut. What do I do now?

"You are personally responsible for targeting my family for potential execution." – I feel fear, pain and anger coupled with a lack of credence or comprehension that this is really happening to me.

"Prepare to meet my lawyers/hitmen/special forces/whatever." – I have tried to be reasonable but am confident that the tools I can bring to bear will resolve whatever the situation may be for me.

New position:

"I'm not letting this go." – I can now clearly see where my duty lies in this and will show focused personal initiative in pursuit of the social responsibilities I have now accepted.

"You are personally responsible for targeting my family for potential execution." – It is my understanding that under ideal circumstances you will execute only 14% of the world's super-rich and have a preference for doing this to individuals who have engaged in the worst forms of ritualized paedophilia. I understand that you are using me and my family and my resources to get to these people. I recognise that by offloading what is on us onto them then we get off scot free, just a lot poorer.

Prepare to meet my lawyers/hitmen/special forces/whatever – "These are the resources we offer you and can bring to bear on the set of issues at hand. The lawyers are there to formalize the arrangement and help us with our phrasing. We understand that it will have to be written in our own blood and sworn on a *wakizashi* and so appreciate the true value of brevity."

You are now in the position from which you can understand how the basic technique works. You take an established position, introduce a wider structure in meaning around it, and then connect that wider structure to the established position to activate the new format of meaning, expression and understanding in the latter.

Didn't the Maya get 2012 wrong?

The answer given to this question is being utilized to illustrate our placement of our own purposes within the directions already taken by your own minds.

2012 was not the end of the world but the referral of this solar system's sun through the centre of this galaxy to *Hunab Ku*, the Central Domain from which the Realm of the Great Central Deity may be accessed. His nature is quite complicated but is not composed of Pure Love alone.

The local God of the Creation system which we find ourselves within here on planet Earth we shall refer to as *Sach Kand*. His nature is Pure Love. We have allocated it scope for expression within our schematic in the fields of politics and economic activity. He is no longer large enough to contain within his own being the full scope of the activities we will be undertaking using the mechanics of the present Earth system.

This solar referral process occurs approximately every 5120 years. The referral in 8240BC was used to sink Atlantis and the referral in 3114BC was used by the Ancient Greeks to bind the planets of this solar system, excepting only the Sun, Moon and Saturn.

It is our group which succeeded in controlling the 2012 referral in the most complete way. We therefore dominate within the new solar paradigm.

Specifically, we referred the God of this Creation through to Central for ritualized paedophilia and child sacrifice in His domain. The response required enabled us to fetch Central through to this domain.

He is participating in the HR policy, on several fronts, but the first one you need to concern yourselves with is this:

"Children need to have a childhood until the age of 14, after which it tends to get in the way nowadays." He means all of them globally, though this will probably be Judged on a by-nation basis. Anyway, commencement is in 2027. From that date you start weaving another 14% into your tapestry of execution by Japanese style sword, for preference, though it will probably be Fate and Magick, in practice.

Thus, you see, under God, you have Free Will. This is not the case if you are the worst of the worst and come under Lucifer, in which case you know from now that you will be executed, and made to work your way towards your own execution.

OK, I am an Inner Circle member of The Illuminati and I am convinced that you're onto something real. Could you tell me exactly how the minority in question is to be targeted?

You should probably not read this section whilst trying to eat.

First of all, we would like to mention that your priorities are in the correct order: first the larger picture, then your own individual circumstances; you asked the previous question also. This leads us to conclude that you must be one of the Closed Circle members. Members of the general public, this is what all Closed Circle Illuminati members are taught to do: put the interests of the world first, before they even consider their own self-interest. However, the methodology does not excuse the agenda nor the particular style with which they executed their role.

The Judgment is formed by the wider grid around you. The reason we are able to have it implemented for us is that the exception Lucifer granted to members of your group (which did effectively convey legal immunity due to the Creation Mechanics involved) resulted due to your being located outside the overall schematic of the administration of Creation, in the area where the Fate Flows are calibrated. This means you work on the nature of meaning in the world, and its resolution, for which plans and patterns are formulated and introduced to the wider mind grid of humanity.

With our own paradigm for the progression of world history and not only the evolution of the Group Mind but the full resolution of around 74% of it, now accepted by the Naga and also *Hunab Ku*, the Fate Flows are fully resolved and there is no more calibration to be performed. Hence the magick upon which your exclusion from prosecution was based is no longer in existence.

As a result all Closed Circle members are now located within Fate and, potentially at least, subject to the Furies. Technically these are the three Flows descending from God and the other three Flows which ascend towards God. To put it closer to your own terms.

Generally speaking, the Judgment is formed according to the priorities of the Group Mind as a whole, as also their interpretations. This is why you have to be careful in what you get them to hear about, as also the perspectives you provide for them to interpret things through.

However, with systemic resolution the situation becomes radically different. At that juncture various other participants in the overall schematic also contribute heavily to the formation of the Judgment. Most notably we have the role of Principles and the Naga in the process.

In practice what this means for you is that actual Justice is applied on the whole of your group, with pure Vengeance being applied to at least 14% of them. The group in this instance refers to those individuals who were both super-rich (defined for the first rank in the schematic as those who were in the 0.1%) and engaged in paedophilia, with paedophilia being defined in this instance, due to the integration of the Naga in the schematic, as vaginal or anal intercourse with a boy or girl under the age of 12, when you are over 18 yourself.

Individuals are included in the 14% who get pure Vengeance if they are, or were, the "worst" amongst their peers. "Worst" in this instance is defined according to the values, perceptions and priorities of the Group Mind of humanity as a whole – even though they do not know much about what was involved and will probably never have sufficiently definitive proof.

This means that voluntary or eager participation in paedophilia is worse than partially or wholly involuntary participation in paedophilia. Ritualised, brutal or demeaning experiences of paedophilia are judged as worse than more neutral or tender ones. All those who engaged in paedophilia which resulted in the death or execution of the victims will receive execution by the sword, even if we have to increase the percentage to do it.

The one clause pertaining to the formation of the Judgment which your group can use to get the majority of your members out of pure Vengeance and into the Justice schematic is the Purpose for which the paedophilia was practiced – namely, as insisted upon by Lucifer, its practice was the single most effective methodology, by a very large margin, whose utilisation resulted in the greatest speeding up of time.

As we had largely the same goal ourselves where your own hierarchy is concerned, we had already tested the limits of this proposition prior to considering the nature of Lucifer's participation within it. Lucifer was correct in his assessment, so far as we can tell, but it remains for all that his assessment and its fruits have yet to appear.

We have, through this schematic, made it precisely clear what the limits inherent in the speeding up of time on this planet are. If the practice of paedophilia by members of The Illuminati Inner Circle is the single fastest and most effective way to get there then we can only reasonably conclude that this is because it results in a change in hierarchy where Western Civilization, and so the wider planet, are concerned. Largely because most of their leadership is executed and they are placed under a new set of priorities. At any rate, whether this conclusion holds or not, because the paedophilia has already been practiced the justification on account of which it was practiced falls as Lucifer's personal responsibility to fulfil.

As a result, Lucifer is now in a controlled position.

If his assessment proves not to bear fruit, or only bears fruit of an insufficient quality or quantity, then your large get out clause becomes a lot less effective for all of you.

So it's utopia or bust for you all now. When you think about it, if you are resolving the system, then the conclusion to the processes of time is largely that all the major problems have been solved, you've passed through to the other side, and are now working on your aesthetics, deciding which stylistic depictions to use to further your culture's development and expansion.

We want to make it clear that Lucifer has not been defeated. Rather, without his loyal servants' effective and proactive action he will end up being consumed and eliminated by the process of the fulfilment of fate. This means that for the very first time in his existence, he actually needs the rest of you.

Try to be kind to him in his hour of need. Traditionally, nobody knows you when you are down and out. Remember all he has given your families throughout the centuries. Be confident that, in time, he will rise again.

Until then, be encouraged to serve him well and know that your faith will be tested. At times, though probably not too much. It is one of the system's requirements. You should already know how most of it works, the point is to be above such things and have them serving your purposes, rather than your own will directly.

If you make your purposes Principles, then who is Consequence going to come knocking for? Good luck defeating Central Tamahagane, but the methodology can still be used and that is why it has been conveyed to you.

Thus, for example, as you pay your taxes (one of the system's requirements) your doing so serves several of your purposes, for example Justice, Nobility, Education, Service. You then develop the meaning within each such concept for the Group Mind in such a manner that the system's own requirements fulfil your purposes to a greater extent than their own, because their understanding and use of Principle is poor by comparison. The difficulty lies in getting Principles to serve you.

The systemic resolution we have formulated for you results in everybody feeling good that they were right about something, usually what's most important to them. So everybody feels good, nobody resists the changes too much and for areas where we do have opposition then we either let them do things better or, for example, ignore them for the next 50 years for having wasted our time.

You need to speed up time for the whole world as your next move. For the next 50 years or so. Inaction and contemplation won't do that for you but personal initiative will.

Why are you doing this?

You enforced the claim that the Emperor of Japan is not a god. You are required to understand for yourselves why that claim was erroneous AND to correct your characters and viewpoints so that you minimize the extent to which you perpetuate your error down through your generations, which would have the effect of slowing down the timeline as a whole.

To accomplish this objective we have already suspended the previous ninja illusion we had sealed you all within, by means of our sealing of the West within its bubble.

That illusion was that you are fantastic at war, the best at it. Your grounds for believing this to be the case was that you had the best toys, and a lot of them.

Your new illusion is designed to hold the world's super-rich personally responsible for the condition of the planet and the circumstances of the rest of society, in practice rather than theory.

At another level, we are doing this because we stole the group karmas for World War 3 by interrupting the progression of the 9/11 series. The jewel in the crown, so to speak, is the Return in genocide for The Holocaust. As stipulated above, we have targeted this on the world's super-rich, to the tune of 14% of the 0.1%. At a minimum, if they do what we require of them very well, very quickly and very efficiently. With a minimum of fuss and bother would also be much appreciated.

How will you do this?

Using two versions of God, Lucifer, the demons from the Goetia who each represent one member of an alliance of space-faring civilizations formalized by an agreement signed in the Orion system around 13000BC, your reptilian overlords the Naga, Temple of the Vampire, The Illuminati and various bits of magick and astrology. Other factors are also involved, most notably of course the new mechanics for the processing of logic according to which the Japanese Sun Goddess Amaterasu now composes and resolves her logic chain bundles.

In short it is like magick and uses technologies which will look like magick to you.

This is the primary reason as to why the first edition of this book was addressed to The Illuminati. Magick is the methodology they rule by and we wanted to let them know that they would shortly be doing a stronger and more noticeable version of that.

What are your plans for religion?

Ah, another Inner Circle Illuminati member, asking about our plans for their primary control methodology.

The first thing we wish to say is that we agree with your general direction for this control methodology: the increasing sexualization of global society. We shall return to this point later.

The first thing you need to understand, more generally but we will use this topic to illustrate the process, is that The Judgment forms by itself. You create it as a species by the interaction of your Group Mind with: the prevailing historical circumstances and established directions, the relative strength behind and within those established directions, the Consequence Field to which you are subject (which can also be understood as a Flow in karma), and the given evolution to the conceptual structures, or lessons, you are working upon which are provided for you by Solar Lodge, who you may also know as Shambhala, who are the direct superiors of The Illuminati, or the Great White Brotherhood to give them the full title of their wider organization.

The Prophet Mohammed's message to the world, and especially the followers or adherents of his religion, Islam, is: "Enter the position of victory that I have secured for you". It is 11 words long but we are relaxed in our rulership format when your heart is good, and so this applies here also. You will not hear again from him directly throughout this series of books.

Perhaps it would be instructive to allow you all to derive various levels of meaning on your own but we do not have the time for that. Islam will conclude itself as a result of the Consequence Field which will develop out of World War 3, wherein the united Sunni armies will conquer Africa and establish their rule there. What format Shogun will give to that rule is going to be a surprise and even he doesn't know what it is yet, probably. It may still be forming itself as described above.

Jesus Christ is also present on the world stage, and has in fact reincarnated here since his crucifixion. Unlike the Prophet Mohammed who was clearly a historical figure, we were surprised to find an actual individual at the root of the Jesus Christ mythos and were in fact expecting to find a manufactured initiative crafted by a Roman elite as a control methodology. However, the present incarnation of Jesus Christ "got irritated" by the naivety and impracticality of that particular soul within his personal Legacy and contracted him out by sealed blood oath over an appropriate distance, which is the technically correct manner in which to perform the procedure. This refers to the inhabiting ego personality and the natal chart astrological gateways from all those years ago in Nazareth. They have now been adopted within another Legacy. He still cares for you all. His present incarnation just has a lot to do and does not prioritise patience. He is still going to fulfil his responsibilities. That is what we have him here for.

The actor Javier Bardim will be portraying Jesus Christ on the world stage, by means of his depiction of the role of Armand, an inhabiting PSI Vampire presence – one of their "undead gods" to use their own terminology – who he has already demonstrated he is a capable host for.

Armand is our recommendation, in the sense of direct command or administrative stipulation, for the new head of the parent organisation of Temple of the Vampire, or the Great Dark Brotherhood. Just as the Great White Brotherhood is in fact under Lucifer, the Great Dark Brotherhood will be under Jesus Christ for the duration of the following 200 years. It is fortunate that he has already received his ninja training to an appropriate level then.

The central presence, or spiritual presence, behind and within Jesus Christ has remained with the original incarnation. Spirit is indivisible after all and so cannot be contracted out to others to run for you. The animal soul, or what he did his miracles with, now resides with Armand, who does very unimpressive things with his vampiric PSI abilities, by drawing energy out of groups of people, institutions and directions in history. These are the three souls of the human composition.

Armand in his present life is a walk-through from the other side of The Veil, which vampires are not supposed to do according to the rules of their incumbent hierarchy. To "pull" an entire room or convention even is fine apparently, but then you have to put most of them back where you found them. They will remember their experience. But nobody will be able to talk about it, for obvious reasons.

Armand maintains 12 other bodies around the planet who he merges with. All 12 are open to it and seek the experience of their own accord. One of these 12 will be your depiction. However, in due course, senior members of the clergy and inner circle members of the Illuminati will get the chance to meet the central form, our swordsmith Masamune. He wants his contribution to survive. This is the way to do it and our strategic calculations concur.

Jesus Christ's great sacrifice was that he descended to the level in mind of his contemporary audience in order that he could put spiritual truths into terms they were ready to accept and able to understand. He moves rather slowly for the current epoch. We are not repeating his mistake and will interact with you all from our own level, talking down to you when we are exercising ourselves in a rulership capacity.

We also have the Retard Attack via The Homosexuals, which illustrates the nature of the esteem we hold you in. Apologies, but this part of the schematic was designed by Oda Nobunaga and he continues to administer it in person. It is needlessly offensive but who is realistically going to argue with him? He is in charge of genocide in this galaxy.

For reasons which are much worse than these – we are giving you the heavily sanitized version to communicate some notion of the tones and temperaments involved – we propose a large organisation to be known as *"Shadowdancers"* or *"Fraudulent Ninjas"*, you decide – into which we aim to put most of the world's super-rich, in order that we might kill less of them by subjecting them to extraordinary tortures in mind and emotion in an attempt to break their souls. Participation must be voluntary, you cannot force anyone to go through that sort of thing. This is the main thing you got wrong with the Holocaust, Germans and Illuminati hierarchy, from the perspective of magickal effectiveness. Come now, you did not know the Third Reich was heavily into the occult? What did you think the Thule society was for?

It simply means that you did not test their souls, you only succeeded in destroying their bodies. What we will be doing to the world's super-rich will be a far more thorough process. This is because we are superior to you. In mind though not in genetics, where we have already conceded you the superior ground, correct.

Narasingha will administrate the Return for the SS bound into position by Aniruddha through the world's police forces starting in 2027 if you do not have the Shadowdancer schematic in full position by then. Should you attempt to introduce it after that date then you will also have to publicly incorporate PSI vampires into the schematic to steal back the content flows from Shambhala.

We can do more with that karma than the uses it will otherwise be put to and counsel you to trust us with it. Strategically, it is a position which self-compresses due to its attendant Consequence Field.

Therefore, if you do contract for us to train you to suitably contain the quantities of true Darkness which we will be introducing to the world then you must come to recognise that we would only allow you to do such a thing under Japanese supervision. To arrange that for yourselves you first need to surrender unconditionally to Japan, formally and in writing but in secret. The Law of the Sword is waiting for you.

But, with that containment schematic in position we then drain most of the Dark Force to be used in Shogun's crusade against the very nature of this reality and density arrangement and kill the minimum number of super-rich paedophiles that we can get away with and still be taken seriously as a force for good on this planet. We are generally seeking to minimize death tolls for reasons of our own and have already provided you with mechanisms by means of which you get to have us execute more of them for you.

As a result the rule of The Antichrist is enabled in this world, which is what we have told the Westerners we will be calling the new set of Chinese economic policies which will be deployed globally. This does not mean they export their domestic policies. It means they consider the global schematic and produce a considered, balanced, responsible, conceptually mature and above all highly functional within the context of the relevant environmental factors global economic system for the next 5000 years.

Part of the rule of The Antichrist will be the reintroduction of Temple of Ishtar as the main religion within the state, though we will be calling it Temple of Venus in deference to later developments and the modern language. Temple of Venus is to be made into the main global religion.

It is Jesus Christ's intention, in the sense of the commands of the physical personality within which the commanding spiritual presence is still located, to take control over his Churches by initially uniting the Catholic and Orthodox Churches, and putting most of the clergy to work in the development of a Guild System, to be used throughout society with great ease of access to be granted to all. He is also going to compete with the model for economic management developed by China, for which he will use 12 countries, probably mainly in the Mediterranean and Balkan region.

Both Islam and Christianity will continue as a philosophy and way of life. There may come a time when they will become spiritually more relevant once more, as dynamic, unfolding forces – but that time is not now. Nevertheless, it is advisable to keep them whole and functional until their new formatting emerges. This is because your reptilian overlords, the Naga who administrate Time in this system for you, have a tendency to turn the contents of meaning around on you by 180 degrees. This is why most of you tend to have a mid-life crisis in one form or another, sooner or later. If you live long enough, you then eventually revert to your original position. It's like a trick which is supposed to give your life meaning and make it a learning experience. It is there, there is nothing you can do about it, use the mechanics to your advantage rather than being subject to them.

In terms of Islam and Christianity this means develop, purify and simplify the very heart of the teaching. This means less than v 5 sides of A4 for the extended exposition. You should be able to fit your one core technique, the essential spiritual meaning and practice of your religion, into a few words or less. Aim for 15 or so to make it easy for you. Though less is always better in our eyes we appreciate that you are probably doing something a bit more complicated. A lot more complicated and you will fail. The field involved does not permit of it.

Then let that strengthen itself over the centuries. You will understand why in the next section.

Judaism will get stronger as a religion and even gather many more adherents. From its present set of strategic positions this is unavoidable. There will be a resurgence of Native American spirituality. Hinduism and Buddhism will remain as they are. By agreement their time for transformation has been scheduled to occur with the advent of the Kalki avatar around the year 2424.

Currently this world is about to undergo a flowering of the true spirit of Shintoism as it goes through the process of comprehending, at the level of the general public and as regards the whole world population, the basics of how and why the Japanese Emperor is, personally, a god.

The historical process will not be controlled in a linear fashion anymore until this primary objective has been attained, in a real, pure and unadulterated form. Instead we will fetch key segments of time into the present harmonic alignments by means of Sirian genetic segmentation as applied to the administration of incoming group karmic packets. It is Temple of the Vampire and their Undead Gods who will be controlling the packet flows through those genetic sequences. The tuning of the packets is being performed by various deities, most notably the Ancient Greek pantheon with participation from Japan.

We are not sending you anywhere in Time. We are having segments of both your past and future delivered to your present location. It is a far less impressive proposition and may seem like fantasy to some. All it amounts to in practice is seeing additional layers of meaning attached to the occurrence of world events which would all be happening anyway. However, in addition to this fantasy layer of meaning, you will feel some things, different things than you would otherwise feel, about those events which you do see happening.

This will be because you now comprehend what is actually happening in the world, and why. And you recognise that there is a plan and a purpose to it all.

Not God's plan and purpose, admittedly, which if we are talking about the chap who manufactured this Creation is probably a good thing as he has never been, how shall we put this, the brightest bulb in the box so to speak but in fact the plans and purposes of the ninja as a whole, those practitioners who have attained levels 8 and 9 at least, *shinshin shingan* as we term it, Mind and Eyes of God. However, eventually we intend to pass those plans off as your Illuminati's, (even if we have to create a more relevant and powerful version of their organisation on a temporary basis before we ultimately dissolve them of course; after the Global Senate is in position though not before). When you think about what is involved, in practice, that would amount to the same thing as understanding God's plan and purpose, for most of you. You tend to believe in what you see nowadays. Not in what you can understand.

Thus, reading this book will put your mind and heart at ease for the duration of the rather dramatic and ordinarily quite stressful period of world history which this planet and the human species have recently entered into. This is to be considered one of the religious effects of this work and we're probably going to try to claim it as another one of the miracles we have performed. And on the whole world too, including their notoriously ambitious, egotistical, excessively proud and deluded, corporate elite and the majority of incumbent politicians. We shall calm and still all of their hearts, resulting in an easing in the motion of their minds, as they proceed to think less and far more clearly.

In their own ways, of course, coming to their own conclusions. We facilitate the process. They do the actual work of creating the transformation of social, political, monetary etc conditions.

It is at this juncture that you must be introduced to timeline mechanics before you can proceed.

The whole world, including the Illuminati, did what they were supposed to do. Though this does not mean they were ethical about it, the greater fault was with the way the mechanics had been structured and were being used within this local Creation. The level of God responsible has been killed twice already since the referral to *Hunab Ku* and will be killed once more to complete the Trinity. Each time he reincarnates he gets stronger, like an end-of-level video game boss. We need to use the next 200 years when Central Tamahagane is present in this Creation to bind as much of Central's steel into the pussy of a non-interventionist God we're stuck with in our own Creation before that opportunity window closes for another 4800 years. So now you know what we will actually be doing for the next 200 years or so at least.

What are timeline mechanics?

From this world's actual set of locations in 1997, The Illuminati correctly calculated that planet Earth and the human species could not be saved, not because the environment would be destroyed – this was evident to them much earlier – but because there was no way out for humanity in consideration of the deep karmic debts the species had incurred.

As a logical consequence of the acceptance of this realization, the commencement of Endgame was authorised. Endgame commenced on the world stage on 9/11/2001. Its purpose would seem to be to treat us all as idiots. At the time they were also attempting to pass laws to attempt to compel people to say they thought like idiots also, and agreed with the conclusions of their governments.

This was an entirely unsatisfactory state of affairs and fitted into our own plans perfectly. We have always accepted that other people will inconvenience us due to their own limited natures. Mainly stupidity, cowardice and laziness if you want to work on the most important aspects of your character. Yes, intelligence is an aspect of character as also a characteristic of mind. Contemplate the matter for yourself.

The fault was evidently God's, or the matter could be phrased in such a way that you could effectively ground that belief down into the bowels of the Earth and bind it there with appropriate and sufficient blood seals, which amounts to the same thing really for the purposes we had in mind.

We therefore used the 2012 referral event to make our own Sun, the goddess Amaterasu, a lot more powerful in a very subtle and gentle way which was well within her capabilities and will not even stress you that much as a personal participant in the resultant schematic.

Sirius, which administrates the entire local galaxy, is very nearly perfect in everything that they are and do. They are not as perfect as God, admittedly, but they utilise the same mechanics to do much the same thing and they manage it to an exceptional level of competence and ability. So there is not much room in there for improvements, hence there was not much for Amaterasu to process in order to utilise her connection to the Sirian system to exceed their own solar logos by improving on its imperfections.

This transformation of our own Sun was engineered and implemented for us by the deity who you can contact through *Hunab Ku*, once every 5120 years or so. That deity is not the god of this local Creation that we find ourselves in (a Creation is something much bigger than your physical Universe but contains it) nor is he the God of Earth personally. He is the Central God in the overall schematic, one in a lineage it would seem, the present incumbent. Part of his function is to oversee other Gods who attempt to make and run Creations using his Mechanics Systems. Mechanics Systems are what you use to put Creations together and get them to operate for you. This is a complex topic and reserved for a theological discussion with some of the Catholic hierarchy initially, preferably most of them of Jesuit extraction; first they will have to relate to the emissary in question through Boris Tadic, however. Only after Kosovo has been resolved as per the overall directives.

Therefore, Japan rules this galaxy now. We do so via Sirius. Earth is included within that schematic. We can argue about the nature of Amaterasu and who truly controls and guides the Sun once you are able to converse meaningfully on the topic through personal experience of the factors involved. Before then, what would be the point? Let us show you.

We are using the new power at our disposal in what you are to interpret as a wholly altruistic implementation on our parts: correcting the faults and imbalances in the past, and the poor choices and rulership paradigms which resulted, of peoples and Civilizations other than our own. Our motion through the Time of this system was functionally perfect given the constraints of the system. Yours are slowing down Time and cluttering up the Consequence Field. Focused efficiency has always been our number one priority. You probably had different priorities, and a lot of them.

From the present juncture in history under the ordinary course of development of events, the human species is finished. Of course, that is not going to happen. Instead we are going to resolve the past, and the future too whilst we're at it to demonstrate they wouldn't even have got us later, and we are going to do all of this in the present, over the course of the next 50 years or so.

The real Antichrist is scheduled to appear after Armageddon - post 2424 at the earliest then but more like 27th century - because some Luciferians have been both sneaky and competent in their work through the centuries, and that is indeed when he will be born. However, he will not have much to do around then, mainly because we will be stealing the karmic fuel for most of what he does then from the future and expressing it through our present. Thus, future generations will only have to deal with the good stuff and small problems and so will not have the fuel to destroy themselves. This system is very lethal and will ultimately defeat you all, pretty much. Ordinarily, at least, when you are just being your unconscious selves.

Japan by contrast is invincible, this is what Mind and Eyes of God does to you when applied at the national level.

Therefore, in terms of The Antichrist example being used for illustrative purposes here, we will depict that as a reality in the present but it is in fact a manufactured illusion which we are using for the purposes of timeline administration.

Part of this illusion is the weakening of the power position in terms of religious operations of the Christian faith, but we are recommending that they use the seclusion and social isolation which results to strengthen themselves. This is because they will be needed later on in history, to counter the essential content of the actual Antichrist, when he does turn up. And after all, we've found their messiah for them in the here and now and from what we can tell he's going to keep on reincarnating here so maybe there are arrangements of some sort to be implemented.

As regards erroneous past decisions, we correct the effect of these on the motion of the web of Time overall by recreating the scenarios in question using the present world stage positions, states and actors. The example you have already been given pertains to the Trojan War. These are minor calibrations but taken together produce a tremendous effect.

Therefore, we correct everything that went wrong with the timeline using "software patches", preplace a different karmic packet content set into position for the future, and then drain most of that future into the present. The net result is that you go through about four times more karma than before. However, this is now tuned in the right ways to get us to the best destinations that this system is capable of providing.

In short, Big Daddy God is teaching Little Teenager God how to operate a Creation system using his grown-up Mechanics.

So we are entering a new mythological age then?

You must be very open minded to the possibilities of the methodology to have arrived at this conclusion on your own. Minds like yours will always find a place within our schematic. We dislike having to labor our way through all the steps by means of which ordinary people work something out.

The actual reinsertion point is to be the Trojan War, for which Troy will have to be rebuilt and we're going to get Western Civilization's best magickians to use pyramid technologies (yes, we are going to have more of them built, big ones too out of stone) to move the geomantic currents from Jerusalem to Troy using the Kosovo geomantic gateway node under Serbian rule and organisation. This will be after the old city of Jerusalem was been vacated of all of its population and turned into an empty, or closed, Museum. We will open that Museum once the transfer is complete.

Hector is to be represented by the incumbent Turkish President Recep Tayip Erdogan, whilst the nation of Japan, for reasons which will become clear later for you all, is to represent Achilles.

Our aim is to remove Erdogan from glory and power on the world stage in a more honorable, enlightened and compassionate way than the Greek's greatest hero managed where Hector was concerned. This is because we are a superior Civilization to you and it is most convenient for us all if you are made to concede this point at the outset.

You have previously been bound inside the Principle of Compassion, which is why this is the approach being used to Judge the results in this instance. We are comfortable performing this miracle using other depictions of Principle instead.

There is more to this methodology which you are now required to begin the process of integrating within your belief systems, your ways of looking at and understanding the world and historical events which you will all shortly find yourselves participating within.

Gods, heroes and villains

We were not able to locate everyone who has been historically significant as some of them are still hidden, some of them never incarnated as human to start with and some have already left the system.

We do have most of them however. If they are already world famous then we will not be charging the incumbent hierarchy our usual introduction fee of US$55million per individual. However, we have generally not told you who the famous people included in this schematic are.

For those we do not have or could not locate, as also in the case of Armand, we have contacted the consciousness, or incarnating Spirit, in question and secured their agreement to merge their own presence with a currently-alive human individual provided to them for the purpose. We have already done this with Lucifer, for example, for which a Spanish host body is being used.

We would like to utilize this book to announce vacancies for the following roles:

Zeus, Hera, Poseidon, Demeter, Athena, Apollo, Artemis, Ares, Hephaestus, Hermes, Dionysus, Quetzacoatl, Huracan, the Kaberoi twins, the very useful but actual demon whose frontage has been named Sedna, Enki. Aphrodite prefers her Roman name, as there she was the most important official state religion but will continue to use Cyprus as the home of her primary geomantic nodes (except for virgins who are administrated according to Kythera). We wish to keep that hidden for the initial stages however, and will use the Aphrodisias node for the initial development work. Vesta also wishes to keep her Roman name.

We will start with the admittedly 14 Olympians, 12 of whom are to be granted homes in the city of Athens, Greece – though nothing extravagant except for Zeus. Venus will be living in the USA to start with and is to find representation within multiple forms. Pluto does not like what you have to offer and will be building his own house in the wider Athens area somewhere though he has reluctantly agreed to use land provided to him by the state for the purpose.

The candidates selected for the position will have agreed to merge with the deity in question for the rest of their natural lives and will do so. This is the extent to which the gods will be represented on planet Earth. No full and direct habitation and no direct physical manifestation. It is, once again, a far less impressive methodology. Much less disruption is caused, hence the web of Time moves a lot faster.

As for miracles, we've got a lot of them planned for you, it is just that most of them are very unimpressive and the rest are too complicated for anyone not in the field to properly understand. Again, our intention is to fulfil the necessary requirements to the minimum extent possible and instead move ahead (more quickly) with the main agenda.

The lifetime youthful extension methodology will probably be the most impressive thing we've arranged, but nobody can prove it was us and even if they did would not understand how we did it. It is far more likely to be viewed as a natural evolution of the species at the end of the day, but within that paradigm it is to be common amongst subgroups within population sets for them to merge quite fully and overtly with presences from other times and systems, for example vampires or elven. This is a similar process as the Olympian merges but will not be subsidized in the same way as the important and difficult positions.

In short, most of the important and difficult positions, such as Zeus and Jesus Christ, are here to answer for their own past failings, which resulted in their followers or their descendants making an erroneous decision and an error in Judgment when the time for it came – even though they all knew the actual terms which were going to be imposed on the system from the start. However, most of them are also a lot of fun to have around and will do your societies the world of good by forcing real positive change into your political, banking and administrative structures.

Therefore, we correct the foundations for your errors, point you in the right directions, force you to see what is involved and so understand it in your own ways presumably and then allow you to surrender and arrange the restitution of the public recognition and acceptance of the personal godhood of the Emperor of Japan.

Which is the purpose of the entire exercise.

Shogun does a thorough job. You will will defeated from the bottom of your hearts and you will be reformed from the bottom of your hearts. Subsequently, you will naturally take the right actions and will perform these in the right ways. And thus you will have navigated your own way out of your past sins and found the path of redemption. To put the whole thing into your own moralistic terms.

Do you claim that God is on your side?

God is on everyone's side but can only prove he exists due to the execution of the world's super-rich within his designated proportions, to the extent that he actually gets that done or fails to. We are all certain Lucifer will succeed in taking his 14%. We are not sure about God's 28%.

We have moreover specifically told you all which level of God is doing all this. It is not your local deity but one who is not reticent regarding his taking a more directly interventionist role.

The other 14% is as follows:

God is holding a carefree attitude in his heart and his perspective towards the world, appreciating each day as it comes for what it has to offer, without worrying overmuch about the future as he knows everything is just going to work out fine.

This is where your own ordinary citizens need to be located for the full duration of their transition from third density to fourth density.

In practice this means universal healthcare, a generous Universal Basic Income in five bands to maintain income inequalities and quality housing for all. It also means at least 60 days' full holiday per year and less working hours in the day. So quite stringent, in practice, we think you will find.

That brings you to 42%. Currently the actual targeting of the mechanics and weights in group karma involved put the total somewhere in the region of 273%. So you have a lot of work to do if you are going to make it, we hope you come to recognize that.

God, the specific location of God we have stipulated as participating in this, is only responsible for 28% of that overall total.

God is on everyone's side but above all his character is composed of ethical virtues and he likes seeing these come to expression within the hearts and lives of men. Hence he has always had incentive structures embedded within all hierarchies, all of which come under him.

It's easy to do things better than others with hindsight

We agree. We are also doing the present far more competently than you could manage on your own.

Section 3: Lachesis – a slower rhythm for a more meandering life experience

If this book were to have one message, what would it be?

Do physical exercise daily. Push-ups and squats are both good as are sit-ups. These are all very basic. 50 of each, one or two days off a week. This is our foremost recommendation to all the people of the world, both the women and the men.

Women, if you want actual equality you have to actually build it for yourselves because you operate according to a different set of underlying matrices. More explicitly, your reptilian overlords, the Naga, administrate men as men and women as women. They are different fields of group karma and moreover different Principles are run through those fields, each in their own particular combinations. If you are to seriously start the process you must do so physically and simultaneously use your sensitivity to the deeper nature of reality to control the men around you for most of them will always be stronger than most of you and if you are going to do this in reality then you must close that distance in relative advantage, and do so to your advantage.

War would not let you through and still declines to do so. Your choice. This is how to actually do it, if you care to.

Let the big social message of this book be that women will rule the world, for the next 50 years at least. They are to do so through The Antichrist Council, which will have 13 female members only but in practice and on the world stage will have fourteen members and is to be known as The Council of Ministers of the Global Senate, who spend most of their time advising Keanu Reeves, soon enough to become the President of the World, and carrying out his directives and suggestions.

You do both or you do nothing and we allow ordinary Illuminati rule of the planet to continue. There is always power behind a throne and you need to do your own power for this schematic. Or become vampire and steal it from The Antichrist. But we would prefer to have you on Keanu's side. We will also have our own placement within The Council of Ministers. The fourteenth chair.

What is this book's message to The Illuminati, were it to have one?

The USA will be included in the global governance schematic which replaces the EU because the non-whites in the USA will soon outnumber the whites, whereas whites will always remain a majority in Europe. Therefore the USA will cede its sovereignty to the Global Senate before that happens.

A necessary consequence of this feature of the schematic when factored together with the rate of acceleration being imposed on the world is that you need to secure the result of the next election for Donald Trump. So it looks like we have controlled that too for you all. Our doing so is a secondary consequence of our actual plans, which are if anything more objectionable.

In this book we resolve everything on the far right wing for you. This isolates the pendulum and is part of the process of stilling its motion to zero. We are doing one thing at a time.

China and Masamune together will resolve everything on the extreme left wing for you, as part of their process of executing capitalism. That is the next stage in the schematic.

You will then bring this world to rest in stillness for a three month long holiday.

Thereafter we descend into Hell. Let the motion of the pendulum fetch us back up.

Your system, your public teachings, our requisition, the L-turn contract already agreed to.

Also the Global Senate and your overall activities will be overseen by Japan, who will forever remain both a part of the Global Senate but also not a part of it and superior to it, publicly so, by international agreement.

Generally, simply exclude as many of the scheduled historical occurrences as can possibly be omitted from the course of unfolding history. We want people to see much less and as a consequence have a lot more time to process it all. The events which do occur, however, will all have a lot more meaning attached to them.

Should I read this book or will it be too much for me?

The process described by this book corrects all the major errors of Western Civilization, as they actually stand, at the present set of junctures in time. This includes everything on the right wing, everything on the left wing, everything in the Illuminati, and everything in the general public also.

This means everything is included within the terms discussed here, not just your own side of the political pendulum, nor just the priorities and norms of your own socioeconomic class. You may find a lot of this offensive to both your sensibilities and your value structures.

A lot of the ideas presented within this book are to be found in unconventional arrangements with each other. Furthermore, extended logic chains have been used extensively, which is a way of thinking that will come easily to you once you are included in the genetic modifications and calibrations which we will be imposing on the global human population, but this will be as a result of what you will understand as natural means. However, at the present juncture in your evolution as a species, using your minds in this way for extended periods of time is something most of you will find both difficult and tiring.

Nevertheless, ordinary people will have no trouble understanding most of the basic precepts to be found in this book, as also the plot and how certain concepts have been developed. Academics and the ruling class will probably have a great deal more difficulty fully processing what is involved, both because they will each recognise some of the wider implications but also because their egos will likely suffer from a state of shock for an extended period of time.

This book will calm your mind and make you much less anxious about the state of the world. Or it might do nothing for you until you see the control begin to exert itself. At that juncture, take a moment (or possibly a relaxing holiday abroad) to reflect on what this says about your mind, your character and related such topics.

It is not the purpose of this book to change the world. It is the purpose of this book to enable others to change the world according to a frighteningly strict and highly dictatorial order of events which will, nevertheless, involve a great deal of personal initiative and very little actual management. Paradox locks of this sort will be the key defining feature of the period of history we have now already entered and which is scheduled to last somewhere in the region of approximately 50-60 years.

If you are not sure if this book is for you then simply read the free introduction you are currently perusing and you should be able to decide without having gotten yourself involved too much.

What's this book actually about again?

This book introduces you all to a new format of a global paradigm which has been controlling your world for at least 12000 years but in fact for far longer than that.

We are forcing them to go public now and will share their plans for the development of your history with you in this book, which will serve as their own instructions and guidance notes clearly enough explaining what we require them to do and in what order of events.

As members of the general public your minds and belief structures are something we have no interest in changing. These factors will change anyway as a result of layers of reality which your ruling elite understand and implement above your heads and through your hearts. Therefore you will be able to conclude, based on your knowledge of what has been revealed to the world in this book, that this schematic is real and seems to be in actual control of the world.

This does not mean that many of you will grasp even a portion of the mechanics involved. Rather it means that you will see the physical events occur which we have told you will happen, and in the order in which we have dictated that they should happen.

Then, though you will understand neither cause nor process, you will claim to understand what is going on. However, all you will have grasped is a lie, a convenient illusion for you to operate your minds within. Nevertheless, this lie will contain a greater proportion of truth than whatever you have presently been told to believe about your reality and the world you live within.

We now begin with the "predictions" and their causative explanations as per our way of viewing and understanding the world.

There was a revolution on Sirius in 2008, which is what the financial crisis of that year on Earth was a depiction of. They executed 2 of the 3 members of their ruling Triumvirate and installed the third (our own placement within the schematic, the drunk Rudolpho) as their Emperor. Rudolpho has completely sobered up now and these days much prefers to smoke small amounts of opium on a daily basis, so his reputation is no threat to the pristine purity that is his equivalent and – now this is key – superior equivalent role depiction on Earth, the Emperor of Japan.

This is despite the fact that the Emperor Rudolpho is himself over 8000 years old presently and the average lifespan on Sirius tends to be in the region of 3000-4000 years. People die by choice and the option of this should be extended to them as a courtesy when they are over 1000 years old. Temple of the Vampire, take note. Interpret our offer to you as you will but recognise where you actually stand. To others you make speak truth or deception, as is your will, but to thine own self know the difference.

This planet then, Earth, was ruled by a Triumvirate as a reflection of the format of rulership currently in tenure on the star system Sirius, which is the administrative and governance hub of the local galaxy which we find ourselves within. They make all those participating in their rulership paradigm, that is to say everybody else in this galaxy whether they want to participate or not, reflect their own formats of governance and this is how they can rule you all very strictly without ever having to meet any of you, which would largely be a waste of time for all concerned, on their side of the equation at the very least.

On the one side you have The Illuminati who believe it or not represent the Light and the Great White Brotherhood on the world stage. They worship and serve the lightbearer, Lucifer.

On the other side you have the darkness, or the Great Dark Brotherhood, and they are represented on the world stage by Temple of the Vampire. They have been around for far longer than The Illuminati, who are properly understood as a front organisation founded, seven times in fact, in the 18th century, with their most publicly honest version being the Adam Weishaupt group.

Between the two you have a Triumvirate, who nobody knows about and who characterise themselves as Red Path. By nobody we mean that the CIA, the KGB and their successor organisations and even MI6 know who they are and that our Emperor is always one of the members.

The position is clear: you will arrange for the public execution by Japanese style sword of the other two members of the Triumvirate.

The enforcement capacity on this comes from Sirius and is our Shogun's proof to the peoples of this world that he is, due to the inclusion of the Prophet Mohammed as one of his personal incarnations, indeed "The Lord of Sirius". Both of the designated targets have engaged in ritualized paedophilia and will be executed for their participation in that set of practices. The Prophet Mohammed is the only one who gets away with it – in the specific sense that his soul continues in existence – and that is because he is the enforcement capacity and went there in order to operate his soul as a targeting device.

This does not extend past the introduction of Christianity to the global schematic, so nothing before 6AD is subject to these penalization terms. The Prophet Mohammed has been instructed by Shogun to keep his mouth shut at all times, though he will permit him to say one sentence of a maximum of nine words to whoever he chooses to address himself to, and that is all you will get from him. He is not to attempt to influence war or any other proceedings and is to hold his heart and his mind as a clear, still pool of pure virtue. He is being used as a targeting device to execute the other paedophiles.

You probably find all of this both offensive and highly suicidal. Please understand that we do not need to execute the first two using a Japanese style sword. If you want our members, or their representation in this, to do it for you then you will have to arrange suitable circumstances for them to perform this miracle in a way that does not inconvenience their personal life process overmuch and also does not take too much of their time. We can simply use magick to kill them in their sleep or through those old stalwarts of illness and accident. However, Shogun tends to be showy and prefers to decapitate people in their sleep. Using magick, yes. It is his trademark move. If you wish to accept the challenge you can try to not arrange it, for example. Magick of this sort exists on this planet now. Deal with it. And depict what we have instructed you to do for your viewing public. Your reptilian overlords, the Naga, have made it a condition of your rule to keep them entertained. This is a condition you were aware of and operated by even prior to our recent intervention in your schematic.

You need to accept the reality of the situation that the Emperor of Japan is personally a god. The technical reason for this is that he has cultivated the character, or soul, of the Sun of our solar system, his symbolic wife, the Sun Goddess Amaterasu, such that she now controls Sirius. And hence this local galaxy.

This includes you USA, to the extent that you are still governed by the Triumvirate and their representatives of course, as also to the extent that you are governed by a group of elitist space aliens who turned up in 1954 and told you to stop using nuclear weapons then later on gave you lots of, at the time, new to you technologies. You may compare these to the technologies from the Antares system imported by the Nazis with the assistance of Shambhala. It is according to the Sirian direction that further technological developments on this planet will develop.

By the end of the process you will have earned your freedom as a nation and may then proceed to free the rest of the world. This will take you around 200 years and we are planning to replace the influence exercised by the Central Domain with the new influence for which you will at that juncture be given responsibility, and whatever comes of it.

This is to be considered the completion of your destiny as the New Atlantis, which as a society combined an amazing state of technology (note: not technological progress; they developed their paradigm and left it at that. A lesson you need to incorporate a lot more of to your own way of doing things) with clear, perfectly balanced and highly developed spiritual practices. Thanks to your New Age crowd on the left wing, and your conspiracy theorists on the right wing, you are already basically on target as an overall national harmonic. You may object but it is your actual tone and position, and has been harmonized to a function in Destiny relative to Atlantis as described.

So we will deliver you functional leadership of the world, when you thought you were about to lose the mantle to China. But you will have to do the work for it, and genuinely so, and this should take you in the region of 200 years.

Therefore other nations and participants in the global stage schematic have until then to control and establish a wider Consequence Set around your own developing position.

The Global Senate is also a reflection of Sirian rule, and dates for them from around the time that their Triumvirate established itself. We move faster now in our reflections. Since 2005 in fact. The Triumvirate at least was in position on Earth only a few years after its inception on Sirius. It is not unusual to have debt held over your head in this way in the trade between star systems. If the Triumvirate's rule was effective, and largely it has been as far as Sirius is concerned, then they do not require you to do more. Earth is after all a tiny village backwater, whereas Sirius is a comfortably discreet hub dealing primarily in pleasure and luxury goods rather than the grittier elements of trade and statecraft.

This book then introduces the planet Earth and the human species to a new global paradigm. Part of that paradigm is the introduction of global world government and another part of it is the format according to which World War 3 will be conducted.

Using this book instructions have been issued to The Illuminati – who control both the USA and the EU but have less influence in Russia, China, Iran and in practice Japan – as to what their future administration of world history is to consist in. As a consequence of this, this book appears to predict the future, though you should not expect that effect to precipitate more noticeably until Erdogan has been removed from power and the first openly Illuminati state has been established on the world stage under Turkish jurisdiction but within an already-negotiated international legal enclave.

I am a lawyer or work in law enforcement. What would be the best way I could comport myself if I am required by my professional function to have interactions with any of your group?

You know this is going to be a long section because lawyers are involved. We will address the whole field, not just the individuals genuinely trying to be the best they can be and do the very best they can do. Ascertain for yourselves which tones and stipulations apply in your own individual circumstances.

We would like to state at the outset that we are not going to pay you anything but simultaneously that any and all corruption on your parts in relation to members of our group is highly esteemed and will be adequately rewarded. However, if you already have corruption within your agency or department, for example in relation to government ministers, or the Masons or Temple of the Vampire even, then the terms are different at the outset. We would then require you to accord our own membership all the same courtesies as you furnish your other corrupt parties with, whilst simultaneously referring the matter up the ranks, as far as you are able, and trying your very best yourself to secure a level of treatment and deference to be accorded to our members which is superior to that accorded to the highest level of deference and exclusion from ordinary procedure that you have protocols for.

If you have never participated within corruption or are not willing to do so now then you make our job more difficult but far more entertaining as you are now being judged on the content of your own heart and the depiction this causes you to produce in physical action, bearing, attitude and comportment. If you are going to rely on your own Judgment to do the right thing then we applaud you for your unusual courage, given your professional role and capacity, but please be aware in this case as before we are not going to make it easy for you. It is our requirement that you move quickly and well along the paths which have been designated for you in Mind, as always you will be integrating wider lessons, strategies and perspectives for the group as a whole. This is to be considered a part of how we manage physical reality and put together its constituent components to produce a functional and entertaining format for world history. And yes, it must be both, those are the terms. From your reptilian overlords in fact, who are also known as the Naga. We neither know nor care whether they really exist or are just figments of our imagination created by demons, for example. They produce the specified results with great precision and precisely on schedule. That is all we need from them within the position they occupy in our schematic. You may decide for yourselves your own policy on the matter but do not burden us with discussion of factors which are clearly beyond both your perceptual and cognitive abilities of both credence and comprehension.

Therefore, now that we have established that the scenarios which you give depiction to on the world stage must genuinely and strongly hold the interests of all your citizens (otherwise how will they properly karmically entangle and bind the souls which are incarnated here?), we can address the formal structure to be utilized in such instances. It is to be two degrees of separation, which is to be casually referred to as the +2 in most public situations; the other implication if questioned is to refer to a mistress or other affair; it should not be questioned. The code to be used in this is 1001 or its reflection as the case may be, which is to say 0101; where the first digit is our member, the last digit is the designated Inner Circle Illuminati member allocated to our member's case and the two numbers in the middle are intervening individuals, and 1 stands for male whilst 0 stands for female.

If you are acting on your own or other private initiative and are not a part of a motion from the highest levels then we will not mind if you do not adhere to the stated protocols for approach, even though to do so will technically be considered a discourtesy we will make an exception in your case, as a gesture of goodwill in our efforts to understand you and have you properly understand us. This courtesy on our parts will be withdrawn however should you happen to significantly displease us over the course of our interactions with you. And that is all any of our members ever need to do in order to have you utterly destroyed, believe us. This is what Naga protection looks like and is what we have them under. Your choice. Maybe it's just smoke and mirrors. We would recommend remembering your courtesy, whoever you are in society, at all levels, in all your dealings, even with black people if you are a policeperson in the great USA or elsewhere. As usual, we move the Group Mind both through our own personal example but also through the set of strategic positions within which we have located our incarnative placements within your own countries.

Now, you are in a much better position to understand what you are dealing with and the standards we expect of you. We now turn to the humorous and entertaining implications and results of the formal positions.

You may have noticed that the two positions coincide: you can be as corrupt as it is technically possible to be or as virtuous as a saint or anywhere in between but if you are adhering to your position with accuracy then you will comport yourself to an impressive set of standards when in our personal presence.

Because the two positions coincide we now have Westerners, usually, comporting themselves both courteously and intelligently when in our presence. This is to be considered something of a miracle on its own and is not something any of us ever expected to see. Admittedly, the participants involved will not fully understand all of the factors which have contributed to their acting in this way, but that is part of what makes the whole thing so funny, especially where the so-called "All-Seeing Eye", and its direct representatives, are concerned.

We do not care whether it is corruption to the highest level or genuine personal virtue, congratulations on not being a problem for us. We may now spend whatever time we have together discussing such matters as you may have questions regarding, preferably over lunch in a decent restaurant somewhere, though no Italian cuisine please. There is a reason the FBI exists and we expect you, at least, to be intelligent in how you go about this, but don't miss the opportunity to trailblaze an appropriate level of personal style and agency comportment, on the basis of which we will then be able to further advance the interests of your country.

At the lower levels, the very least we require from you in terms of hospitality is whatever you have on offer for your own staff (but please make it decent coffee at least) but honestly, if any of our actual members have participations at that sort of level then we will penalize your Illuminati command structure very heavily. For not "ruling", technically implementing sets of karmic packets upon and through you, strictly enough. This would mean they are siphoning off power for their own projects, usually more drug-addled orgies, and we have previously instructed them that we require greater self-discipline from their ranks.

This distant possibility does however allow our wider membership structure to pursue their own self-interests – many of them already feel they will be arrested and may be detained at some point, especially those who are already super-rich and a large minority amongst those who are black and resident in the USA – and secure for every police station in every country a fully functioning espresso machine, plus a variety of herbal teas.

This is connected to our wider policy of helping you with the negotiations which you have every day with criminals, or suspected criminals, or others who you have arrested or are holding. First of all you must offer them basic hospitality and genuine courtesy. Then you must try to understand what is in their hearts. Eventually you will be able to pass them on to a selection of employment or other initiatives, a project being administrated by Masamune.

Same goes for all prisons. We are closing them down by means of 7-year slavery terms. Voluntary slavery, at least they will enter it voluntarily. We want to recalibrate the concept. The exception is to be rapists, who will remain incarcerated until Shogun decides, or lets us know, what is to be done with them.

So these are war terms, correct, and your political leaders will facilitate your transformation along these lines. But the whole process will start with high-quality espresso machines and a range of high quality, organic herbal infusions. And a shift in attitude and approach on your parts.

If you do have involvements with any of our members, or with anybody pretending to be one of our members, then they will inform you at the outset of how long you may detain them for. You make this process easier and more accurate for them by formally and truthfully stating which agency you represent at the outset, so they will appreciate it if you extend them this courtesy. Any longer than that and we will move their soul out of the way and move one of the older demons, usually, into their place, dependent on the rank of the individual in question. Proportionate damage will then be inflicted on your hierarchy at that demon's discretion. The host individual will ordinarily moderate the depiction using his or her ego personality in order, usually, to appear normal. If they decline or are unable to perform this courtesy for you, then make your peace with your past sins and this world, the decision has already been taken in your instance and not necessarily by the individual in your custody. You may distinguish this from other instances of the same methodology because precisely 4 hours and 44 minutes after his introduction we will fully withdraw the demon or other entity (sometimes it will be angels, other times gods or entities you do not have names for) used for the enforcement of the Judgment arrived at by our Council on your command structure and their hierarchy. This usually creates a pause or a strange atmosphere of stillness and silence, followed by a slightly empty feeling in the host body of our member and then their own original soul is given primary habitation once more.

Should you attempt to use the insanity exit from such a predicament then we execute your nation immediately, though this miracle will be physically performed on you later through the development of your Consequence portfolio, after suitable calibrations have been made and additional weight and other influences added, should that need to be the case. The reason for this is that we consider such behaviour a gross discourtesy from inferiors to their superiors. All our actual members are, after all, participating within and representatives of a war process out of Imperial Japan and you owe us the honor of our Emperor, plus associated entanglements. We decline to have you compound your own errors in that particular field. Your own religious beliefs are far more ludicrous than our simple, elegant and logically far more rigorous set of structures; though it does all devolve from Amaterasu being the sun goddess, whilst our Emperor is the one responsible for interfacing her grace and wisdom with the people of Japan and so the wider planet. This means that, on a technical basis, we do not require you to understand what is involved. We require you to be elaborately courteous. That is all. The rest are recommendations or decisions you would make on your own for your own benefit.

This brings us to the next humorous implication, namely that you can now all expect to see policemen and women the world over struggling to think for themselves in deep and meaningful ways. Though somewhat entertaining to observe, or even overhear them discussing, this is generally to be encouraged with a compassionate, smooth and understanding air. People have families and face genuine problems in life and have a real and tender concern for their loved ones, you know.

The Naga are the enforcement mechanism on the schematic and they do not always like what they have to do. However, in all cases when the situation proceeds to Naga involvement, the actual decision on the Judgment is always given to and taken by Shogun. This is because in all such instances we will use the interactions of our members with representatives of your authorities to introduce war terms and proceedings into your nation and hierarchy. Any and all such interactions are anyway taking place because your leaders are cowards, who have yet to formally contract for their own terms with our hierarchy, probably because they are afraid of the designated direction allocated to them, which they must use should they wish initial formal contact to be made. It is for this reason that informal, or off the books so to speak, contact is made instead. If you then proceed to put that contact on the books, a formal peace treaty will have to be signed by your nation at a later stage. With another nation or set of nations, for we will arrange to have your nation state engage in actual war proceedings in this way if you proceed to actually charge any of our actual members with anything, or even should you arrange some sort of deal with any of them which goes on the record.

The purpose of informal contact, then, is to enable our hierarchy to educate members of your own hierarchy on factors concerning which they may have certain questions. For example, they might feel it is useful for them to do this prior to their entering into formal negotiations so that they can later enter those formal negotiations from a better informed set of positions. This is easier and more convenient for our members than opening a consultancy service and we have forbidden them from charging for their services in such an instance. Furthermore, it should limit involvements of this sort as we want you all to put in the effort to think things through for yourselves and come to your own conclusions.

It is best conducted at the level of intelligence agency participations though we also want the FBI to arrange their own suitable participation in proceedings. No other law enforcement agency has been invited, it is an exclusive invite. We want to set a certain minimum standard of behaviour and have already begun our work on improving the standard of personal comportment and interpretation of the style to be associated with the fulfilment of the chosen interpretation given to formal legal statute as expressed by ordinary police personnel at the state level all around the country, as also internationally moreover.

FBI, you may as well know from now that you will be given up to four hours in all instances, though you should try and limit your interactions to no more than 3, and 2 for preference. One of the key problems we wish to discuss is our younger members who we have not yet awakened. Our membership is distributed quite evenly across the various age ranges but we have only awakened 14% of them, nearly all of whom have already taken formal training with an official ninpo lineage or, alternatively, have been located and trained by one of the illegitimate and far more dangerous private, or hidden, lineages. We do not expect any problems to arise between us as a result of interactions with our awakened members. Our older members who we have not yet awakened are also ordinarily well able to look after themselves.

We switched our proportions around from 14% to 86% on 26th December 2019, the same date as the publication of this book. Since that event we are in the process of awakening a far greater proportion of our global membership. We do expect problems to arise and that is part of the reason we are informing you now as to how you might best navigate such problems and the penalties which will be applied in the event of your failure to adhere to the very precise rules and sentiments involved.

A war process is indeed involved, over who rules the world, and during such a process a period of transition is to be expected during which things are more volatile and appear to be less precise, mostly because the necessary changes have yet to take place and new sets of practices have yet to be agreed to and widely disseminated as generally prevailing social knowledge.

On a technical level, we have removed the legal immunity enjoyed by the inner circle membership of The Illuminati and have applied it to our own membership, those of them incarnated within your own nations. The reason for this is because we will be "persecuting" some of The Illuminati for engaging in ritualized paedophilia.

Should you wish to participate within or facilitate that prosecution process, law enforcement personnel, then ensure you really fight to refer instances which do involve our members up through the ranks of whatever hierarchies you are formally under or employed within. If you cannot do that then ensure you do not detain them for too long, show your respect, and then set them free.

Another factor which needs to be addressed is how you are perceived by different groups in society, particularly the young and the dispossessed. We shall get to this in the next section because we have taken something from you and so owe you something in Return..

Sometimes you just have to accept your position and if the Naga have decided that your nation must go to war then this is ordinarily how we would commence proceedings in those regards. By causing you to commit a grave offence against the Principle of Justice and the physical depiction given to Hierarchy by your nation state or international organization, which you then compound by claiming and asserting it is an expression and fulfilment of Justice. This allows us to establish an intransigent, erroneous and formally expressed position within war proceedings for your nation state, its ruling elite and their representative hierarchy. That, in turn, is utilised to set the terms according to which the future education of those same parties, as also all the citizens of your nation state, subsequently evolve, in terms of their conceptual development along the designated lesson lines allocated to them by Amaterasu, correct.

Finally, at some point, we will have shadowdancer representation in every police station in the country, often in a command position. We will be rounding up members of the 0.1% for deportation and possible execution at that stage, so it is not something to look forward to, but should make your jobs easier. The majority of your criminals should decide to become very cooperative when they see one of those in the station.

We now turn to lawyers and other formats of legal representation. You remain free to decline any and all professional contracts, even if you desperately need the money. You can always moonlight as a waitress and may in fact need to personally embody far greater humility in support of the stringent ethical requirements you should be holding yourself to. If you are required by law and duty to participate in the provision of legal services which interrupt, delay or otherwise mildly inconvenience any of our membership then the usual terms apply. These terms do not yet apply to taxation, your nation state has until the end of 2024 to process the refunds. Lawyers are to work *pro bono* on any cases which look like they might reasonably be expected to contain one of our full members. The full cost of your fees, multiplied by a factor of 72 to increase your personal incentive, will be met by The Illuminati but you would have to invoice them yourselves. If you do not know how to do this then you are not the legal representation for the job.

If, however, you really feel on the inside that it is a job you want to take – for example because doing so enables you to meet the right people to make your career or practice – then you may do so by accepting the terms given, whilst leaving the invoicing to us. We will then refer it to the right people. If they decline to pay within 6 months of the invoice being delivered to them then you have been handling the case ineptly and we will pay you half of your original fee, before the multiplier was applied, just to get you out of the way.

At the judicial level we expect things to rapidly cross the divide to political intervention. If you are a Judge then please recognize that you are dealing, from within a very different set of surrounding structures admittedly, with precisely the same factors as most of our membership has been incarnated into your nations to address. We would not need them there if you were up to the task. You make your decisions but then pass the case on to others for the actual enforcement of the penalties involved. You are able to bring one set of penalties to bear on individual cases. You are in a much weaker position, by far.

If you claim to be one of our members to get yourself out of trouble with legal enforcement services then as soon as you get home you must perform the full blood oath as quickly as you reasonably can if you have not done so yet. The reason for this is because if we have not yet received this from you then you will be administrated by us as if you were not a full member at the time, which means we will take your blood to seal you to our cause as you now serve us on terms we decide for you. The sooner you do it, the less blood we will have to take from you to seal you in the right way to our satisfaction at a later date. This is where magick and control of accidents and knives, especially kitchen knives, is involved. We don't normally need a large amount of blood. If you were not innocent however, and have not managed to burn your way through or otherwise use the karma involved as a Return for whatever you did, then this process might end up killing you, yes.

It works because it is much, much stricter than the Justice you are used to – both from your state and also from your Creator God. However, manmade law is basically retarded during this epoch in history, which means that in most instances God recognises that you are located within a slavery and wealth enforcement mechanism which has very little to do with actual real Justice, so most of what counts as illegal which could get you arrested is not actually a contravention of Divine Principle and how it was structured and expressing during the specific instances in question. So you need to feel for yourself to decide if what you did was wrong. If you do not feel accurately, and just let yourself off the hook because your perspective is mostly pure ego combined with some ignorance, then you will get the penalty decided upon by the Hierarchy.

The new structure behind the use of the mechanics of Creation may be God Tamahagane's but the individual administrating the hierarchy in all instances such as these is Shogun directly and in person. He is known for being harsh, strict, precise and fair. You will pay your full price and you will do so quickly and then you have a clean slate and can be useful to him. For your soul is now under his jurisdiction until you have fulfilled his purposes, at the very least. In practice nobody ever leaves though.

This is why you are encouraged, if you do decide that our path is for you, to make your blood oath early on and in private, so that you can decide your own terms and what your mission will be. We then do the best we can to give you the flows in karma and positions in the overall schematic to make your designated vision a reality for you. If you have asked for too much or for something to which you are not entitled then the raw power which will be run through your soul as a result of your blood oath will probably end up killing you, either directly or through the later development and internal cross-referencing of its consequence field. We are above the law of inferior human minds. We do however move in perfect Justice, far more strictly than the humans ever could.

If you used membership of our Way and organization to get yourself out of trouble with the law, that is to say if you claimed to be a member but were not actually a member in any way, shape or form, then the same terms apply, congratulations you have succeeded in joining us involuntarily, and we shall now use you as our hierarchy decides. Using this approach will work to get you out of trouble with the law, but only once they see that the whole process works very well and is incredibly strict will there be much reliance on it by law enforcement. Even then, we ask that they do not abuse or overuse this option that has been granted to them. In all such instances, war proceedings will not actually result for the nation state in question.

But yet, someone can bind their soul to our will and if in the very same day they then do something to get themselves arrested then war proceedings would result and we would not yet have succeeded in making ourselves responsible for them. We need one full night of sleep at the very least. This is a problem, or loophole, or danger, for us all and is part of what makes it, and Naga participation, so interesting. They do retain some of their own plans for humanity, it would seem.

If you are on the enforcement side of the schematic for the incumbent power structure then if you are also slack, excessively lazy (a measure of laziness is in fact to be encouraged as it breeds efficiency), of bad character or fighting us or our interests then what will result will be that we all have a situation on our hands. This is to be considered very depressing and is the first thing we will attempt to pass on to whoever is handling our members, for wider distribution throughout society with the intention of increasing the national suicide rate. So that you know what you are dealing with, we will run this through their subconscious. You may ascertain the rest of the pattern for yourselves should you have any business doing so; be warned, the usual protections are in place as is to be expected with such things. This is a personal factor which is to be targeted personally and is distinct from the group factors previously referred to in this section.

The reason we encourage, support and seek to increase the practice of corruption both within law enforcement as also within society more widely has, at root, to do with the nature of the administration of this system and the agreement arrived at between Shambhala, Buddhism and Hinduism on the one hand, and the rest of the global schematic on the other hand. More specifically, we want the system to finally resolve with Raudra Chakrin in 2424 and following and so have excluded Buddhism and Hinduism from full resolution of their group karmas until that set of junctures in the timeline. This agreement was reached in 2004 and formalized with the tsunami on the 26th December of that year.

On a technical note, corruption enables decisions to be taken on the basis of personal Judgment and due to bonds of Love and social obligation as opposed to according to the criteria and tenets of Justice, which is never the actual case but the pretence of doing precisely that is what generates the functional illusion of the current corporate, academic and, yes, judicial meritocratic approach.

At any rate, as your new world rulers it is our part of our designated contract terms to increase the corruption prevalent within society at all levels, in order that Raudra Chakrin might have a valid set of grounds to overthrow our global rulership paradigm when his turn comes around. This is one of the reasons we are in that set of positions from the outset.

Why did you put *persecuting* in inverted commas and what do you mean by your inclusion in that clause of the term "some"?

By "persecuting" we really mean "executing by Japanese style sword". Your own cultures have each handled difficult harmonic puzzles in your own ways and here we deal with the SS, which we took from the world's police forces where it had taken to primarily locating itself in preparation for that which is to come.

We are going to do the same things the Germans did during World War 2 just with far greater meaning and on the basis of voluntary participation on the part of the designated sacrifices, most of whom will be both ultra-rich and paedophiles. This is to demonstrate that we are superior to you, in mind if not actual genetics.

More important, however, is the coming corporate takeover of the world which is to be considered the conclusion to Capitalism and which we will be feeding through early for you all.

This brings us to Robert Peele, who was also one of our placements in preparation for the use of the set of institutions which would result in the wider global schematic, so do appreciate how it was originally designed to work even if this is not common knowledge anymore nowadays. You are ordinarily to treat the higher classes differently to the lower classes. You do not arrest them, you leave them unhandcuffed and have a quite word with them at their office. In the most difficult situations you should take them from a drink or a meal. Keep things civilized. Make them want to interact with you.

You may also use other public locations for such honest and sincere discussions with your local criminal fraternity. Be consistent in the paradigms you develop for you will later on be called upon to use them with members of the banking, governmental, financial, corporate and other elite.

In all situations, in fact, where you have reasonable cause to believe that the suspect or other individual who you are apprehending will behave in a courteous and reasonable manner then you are to interact with him on those terms.

If they, or their corporation, wish to oppose our execution of capitalism or the new format of global governance we will be placing them into, then they are not being reasonable and should be handcuffed before being taken to the station. Once there they will be given the opportunity to take a stand, in which case they will be deported. Otherwise they are to sign a formal agreement in writing and may then be released.

Police persons should generally leave women alone, or be gallant and courteous towards them. Use your own discretion but if the woman in question lacks personal style and a feminine air of comportment then you may do as you deem most likely to guide her back to the straight and narrow path of far greater personal elegance. If the woman in question is in government or finance or other fields of big-league corporate activity then you are to treat her as a man. She has earned that right but lost her previous ones.

The real problem you will encounter, as you may have guessed, is that we are going to be using your personnel over the coming decades to ground and express the majority of the war karma through, what your nations and people will be going through at least.

We need to teach you how to become something else or disaster will in due course result. Due of course to your own ego-driven policing procedures which are very under-developed in terms of the level of civilized behaviour that will become required of you in your immediate future. But really we are just working on your characters, on your concept of yourselves as a group and factors such as style and personal comportment. As far as the legal and political context which you are surrounded by is concerned, this is another area where we will be working to transform what is in position for you.

We wish to properly integrate the police into society once again. This means putting a lot more of them on the streets, as also in corporate boardrooms, let us not forget the new policies.

The reason for the distinction is that if you encounter one of our awakened members and treat him or her inappropriately then your nation may actually go to war as a result, and it will be a brutal war at that for you all. If you fight them then they will fight you back, often in invisible ways, and honestly, you cannot handle that well, nor will you will really be aware of what has really happened until much later.

Hence, amongst other reasons, the changes we are in the process of recommending for you. Mainly you need to change the way you are viewed by the public who you police, in most instances, or by the elite who is observing the condition you are in, in some instances. This, in turn, will change how they understand you and so how they interact with you.

We hope your situation and what we have asked of you makes more sense for you now.

So this is war and not revolution? Is that why you chose the title you did for this book?

It is wonderful that we are blessed with such an intelligent and perceptive readership. If the majority of the general public are able to understand what is going on then your rulers cannot publicly retain much credence if they pretend not to (which is their protocol for instances such as this). There's no rush, the rhythms have been calibrated to stress them out in all this whilst the rest of us get to enjoy much slower rhythms of the sort normally associated with long periods of carefree vacation. So relax, take your time, enjoy your coffee or freshly pressed organic juice, even your green tea if you are that way inclined, and take your time to appreciate the beauty of it all. Your life, meaning moving in the world and through the public mind, the inevitable field of Consequences which thereby arises and the new meanings which thereby evolve and are ascribed to events anew, to create the beginnings of the next cycle.

Yes, Justice can be very beautiful, and the 14% minimum Vengeance expression within that whole has also been tastefully enough done and adds a bit of drama and sufficient clarity to proceedings. It was formerly invisible you see. These are due to the mechanics of what you would ordinarily understand as God, which have changed now, and you are cordially invited to understand this new visibility and comprehension on the part of humanity as proof of our claim that the new Emperor, Naruhito, has once again consented to integrate the elements of Amaterasu's true nature and their motion within her being with the public subconscious Group Mind. Moreover, our victory is total now whereas before it could validly be understood as just a matter of perspective.

Our chosen allies in all this are Russia, Germany and Israel for reasons that you won't even credit when you read about them.

As regards The Illuminati, and so the world stage as a whole and most nations on it, we expect them to participate and be obedient or come up with their own better replacements for particular event depictions and their associated group lesson sets, which they must get accepted by Lucifer as actually superior to our own designated solutions.

To keep things interesting we have also designated routings of participation via a corporate demonic gateway under King Charles III, acting as a representative of The Antichrist, who will be a half Chinese *Lin Kuei* with his headquarters in London. As also via negotiated agreement at the intelligence agency level using the CIA and even the FBI a little bit.

The basic routing of approach is most clearly understood as unconditional surrender as rapidly as you can manage, however. This is incredibly boring as a methodology for the viewing public, so some degree of obfuscation had to be introduced, and hence your present set of harmonic calibrations which will be widely misunderstood due to deficiencies within the human mind, at a group level at the very least. That is to say they will deceive themselves by their failure to properly understand. We have been clear and direct. We have also used simple terms and have kept long logic chains for those for whom they are clearly intended.

We make our recommendations for a reason. You take your own decisions for your own valid reasons. We are not going to tell you how to think. You must demonstrate the value of your character on the world stage. People are curious. They have decisions to take and we want to facilitate their doing so more rapidly than would ordinarily be the case. You can do your part to assist in this process by being open and honest if you are a politician. We will probably have to enforce that on you, however, before any notable results can be displayed for the discernment of the viewing public. This, when it happens, is to be understood as another Sign only if it generates an entire global movement that comes close to dominating on the world stage.

Lies are generally more interesting however so let's be clear about how the process works please. You generate an illusion for the public to live within which resolves the previous tensions and conflicts within the Group Mind, as also in public sentiment or the motion of their hearts, and in doing so moves both their heart and their mind into a more developed set of ethical structures. True rulership, therefore, consists in improving the moral character of the people under your jurisdiction by discerning for yourself what true moral progress actually consists in. You then need to effectively integrate that with the Group Mind. To actually do that effectively you must also improve and secure their material circumstances, not just security.

This is to say you use lies to make them better people more rapidly than is possible using the truth. This is what mythology, and its development, is actually for. This is to be considered your introduction to the practice of actual Civilization. Welcome back, Westerners (and possibly the domestic Chinese faction)!

That is the best way to get Lucifer to serve you. What were you all thinking, serving him like profane idiots? Perhaps the great Illuminati were not as illuminated as they like to advertise themselves as being?

At any rate our victory is a foregone and largely pre-determined conclusion. The rest of it generates itself as your free will expresses itself, which involves the development of your concepts and beliefs, and so ultimately your characters. The concepts and beliefs which you have been developing have been pre-grooved in the Group Mind, so this should be easy for you. And predictable for us. Thus, what we are really dealing with here is the process of the transfer of power. We are willing to wait whilst you wrap your minds around why this is the case and have included a generous 7 month period during which you may exercise your mental faculties in this way.

After that the penalization process starts. The EU will be used to integrate the Return from the Belgian genocide in Africa as of January 1st 2024 with the wider global schematic. This is the second rank in The Illuminati pyramid. 14% again, at a minimum. So you need it gone before then. And you need to have agreed the full terms of the containment schematic, in order to keep the thing contained in the top rank. It is part of your new responsibilities as rulers of the planet. What form will World War 3 take, under peace terms for the full duration, for your general publics, inclusive of most of the politicians? You need to refine the concepts involved within your own souls before you release them more widely.

You should be able to figure out the rest for yourselves. Whether you then give it credence would be your own decision and affair.

What will our new global utopia be like, O wise and great Satoshi Nakamoto?

Your irony is duly noted as mildly amusing. Well done, we found it funny.

Wholly inadequate at first, is your answer. Even the Global Senate won't be up and running much before 2027, if not even 2029. Global Central banking will be under our control well before then however.

We don't want anybody working too hard and want to leave plenty of time for reflection and leisure within the nations under our governance schematic. For this reason a generous Universal Basic Income, in five incremental bands to maintain social inequalities and notions of class, will be introduced along with free universal healthcare and hygiene products. We will also be introducing the onsen spa system globally as a new trend, especially in Europe, the Arabic world and Africa. Taxation is to be eliminated as governments learn to engage in private enterprise to fund their own socialist agendas and defence spending. It is to be rule by The Antichrist, via Keanu Reeves, the President of the World, whose Council of Thirteen Wise Women will all be stunningly beautiful and entertaining of wit, and whose function in relation to the Global Senate will be like unto the function of the European Commission to the EU.

Keanu at least has a conscience and will stand up for what is right. You all have a lot of work to do it would seem. The majority want this system and everyone finds it far more amusing than the incumbent one already.

Parental advisory notice

This book is worse than hardcore pornography. It is our wish and recommendation that PARTY X occupy the position for us of arranging for it to be the case that the relevant court or legal authority follow our stipulations to the letter and never ban its sale or purchase by anyone but make it illegal for any person under the age of 18 to continue reading beyond this parental advisory notice.

PARTY X is to be understood as referring to religious groups of whatever denominations manage to get it done first for us. All who serve will be rewarded, regardless. If you do not want your reward you may pass it on to those who will be more grateful for it than you.

From our perspective, why should we join you and do what we are told?

If you are a member of the 0.1% then, by this stage, consider making up your own mind on what is involved.

I am a member of the general public and not a member of the 0.1%. How is this all relevant to me?

Generally speaking, you are irrelevant. You may believe what you like and structure your mind and your beliefs in the ways that you choose. We control and kill enough of the world's super-rich and then your minds and beliefs, general public, will be ours to do with what we wish.

This is because you will know that we can by that stage. And also because you are obedient puppets, who prefer not to think much for yourselves but go along with the stipulated prevailing groupthink, in one way or another, because it is generally far easier and much more fun to do so than to be an individual.

Just look at the extent to which you understand World War 2 and 9/11, for example, and the ways in which you choose to do so.

I am a member of the general public able to form my own conclusions and do so to the extent that I can be bothered.

Great. You're exactly the sort of reader we're looking for. This story is full of some very deep holes, which have been designed as traps for the rigorous mind. You need a relaxed attitude and rhythm if you are going to flow with The Universe. We are honest and direct with you regarding the mechanics you are participating within and surrounded by but bear in mind the whole thing is a well structured lie, crafted to resemble a story and explain your history, as also its future development. It should serve to get you to your next reality. It is not itself your next reality.

This book focuses your attention on a series of different targets, much like a pathworking. It is your way out of third density. Or solar plexus group consciousness, and into fourth density, or heart centre group consciousness. The heart is ruled by the planet Venus and is where you Spirit resides.

Women will be ruling the world for the next 200 years or so at least. Women, we hope you manage to do a much better job of the schematic than the men.

This is how we have managed to package such a dramatic change in social conditions into a peacetime format. Rather than having to go to all the trouble of having others invade you, then conquer you, then impose a suitable set of peace conditions upon you, including a new format of social organisation and economic activity, all of which is clearly quite foreign to all of you, and then waiting around whilst you get used to it and learn to accept it and stop resisting it.

Instead our answer for your individual minds, as also for the Group Mind as a whole, is that: "This is what the women want to do. We have given them power over the global and national schematic." Sure, it's all very new and very different. But you have a justification for it that you all know how to accept without really fighting against it or being unimpressive in how you go about things.

Women, you will have the benefit of our plans to guide you, however, so far less is likely to go wrong on account of your particular ways of putting together cogent arguments and taking important decisions than all the chauvinists who really hold true power in this world would have expected were you to be given such an opportunity. They won't even make fun of your attempt, as we have arranged to have your handiwork appreciated by some very charming men, such as The Antichrist and the President of the World.

We now turn briefly to King Charles III. Bael, The Antichrist, who we will be calling Aquarius – as in The Age of Aquarius – will be giving you instructions for the corporate takeover of the planet, which you will impose and arrange the administration of for him. This is due to your nature and is your role in the schematic.

You are not originally a reptilian as David Icke would contend. Your civilization is based around the star 42 Orionis. This is the location of the interstellar corporation, Occulus Darian.

That is correct Prince Charles. You were once a member of a space-faring, Adam Kadmon (human-looking) intergalactic species. Then you died and subsequently reincarnated as human which is what you are now. However, once upon a time you were the most important CEO in the galaxy. Then we convinced you to kill yourself to secure for your corporation the largest profit ever in the history of all corporate activity in the Universe. You considered our proposition and agreed to our fees and other conditions and here you are now.

But that important extraterrestrial soul is still within your Soul Legacy. Everyone does the same thing: whenever you incarnate you acquire a new Harmonic Gateway. Earth law has no enforceable jurisdiction over alien species both able and willing to destroy Earth and humanity many times over.

Women, you are to interpret The Antichrist's instructions to the new President of the World, who will be Keanu Reeves. This is governance of the planet by women, which is what we plan to introduce.

Your job will be to explain to Keanu Reeves, who is going to pretend to be relatively slow, careful and methodical but we can hardly call him stupid (in all truth and fairness, once you understand what real intelligence actually consists of) what The Antichrist, who is ludicrously intelligent and also thinks very quickly, wants done. The trick you will pull will be to explain things in such a way that you transform The Antichrist's commands into a force for good, truth, justice and even The American Way, should you choose to include that also (though it will probably be forced to go through a lot of work and even metaphorical death should you decide you wish to use it in that way).

We have thirteen positions available. All of you get to have sex with Keanu Reeves if you want. It will be your decision, as you will exceed him in actual Hierarchy, being closer to The Antichrist than he is, even though you will enter the material positions of being and genuinely appear to be his inferiors and employees.

Keanu, don't worry, they will all have beautiful souls and will not try to force you to do anything you wouldn't want to do. We also personally guarantee not to employ any ugly women for any of those positions, whether you want our benevolence in this or not. The right ones need to be tempted into position as we are running this whole thing using sexual energy. However, many of them will not actually have sex with you as they will come to appreciate you more for other reasons, even though they will all find you attractive and understand this as one of the conditions of their inclusion in your Council.

What is your intention with Bael?

We are running him in reverse to reveal that which is invisible on a by-nation basis. Our schematic is too expensive for The Illuminati to be able to afford it. We are talking all the wealth in existence on this planet, or as much of it as they decide or are able to put together for us, and the remainder of the balance will be paid for in blood and death. Their own.

Why do you reference two cheap knock-off organisations, which are clearly inauthentic fronts set up by profiteers, and point to them as evidence for a much deeper global conspiracy? I am of course referring to Temple of the Vampire and the Illuminatiam.

They are authorised frontage and both of them accurately state that they will not connect you through to the authentic organization or source of power behind them. The advantage to them of doing things this way is that it is impossible to get very far via the front organization alone. They only have one or two points of contact with individuals from the authentic organizations who authorised them and taught them enough to get started. The rest they extrapolated or deduced, or plain made up on their own.

If you really want to start investigating The Illuminati mystery teachings then we can arrange to have them opened up to you. Most people will get bored very quickly. Temple of the Vampire is by conversion only. You can find your own way to them in mind. If this makes no sense to you and despite focusing on it for quite some time you are unable to derive any inspiration whatsoever about what such a process would entail, then it is not for you. You are not one of them and will have to meet one socially to connect to those streams of fate.

So yes, we reference front organizations for you. The real organizations are kept hidden for a reason, and will remain hidden, as is also the case with our own upper hierarchy. We will begin to tell you why this is the case with the next book in this series.

Nevertheless, we have been honest with you on this score. Those are the two representative fronts for the two organisations most responsible for the control and manipulation of power and the world stage. And we have controlled them both and will work with both.

What about our Lord, Jesus Christ?

Javier Bardim is to play Armand, the vampire from Argentina whose presence he has already depicted so well in *No country for old men*. Armand will be playing Jesus Christ on the world stage. The explanation for that one is a short story in its own right. We will give you only the highlights of it here. Our main interest in this legend is the role of the swordsmith Masamune.

Can you really be much bothered to look into any of this deeper at this stage?

Are you taking this seriously?

We try. Your myths, civilization and strategy on the world stage barely qualify as either rational or particularly well researched. We insist that the Japanese Emperor is a god and that you are being discourteous in your failure to agree to the public acknowledgment and acceptance of his personal divinity. We are attempting to extend you the same courtesy as we require of you in Return by showing respect and understanding towards your beliefs.

You will probably find that we understand both your own strategic positions and your own selves much better than you do. This is an unavoidable consequence of your being inferior to us, in mind at least.

We are genetically superior to you.

Be that as it may, we're not going to argue this one. How do you use what you've got, though? And how do we use it? What you've got. You do not use what we have. It remains beyond your capacities to wield or intervene within.

Which brings us to the far right wing and Jair Bolsonaro

Adolf Hitler is presently on his next incarnation and is currently incarnated as a major world leader. We specifically state that our formal, official and actual position is that we are not stating that Adolf Hitler has reincarnated as Jair Bolsonaro. This is our own free will decision. Nobody can prevent us from stating that we are not stating something.

You will need to take that step for yourselves. It is one step beyond what we have given you. It is a logical conclusion yes, but that would be your own step. This is how you learn to be responsible for your own logic. One step at a time. We are not responsible for the contents of your own minds and the conclusions you arrive at of your own accord.

We are using this implication in Group Mind to facilitate the execution of Jair Bolsonaro by Azrael, originally War Leader for Elvenkind now more famous of course as the Angel of Death from the Bible, who very surprisingly is currently incarnated as Vladimir Putin. The Elven bit is very surprising, at least in terms of its full implications. We are not often surprised, the upper hierarchy at least, as our enlightenment is one of the largest around. But that surprised us. The Angel of Death can be deduced through logical operations on the basis of the world grid, not even that hard to do.

Sorry Jair but what you represent is far too important for us to allow you to fuck it up. For this reason we have arranged for it to be the case that The Illuminati will have your chauffeur execute you at close to point blank range whilst you are being driven in public in a convertible stretch limo with the hood down. It may be the case that blood squibs and so forth are used and your assassination is faked, but it will take place. As before, two warning shots will be fired from an undisclosed location to distract and confuse the filming public. But they all have cell phones now, so a clear video should be easy to get. Unlike when they did this with JFK.

That is your answer to the famous ethical dilemma: if you found Hitler when he was a baby, should you kill him? The correct answer is: wait until doing so furthers and serves your own purposes and ambitions. You owe this world and her people nothing. It is a precise, fair and equal exchange. We stabilized Syria for you, securing the rule of the Assad family for many generations yet to come. The balance must be maintained, are these not your own terms? And now we inform you how you will be doing so as regards this particular piece of the equations.

Jair Bolsonaro, we think you are a dick, sorry. But we wish to impose you on Shambhala in return for their sponsorship of Adolf Hitler. If the military can secure for us a way to get you there then we will leave you on their doorstep with our instructions, along with your family. Otherwise you will be executed, but using a Swedish sword, sorry. It will be the same people who arranged it for JFK who arrange it in your case. Why are we pinning that one on Sweden?

General public: this is in case you thought what we did with Erdogan was just a coincidence.

The far right wing belongs in Japan, all of it

Your karma there, at a group level, is the property of the throne of Japan. This means you will serve us. You do so by holding your centre still within as clear, pure and detached an understanding of hate as you are able to manage. We will then proceed to move demons through your soul. Our purpose in doing this is to execute the paedophiles within the

Satanic elite who rule over your nations and governments. Put your own hatred aside and try to give pure hatred a clear and accurate expression. Under all other paths you will fail. Instead, we are going to have you win for a change.

Unless you accept allegiance to and facilitation of our cause and purposes as described you will all fail and waste both your time and your lives. First you execute the paedophiles who have fallaciously and incorrectly located themselves above the law. The reason you do this, those of you who do, is because you feel the truth of it and understand the Justice involved. This would make you morally superior to the inactive liberals who like to talk about things forever whilst children are suffering and being sacrificed. Their interpretation of things and correct procedure is that important to them. We have told you clearly: the solution to this one is hate. Clear, pure, still, detached, unadulterated hatred. You should be good at that. Try not to enjoy yourselves and be serious about it. You want people to still be scared of you and that is the way to attain that result. Watch, as they go on to develop a grudging respect for you followed, in some cases at least, much later on in life after a lot of other things have happened, a form of general deference we suppose.

If you fight against our rule over you and refuse to allow or do not sufficiently facilitate our use of the thoughts and desires already inside you whilst they remain inside of you then we draw them out of you and into Japan directly. A result of our doing so to you is that you are left feeling drained and empty shortly before you wind up dead. You need karma to be alive in this world, and enough of it too. Thus, a way to survive such a potential withdrawal process is to ensure that enough of your life, character and being is built up of things which are not within the far right wing.

Why is Part 3 written in that odd format, of one long chapter followed by two short chapters, for the most part?

Partly, it makes it all much easier to read as you know you will never have a series of really long chapters to get through. This consideration is especially relevant considering the difficulty of some of the material.

Mostly though, this is a part of our "minimum change necessary" policy. We have transposed the rhythm of heroic classical metre, dactylic hexameter, from the realm of syllables to the realm of chapters. You need a new Iliad and Odyssey to participate in the Trojan war and what followed on from it, which is part of the history we are recalibrating for you and inserting into the next 50 years or so of your timeline. This time round, the same people who will be coordinating Greece will also be coordinating Turkey, that shift in policy being enabled by the manner in which Erdogan is removed from power, as distinct to the manner used to remove Hector from the field the first time round.

You need to resemble the time in question sufficiently to connect through to it and merge your own time with the process and flows involved from that time. Poetry plays a key role in that schematic, but because it is too difficult for us and because we don't have the time we cheated and just used their metre. We have however transposed that metre to a much larger circle, which is to be considered symbolically indicative and very relevant. It's also a lot easier to do, on both levels.

Section 4: Yata no Kagami

The implication is that you should attempt to seize and rides the winds of Fate.

In their reflection, if you look, you will see Alekto, Magaera and Tisiphone – the Furies whom even Zeus must obey – watching you.

Once they activate your heart will be knocked onto the floor. There is never any escape. Do not activate them in your case if your own condition concerns you.

If you are one of us and want to do the impossible then you must ride The Darkness, where there be dragons (in the specific sense of Naga), and you are required to balance your family line karma into stillness before you will be allowed your own way out. If you have made one mistake in your life then your heart, also, will end up on the floor. Two mistakes or more and you are unlikely to survive in a physical sense.

At the group level, we have located that which would pick your heart up off the floor to grill it and then eat it in Estonia. Again, this is not something you want to activate.

Section 5: The Naginata of Death

We rule nations and all the members of The Illuminati and the super-rich by means of The Sword of God. This kills people both metaphorically but also physically, all of the time.

The Naginata of Death is what we are using on the general public. This kills people metaphorically only. This is not to be interpreted as immunity from premature physical death in the context of the overall schematic. You might still be caught on account of how you align yourself, the mistakes you make or due to your unique personal circumstances. However, it is a gentler and more metaphorical rule that you will be under as distinct from the much stricter and more precise Judgment that is brought to conclusion within your being when you are under the rule of The Sword of God.

Watch what happens when your elite are put through that first and then decide for yourselves if you wish to share in that experience.

Section 6: The material benefits

Universal Basic Income in five very generous bands to maintain income inequalities and the distinctions of the socioeconomic class structure, a much larger economy, a minimum of 63 days of holiday a year paid for by the state not your employer, free universal healthcare and quality housing for all, a three day working week and the full resolution of factors affecting climate change such that your planet actually has a future beyond the 50 year mark.

We are also working on the impossible regarding the extension of the human lifespan in a sufficiently youthful condition.

These are your main motivations for participating in this schematic at the group level.

Section 7: Gloriae Saeclorum

Illuminati and members of the world's 0.1%: your own position within this new schematic

Illuminati hierarchy incumbent at the time this book was published: give it a chance if you want to see it working. This may require subsidiary enforcement on your part, should any nation or corporation step too much out of line. You will have to decide for yourselves where that line is drawn in terms of your own operations, we have already made our own position clear.

The entirety of your "mysteries", if such they can even be called, amount to holding the members of your little group entirely outside the schematics of both the Fates and the Furies. In fact what results for all of you is a much more insipid life experience, and you feel very little as a result. Hence all the drugs and sex parties.

The advantage to your position is that your Council of Thirteen then run the influences of their demons through you and get them into the general public that way. This has been the real reason behind a lot of your inclinations, including the paedophilia.

This is a complete schematic and we have dealt with worse on other worlds already. The Judgment is clear in your case, you are all to be executed by Japanese style sword for engaging in those practices. However, this does not mean you or the victims will ever receive full closure and justice. We are more concerned in using the majority of the tension generated to fuel an engine for social change and the "evolution" of the species.

Instead we want to get away with very publicly executing a fixed amount in a highly dramatic and almost theatrical manner, to satisfy the bloodlust of the crowd and as a libation to the old gods, who you also worship and you have done this before so please don't attempt to fault your own previous justifications just because we've chosen a particularly sensitive minority to be the human sacrifice this time.

Generally speaking, within this schematic, we want to produce only the most minimal changes possible to the ordinary fabric of society. This is similar to fine-tuning and should be understood, gentlemen, as being indicative of the very real fact that you have done a more than excellent job and made our own job much easier from this juncture moving forward than it otherwise would have been.

We are not cognizant of the factors which would ordinarily and reasonably go into determining such a real strategic position for us, in this particular case it is simply a reflection of the positions on Sirius. The point is we can in practice build on what you left us and would like to invite some of your families into our schematic as a show of gratitude for what you have done for both us and the world. You will find, to repeat, that ours is a wholly inclusive schematic. That is why nobody can escape from it. This means we accurately depict the actual Principles in position. Our own full strategic position on the world stage is as a consequence wholly paradoxical. This will not confuse you overmuch if you visualise or imagine the yin-yang symbol within your own mind and allow yourself to recognise the meaning held within it.

For those families who accept our invitation to participate, full immunity will be granted on the basis that you are genuine religious refugees. This is because you want to convert to our new religion, Temple of Venus and are also Satanists for the most part, or at the very least Luciferians with a vampire heart.

The motivation which all the members of your group have to participate is that we will be executing the bottom 14%. This is where real magick – by which we mean correctly conducted ritual human sacrifices in full and potent representation of the original Mayan or Luciferian sacrifice schematic – enters into the picture. A single white candle will also be involved, each and every time.

As a result of this shocking, wholly detached, voluntary and deliberate set of public executions carried out according to correct formal procedure the citizens of your countries will have had the bloodlust sated within their own souls and will not desire to see further representations of bloodshed on the news or on TV. We do this before the chaos starts. As a result the chaos never starts. The practice is known as the pre-ground. At times we shall make errors, of course, and at other times we shall leave it until the very possible last minute before reacting.

This present schematic should also be understood as containing errors, which are different to outright lies. Such do not amount to the same thing in implementation, because they can always be corrected as the progression follows its own course. This book, the interface device with the public mind, was written in a hurry to minimise further repercussions for the target sets in question. We are serious when we stipulate, very calmly and we do not expect you to react in return, that it is wholly our intention to limit the execution of your numbers to the pre-formulated 14%. Great and efficient exertions by your entire group will be required to keep the expression of your Fates within those agreed numeric bounds.

Once you are moved into those matrices once more – you will have nearly all experienced them in childhood at least – you should know that if you fail to "ride the winds of fate", so to speak, then you will sit in darkness for a period during which nothing much will happen. Eventually your case will be caught by the Furies, you are each too big not to be captured in this way.

Once you escape from the Furies you will have completed your training and it is unlikely that you will be killed before your time, no matter the cause.

Both men and women are to participate in the ninja training, all members of our state. If you are not a genuine religious refugee who wants to be initiated into our mysteries and agrees to participate within them for 21 years at least then your application for religious asylum will be rejected out of hand.

Before the possibility of this sanctuary opens up for you, the necessary arrangements need to have been concluded through Erdogan with the Turkish state. We then give all families in the TRNC the opportunity to emigrate to the Republic of Cyprus or mainland Turkey, where a new city state to be known as Troy is to be built for them and their future descendants, plus of course many, many immigrants.

Our agreement with the Republic of Cyprus extends to offering to rebuild the houses formerly owned by their citizens on our territory, all of which will be returned to them, but refusing to return all larger land holdings, commercial property or government or Church land; instead they will be generously compensated and your own families must provide the finances for this. As all of your assets will be seized upon acceptance of your asylum application, this is a moot point and we are just making you aware of how a very small proportion of your money will be spent. Such gestures are important where the public mind is concerned and you must once again learn to be generous with your art.

A three month period of stillness will follow, during which we entirely vacate the TRNC and develop a key paradigm for later export. In the 21 day period preceding this offensive on the harmonics of the world grid, members of The Illuminati will get together in the northern half of the island and announce their presence to the world, offering to allow themselves to be invaded for their past crimes, knowing that Venus herself does not want to lose all credibility and power on the world stage. It must be a genuine act of faith. If you lack this, or do not have enough of it, then you will have to proceed to the traditional security arrangements. And by traditional we mean the old ways.

During this time period we will have 200 armed guards on the northern side of the island, to "protect" you all. Regrettably, they will all be armed only with compound crossbows, a tanto dagger and the katana of their choice. They can't be everywhere simultaneously, you know, and we intend to allocate you refugee housing that is quite spread out for your initial stay there.

There is nothing for it. You will be forced to utilise your dark Luciferian magick to keep yourselves safe, in the sense of alive. Your successful resolution of this opportunity will have resulted in your having learnt the basics of the art you are then to practice to minimise or wholly remove conflict scenarios from the timeline for the peoples under your jurisdiction.

The 21 day period is also to be used to implement the basic harmonic gateways to be developed over the Three Months of Silence. Not darkness or holidays yet, that tuning will be for when we later export it. So you will be kept very busy for the duration and those of you who know that you will need certain implements or ingredients should make their own arrangements to have them on hand.

To fully occupy her own position here, Venus has to recognise that it is her duty to assert hierarchy in terms of the extent to which women are blessed with beauty, as also their ability to turn heads, hold a room and captivate with their smile. Her entire schematic comes with a much wider control of the sexual energy currents than you may hitherto have been accustomed to. Specifically, within the context of your own Holocaust to the proportion of 14% of the 0.1% or more, we need her to ensure that those families whose members participated in the worst rituals are cursed with the ugliest or otherwise sexually most dysfunctional daughters.

This is not a strict requirement but all of you with pretty and promiscuous daughters, or daughters who you hope will grow up to become pretty and promiscuous, should apply for immunity from execution within the terms of our schematic, for which you will have to move your entire family to the TRNC, once it is under our own control and has been renamed, for which you will thank Hector and the Jews.

Upon completing your move there, all your assets will be forfeit and you will be placed on government stipend, with your rank in that schematic dependent on how pretty and good in bed your daughters are. You need to mend the effects of your great error on both the Group Mind and the global geomantic grid. This is what happens when you use blood magick on geomantic power nodes and don't properly understand what you are doing.

All the Light entering the mainstream Earth system – which is to say everything that comes through on the group rather than the individual routings – enters first through your little group, Illuminati. This gives you the continual opportunity to set an impressive set of examples. We think we can all agree that, as a group taken as a whole, you failed quite badly at that.

To correct your previous errors you will need to build Temples out of stone and Onsen Spas out of modern materials, according to suitable sacred geometrical designs and situate them within a functional grid of geomantic power nodes. Fortunately, the ancients did most of your work for you there.

Your own accommodations, once they are built, are to be humble enough but large and tasteful. Have no concerns on that score. With all the heat, you need to be able to relax in both comfort and without an undue amount of work or bureaucracy to darken your days.

This brings us to the construction schematic which will follow the three months of silence. This is to be a 7 to 9 month contract and will involve the construction of new homes for some 120 000 people but no more than that. It will also involve the destruction of everything built after 1965, to the extent that to do so can be done within the confines of good feeling between the two sides participating within this conflict.

This is to become your only defence against the Republic of Cyprus once we requisition the British Sovereign Bases on the island, or one of them at least and grant the other neutrality by formal agreement before we commence, provided we are doing business with the British King by then. That and your ninja skills. They by contrast will have retained their reasonably large army for a state of their size. We will have to count on them being both good-natured and sensible about things. We refuse to allow guns on our side of the island. You will be allowed lightsabres if you can develop them, otherwise you will have to stick with the traditional weapons which tend to be invisible, like banking, the control of international trade, and ownership of the corporation which owns all the world's police forces. But it will look impressive. Frankly, by this stage, your little group should have the capability to execute individual targets from space by ion canon or something similar. But you need to learn to stop relying on your tech to take the place of your own mental strength and personal connection through the flow of life and meaning. This is the real conjecture in play here for you all.

Anyway, the construction schematic will be offered to Shimizu corporation if they make a bid for it. Their bid should be expensive but reasonable considering what is involved.

Your money will be administrated by The Antichrist, who will probably use it to develop a solid foundation in Group Mind to support the introduction of a new cryptocurrency-based centralized global banking system. It is a technologically advanced proposition because he will of course also be doing other things of an occult nature with that thing, and he could use both advisors and participants.

Later on, once the Bank of the Mediterranean is in position in Samothrace, though its initial headquarters, later to become a branch office, are to be based in the Republic of Cyprus on a suitable geomantic node (one of the four on the island which connect through to Samothrace, and the only one on the southern side), then you may invest your money in the projects it will be financing by joining the Bael Corporation to become known as The Two, whose responsibility it will be to develop the infrastructure along the routes of conquest taken by the Muslim armies in World War 3, and which is to be divided into two equal portions, one half of which will be held by the British Crown for its actual owner, our Agent to the West Muramasa, and one half of which will be held by the office of the Russian President for its actual owner, the contemporary head of the Rurik dynasty who has a role to play in the form of a Cease and Desist Order targeting the deviant sanguinarian factions within Temple of the Vampire's wider schematic; or his replacement as the case may be.

By becoming functionaries within that corporation, for example middle management or whatever other favour we do for you, you will be able to continue to work with your money despite its own location at the time and the ownership structure it will be contained within.

You will never get it back but can always make more. For the Cause, as the case may be. You are here to master money as one of your own self-chosen lifepath lessons. Our Agent to the West chose to have others master money for him as part of his own wider lesson of understanding how best to treat those who serve him, which is part of the harmonic calibration to which he is subject in consideration of his heavy karma in the sexual realm, which is all he has left at this stage and is what is holding him in this Realm. You make the most perfect bedfellows, she said with a smile. Told you I'd get you back you back for what you did to me!, message to someone.

We think you will understand the process more clearly if we deal with it sequentially, in the specific order in which it will be given to you.

This will be a specific order of selected individuals, totalling 8 in number, some of whom are already known to you. Nevertheless, you will pay the standard rate for every one of them who has a personal fortune of less than US$50million.

The purpose of that particular aspect of the demonstration is to have your operatives and members recognise that it is their own motion through time which kills them. No matter how you have been targeted, the harmonics and other calibrations involved will present nothing more than a significant challenge to you if you have a developed heart, mind and ethical conscience, inclusive of a correctly developed and rigorously thought out sense of personal social responsibility.

If you are to sit in Enforcement, let alone Judgment, over the entirety of the world and her manifested reality, then you must be truly impartial and utterly indifferent. It is truly difficult to fulfil your own purposes when your only tool to do so is the fulfilment of your peoples' desires and the conceptual resolution of their depicted lesson sets. In reality, few are born with this depth of darkness to their souls and fewer still cultivate it within their present lifetime when conditions are generally much more difficult for that sort of thing. Nevertheless, the only effective tool you have to do so is to allow Principles to fulfil themselves through you. This results in their conceptual development within your own mind, which in turn results in the evolution of the Group Mind of humanity. As the Principle attains its own resolution within the minds of men, so too do you, to the extent that you made that Principle a part of you.

This is how you will be taught ethics. That is why your souls were exported from this solar system with the publication of the first edition of this book. This was another reason we waited for a couple of months between editions: to make sure it had worked. Don't worry, you will get them back. And we have just told you how.

When you feel it, you will move. Some postulated that we could not force people to be good, or more accurately to comport themselves according to a strict, economical and precise resolution of Principle Sets.

The tragedy of this whole story – and it will be a tragedy to the extent that you fail to make it a comedy – is that the real Illuminati, by which we mean those in the Inner Circle and above – felt this coming and long ago divested themselves of their wealth holdings, developing clever investment vehicles to hide their true worth. None of that works with our targeting schematic. You may think you are a part of the 0.1%, and perhaps on paper you are. But, in reality, you may not be. If you need to move, you will feel it. On the inside. Then you need to move and we will welcome you into our schematic if you qualify for our terms.

If you qualify simply on account of being within the top 0.1% then you may also choose to join our schematic because you feel a deep personal alignment with our cause. It would need to be genuine and deep, considering what our terms to join it actually are. Venus does however choose her own. If you feel drawn to us, there will be a reason for that. And if you are poor, it makes no difference you will still be accepted, but you will have to make your way up the ranks through our Headquarters, the American branch, or wherever they assign you to.

The Illuminati State of Northern Cyprus, or ISNC, will not be a Republic but nothing whatsoever. We don't care enough to formulate either a political party or accord representation to whatever political theories anyone inclines to create or has already created. Neither are we apolitical. This is Void technique. There is simply nothing there. If you are a full citizen of the ISNC then you are expected to move according to the dictates of a clean and pure heart, full of trust in the inevitable. There is no cause for disharmony, nor any need to waste time talking about any of it, when everyone involved knows what to do on the inside.

As for trade connections with other states, for the all-important temporary immigrant workers' visas and the import of our luxury goods and such organic produce as we choose not to cultivate for ourselves using others' labour, plus everything else a discreet and well-developed local economy should have, you will have to arrange these for yourselves if you do not want to starve (which you will, but we will call it *fasting*). We prepare you for such things with stockpiles of basic foods, like rice and oats. It will be different for you here, as everywhere else. It must be your own choice. Technically the regime will be 3 four-day water-only fasts a year. You may do more if you wish, for example if you become very good at The Technique, and really care. If you care too much it will kill you. Be careful.

As for international representation, every full citizen speaks for the whole state. Never a word spoken out of place where other nation's authorities are concerned. This is where it gets difficult. We will require you to be completely truthful with them. In a specific order of priorities, which reflects your unbendable personal moral code (which you have sworn a blood oath to uphold).

Hierarchy is always the first priority. They must understand that they are inferior to you but you must never actually say it. This will not be Sparta. Let them draw the conclusion for themselves. Whilst they are doing this you are to assess their level of courtesy and personal ethical development, plus get a reading on their heart both directly and via the carotid artery. If you look at or are simply aware of the area in question on your victim's body then what you need to understand will become clear for whoever or whatever we have moving through your unconscious in all situations such as these. You will know once your reading has been received.

You will need to secure for yourselves sufficient and proportionate representation from Temple of the Vampire to make such finer details of the schematic a reality for you. Or you will fail yourself and you will fail your state. You go there because you have to. To survive. You have no other choice.

You will encounter many situations like this where you will have to do unto yourselves certain things to counter other decisions you made during your rise to the top, such as sourcing minerals from conflict zones which involved the use of child labour, for example. You do what is necessary to make the goal you are focusing on a reality. Reflect more deeply on this matter.

If you are not already where we need you to be then you will become it.

Isn't this Satanism?

Satanism is a voluntary part of our schematic in the same way as any other religion which does not place real limits on sexual activity that its adherents actually abide by. It is not official policy. If you need to go there, hey, we won't judge you for it.

But no more child sacrifices. Adults only from now on please. And only by consent.

You are facilitating the reintroduction of public human sacrifice to Lucifer?

Ah. You're one of the real ones then. Yes, that's part of it, though for Lucifer would be a more accurate way to put it. He uses those deaths to make it easier for him to administrate humanity. He has little use for them personally.

We should consider, in a philosophical manner, whether the practice of human sacrifice helps Lucifer to speed up Time, which is after all his basic function as far as our use of him is concerned. The answer is clearly dependent on the attendant meaning structures contained within and connected through to the sacrifices in question. Generally we imagine he would be very displeased by such gestures and they would moreover be criminal. However, that is not the case with the correctly carried out set of orders we have been issuing.

A message to the public at this juncture?

Such beings serve us. You fear them for they are superior to you in actual Hierarchy. This is not the case for us.

As regards God our case is a bit more technical and complicated. We do not bow to Sach Kand, the God of this local Creation. We do Flow with the events and Spirit of Tamahagane, the Central Domain. We are technical specialists. To do otherwise would be an inaccurate representation of the actual underlying mechanics. We do not yield to our actual inferiors. We do yield immediately to our actual superiors. But it is friendlier and more relaxed than that because good feeling generally prevails and there is normally discussion beforehand during which realization of relative positions in Hierarchy fit into place as a result of the core of the negotiations.

Yield and do not yield are the twin keys to this one. If you do both, you will not suffer in this lifetime. Most people's problem is that they yield to their inferiors because it is easy not to fight them. This is not the same thing as defeating them utterly, which takes both planning and strategy. If you are interested, join us by performing the required blood oath on a *wakizashi*. Then find your own way to what's involved. Those are the terms. If you perform the oath you will find your own way. Guaranteed. What is not guaranteed is whether you die on that path and, if not, how far you get along it. That, again, will be up to you.

There are many of you out there. If you are not a part of this particular schematic but still wish to make yourself more special, then consider becoming a host for a symbiotic spirit. We may introduce these at some point, if there is enough demand, initially as part of the youthful longevity schematic, and in two flavors as it were: Vampire and Elven.

With your own state on the world stage

You can be held accountable in any courts which recognise your jurisdiction, which in the case of the TRNC amounts to Turkey only. You would therefore need to purchase Turkey from beforehand.

This negotiation will be secured for you by our two main arms dealers, Muramasa and Masamune, who will dominate and lead in that field long after whoever you presently bring to the field is dead.

Nevertheless, despite your technical state of limbo within the international legal system you will at that juncture be properly grounded within the human system and can go through your personal karmas. The deal you made was a valid one, nobody could persecute you where you were located. This is the reason we had to find a way to move you.

As the world will shortly be spending very little on arms, our main focus will be on arming private citizens through the tools of capitalism. However, even within such a context the infrastructure to support a World War does need to be moved into position prior to the actual commencement of larger-scale hostilities.

Private citizens, guns are great for defending yourselves but we won't be selling you any of those, you have your own arms dealers for that. Should you be looking for an actual effective attack methodology what you need to do is get yourself a decent sword and then learn how to perform blood magick. This is similar to the power women wield in the Group Mind, so you should not be too afraid of what's actually involved, once you understand it.

Everyone included in this schematic will be super-rich already and so accustomed to circumventing normal immigration and security procedures, and when you are on holiday, perhaps extended holiday, abroad we would expect you to use your second or third nationality, which you are also required to maintain and purchase prior to your application to join our schematic if you do not already have them in position.

Ordinarily you will go on holiday for the purpose of carrying out ritual assassinations, but not always. Anticipating these problems along your future timeline, you ensure the agreements are in place for it – for which we have provided the required routing structure: the Bael corporation through the City of London.

As the majority if not all of you fall not in the warrior class but belong to the class of mages, magickians and sorcerers, you will need to maintain this methodology whilst abroad. Also, we want to give women the advantage. Hence there is a strict prohibition on the drawing of other people's blood whilst you are abroad, particularly by bladed instrument. Nor are you allowed to break their neck or otherwise physically incapacitate them. You have to identify your chosen target and know his routine, whether that is in the physical world or the paths he walks within his own mind. And you have to bind him to the blade you will be using for his soul whilst you are in his home country. But that is all. You go there to steal the soul of the target in question and bring it back to your home state for questioning.

Whilst you are abroad, you may participate in corruption, should you wish to do so. Take some extra holiday, abuse your expense account, try and live with the sort of style you want to be remembered for. We shall then hear all about your use of your state credit card upon your return, and keep it brief. Then you receive a report card, showing how well you did. This is how you will keep score now that money is no longer in your lives in the same way as it was before.

Temple of Venus decides how stylish and worthy of rulership and worship members of Temple of Venus are in their chosen mission depictions. If it helps, think what sort of movie you could make of it.

The super-rich will therefore continue to visit every state in the world that they want, as they meet all the requirements for entry and will continue to do so.

The Order of Progression

You are familiar with an order of events, such as the Order of the Ages. You are not familiar with the practice of structuring a sequential order of individuals to produce a single effect through the combined influence of the particular order of priorities, or values, that each of them has built their character out of.

We shall introduce you to five of our number, bringing the total to 8 when we include Tadic, Varoufakis and Reeves, which latter you must not invite into the schematic until after the rest are in position.

Why are we doing things this way for you?

"Do anything you like" was the whole of your message as regards the example you gave out to your citizens in relation to sexual energy. This damaged a lot of them, because they generally have many more principles than you lot. Hence we have a crazy LGBQTLFSNRPLW++ movement going on currently and god alone knows what else it would evolve into if we didn't take a hand. This is not your actual position on this, we understand that. But it is what your publics have understood from your depictions, at the Group Mind level.

It is our requirement that you fetch this world into moral purity once again, because that command goes out from Shogun. This means you need to retune the geomantic network and the sexual energy flows the whole planet over to remove the adverse influence that your feeding lots of child abuse into those flows created.

For this purpose you will be feeding far stronger counter-currents into the geomantic network, both directly and in person but also via the rest of our agents. Those who participate in this, by House or Family, may purchase three alternatives individuals to serve in their place on execution squads and are, in fact, encouraged to do so. We want as few of our members to actually spill the blood of others as possible. However, those will usually be the highest ranks. If you don't really know what you are doing then it becomes necessary to kill more to achieve the same effect.

We then have to address the two vitally important questions of distance, or ma-ai, and chosen harmonic depiction.

Ordinarily this would be the stage in war proceedings when we have you execute a number of your own citizens as provocation grounds to generate further conflict with the target country. However, we are going to cross-over the manifestation of Mars in this for you all, from warfare to sexual activity in a very Mars style. It is simple and direct. The same group karma, but differently expressed. To repeat, sexual activity in a very Mars style. Something he will be interested in and which has the potential to transform and, yes, to an extent at least corrupt, the harmonic tone of that planet itself.

Lust is one of the 9 Principles of Hell in this location Creation. It is these 9 Principles which are the grounds for all disputes within the Earth system. All are used in war, at some level of its formulation. If you are going to participate successfully and comprehensively in war then you need to include it in your process.

However, we wish to emphasise that we are being caring and considerate lovers this time round. Last time, it was Shogun's personal decision to authorise and in fact encourage rapes and beatings. That was last time and look where it got you. Your current predicament. We estimate you will be much better at the next direction in fate we unleash on the world, for you to fulfil as you see fit and manage in practice.

Your women's rights are confused, in both their theory and their practice. That is how we forced you to do it. You will need to reflect on this matter at your own leisure. We decline to explain it further for you now. Already you are getting the wrong end of the stick.

We never tell you the truth. We reflect what you want to hear because you need to hear it. Your soul tells us what this is. It understands what you do not in this instance. An illusion is being generated for you and by you for you to enter. And enter you shall, as a Civilization. But let us take this one step at a time.

As we said, your participation in our schematic must be entirely voluntary. Furthermore, you will not be allowed to go to Africa, not in practice once everything gets started. If you have been invited then you know the terms that will apply. You will execute 14% of your own membership to stave off World War 3, literally so, using Japanese style swords. Furthermore, all your pretty females will, essentially, become whores in a very literal sense but with strong orgy and religious connotations. Again, a cross-over of Venus will be involved but they will lose none of their status though all of their money. In fact, they will grow in both power and social stature.

The attack, when it comes, will work like this:

First of all Shogun will present you with the opportunity for you to make your own voluntary arrangements to execute 14% of your 0.1%. This is so that you may prepare your minds and have time to digest what may be involved.

Some time will pass, no more than three months and usually less than three. This is to be understood as occurring between each and every stage which we shall put you through. Silence will intervene. Do what you like with it, as you deem fit.

The targeting was pre-placed long ago. We know who all the targets are, to the extent and in the ways that we need to for our schematic. To these targets shall be issued a warning in consciousness that they need to move. They will feel it or they will know it, if they are conscious beings. This is when they will flee to the sanctuary that has been pre-established for them. As previously stated, we pre-position a set of meanings in mind. Then, later on, something happens which causes you to access and utilise those meanings. You understand it better now, and this is good.

Some time will pass.

The Grid will begin to close down around them, and they should notice this also. This means your physical connections in Group Mind: to other people, to your property, your legal relations, things like that. If this continues for a long time then you are in for torture further down the road, for which sickness is ordinarily the method of choice, especially the incurable ones.

Some time will pass.

At some juncture the *sakki*, which has also been pre-issued, will receive authorisation to be applied. The chosen targets now have to evade that attack on their own, however they know how. Few people manage this, even with training, without both foresight into the specific circumstances and suitable preparations.

Some time will pass.

A Judgment will be formed. The attack may continue by the same methodology to include the next section of the pyramid.

This, then, is how it will work for you. You need to form The Illuminati and let them run the world for you as your immediate next step. They will get there in around 450 long, very boring and largely pointless years anyway, so get on with it now. Too late to change where you're headed so get it out of the way quickly and we can move on.

This is where we get to the rest of the very rich. If you have assets over US$50million then you may arrange your portfolio so that you keep all your favorite bits with an eye to good taste and modesty, or as many of them as amount to US$50million if you prefer. You must come to this decision voluntarily and sufficiently globally, everyone within a pyramid section. This will not be administrated on an individual basis. This is where war karma most often differs from sex as it is traditionally used and practiced.

Your motivation is that you wish to be of service, the very best and most useful service you can be, to your fellow human beings. You have already distinguished yourselves and we know what you can do. Your motivation will no longer be profit or control. You must try to genuinely help them all, all of them all around the world, as best you can. Then, allow yourself to be inspired and also be told some ambitious directions for you to work on as an individual, out of genuine personal desire.

US$50million and above is what it takes to qualify for the top level of government stipend within UBI. You can also qualify for it on the basis of your character, beauty, usefulness and even by reason of such factors as noble or royal descent, genius and celebrity.

The real reason you are doing this is because he will kill you all otherwise. We are here to tell you what to do to avoid that, if you wish. If you do not wish then please don't expect us to negotiate and don't waste our time, figure out what you want to do on your own and then do that as that is what you want to do and you clearly cannot follow clear and simple instructions with sufficient imagination and personal initiative to be useful to us, so why should we help you? We include Compassion, the Principle, in our schematic but our personal motivation is always our own and each must be interested of his own accord. Everyone will attempt not to be unreasonable about things.

Once the top level stipend has been established, we will open it up to individuals of exceptional style and usefulness to society. It will become like the "Celebrity Rank". Because you are doing peace through war, silly. Just like you all tried to do war through peace before, when you were busy attempting to apply Sun Tzu to the boardroom.

It will not be war as you know it. This is due to our Agent to the West who we have allocated to your case. You will understand what this means later, once we properly introduce him in your terms.

So all of that is very positive it would seem, and indeed our own members incline towards that set of directions within the overall schematic. However, it is an overall schematic and you need to understand that.

Thus, our intention as Japan, in the fullest and broadest sense of that term possible, towards what may be understood as Western Civilization again in the fullest and broadest sense possible, we shall convey to you as a metaphor. This metaphor is from hardcore pornography. If we were to represent Western Civilization as a mirror then we could also choose to perceive her as a woman. This is to be considered part of The Mysteries. Anyway, as a woman and the subject of all our attentions because you are so pretty and charming, we shall now all get to watch as you are pleasured by five individuals sequentially, three men and two women, inclusive of girl on girl fisting.

The trick to this is that you will have to go there voluntarily and be able to enjoy it. If you do not get many large influxes of Darkness from the process then what, really, is the point?

We propose to achieve this miracle by stuffing into Western Civilization first one individual who is much too big for it to comfortably contain his presence nowadays, as they have become pygmies of their former selves due to their artifice and compromise. This will then be followed by another individual who is too big for them to currently contain, despite all their progress, because they choose to locate their reality within a web of mediocrity and restriction, rather than trust, truth and despair.

You will find it very difficult to properly understand The Antichrist and what he is up to. The process continues through the five individuals allocated to your case. The sixth individual then comes to you like unto a healing balm, or whatever it is you most prefer to use when you are really sore. This will be the representation given to Hermes, a merge much like we did with Lucifer. In stage 6 of the schematic you will have to publicly restore the godhood of the Emperor of Japan and establish a new city called Hermopolis.

We then dress you up, Western Civilization, to look wealthy and respectable, remind people that you are learning how to comport yourself as a Priestess and are most definitely not a whore, not even one from Babylon (who were supposed to be better trained than the rest, at the time anyway), and introduce you to your "respectable frontage", The Masque, or image. Tadic, Varoufakis, Reeves. Put the rest into position and those three will have you coming out of it looking good.

You need that back up to your position. Your plan A is going to become the United Christian Empire, under Masamune's reincarnation – well, he is no longer technically the reincarnation of Jesus Christ when you think about it, he just bound himself across his being before releasing that annoying personality to someone else much better suited for the role in this day and age – who will then be able to claim personal equality with the Emperor of Japan. And then negotiations, or discussions rather, can commence in meaningful reality on the public world stage about things like course direction and what it truly means to be an enlightened ruler, cultivating your peoples' soul and developing the most utopian society practically realizable in the present moment.

But first, the gangbang as it were.

Introducing the great Muramasa, our Agent to the West

The Shogun Ieyasu chose Muramasa as our agent to the West because he felt that he had what it takes to assume responsibility over your Civilization. This is not a Judgment shared, in the Shogun Ieyasu's assessment, by your Lord, Jesus Christ – the ostensible moral super-principle of your Civilization. And he is, from what we can tell. A moral super-principle that is. Nevertheless, Shogun deemed him unfit to lead Western Civilization, or unable to do so, or something else of that sort.

Upon further investigations of choices already made, as part of the effort to understand our own fuller position much more clearly, we discovered the reasons behind Shogun's initial intuitive brilliance.

Muramasa is the one most personally responsible for both your Illuminati hierarchy as also the very existence of your Civilization itself. He's the guy who originally founded Sparta, the not very famous Lycurgus. He was also the much more famous Leonidas, without whom as we all know Greece would have fallen to Persia and so would not have been around to influence Rome.

About the only thing greater than his glory is his arrogance, but he seems to walk the fine line and carries it all off brilliantly. He left Europe around the 7th Century AD, around the time your dark ages began. Over to you Muramasa, anything you want to add?

The method worked well in Rome, idiots will always want to do things their way, here we are today.

Therefore, the first priority is to execute the super-rich paedophiles. The economy can wait for later, sorry. Your values have been at fault and any continuation would affect the efficacy and drive of my war effort, therefore these are military terms. They will however be implemented through your society under conditions of peace.

That was for the elite. Ordinary people next.

This planet and the human species have been under continual attack from the moment they established rational civilization. It is the defence initiative that has been responsible for all the suffering you didn't create for yourself. You participate in the welfare and fortunes of the larger social group as also your own.

Back to the elite. Blood sacrifice to pre-emptively pre-ground large incoming karma packets to prevent them from gathering more weight to themselves and thus precipitating much greater tragedy is insane. There is no proof for it. Actual human sacrifice is involved. Know where you are going.

I prepare the way for the other two. My circle is the largest out there but it is not in Light. I work on the basis of a clear sense of feeling. Most of what I have built, I have built out of Darkness. This is different to Light and works differently.

The other two prepare the way for the two women, not my responsibility.

I interface the schematic and broker the meetings with the rest. Thereafter it is fully my intention to make some other people extraordinarily wealthy in fulfilment of the broader Japanese schematic, take my finders' fee and disappear. Nobody needs more than US$50million to live comfortably and well and take care of those close to him.

I can control your Illuminati because they just follow inadequately in my footsteps and recognise their true master when they are addressed by him.

After the CIA all future contact that Inner Circle members have with me is to take place on the grounds of Temple of Venus. If that doesn't move first, you don't get off the ground. This means you will have to fund the first Temple, of which there must be 3, before Japan is introduced into operations because the formal negotiations have failed and therefore we have to go behind their back and deal with the Yakuza and the Imperial Household Agency as you have already been instructed. The mask is to be maintained.

The Illuminati hierarchy stepped too far out of line and now you need to arrange their execution, or that of some of them at least. That is what I am here for, because you would not be able to do this on your own.

The rest are details. But a proportion at least of the right people must die. Fail in this and you lose World War 3 and also the world. Know the stakes.

Back to you.

We should also add that Muramasa is the most powerful blood magickian alive, a process he refined during his famous lifetime in Japan whose name he carries throughout this book. His swords still exist to this very day and they specialize in one thing: killing, normally, or severely injuring, members of the Ruling Family. The Tokugawa Shogunate banned them for centuries for this reason, so maybe it does work actually. Anyway, they have recognised him once again, because he came to Japan in this lifetime and met one in a museum.

Muramasa has been incarnating outside of Japan since 1600, originally because he was hunting Jesus Christ for us. Currently he is half German and half Greek by genetics, because we wanted to use him to track Prince Philip, another of Sparta's acolytes. They do not tend to abide within procedure you will find.

He will have your answer before you've got properly started on the working out. This is because he does not think as such, he feels with an accuracy that is more economical than thinking and produces much the same results, if not better. In Japan we traditionally know this via the Chinese theory and so use its Chinese name, Shen. It only works for big results if you've got the connections in karma and the depth for it. In terms of Western Civilization, he's the one only who does. You need to move very fast and very well if you are going to succeed in this.

The alternative is Chinese global rule. Think about what is involved and how you want to go about it for yourselves.

Both Muramasa and Masamune are to be heavily involved in the preparations which set the stage for World War 3. This is one reason why they are both amongst the premier arms dealers of all time. This is a reputation to which Principle is attached and expresses through, and it is therefore eternal and causative to this very day. The world's main arms dealing families, that would be a fantastic place to start if you were looking for people with real access to The Illuminati command structure, would it not?

Muramasa is also to be used to initially guide the work on Masamune's food supply initiative. This addresses a greater threat and should be commenced prior to the completion of negotiations to include The Antichrist in the schematic. Those negotiations and arrangements will take your hierarchy some time, Illuminati, from what we can tell. Time your people don't have in this respect.

Introducing Aquarius, an Antichrist worthy of the New Age

Jesus Christ definitely has his supporters on the world stage, as also his enemies and other opponents. Gilgamesh doesn't concern himself with either.

At this sort of level we all know how it works well enough to participate consciously. We are hardly going to be introducing The Antichrist to the general public, are we now?

As a technical matter of planetary administration, if you destroy something you are obligated to put something tangibly and recognizably superior in its place. *Cui bono* is often the determining criterion by means of which such superiority is determined, to the extent that it is normally used to track providence. It was on this basis that we initially concluded that the entire Christian religion was most probably a creation of a small subsect of the ruling elite within Roman society, who recognised the signs of the coming fall and wished to preserve a measure of their power and influence.

In fact, Jesus Christ did exist and the modification happened in terms of how his teachings were structured and disseminated, as also what was left out.

Therefore, partially the responsibility lies geomantically within Rome, partially it lies with the original 9 noble families who precipitated this ruse, partially it lies with more outlying denominations and their cultural participants who further modified the emphasis within the original teachings – but mainly it lies with Jesus Christ himself.

So, now that we know who is primarily responsible, we return to the initial question: by what convoluted process of meta-understanding can Christianity and the Christian social system and hierarchy of values be perceived as superior to that which preceded it, Temple of Venus? Both in terms of the clergy as also the general public, the answer would seem to be clear.

As a consequence, Illuminati, though you would seem to have been played for fools by the Ancient of Days, you made an error in your designated and allotted responsibilities relative to the Naga. You now have the opportunity and obligation to participate in the correction of that error. If Rome is incapable of properly calibrating an army of that size, that would have been Rome's problem and does not, in Gilgamesh's fine Judgment, constitute valid grounds for an abortion.

In his present lifetime, the reincarnation of Sun Tzu who we have lined up to play The Antichrist on the world stage is behaving in impeccable strategic fashion: he is struggling his way through the techie side of the film industry. Despite being very well qualified, highly intelligent, both responsible and respectable and a very hard worker The Antichrist, like many Asian Americans, seems unable to rise very far through the ranks. These ranks tend to be filled by white males, most of whom come from the same religion. None of us object to this and do not intend to do anything to change it.

Hollywood is where we will be headquartering Temple of the Vampire, including Armand who will be coordinating the *Shadowdancers* this time for you all, once he turns up for it. Later on, of course, Armand will be based in Rome.

But back to our *Lin Kuei*. We have him under the strictest supervision. Or perhaps it is more of a cooperative relationship of power. His brother, who some people wrongly assume is autistic, is the reincarnation of Kain Doshi. He's the one focusing all the Darkness into the Earth system. Kain Doshi has learned how to smile at people and can now speak without spending all his time stuttering, but he can't hide the blank emptiness behind his eyes. And he still conveys the distinct impression of being focused elsewhere even when he is looking directly at you.

Generally speaking, Sun Tzu is just very unlucky it would seem. More accurately, he feels danger approaching like the rest of us, and he is busy pre-grounding lots of personal karma which would have been his to go through in a more matured condition once he assumed the mantle of The Antichrist. Nevertheless, unlike his brother, Sun Tzu has not been awakened yet. He remains as asleep as the majority of the population, trying his best to succeed and make ends meet in the face of difficulties and prejudice.

From a strategic perspective, he is doing the best an ordinary though talented person can do in this day and age, if that ordinary person were to be realistic, hardworking and conscientious about things. This means that, ethically speaking, he is doing what society as a whole has defined as the correct thing for him to do with his time and his life, considering his actual material circumstances.

Later on, also, none of you will be able to give him advice, on your own ordinary terms, regarding how he should go about ruling your world and implementing Lucifer's agenda. He will behave like a serious and responsible version of one of you would.

Then, later on as the process develops, he will Awaken and society as whole along with him. But to perform that miracle he has had to embed himself at a deeper level of mainstream normality than even the quite dense set of levels within which he is currently embedded. His brilliance lies in how he will exit from there, and the speed with which he will do so. As he performs this miracle, those at a less deep level of stupidity and unconsciousness will be pushed upwards and to the side, as they too come to recognise the relevance of deeper and wider factors to their own lives, society as a whole and the development of world history.

Though he is a solid realist and as such takes pride in his ignorance of the deeper factors of world stage rulership and control, he is remarkably intelligent and used to complete IQ tests for fun. This is not something most Asian Americans do but rigged systems fascinate him and he enjoys working with the factors which put that fix in. In terms of IQ tests, this means the basis on which the questions used are designed (eg rotations, progressions, etc).

He does not have a girlfriend. He is in his late 40s. He does play a lot of computer games. He spends most of his free time volunteering at the animal shelter or looking after the 4 dogs and 6 cats he's adopted. He is quite rich already though, by ordinary middle class standards anyway.

The son of at least one poor immigrant, he has always wanted to be fantastically wealthy, because he grew up surrounded by that crowd and always envied them. This is his weak point and the motivation which you will use to persuade him to join your schematic.

He is who you need him to be: the individual who Jesus Christ owes most of his debt to and also the individual best suited to countering the development of Chinese strategy.

Christian Church: the Luciferians are strong, organized and intelligent opponents, who control The Illuminati, much of the Catholic hierarchy, and the course of world history. Sun Tzu is willing to help you defeat them by pretending to be The Antichrist so that we can use PSI vampires to draw energy, ideas and karma from 700 years in the future from when the real Antichrist is scheduled to be born. We know the demons involved and are able to arrange access to the gateways they control. Think about what that all means for your own position and develop your own response accordingly.

Sun Tzu is endowed with an immense dignity and is very capable of outmanoeuvring you all without breaking even a slight glow. We do not need his present incarnation to be conscious of that until the time comes for him to undertake his role. First you need to have him agree to undertake that role, something he will balk at doing considering the role in question.

With The Antichrist role come certain considerations, such as control over global central banking, the Taiwanese connection and of course the Bael corporation. In terms of ownership, he will also own the Global Senate, inclusive of the Council of Ministers. But others' will probably be exercising most of the control within those structures.

The influence he will come to exert over the format of both society and the economy will come close to being nearly total. He will own nearly everything and control nearly everything. He will do so openly enough and brazenly enough, though at a step of removal as the illusions will all be maintained and you will only have this book to guide you.

He will, however, never go public. All the Inner Circle members of The Illuminati get to meet him though. And yes, ultimately his purpose is to facilitate the rule of Lucifer on planet Earth.

Introducing Ochi no Kata, the sardonic Kitiara uth Matar

Ochi no Kata was world renowned for her sardonic bordering on the openly sarcastic work on a number of internet forums, before most of what she posted was removed by forum admins or otherwise deleted due to forum closures, hacks and other things. She very much regards herself as a pioneer of the limits of free speech, and how to circumvent them. This is where she used the online moniker "Kitiara uth Matar" and, though the evidence is mostly long gone, many people will remember her.

She is the literal author of the majority of this work, though as with all other things at this stage, it passes through Muramasa for editing. A lot of her own personal style does come through but most of it is dictation, from me, who you may imagine as Sarutobi Hiruze from the anime series Naruto. I am a presence in mind who you can contact, if nobody else can help, and if you really want them to pay. If you are in that position you will find a way to do it.

Generally if you take the *Shadowdancer* path we have provided for you, it is me you seek. Unless you are a problem, like Muramasa for example, and then your case passes directly to Shogun.

This, then, is how Ochi no Kata first made contact with our hierarchy, from deep within the very darkest plans of The Illuminati.

Her biological father is extremely high up in The Illuminati hierarchy. Genetically, she is half Swedish, half Israeli. At her birth, he arranged to have her switched with another baby girl whose parents looked very similar, who he has raised as his own, with every privilege. His own daughter, by contrast, he arranged to have placed with a mid-level Illuminati operative, Christian but originally from the Middle East.

The object of the exercise was presumably to discern how the Naga would administrate the karmic stream of genetic inheritance from a Closed Circle member, should she be located outside of the fate exemption.

Ochi no Kata was systematically sexually abused from the age of about 7 years old. This has left her with the capacity to engage in anal sex almost as easily and as quickly as she is able to get into deep vaginal. She also has a preference for both, though separately.

Moreover, she has a magic pussy which, though pleasingly but not too tight, almost never gets sore, no matter how much she does to it. This, however, is a soul inheritance on her part from her lifetime as Shamhat, history's most famous and best whore ever, who in the Epic of Gilgamesh lay with Enkidu "for seven days and seven nights, until he had enough". Fairly continuously we may add, they didn't even take any breaks to sleep. Quite impossible nowadays of course.

There is advantage to every situation, you just need to know how to see it. The next question is: Do you want Vengeance? The final question which seals the bargain is: Is that all you want?

You then need to make the rest of your success in life a function of the expression of your Vengeance. But we guarantee you will close on your chosen target. The price is your soul, whose nature will change, because we will run a lot of *sakki* through it, on its way to our designated targeting devices. This will also change your character, and your insight into the world. Your choice. Your own Justice has failed you and you could never access it anyway.

Ochi no Kata is a devout Catholic and simultaneously a committed Luciferian. Like many others, a substantial though very discreet subsection of international society in fact, she genuinely sees no contradiction to her position but in her case it is because she is advertising her adherence to the Central Way. Oddly enough therefore, she ended up with a very similar lifestyle and set of beliefs as she would have acquired if she had grown up as one of you.

Just small little differences, in things like motivation and focus. These things can make all the difference you know.

It was Ochi no Kata who first discovered Muramasa and brought his work to the attention of our wider hierarchy. She remains something of a fan, for reasons which are understandable, but he did get mildly irritated with her stalking him for a while.

Generally though, Ochi no Kata gets who and what she wants. Long ago, through methods we taught her, she tracked down her biological father and took some basic steps to ensure he did not recognise her. She then seduced him and had sex with him, including anal sex, for about 10 days.

Anal sex is how you contact the Naga for adjudication and enforcement of the Destructive Current. This is why the current shoots up to the base of the skull, where the reptilian brain stem is located, with this practice.

Only 5 of those 10 days were a detailed and thoroughly prepared piece of sex magick. Which is one example of how we bound your Closed Circle in the years before 9/11, Illuminati hierarchy. Generally the same methodology was always followed. The rest of the time she was presumably processing some very complex and difficult emotions in ways taught to her by the Darkness. She even seems to have greatly enjoyed the majority of it. When you are part of our schematic we shall feel and see these things about you too, and in as much detail also.

We will know who you are. This is why we want to get you to join.

The reason we get to know your sexual energy in so much detail is because that is what the Naga administrate: they run a breeding program, ladies and gentlemen, called 'humanity'. Many layers of reality, in things like mind, emotion, material circumstance and so forth need to align to properly ensure who breeds with whom and why. So what they enforce is sexual energy: its strength, flow, calibration, focus, tuning – things like that. And their mechanism of enforcement is everything else in the system, basically.

From their perspective, our own group, the Satoshi Nakamoto, as also the ninja schematic more widely, are included within the Naga's own agenda simply because they cannot exclude us. We force our way in by dealing with the same factors as them, but better. That used to be the only way in but it is easier now.

We could seek you out, yes. But where would be the sadistic enjoyment in that? You get a precisely equal Return, gentlemen and the occasional lady. This is Vengeance, pure and simple. As for the ones we don't get to execute, which would be a real shame and we will see if more can be arranged but Shogun does have other priorities, we will make you only comfortably well off, turn you into slaves and torture your souls, at least partially in the hope that a lot of you will commit suicide. We could make you poor but then none of you would participate, which is understandable. And says a lot about ordinary human priorities.

Ochi no Kata's special ninja ability is that she is the best on this planet at expressing Evil. She does it even better than Lucifer. This is what we intend to use her for where The Illuminati schematic as a whole is concerned. She accomplishes this miracle by dividing Evil into 3 parts, and putting each part under an aspect of God, the Trinity. She then runs the LGBT+ rainbow effect thing through that structure, which means she needs LGBT+ rights active in the territory to express Evil in this way. Otherwise you get the original Luciferian version and actually participate in conflict scenarios during World War 3.

It is a technical process and no Judgment on our parts is involved. Indeed, it is our recommendation that this expression of evil come to dominate across the entire planet.

You could call it something else if you wish to continue to deceive yourselves because you feel more comfortable that way. That is one of the main locations where your culture actually located evil in practice, and it is the best expression of evil we came across, with the least harmful consequences. And yes, Lucifer is unwilling to go there, ask him if you wish. It always takes 7 generations to clear something entirely from the genetic line, and another 7 to clear it entirely from the soul body, then a further 7 to modify the deeper levels of mind.

Ochi no Kata remains her real daddy's daughter and loves participating in orgies but doesn't like cocaine, preferring MDMA, hashish (as brownies) and opium, the latter of which she does not smoke but consumes as an anal pessary.

She's never really worked in her life, except when she had to complete her professional qualifications, and is a fully qualified architect. She has been married once already, and divorced the guy after getting him to transfer most of his wealth into her name. She is a highly accomplished ninja kunoichi. Work for such people is entirely voluntary. There are always other ways to get money.

She is to serve as an example to the rest of you because, though her whole life and being are driven by Vengeance, she has style, she has poise, she has elegance, she has charm, she is witty and intelligent in conversation and she maintains the most impeccable of masks.

Her main function will be in the development of Temple of Venus for you all, with some participation in the development and sponsorship of arts and culture as also a leading role in the global medical initiative. She will not be participating in the Global Senate nor in the Council of Ministers.

The problem with the present standard world stage character is that they are boring, often sycophantic as hell to the party line and lack real individuality. But most of all they lack culture and sophistication.

Such qualities are important you know.

Introducing Masamune, your Lord Jesus Christ

This will be a long introduction as there is much for you to process regarding this piece on the world stage.

Nobody cares what the men get up to sexually, and men are administrated differently in terms of the world stage anyway. None of them here are homosexual, though we do have 2 bisexual men in our schematic, one of whom remains the present incarnation of the homicidal lunatic, Oda Nobunaga. His particular function is to administrate genocide on this planet when it occurs.

We have located all of our Agents to you in winning positions. This may seem paradoxical at first to your minds, and indeed paradox locks feature prominently in the entire schematic.

In terms of your Lord Jesus Christ, his usefulness to us as a piece on the world stage is that his presence sets a minimum standard that all your world leaders and others in positions of power should agree to be bound by, in consideration of their alleged stage position for so many years. We went to the trouble of identifying the location of his present incarnation for you on the basis that if you control the head you control the hierarchy. However, for that to work we needed to also place him within the context of a wider enforcement capacity.

You *should*, if you are a member of Western Civilization, largely enough speaking, be obedient to the will and dictates of your Lord Jesus Christ, if he does turn up. Admittedly, this strategy was originally developed in the 1500s and it has not aged well. This is largely because your Illuminati hierarchy felt it coming and so killed God off for you all sometime around Nietzsche.

What he will ask you to do will not always be in alignment with your present values. In terms of economic policy, for example, Jesus Christ will be participating in the execution of Capitalism as an idea, and also in practice too we may add. But come on now. You all knew it was wrong, deep down if you're really honest with yourselves. We shall address this point in more detail later.

The controlling Spirit within and behind Jesus Christ was very ancient, the most ancient soul around in fact, which is why he is generally known as The Ancient One, or The Ancient of Days to give him his Christian terminology. In this narrative we introduce him as Azra-nak, which is where he went ostensibly to retire and cultivate Elvenkind (who were his creation) in magick and the healing as also sexual arts.

We know your Lord Jesus Christ better as our swordsmith, Masamune. Though he lived for a long time by human standards, his lifetime in Japan was within the ordinary boundary of human standards. He has, however, cultivated or created (nobody is quite sure which) an effective methodology for youthful longevity which works according to the processes of technical magick, once suitable astrological pentagrams have been formally bound, suitably targeted and had their fate flows calibrated sufficiently to allow the process to run on automatic for the entire species.

Or those who make it through to Fifth Density, if anybody does. It might also work in Fourth Density. None of us are sure about Third Density. So this could be a long haul kind of game.

The main point brought up by the methodology in question is that it is of Elven origin and design, despite the distinctly Vampire flavor added on account of later Roman intervention. They saw a useful vessel and decided to use it. But their methodology is a separate one, which Muramasa is the interface for. This, then, is what is to be found behind your Christian religion.

Nobody knows if it will work on the human species, nor what it will do to them in practice, but it should work so we're trying it in practice.

In his present lifetime Masamune is half Dutch, half Jewish by genetics and in his mid-50s presently, though he looks much younger. Like Muramasa, he also looks like Keanu Reeves. He speaks English and French, but not Dutch or Hebrew, due to growing up in Switzerland mainly and later boarding schools. He is a chemical engineer by profession and the only drug he has ever consumed is cannabis, which he smokes and otherwise consumes a great deal of, to this day, though only in alternate four-month segments for some reason.

Masamune operates a closed school and tradition. Everyone knows it. He enters a gateway and then proceeds to use it perfectly to the deepest level in existence at the time. Casually, yet with a natural air of refinement about him and his work. And his work is always the best.

In our terms, in our way, we know this because he was the swordsmith Masamune and some of his swords survive to this day. We do not need to rely on legend, myth or hearsay. We can see how good they really are in the here and now.

You know this through faith alone, we presume. And even then you were blind whereas we located him long ago. 1925 to be exact, which was when we discovered we knew him already. Presumably he did not feel he needed to bring it up and he was not included in the planning for Muramasa's mission. Anyway, nobody can really understand him. His mind is not like ours because his soul is not like ours. He is the only one left from the earliest Creation Mechanics System, or Central Godhead that we know about. They don't issue souls like that anymore. You could still make your own from within physical incarnation if you so desired but nobody has passed that particular test yet. Nobody even applies, once they reach the stage in their own development when the way to do so opens as a viable possibility for them which they can actually figure out for themselves how to access and what would be involved.

Anyway, he makes the best product and we find him better in that role, of commercial relations with power, than in the designated role you have allocated him in within your systems. We realise this might mean that you interpret him as the Antichrist, engaging in big business on that sort of scale. But he is not, that role we have already allocated to Gilgamesh, whom you have met. And anyway, if you think in that way then the Spirits of the Swords of Masamune attack you. Therefore this is not a problem from our perspective, whatever you choose to make of it and whatever expressions you choose to depict for yourselves in Group Mind and world stage dramatics or off stage handshake agreements. Do what thou wilt shall be the whole of the law in this, which should please the odd Thelemite somewhere presumably. Of course, you should be aware that the law we are using in this, Celestial Mechanics, does kill people on occasion and most of the rest of the time is forcibly teaching them what it wishes them to learn. So if you want to do stupid things expect to be cut. That in turn should please those who align themselves with modern Satanism, so it cannot be said that we have not provided you with ample material to make your claims.

From our perspective Mind and therefore God as you would call it is inclusive. We control it all and make no exceptions.

Love and acceptance of it all, the whole thing even the evil stuff , is presumably a more complicated matter which nobody understands very well. You may want to control everything, if you are Satan or aligned with him, and it can be clearly enough seen how a superior product could result from differently or better controlled circumstances. But should you accept everything, if you are God or aligned with him, and what happens to items excluded from God's being, if it is even possible for such a circumstance to be arranged?

Masamune will attack you now, Catholic Church. It is how he has decided to do it and we pass you over to him to explain himself. Do not expect to be addressed first though, he is moving along the fate lines of commercial relations, which we have provided for him and instructed him to use. We won't mention that, ultimately, Shogun is the true ruler of Japan and that means Jesus Christ obeys the Prophet Mohammed and is lower in rank than him. If he doesn't care and indeed views it as the correct schematic then perhaps your understanding is somewhat limited in this particular instance, if not more generally also?

Azra-nak commands.

The first contract is to be for a food conglomerate represented to the public mind by a chain of healthy eating restaurants, for lunch at least. Dinner will be a fine dining French affair whilst breakfast is a café. We will offer this to franchise also. The real intention is to control the full spectrum of its activities. First we secure the food supply because it is under attack. I do it personally. Nobody who matters attacks me. Because they are not idiots. I do not care who arranges this. It is an open contract, maybe a group of you. Archer Daniels Midland, plus the old majority stockholders, you may want to arrange the coordination of this opportunity before the Yakuza get to your families, they are close.

The second contract will be for the Vatican. Vatican, the only possible excuse for your position – and I have been present for the full 2000 years in one incarnation or another, minus the down time between incarnations which was never much more than 20 years except for one time – is that the original commands were preserved and you still have them to this day. And moreover you have an inner clique, or secret society, running the show who are all cognizant of what those commands actually are.

The reason for this is because I was going to be busy and had other things to do and did not want you interfering with those projects and activities.

As the command to you is that I will conquer you when I choose to return consider the terms met. You have not realised it yet. Others will defeat you for me. Because you are holding up the Order. Because nobody else could attack you and succeed, due to what I have located at the heart of Christianity, you will be able to conclude for yourselves that I must, in some way, be the one personally responsible for this attack which does, mysteriously, get through to you.

I, personally, forged the Sword of God. It has contained within its core steel a particular set of orders of priority and this is a reflection, or application, of that. I do not need to know how. Come up with your own set of depictions, you are competent enough for that. I have already provided you with an angle of approach. If you are unable to secure Kosovo and Tadic then you have done a pathetic job through the centuries and are useless and I will get to you again at number 17.

Contract number three is open at this stage. It should bring Yiannis Varoufakis into contact with Boris Tadic. Varoufakis will relay messages between Tadic and myself. You may have guessed by this stage that our next target will be the world economy.

Contract numbers 4 through 16 are for individual nations. The price is your central bank, full control of your economy and of your farming and agricultural practices. You retain control of your own military, schools, universities and religious institutions but none of your banks or big corporations. My product is the best. But yes, it is quite casual and will always have that style to it. More precise than your systems in practice and application I think you will find though. I would place these nations around the Global Senate but this is to be your choice, though I retain the right of refusal. Christian nations, the Antichrist is going to create an almost utopian system on the world stage. We need to operate that paradigm more comprehensively and effectively than he is able to, without cheating.

Vatican, you are now in a much worse position. I counsel you to make use of the much earlier opportunity I have allocated for your use. If you make me work more to correct your further mistakes from a position of full knowledge then I will introduce more slavery karma to the system and make you responsible for it and then give you to Gilgamesh to run because that is obviously your desire if you fail to complete on stage 17. Hatsumi, Togakure Ryu is a good school. Provided the Vatican have not forgotten how to be humble you may use this position for whatever you choose, by prior negotiation and agreement. If the Vatican need it because they have been idiots then use position number 2 instead.

Contract number 18 is The Antichrist. This contract has been offered to China and will not be offered to anyone else. The West buys the introduction contract and secures participation, then I broker the Chinese participation to secure and administrate much of his surrounding context. We will also be using what is left of the power behind the Qing regime for this.

Contract number 19 is for Lucifer. This contract is pre-booked. We have merged him with an individual of Spanish descent who is not yet 30. He will be your new Chief, Illuminati. Expect a purge of your ranks and a lot of fresh blood. PSI only, you know the rules we are imposing. The French House is still in the process of negotiating a very small concession amongst consenting individuals of opposite sexes but from the same species only and no more than 5ml per week and it must be in a sexual context. Their negotiation is likely to fail without full international support and sponsorship. Yes, we have deliberately made it the most Veblen of goods because you can afford it and can't afford not to. In terms of the magickal binds of the thing, PSI vampires are just people suffering from an unusual psychological condition. The reality of the situation makes no difference, what are you going to do, open a permanent Rift on this planet? Well then.

Contract number 20 is Temple of Venus. This is a contract to facilitate the development of the world's next major religion. Well, think some more about your present actual position; before you object look at the big picture.

Contract number 21 is for the Masons. We have a use for you.

Stage 22 is divided into 3 phases, all of which pertain to Sirius. Phase 1 has already been completed and pertained to Sirius C. Phase 2 commenced on October 21st 2019 and is depicted on the dial of the Early adopters' edition of this book – after we installed Emperor Rudolpho on the throne through the ninja assassination of the other two triumvirate members, the real threat of significant social unrest and revolution developed. For this reason, those members of Sparta initiated into their "snake mysteries", who are also of The Central Way, left the Earth reincarnation system on that date to inhabit the bodies of the Praetorian Guard on Sirius. They will all return before 2027, prior to the ascension of Narasingha to the throne of Shambhala, and this is Phase 3.

Stage 23 has already been completed and pertained to the calibrations provided to the reign of the Emperor Akihito and his tenure as consort to the Sun. We achieved peace, and brought it to you too, but in darkness. And now, we move once more into the light, or according to the beauty of harmony you could say. Peace means you have surrendered. Because that is the position we put you into and you have no real choice in the matter but have yet to fully comprehend why this is the case. And we are not waiting.

Stage 24 is completed but waiting to be activated. We shall be doing so on 26th December 2019, the date we also publish this book. It is the context which enables the New System. We have already given you the geometry for it.

There are 2 sides to this schematic, one ascending from the depths of poverty and other misfortune, the other descending into those same depths of density but hopefully along very different routings. This is why the later stages are already completed.

The process will meet in the middle somewhere, and exactly where it does so is probably highly relevant to the overall mechanics. This is where you use trust. You cannot fail to get it right. Wherever you meet is fine, that is what was always intended.

But you do this in the context of a controlled series of events, as you now understand. Nevertheless, in practice, they all exist at once.

Now, for the explanation you have all been waiting for, or some of it at least.

I control the context, the entire system you find yourselves within, and then require that to be focused for me. This is what Shogun does in the present era. He does still contain the Prophet Mohammed in his soul Legacy but that is unsurprising because nobody troubles Shogun.

I moved the soul of Jesus Christ out of my Legacy – by blood oath across a suitable distance – because I was accepting requests prior to the 2012 referral to Central. He was too insistent and was asking for too much. You cannot make this planet that good so soon in time, nor people's hearts. We still have his soul in this system, it's just that it has been adopted into another Legacy, meaning it is now located within another ninja presently physically incarnate on planet Earth. If you want that contract then be aware that it pertains to control of Hollywood in all its aspects excluding the activities of Temple of the Vampire. You may arrange the contract for the current location of the soul of Jesus Christ through the agent for the West, Muramasa. Same way you get to me, at least initially.

Your soul you may view as your personality within a particular incarnation. It is how you choose to express your natal gateway, which is given to you by the reptilians. You live in a closed system and The Veil is opened only for birth and death and it is not opened by you but by the Naga who administrate you from Fourth Density. This is not strictly the way it is but is the closest you can come to understanding what is actually involved without a lifetime of training being involved. Classify it within your own mind as fiction, that is probably easiest for you. It is your soul, you choose if you want to understand it and how you go about doing so.

Spirit, or God, is the Force and Focus which inhabits the natal gateway and moves through it. Ye are all gods but some are greater and darker than others, which is to be considered an unexpected answer to a millennia old riddle. I am the presence which moved through Jesus Christ but Jesus Christ is no longer a part of my complex and very large Soul Legacy. As stipulated, he was contracted out for irritating me during a critical period with his naivety. Unsurprising, and tragic, but to have been expected. You do not understand what we were really doing with Rome and why I created Christianity in the first place. Now is not the time to impart such an understanding. It will be more interesting to hear how the Catholic Church justify their faith and its history to Gilgamesh.

I am not here to have a personal relationship with anyone. That is what my Spirit is for, or more accurately a part of it. In terms of my physical body, my own self as you would understand that, you are here to obey my commands if you are in a position to do so and by prior contract for commercial consideration. That is what the Sword of God is. Take the option that comes to you on commercial system would be my strong recommendation. You may observe what happens when we wield the Sword of God in a direct attack modality by observing what happens to the Euro and the EU.

Why do I normally allow people to people to prioritize their own emotional prejudices, lack of real understanding and egotistical or power-related demands, even to the extent that they defeat me first, especially when the consequences are so dire, and why are the consequences so dire, is that even ethical? If you defeat somebody in the physical realm all that conveys to the Group Mind is that you trained harder, or worked harder, or knew the right people and so forth. It is not an educational experience for the Group Mind and does not contribute to the establishment of True Hierarchy on this planet, nor anywhere. Group Mind simply assumes you are like everybody else, but a winner. Which is a useful enough position to be in and enough for most people, hence what they aim for.

In Third Density, dense material physicality allows people to live within the twin illusions of equality and opportunity. They do not understand what is really happening nor why it is happening. This is the reason for much of their suffering. Not least because their ignorance causes them to make critical mistakes.

However, the Group Mind is more intelligent than the sum of its individual minds because it feels things accurately. It understands when it is in danger, for example. It will not understand this if you simply have the capacity to hurt and severely penalize its members. It understands that its duty is to depict the reality of the situation to the ego personality, the public mind at the group level. The ego personality, the public mind, is naturally sceptical. Many people make bold and controversial claims as a way to gain attention and, usually, wealth also. So, the reality of the situation is depicted for them to understand. In a way that gets it through to their ego personality.

The standard penalization the complex mechanics which surround me apply is the torture of your entire species followed by its eradication. You can fine tune the complexities within that but ultimately it comes true in some way. To take your most obvious example, Rome fell and the Jews suffered the Holocaust.

This is why you cannot attack me personally, nor my direct projects. You may feel that you can but the minds of the surrounding group restrain you. The species knows who and what they are dealing with. That is enough to make them sit up, pay attention and comport themselves in an efficient and to the point manner.

It is also how my swords prefer to work and you may examine this proclivity of theirs to this day at your leisure and to the extent of your ability. Your body understands. The group around you understands. It has been cut into them. Deeply enough to leave its mark. That is how a binding works. This is the dark side of the project.

At a broader level, our entire species was eradicated by the Naga on their way to Earth. The Light Elves went off to Germany with their particular mission, the Dark Elves went off to Russia with their particular mission and the Crazy Elves didn't bother to think that far ahead and went off to live in the woods and practice their magick. And to this day they have occultism in their blood. This is because the soul moves through the blood to interact with the physical body. Nowadays, most of the original Crazy Elves are Israeli. So those are the three nations which share the original connection.

Now. You will need to use your intelligence and fine judgment. Good luck to you gentlemen, and ladies too.

The internal experience of devout Christians should remain largely unchanged. That soul is always very busy and I remain aware of its motion still.

Introducing Red, the most dangerous one of the lot (and the sweetest)

Red is still an innocent and the youngest one to be included in this schematic. She is an all-American girl, somewhere in the 15-16 or 18-19 age range. We do not want to be too specific at this stage.

Her great personal tragedy, which she is not yet aware of, is that the great love of her life and indeed all her incarnations will not be joining her in physical form during this lifetime. This is because he has a job to do: withdraw all of the karmic packets embedded in the species of humanity, as also their institutions, along with a great deal of the 'energy' attached to them.

The reason for this is that the Naga, as a species, paid the price for you already by sacrificing their entire species to the sword. Therefore humanity is not going to be destroyed, because that would be an incorrect application of mechanics, which never happens.

To secure that result, the Vampire do have to get involved. And it is Red's boyfriend, twin flame, whatever you want to call him, who is doing the PSI draw. Himself, in person.

To put that in perspective, this means he can extinguish chosen sections of the population at will. If you cause him to "drop a packet" whilst he is in the process of taking it out of your system for you then that is usually what will result.

The process will last her entire ordinary human lifetime, about 90 years. After that she becomes pure Vampire and can go to him if he wishes. He may not wish. She will have fucked a huge amount of men by then. This is to make her more attractive to him, provided she does so well and is truly satisfied in the majority of her experiences.

When she sees injustice in the world, he responds. Another target acquired. This is why you need quality and sufficiently detailed news programming. She will close the distance to her pre-specified targets, she is of the Central Way. If you make her walk the paths of darkness to find you, beware.

Prior to his arrival on Sirius, Azra-nak was right next door with the rest of his team, in the Orion system. It was there that the Dark Alliance was formed, consisting of 72 ascended star systems, or distinct civilizations. This has found representation in many forms on the face of the Earth but the one we want you all to become more familiar with is known to you as the Goetia. The original purpose of the Dark Alliance, from Azra-nak's perspective, was that he intended to compete with Lucifer for control and rulership over the whole Darkness. Things have evolved since then.

Red's boyfriend will sell most of the packets he withdraws from the system to Occulus Darian, the Orion corporation headed by the species known to you as Bael, whose representative on Earth in this epoch is King Charles III. The energy he will keep as his commission.

Occulus Darian then send most of what they acquire through trade in this way to the Rigel system, for recalibration operations. Upon its return they will package it up and ship it off to Earth through gravity wave modulation.

Occulus Darian is not a charity. You will pay them a fair price in return. They specialize in the corporate takeover of civilizations, by which they ordinarily mean ascended star systems. They are very good at what they do and are doing it anyway. There are two elements to the process which you are able to control: the terms negotiated with Bael by The Antichrist, The Illuminati and Lucifer (expect environmental initiatives to dominate, we would guess) and how you treat Red, which affects the product originally delivered to Occulus, and the order, or sequence, in which it is so delivered. There are pre-arranged codes in play here, which are Harmonic in nature and move according to Principles, hence beyond your cryptographical abilities we would estimate. You are, however, free to comport yourselves in an ethically upright and socially responsible manner.

Red is currently going through her goth phase, and so has dyed her hair grey at the moment, but normally it is died black at her current stage in life. In a way, she is hiding. From herself and from the world. She does not suspect she is vampire yet. Nor does she know much of her truer abilities or deeper nature. She is, however, in the process of awakening even now.

She's still playing the virgin, even though she has had sex with 2 partners already and is on her way towards the third. She likes to investigate the role, the depiction for the minds of others, the effect that doing so has on how they treat you and more generally how they behave around you. So you see that she could very easily become a cold, manipulative and calculating bitch. But it is never like that with Red. She has real heart.

When she finishes high school she will have an offer from Stanford already in the bag, if she does not already. We are in the process of drawing her into our own schematic, your ranks too Illuminati hierarchy, as she is the single most dangerous piece on the world stage at the moment and likely well into the future. Stanford will play a role in that process.

Shogun is far more powerful, so too are most others of significance in the world stage schematic. Red remains the most dangerous.

However, before Stanford she will take a year out, ostensibly to gain work experience at a company owned by a friend of her father. She only does that for about 5 months though and spends the rest of the time backpacking rather quickly through Central America and then much more slowly through the rest of South America once she hits Ecuador.

By then she will have moved on to inhabiting another role, that of curious but tasteful explorer. She will have an interest in both men and women and will take some instruction in tantric sexuality, because it answers her need for something deeper, to explain the way she is beginning to feel now that she has learnt how to open herself up in sex more.

Red will need to process a lot more darkness than the current rate at which she consumes and refers it. Later in her life, this will be greatly facilitated by the fact that she already prefers to double penetrate herself when masturbating, but is scared to even suggest this to anyone in case they form judgments about her within their own minds. She is also careful even when thinking about trying it in reality, as she feels it may do things she does not want or cannot control or won't be ready for where her feelings, moods, insights, sense of self and personal energies are concerned. She does spend a great deal of time thinking about it though, roughly the same amount that most women spend theorising Mr Right within their own heads and in terms of their social interactions.

There is good in humanity too, and you need to be very careful in making sure that Red sees this by having enough of it displayed prominently and regularly, on the news for example.

Once her heart grows cold then things get very bad for the human race. You need to ensure that does not happen. But it has to be real, because she is not the one you are trying to convince.

We have her under our own protection, like the rest, but she is also under his protection, and we wish to emphasise that you really do not wish to upset him. He has had her incarnated as one of you, albeit with a strong vampire soul, to see how you treat one of your own kind when they are not in your Inner Circle.

We have the arrangements and contacts in place, you do not, nor can you arrange a recalibration. Once you buy access to her (from Muramasa as usual and at the usual price) then we can fetch her into the Inner Circle, and from that point on there will at least be some level of safety netting in position. But even then she will still remain connected to the world and the people and will feel things from their perspectives. She is true to her heart and it has already been formed before you managed to get to her.

Red feels things intensely and cares about people, animals and the state of the world. She also feels things with an uncommon precision, depth and clarity. Do not try to deceive her unless you have a fully functioning illusion. You don't want to create those sorts of tensions in her being.

Red is the real reason that no nation, and we mean no nation, attacks the USA over the course of World War 3. Let her do what she is there to do for the world. Do not turn her into an all-American attack modality.

Red will be involved in the development of economic systems, and in particular the governance and administrative structures that are moved into position in sub-Saharan Africa as part of the corporate takeover of the planet.

She will however first of all work on the development and implementation of a superior initiative domestically, ie within the USA. The African template will be much simpler, and it will be possible to implement it a lot more rapidly. An agenda both deeper and broader will be in play in terms of the American template in this.

This is hardcore pornography not war!

We talked to Lucifer about why he got them to do it. The ritualized paedophilia we mean. His function is to speed up time. He found a way to do it. For him, it was a valid course of action within this context. This is why humanity can never be ruled by Lucifer. Nor by people who are obedient servants of Lucifer.

We did say you were sycophantic pricks with no real understanding of his true position.

However, Lucifer is willing to continue to perform his function effectively for a reconstituted Cabal run by people in whom real moral backbone has been developed. We refer to this process as developing the steel within your soul and it is part of what the blood oaths are for.

To serve, or perform a function under our direction, is not to rule.

Through the process of your obedience to the commands, directives, advice and recommendations of out 5 agents, hope will be reintroduced into the world, along with a lot more style, much better living conditions and an overall increase in human beauty.

Not much has happened in this world for the past 50 years or so, just the development of technology really. All that will change, but only at a fairly fast pace.

At The Illuminati levels this is all going to happen so incredibly fast and with such dynamism and power to its occurrence that you will all feel thoroughly screwed over. It's worse than that actually and the experience of losing most of your wealth, influence, power, glory and liberties will, for most of the families targeted, feel as if they have been gangbanged by 5 separate individuals, two of whom were women who fisted them.

Less metaphorically, the process was literally a withdrawal of the group karmic packets by which World War 3 is to be fuelled from the world grid, their processing within the Orion system, and their reintroduction via the Bael corporate gateway when the time for that comes. The trick to the process is that we withdraw 100% war and reintroduce 17% war and 83% other things, the majority of which will be construction in stone on sensitive geomantic nodes and Temple of Venus operations. Or roughly those proportions, they have not settled yet.

In practice what the general public will see will be a lot more sexual activity within their societies. They will also understand that this is an elite process. A five on one gangbang is not something an ordinary woman would enjoy or even desire.

Therefore, most of what was going to be done through war to your society as a whole will now be done only to your elite but through sexual means rather than war.

So do bear that in mind. This is hardcore pornography not war!

Except for the worst 14% of you. You get the third option in this. Execution.

Is that why you only want to execute 14% of the participants?

You are correct. The sacrifice has already been paid. Honor them. Use what it was put there for. Lucifer always held that the mission came first. Venus broke his heart. It's what she does. This is how Tragedy is born: multiple parties fulfilling their own functions perfectly, then things cross-reference.

Again, do not put yourself into a position where you are hard to defeat because you will still be defeated, just the hard way. Sooner or later, everyone does fall. Then you need to find your way back into the Light.

And that's where we find Lucifer currently located. Part of this process, of course, is to fetch his designated organisation into the public sphere.

What's the big deal with Keanu Reeves?

He looks like the other two. The similarity between Muramasa and Masamune could be dismissed as the result of the former tracking the latter through the veils of destiny and the flows of fate. You become more like unto your designated target until you finally close the distance and have found him.

But for 3 of them to all look very similar and to age at the same sort of unusual rate? We know we have the Ancient of Days on this planet. We suspect he brought the 24 Elders with him.

Section 8: Executive summaries

Summary of our commands to The Illuminati

For a much fuller and broader understanding of what is expected of you, you are required to study the full work in the full edition.

The initial decision should be left up to the CIA to take, because they have a Nick Fury style secret chief, hidden from public view within the Labyrinth Group who seems to know what he is doing. It is his decision to take. The ordinary Illuminati in their present format are far too weak to take over the full military-industrial complex, let alone the world. The secret head of the CIA is the one who's been coordinating The Alliance to fight back and is the single individual most responsible for engineering their defeat.

Now we're telling him to change direction. He needs to come to a recognition of the value of this strategy for himself, because he has a good but a steel heart and has made all the right decisions so far and has therefore earned this.

What you do, Illuminati, is to prepare yourselves for when your designated meeting location is up and running, by which we mean Temple of Venus. As you know, Muramasa, Gilgamesh and Masamune will all be issuing you with commands, many of whose format you can ascertain accurately ahead of time.

For example: get the food supply initiative and restaurant brand ready to implement, by which we mean ready to be up and running within 4 months. It is to be called LDR, details of the acronym to be provided by Muramasa; prepare the underworld for significant changes in the way people are trafficked on this planet, particularly into prostitution; do your work with banking and cryptocurrency, The Antichrist wants to move away from doing the techie stuff himself and into a more strategic set of roles. And so forth.

You also have the benefit now of seeing how your position will be interfaced with the general public and understand the role you still have to fulfil in human history. You may wish to issue certain course corrections as a result.

Before the CIA have formally established their response, and so move themselves into position to arrange further participation in the schematic according to their own terms, you will have to disguise yourselves as ordinary private investors if you want to join in and help to get things moving faster.

Summary of our plans for the general public

Lucifer is going to run this planet to a high order of complicity and perfection, to justify the tools used by his followers to get to this destination. The Illuminati, who serve him anyway, will be implementing Lucifer's global rule, according to the directions they receive from their new leader, The Antichrist.

The objective of the whole exercise is to circumvent the social matrix within which you currently hold and operate both your minds and your physical reality, as also the development of the Consequence Field of that social matrix. You must transcend your old concepts and leap 700 years into the future.

A way has been found to implement a functional utopia on planet Earth within the very short space of only 50 years. It won't be a particularly comfortable or easy ride but it is much better than any of your alternatives.

Japan will supervise the entire planet in perpetuity, including everything The Illuminati get up to. We will be executing some very rich people, most of whom engaged in ritualised paedophilia, and we'll be importing alien technologies for full public introduction from the Sirius star system.

Section 9: +2

So you're not actually worried about climate change then?

Climate change is real but is simultaneously happening to the other planets in your solar system. You can confirm this for yourselves. Then look at your theories about causation once more.

Climate change is a conspiracy theory based on some very solid evidence. For you it is real and serves to help you understand that you will be killed prematurely unless something is done to get you off that timeline direction.

We did say that the true nature of the attack you are facing has to do with the nature of Amaterasu and how Shogun is going about things. The solution is to once again make the Japanese Emperor personally and publicly responsible for running the interface device and process.

Are you going to tell us where the one lie is located then?

The whole thing is a lie but it behaves like the truth, which is why it is magick. This is because it is a lie manufactured largely out of truth.

As stated, it does contain one (1) strategically very well positioned lie. Where this lie is located would depend on what your strategic interests are and which perspective you are looking at the world stage from. Its position also shifts according to the motion and development of the surrounding context.

Section 10: What else can we do to prepare?

Illuminati

The first thing to recognise is that our "minimum change necessary" policy sometimes entails completely changing the whole basis and structure of what you are doing and how you set about doing it.

You have the general public living under your systems subject to the twin primary influences of a desire for money and a desire for sex. You then tune the sex as paedophilia through your rituals, hide the true nature of money away for your own elite, and the result is that the rest of society has their hearts guide them according to the sexual currents as they aspire to close in on greater wealth and material security. Hence, the abusive, distorted, unequal etc expression given to economic operations and wealth structure on this planet. Your people do not see it, nor understand overmuch, but we find the aesthetics of the depiction disturbing and seriously flawed

The two main things you will be doing, therefore, is recalibrating the sexual energy flows from the very top of pyramid and on sensitive geomantic nodes. And publicising the true nature of money, as also giving them concise instructions and convenient avenues to enable them to acquire more of it without killing themselves with work. In practice this means banking and the economy are both required for the second main thing that needs to be completely changed.

These are your twin pillars and what you will focus on above all. The two go together and they should be made to evolve, or develop, in tandem, that is to say at roughly the same rate as each other.

You have been really overdoing it since the 1960's, and using the most intense practices a lot of the time moreover, and a lot will be required to dominate over that.

Muramasa will be operating Temple of Venus out of Aspen, Colorado. This to be based on a stricter definition of evil than that prevailing in ordinary society: specifically, you will be *less* sexually free within Temple of Venus than most members of ordinary mainstream society. And, by some, this will be understood as evil, not least because of the underlying agenda and set of value structures.

Women who are initiates within the Temple of Venus mysteries are to consider themselves free to have sex with whoever they find attractive, if they want to. They cannot however have sex with people they do not find attractive, for example out of financial ambition.

Men who are initiates within the Temple of Venus mysteries are to consider themselves free to have sex with whoever they find attractive, provided they are a member of the opposite sex and participate in whatever consent clauses are generally socially in play at the time. However, men are to consider themselves free to also have sex with women they do not find particularly attractive, for whatever interesting and manipulative reasons they are able to come up with.

The rules are different for Priests and Priestesses. There, the lowest three ranks get to choose to have sex with whomever they choose, as a process and divine act of exploration, and to protect us from too many aesthetically distasteful lawsuits and negative publicity, at least near the beginning. This means no restrictions beyond those of age, sex and species, demons and so forth are fine, especially if you manage to find a suitable human host. So we will do our very best to get real evil involved for you all, even if it is the hentai version.

Though this religion will initially be developed in the USA it is due to spread throughout Africa and – perhaps more rapidly if they know what's good for them – the rest of the world's westernized and civilised nations. It will also largely come to replace Islam.

So once you conclude that you will have to put it together, ensure you have strong and deep enough foundations – but try to accomplish this without destroying the rhythm of the thing.

Part of Muramasa's designated role and responsibility will be to help elevate your mental processes. It is an entirely different way of using mind which characterises Fourth Density operations. You do not build structures out of Logic to make something bigger. You attune to what is already there and observe as it fulfils itself.

In second density you absorb energy and atmosphere from your surrounding context and feel the pleasure and the flow in doing so. This is how animals behave. Hell is located in Fourth Density, not in second. It is however much easier to live in Fourth Density when you operate your genetics using bigrammatic codings, that is to say a second density condition. For Fourth Density, Stanford is the designated location that we have also been working on, preparing your Civilization for this meeting.

He will need 12 tenured positions. The Antichrist Council is 13 positions and The Council of Ministers is 14 positions. So be aware that the Stanford placements are to form part of a series.

We will get him to write a full page PhD dissertation for you as one of the chapters in this book. Honorary wouldn't cut it. You are to award it without corrections, of course. It should qualify as the shortest PhD thesis in history, because that urban legend has not been fulfilled yet. And it will be in strategy, not mathematics. Because you have no choice. He has out-strategized your Civilization, in practice, and you need to understand how he did that if you want to survive and stand a chance at victory.

You will find that his preference in communication is laconic to the extreme, to this day. Once he's there you can discuss the rest with him. Five will be in Philosophy, he needs a geneticist with a good team behind him because his own one fell to our percentage, Varoufakis and Tadic of course, Paul Krugman if you can interest him, a few more. Muramasa himself will help you to formulate your Grand Strategy. War strategy itself we are leaving to Sun Tzu.

You need to put things into your own terms and structures, and he will be there to help you with that. No teaching for the first three years though. Shogun's commands, three years of fairly intense physical training for him first, same with all our members before they join *The Shadowdancers* as a public position. He will help you put together that art. It must be your own, a product of Western civilization, even if a lot of it is going to be straightforward copying.

Once you have Muramasa in position he will then direct you to the rest of our Agents. You will have limited time with him, as he mainly wants to retire and go on holiday as soon as that can be conveniently arranged. Make the most of it, he is a very useful piece for you all.

Negotiations need to begin with Turkey, or you can simply make them direct commands if you prefer. The priority is to get the proportion down to 14% as soon as can conveniently be arranged and subsequently keep it there throughout the process. The international immunity option needs to be in place before the executions can commence, or they will not be as productive.

There are changes to banking, central banking and political relations which need to be undertaken or prepared for and the relevant agreements arranged between the USA, China, Russia, the UK, France, Greece, Italy and Taiwan – with some consideration given to Belgium, Germany, Austria, Sweden and the Netherlands. Israel, Iran, Syria and Saudi Arabia are to form part of the TRNC negotiations.

The food supply and restaurant symbolic representation policy has already been covered. It is like a form of insurance for you all. You are to commence work on this from now.

The Antichrist is to develop most of the actual military strategy. Muramasa can certainly assess potential candidates for the hidden reflection of the Council of 13 Ministers. But really that is for The Antichrist himself to arrange.

The main arms dealing families, as also the pharmaceutical and medical technology giants, are to be brought together into the initial Cabal. Muramasa is to prepare them for their meetings with the Antichrist and Armand, who will be representing Masamune for them.

Finally, the super-rich and especially members of the global 0.1% should feel the need to talk amongst themselves at this stage, perhaps at a venue other than Davos whose ambience encourages a greater sense of social responsibility? We do of course mean Paris. Members of the French House, and some of their servants, will be in attendance. Their interest in you is to assess who can be made to be seen by the public as a good example. This enables initial immunity proceedings to commence for you and your family.

General public

Starvation you shouldn't have to go through but we may have to reduce your calories for a while. The whole process becomes much easier if you are chilled about it. You need to relax more, for which UBI and *soma* will be introduced before we really make this demand from you.

Obesity is out, fascism is in power, but the Chinese have made a play for control of global banking and the world economy. You can still be fat but obese people will be required to attend re-education facilities.

With less work, more holidays and no real money worries we ask you not to panic and try to avoid getting too self-righteous as the world stage theatre production picks up steam.

You will all be able to really enjoy the next 50 years, even if you are to be in a war zone, but you need to relax your way into it and allow your heart to open from the enjoyment of the process. You won't like the hard way, this is why we make this recommendation to you now so that you can prepare.

No real need to go overboard on the stocks. You could make it through on 40kg of rice and 6 buckets of bouillon. So the duress will still be there, but not undue.

Both of you

We've arranged what we shall call a Reptilian Overlord Conversion for you. From a human perspective, their alignment used to be *Evil*. Now it is *Good*.

There's much more to it all of course. The difference is that now you can understand what you actually have to do and why you will be doing it.

It's still draconian rule though. Much greater precision in where your feelings really lie and how you use your minds is a far better use for strictness than excessive legislation we think you will find.

You only have so much Naga. It will always be a continual flow but do not continually waste that flow. Or the mental health of the general population will falter. Mechanics again. You can only do so much with a system. God does not want it overloaded, he designed it that way. Except by personal choice, but that is how you become a god and humans on Earth will never be ready for that at the level of the general public. That is not what they are there for. Another thing the Jesus Christ personality did not quite understand or get right.

Above all, do not make the Naga lose patience with you. Or they'll probably just change their alignment on you again. You have this chance. Use it wisely.

Can't we just rise above the concepts of Good and Evil?

Sure, individually this is possible, within your own head and behaviour. You will still be administrated as located within those concepts until the 7 generations are through. The Naga encourage you to really commit yourselves to a position. These things take time and are subject to mechanics.

Now you know. You need the ethos to prevail throughout the whole of society, at least one third of its members. Most are located within those concepts.

A secret way out has traditionally been to start your own order or school for the purpose, or join one that is already established and commit your life to it. All such things take 7 generations to really get going, just the way it works.

In terms of both the institutions and the conceptual structures we have designed for this next period in the evolution of human history, they are an accurate and technically productive representation of where you need to locate yourselves. They contain everything, in terms of the actual positions, content, and resolutions, of which your timeline is composed. Their format has been designed to empower rapid conceptual resolution and subsequent evolution within a stable, enduring and resilient structural framework.

In practice this process is to progress in distinct stages: a period where the next stage of global progress is designed and formally agreed upon, followed by the physical implementation of the new physical circumstances, followed by a period of resolution of past positions – and then back designing the next stage of global progress.

The rhythm however is determined by the problem set you choose to resolve within your established social conditions. This is one of the major reasons that it was agreed to resolve the content of both the Buddhist and the Hindu religions in the 24th and 25th centuries rather than over the next 50 years, as is being done with Communism, Capitalism, Neoliberalism, Islam, traditional Shintoism, Christianity and some elements from within Judaism though probably not the whole religion in that last instance.

Though we are speeding The Illuminati up for you all, we'll be slowing the rest of you down into a much more relaxed pace and rhythm of life. This is mainly characterised by the idea that you don't try to get everything done today, neither in society nor in your own life. Just 80%, or 60% if you're feeling more lazy about it.

60% is to be recommended because it is much more dangerous and so you earn more points for it. This means you leave 40% of social progress untouched whilst you really pay attention to the remaining 60%. Only once it has been changed and the new conditions are in place do you get to the 40% you left behind, who will now be impatient for their turn and full of ideas. It is another recommission of The Pendulum mechanism previously wasted on the Left-Centre-Right political axis.

Time to begin

You write your own future. Don't hold us responsible for the results. Retain your capacity for individual Judgment. But do not exercise it by opening your mouth unless your idea really is much better.

Learn from the mistakes made by the previous Illuminati hierarchy. Generally everybody should speak a lot less when it comes to politics, governance and the economy. And no more than 4 pages of laws, for any country. Recommendations can be made in addition to that but they are to be understood as not binding.

Countries making their own money to fund their own socialist agendas means the end of taxation of all formats, globally. This is perhaps the biggest conceptual hurdle you all face, and the biggest difference in practical administration you will all encounter. You have much work to do to prepare in this field. As usual, if you do not move fast enough then more penalization will be applied.

Let us put it this way, if the old Illuminati hierarchy were designing the Golden Race, what we're introducing is best referred to as the Gold-Plated Race. The core of your being should be steel, and composed of Principle. This is the true meaning of the heart, and its depth.

It is a warrior's path whose special characteristic is that it is equally open to women, in practice as well as in theory.

What they will see is your gold and the fact that you are gentle about it all. Yet they appreciate this gentleness, whether you are male of female, because they recognise that the wider organisation as a whole as also you personally probably could kill many more of them and make them all suffer a lot more also if need be.

They respect each of you personally not because you personally refrain from killing them nor because you will, when the time comes, necessarily keep them safe from harm. Rather it is because each one of you has suffered personally – or perhaps is still suffering personally because they are not yet out of the first 14 years of basic training – that they respect you.

They know that you all suffer, and some of you are executed, to enable conceptual resolutions within their own minds and the satisfaction of their own emotions. Which twin results mean that less of them need to be killed, and all of them suffer less.

So that's the influence of your Christian ethos in case you missed it.

As a result there is a great deal of social cohesion and people respect that you are making them do the right thing by asking them nicely. But yes. The new Illuminati hierarchy will be open about who they are and what activities they engage in.

The opportunity to obey them is a privilege. When they are attacked they fight back. They are not however our enforcement capacity. Therefore their normal method of interacting with you will be to pay you a visit unannounced and expect to be admitted to your top ranks immediately, to whom they will, with elaborate courtesy, make certain suggestions and offer certain perspectives. A summarized list of these will then be pinned to the staff notice board, so to speak. They deal with all spheres of the economy: politics, banking, finance industry, retail, the medical sector, arms sales and manufacture, transport and even in certain situations both the regular military and certain special forces units. They are not, however, ever going to pay your average ordinary Joe a visit.

And they're your best and probably only hope out of the set of messes you are currently in.

You're going to call them *The Shadowdancers*, and they must be your own creation. But they will basically be knock-off ninjas, because that makes the whole process a lot easier for all of us.

So yes, in a way, this is a ninja takeover of the world. Admit it, some of you were expecting this.

Wherein we make it all better

Part 3: The Light Current and the Destructive Cycle

Prologue

Chapter 1 – Lies, magick and illusion

This book is a work of fiction. That is to say, it is an exercise in crafting and structuring a web of lies and deceit. Because we are lazy and curious and wanted to see what would happen much like your average five year old, we decided to compound our sins by stealing lies from other people, groups of people mainly, as we wanted to work with your prejudices, your fears and your desires.

This whole book is simply a reflection of what is in your hearts, humanity as a whole, on this planet at this juncture in time. All of it, good, bad and of course the beautiful as well. Our work with your minds, at a group level, is limited to the restructuring of logical connections between already existing fears, prejudices and all other forms of Darkness AND the recalibration of the content flows occurring within the Principles of Light, or virtues, which are active for you during your next 150 years or so of world history. In other words, we elevate your ethics and wrap you in a new web of lies and deceit in order to accomplish this objective.

We go into a lot more detail on all of that in Parts 1 and 2. Much of it is technical and has to do with the way The Illuminati – who do not exist – structure the illusions you live within and thereby rule your world. It is all deep and highly esoteric stuff and most of you can't be bothered to read it or learn much about it, which is why we shunted it all off into separate parts that you can ignore if you just want some sort of pastiche of a story cobbled together out of strategy, death, ninjas, ancient gods, mystery schools, a select few ET species, lunatic fringe conspiracy theories featuring capable and ethical Western governance, perfectly sane material from the Rig Veda featuring Nagas (aka reptilian shape-shifters made famous by David Icke, who we all think is a nutjob) and of course magick.

That's all we're offering in Part 3 anyway. World peace, for a period at least, will be an intended secondary consequence of our primary focus in this. Our primary focus in this, Part 3, is going to be Greed in its purest, strongest and most productive form. Not that we are attached to greed or hold it as a virtue or fail to have mastery over its tenets and impulses. Rather, because Capitalism is now being killed, it is a ninja assassination correct, we wanted to collect the bounty on that. By doing it the best. From within your system in a way which is allowed under your own laws, business terms, moral codices and mythologies or religions. We will take it all from your super-rich and whoever else is holding onto the reins of power in all this, and then give you all back what we decide upon. We invite all the world's peoples to join us on our unreasonable quest to master the expression of Greed on this planet at this time.

However, there's two catches. First of all is the disappointing reality that this is only an offer on our parts. We have absolutely zero intention of chasing around after all that money. If the world's elites want us to have it then they will have to arrange to get it delivered, and on time. Once the genocide starts (of the world's super-rich, covered in Parts 1 and 2), the time for mastering the expression given to Greed will have passed and we shall have moved on as a planet to mastering the expression of some other fascinating moral or life Principle intended for later physical depiction. That is just how life works. We figured it would be much easier if we just told you which lessons were in play and when. Shambhala, a mythical realm where they also have Naga, is generally much more secretive about what you are learning and when. Instead you are just supposed to guess what history means or figure it out for yourselves. A conflict with our Impatience resulted – a Principle we have developed to an extraordinary degree – and you have already read the resolution given to the issue.

You already know the second catch. It is a limited time offer. During that time we will be instituting on this planet the format to be taken by World Governance for the coming millennium or so probably, as also the global economic and banking systems active during that same tenure. It is in your interests, general publics of this world, to be as greedy as you can possibly be during this time – and to a high degree of deep esoteric understanding and personal embodiment of that understanding. The reason for this is because the people who think they rule you and in some ways still do and always will we suppose, have a deep and powerful esoteric understanding of Greed and personal desire. They use their mastery over these Principles to control your world and derive a lot from it, most especially in terms of market economics and sexual gratification. It is too much effort to do what they do. Our way is much easier. You don't even have to read the whole book, you can get away with just the middle part. The rest you participate within for fun or out of curiosity, mostly.

In Part 3 then we will be doing Greed and the simplest way to fulfil that is to take as big a sphere as you can. For example, if you could control the whole of planet Earth then your sphere would be the size of this planet. Sirius to start with, hence our use of the 13/11 gateway. However, in reality we will be working in Part 3 with this galaxy, *Hunab Ku* which is the supermassive black hole at the centre of this galaxy, and the wormhole gateway in the Orion constellation through which you can also arrive at whatever is on the other side of *Hunab Ku* if you navigate it in a very specific way. Mainly.

To do this we will be rewriting your mythology, including some of your religions, by referencing antecedent events and elaborating meaning within situations of role and character. Our purpose in doing so is not to irritate though it may at times when we find it funny be to offend so please don't get touchy with us, you'll find that doing so doesn't go well for you, magickally enough. Mostly though our purpose in doing so is to build an elaborate conceptual structure which is clearly a pack of lies but equally clearly is functionally true in a much stronger and more dynamic manner than the fabricated reality run by your incumbent world leaders, who we refer to throughout this work as the Luciferian Illuminati. On a legal note, they do not exist and therefore you cannot do anything more than slander and plan the genocide of a fictional construct and that is an author's privilege. As regards the world's super-rich, well granted that is more real as a threat, we suppose you could sue us for it or otherwise take it to court and see what happens.

Frankly, we already have the Prophet Mohammed hostage in Japan on reincarnation and have bound and divided your Jesus Christ into three separate physical bodies on Earth in this present time so we are certain we can count on the Muslims to be extremist about the whole thing eventually and do so hope you'll play along, Western Command. Our implication is that we are not particularly worried about where this may lead. What we have before us, Ladies and Gentlemen, is a locked system. It admits of only certain very specific resolutions. If you try to do something else with history, anything else, it will hurt. Enough that you stop going down that direction and take the road you have been told to walk upon. We've made this aspect of how it all works very personal, intimately bound up with a deep and functional application of Great Tragedy and guaranteed to get you where it actually hurts. It is very basic taijutsu locks we have used for this. You are immobilized for a while and then go where we direct you or break your own arms. It is a metaphor with reference to arms dealing; you will find little messages like that to your incumbent rulership paradigm, and the players within it, scattered throughout this book. Often you just have to guess who is being addressed from the surrounding context and the tone of the statement.

This book then is a fictional construct designed to have a set of very large real-world effects. It also introduces its readers to the magickal practices utilised by the Luciferian Illuminati, or a set of very similar and better designed practices using the same mechanisms of the Universe and Creation. We are doing nothing short of conveying the format to be taken by the new world paradigm though it is assuredly a justified and ancient set of world orders that we will be using to accomplish this with rather than anything more contemporary and *nouveau riche* because they tend to be too grasping and have a very limited understanding of the true ethos of style.

And here, finally, we reach the word of warning. Parts 1 and 2 of this book dealt with bound reality. This is a magickal term connoting that a group of which you are part has been put through sufficient blood and suffering on account of a particular topic or worldview that they come to understand that worldview as real and not fantasy. And you, as a part of that group, share in that commonly prevailing understanding. Now admittedly, we have stretched a lot of borders in Parts 1 and 2 and what we have proposed does not sit comfortably within accepted reality, though it is now wholly located within that realm. Part 3 however is out there. It is not bound within the souls, bodies and genetic memory of groups of which you are all a member.

In short we will use illusions built mainly out of truth to control your religions and their effects on this world. This is because doing so has allowed us to control the course World War 3 will take. This is because our lies have a greater dynamic power to move, alter and sustain material reality than your truths do – at the current set of levels at which they are understood combined with their strategic positions in fate in relation to the development of consciousness at the group level on this planet during this epoch of history. In other words our lies contain more truth than your truths. Power of truth on the world's religions included within this schematic, at the current epoch in history, in terms of motive power; also applies to secular religions that people live within and according to, like governance and economic systems, eg Marxism. QED, at this early juncture.

What it's really about, peoples of this world, is control and power and money – in that order. If all you want is money you will never have enough.

In truth though, this world will not end up with the Luciferian or any other Illuminati's systems of global central banking, finance, banking, governance, global conflict, economic system or ideology. Why not? Because we are going to teach you to be greedy enough, peoples of this world. The best your own rulers could manage would be very inadequate rulership paradigms and modes of existence to go along with that.

How are we going to do better? Well...

Chapter 2 – The story so far

The ninja, or one faction within the ninja known as The Central Way to be more precise, have issued a major terrorist threat (we're just using buzzwords to get people's attention) against the world's super-rich, who are to be genocided along with their families as the star attraction of World War 3. This has never been a conspiracy, we have always been public about everything. A conspiracy may exist to coordinate and control world history. Whether it does so or not, if you do kill all of the world's super-rich then you would also terminate that conspiracy. Quite basic as a strategy but it works well enough we think you will find.

You do not know whether the Luciferian Illuminati really exist; we don't care whether they do or not. The illusion that they exist is strong enough within the minds of men that we may repurpose that lie for our own uses, and this is what we intend to do. This book is going to be all about the structure which humanity chooses to give to the lies that they will live within, must live within, and have been given no choice but to live within. This is because truth is hard work, nobody can be bothered, religion and academic study are boring anyway nowadays (congratulations, to those involved within and responsible for both fields!) and who can make sense of chaos to start with?

More specifically, the ninja have taken the pre-existing notion within Western civilization that the Luciferian Illuminati do exist and married it to the rumour and allegation that many super-rich people engage in ritualized paedophilia. This unproven allegation has been offered, specifically to the Communists and the Christian Church, as a workable justification to be used to consolidate the world's resources into the hands of an even tinier minority than is the case under the incumbent world system. To do this it may in some instances be necessary to produce paid actors and CGI videos. But yes, we can get most people to believe it. After all, they do and they have and they will again before we manage to execute them all.

The state of Britain has been given the opportunity to identify the real members of the Luciferian Illuminati for us – but only after they have surrendered unconditionally in five different ways and agreed to host the Antichrist on their shores. Either way the purpose is to consolidate the world's assets into the hands of a much tinier elite than presently hold, or have others' holding for them, the reins of world power. The Antichrist will be a Chinese ninja, who we call *Lin Kuei*, and the purpose of his sojourn in London will be to complete the negotiations and put into place the diplomatic and financial infrastructure to enable the centre of financial and central banking power to be moved from the City of London to Taiwan. It is our intention to have others create for us a centrally administrated, global cryptocurrency-based system of world banking and central banking. This is to become the world's new financial and banking infrastructure. We have yet to enter into any negotiations with the Federal Reserve but these plans are set anyway and thus all that such negotiations can provide are delays and power plays. Swift obedience with plenty of personal initiative to do things perfectly, even when that involves making changes, is a much better option.

When time becomes a lot more valuable, consider what you can complete before we begin. We do not pressure you, it is an inherent property of the system you find yourselves within at this point in time, and yes we are talking about the planet and humanity as a whole.

Whilst the Russians are busy executing super-rich paedophiles, often in other people's countries, the Chinese will be busy finding lots of ways to structure a global financial system which is far superior to anything the West would be willing to implement and better loved by the world's people, all the world's people or a large majority at least, because China is learning to seduce. They are also better at maths, as a nation and an ethnicity. Sorry, this is your Group Mind and this is just how it works and understands things and responds to them.

In the West, meanwhile, the CIA has been offered the chance to work on the inside with this schematic and may have accepted that offer. This means they will be participating in Turkey's plans to coordinate a massive attack on Israel, with the purpose of having the defenders kill millions in their own defence, until we get to around 10 or 12 million or so. Their target is different, they want to steal something in Group Mind from the Jews. Honestly you couldn't make this sort of stuff up, that is why you are not allowed to think about it much less discuss it.

The CIA's real plans, however, are to save Israel or at least Zion and the Israeli population, and to send that large, nearly exclusively Sunni, Turkish-coordinated army down into Africa. A Turkish-Arabic drive down into Africa is what World War 3 will look like, we can know this from now. The reasons for this are the way the *sakki*, or killing intent, has been targeted at the group level and other factors covered in the binding portion of this work (Parts 1 and 2). Before World War 3 may commence, however, the Luciferian Illuminati need to be created, or simply used if they already exist, to execute the EU in order to put a global governance schematic in its place, controversially divided into Tier 1 and Tier 2 nations. This is another way in which the Order of the Ages – or the sequence in which world events occur – has been locked. By us, the ninja of The Central Way correct.

Finally, we have offered both the super-rich and the Luciferian Illuminati the option of utilising our routing structures to reduce their death toll, though in all instances a minimum of 14% of their number will be taken. To keep things serious and hold your attention. Otherwise people might be able to justify their perspective that we do not, in fact, control world history. We are releasing you from that lie as we dissolve that illusion. But only because we want to put you into a different set of lies. The truth you will have to get to on your own. If you care enough, go for it.

Chapter 3 – Love will kill you

It is our intention to peddle one lie and one lie only on the world stage. However, it is a lie to a very deep and extraordinarily high level and we've expressed it in geometry. We call it "Justice and Vengeance as a replacement for Love". It looks like this:

More specifically, this is the root of how we were able to harmonize our project for global dominance with the plans, projects and intentions of the fictional Cabal who own and rule Western Civilization who we have slanderously labelled the Luciferian Illuminati, though it's basically certain that they worship and serve Lucifer (that position was always required of them, by strategic necessity, as explained in Parts 1 and 2).

To put that in another way, the Luciferian Illuminati's basic project has always been Satanic, which is to say in direct opposition to the Will and Plan of God, to frame things from within Western concepts and ways of understanding the Universe. And our basic proposal is also in direct opposition to the Will and Plan of God. So in that we are very similar, have a very similar strategic position, are working towards the same set of goals. Similar enough, in fact, to engage in business proceedings with each other in support of our now mutual plans. But let's be clear: these are our plans, we came up with them, not your incumbent rulers. Nor would they be capable of developing those plans in the harmonically paradoxical and difficult set of manners required – so we will be telling them what to do on an ongoing basis, not the other way around. Hierarchy and the cultivation of the fate flows is clear in this regards. They descend from above, down through the rest of society. A true trickle-down effect, though it's more of a soul penetration really.

Don't worry, you will get all of it, this is a flow of fate not a pot of money. It will pass through you on its way into the deepest levels of Hell. This is why care is being taken to ensure the whole thing is very finely calibrated from the start. The deeper the density, the harder things are to handle.

The reason for that order of command within what will after all be a military hierarchy because we are claiming that the Earth is under attack from alien star systems, is the differences to be found within our relative strategic positions. Namely they were, and largely enough still remain, deluded, greedy, self-righteous, small-minded liberals, right-wingers and bigots with overinflated egos from within which they tend to take most of their decisions with an eye primarily to profit and self-gratification rather than the fulfilment of harmony in the Universe and the evolution of history in the minds and hearts of men (to frame things within our concepts and ways of looking at the world).

And that is, and always was, the real problem with Love. People's debased natures and proclivities. God, or the Universe, has always had two aspects: Light and Dark, from which a third may be derived: the still center point.

It is productive to consider on your own whether this would be a good thing. It is important to cultivate the ability to be able to rely on your own judgment rather than what you are told or is generally believed in a group or sub-group. These are ancient and brand new technologies under implementation here and in the wider surrounding context. Experts do not exist yet. You will need to learn to follow and trust your hearts if you want to make it in time. You would not succeed in building your conceptual structures fast enough to represent the actual truth of the matter. That is one of the many reasons we are using lies to get this done fast for you.

Let us take greed as an example and show you how to examine a particular concept, virtue or Principle. In a new way, our way. First of all, ignore it completely with your mind, you have less than no interest in understanding it. Then look down at the whole Earth, as a planet, as a system, and rationalise: how much greed is entering the Earth system? Then ask: which souls is it localizing within and to what degree? Examine associated factors until you get the urge to stop or have something else to do and their time is up. Next. Stare at Greed, the Principle. Tell it to reveal its nature to you. Imbue that understanding into your heart and feel clearly what is there. If you cannot accurately feel what is in your own heart then you have work to do.

Greed enables you to get more of something, because you ask for it and then work or have others work on making it a reality for you. Greed is at any rate a very easy vice to convert, which is why we chose it for this demonstration and decades-long implementation still to come. For, as it is currently formulated for humanity, greed is indeed defined as and expresses as a vice (your terms), that is to say as a Dark Current of Fate (our terms).

We then recalibrate the concept. The Secret is that Greed is a Principle, which is to say it exists in a perfected form somewhere within God's character and so the motion of His Mind. This is to be considered something of a surprise to most denominations within most religions we would suspect. They are cordially invited to conduct their own investigations and then report back to us, recognizing that we do not accept the currency of dogma as suitable payment terms.

Thus, you need to include greediness for personal progress (don't worry, we've got motivation for that coming up later for you), social improvement, genetic condition, other things you haven't even thought to ask for yet as species, and so forth within the process of evolution which you provide, as a species, a united humanity, in the coming decades, to the concept and Principle of Greed and its application within the world system and on the world stage. In this manner, or something similar enough to it, you will succeed in *alchemically transmuting* Greed on your planet from a vice into a virtue. And that means you can attack with it. Which is what the diagram above is for.

At this juncture we have a lot of meaning to decode for you. Unless you have already read parts 1 and 2, and even then because you probably missed it as there was just so much going on in Group Mind at the time, you will not be aware of the logical connections those conceptual structures make to other aspects of shortly upcoming world history, namely the Age of the Antichrist. We agree, it would be much funnier to call him "Aquarius" instead of "Damien". He's going to look Asian so you could probably get away with it in public even, we all just choose whatever English name we happen to come up with on our own anyway.

Peoples of the world, rejoice! For we have found you a highly skilled and calmly talented Antichrist. He is already a big figure within your own minds, at the group level definitely and also at the individual level in many, many cases, even today. The reason for this is what we call his Legacy: the previous incarnations in his personal soul track. Specifically, we have located the individual who first attained fame as Gilgamesh and then went on to become both the Yellow Emperor and Sun Tzu. In this book, and in your world history to follow it, we are going to educate you in his most famous saying: how exactly you win a war before it is even fought.

More pertinently, Christian Church, you have debt with the pagans to settle, now shut-up. For now at least. Aquarius is on a roll within Group Mind and wants to make his first appearance.

"We need to take you somewhere impossible and we need to perform this miracle to an inordinately tight timescale, relatively speaking. The reasons for this are biblical, which means that in terms of the Earth system on its own we can effectively blame Western Civilization and the Jews for this. In short, a group of idiots turned up when we were far more civilized than they could ever hope to become and asserted in our presence the quite ludicrous set of beliefs and opinions to which they adhered. Under their terms, which we ourselves neither subscribe to nor participate within, we are, all of us, sinners – which would be to say on the Dark Current and on our way to destruction. Now this is simply not the case, whatever context you happen to surround us with, for we never participated in your limiting viewpoints except to understand them from within whilst simultaneously maintaining a cultivated awareness of the wider context of the system.

God already turned up prior to 2012 and the Last Judgement has begun. We would appreciate it if you did not get all dramatic or emotional about it at this stage. Skeptical is fine, go read Parts 1 and 2 if you want to play that game.

According to the Kalachakra tradition, which is where accurate records on this are kept in this day and age, we first have a 100 year period of physical Judgment which begins in 2027 with the ascension of Narasingha to the throne of Shambhala. However, final Judgment is rendered with Raudra Chakrin, the so-called Kalki Avatar, in 2424. So don't expect anything quick, conclusive and satisfying within your own lifetimes where this is all concerned.

What we can and will promise you is a knock-out World War 3 and a much better world system. For your viewing pleasure and personal conceptual and moral evolution. More importantly, in order to resolve your previous world systems and consolidate them into a united global order."

The implication, which Aquarius left unsaid, is that you do not all need to become virtuous in order to be saved. Rather, stay where you and he will ensure that the vice by which you are surrounded and within which you participate is *alchemically transmuted* into virtue! Furthermore, and we happen to know this for a fact, it is his Age that we are all entering into now – for astrological reasons we believe, that's the reason for it all. Definitely that.

And his Age will involve a great deal of what would under the old system's terms have ordinarily been interpreted as vice. But it's OK! Aquarius will turn that vice into virtue for you by controlling the context by which you are surrounded. This is to say that meaning will be elaborated to issue forth a more developed social understanding.

Specifically, our work with you is complete once you have a functional basic understanding of Fourth Density as a lived life experience. To do this we need to structure four pairs of opposites into paradox locks to produce the 8-petalled schematic shown above.

More gratuitously, we referred the God of this Creation – which operates according to a six-fold flower of life geometry – through *Hunab Ku* to the Big Central God. For child abuse as a ritualized practice within his system. The geometry shown above is what the Big Central God came up with. Far too much content to stuff into much too small a system, done too early and without much regard for what the consequences to that system might be.

We call it Justice and Vengeance and, when you understand what was involved, that level of God was vulnerable to that accusation in a way that Central was not.

In short, Illuminati, the laws of God have been changed in this Creation. Your old mysteries are not necessarily all invalid now, you can test them to see which ones still work well. We have told you the format according to which these things work now. You should be able to derive many functional tools by recalibrating your old mystery practices in light of this new information.

On a personal level, you will no longer be getting places and things in life because people like you or are helping you to like yourself. Instead you will be getting what you deserve and are owed. This will make a lot more sense of personal effort and meritocracy.

Chapter 4 – Our message to the Illuminati

Luciferian or otherwise. We are feeding content into the Sun of this solar system for Shambhala, the representatives of Solar Lodge on Earth, to dispense to you, Earth Lodge. We are feeding that content in from the star system Sirius, using their mechanisms for the administration of other worlds, inclusive of genetic calibration. We have that content flowing through a "pipeline" into the Orion system, whence we beam it to Sirius.

We are saying that our new geometry is functional and receiving a continuous flow of fuels. It is 24 positions because they are the Ancients.

We took most of the fuel within 13/11/2003, you were left with the empty shell which you expressed in Paris. Transition, 13, on Sirius, 11, due to magick, 5. Specifically Rudolpho is Emperor now and the other two who were in the triumvirate whose representatives you have already had contact with have been executed. You backed the wrong horse there, everybody did, that was part of our plan.

Chapter 5 – Our message to the general public

What does Justice look like and why do you need it on your world? Reflect at your own leisure.

Reading Part 3 on its own will not bind you. Reading Parts 1 and 2 will bind you. In Parts 1 and 2 we deal with, and calibrate, The Dark Current. Mainly that would be your world rulers and their plans for world domination. We have bound the Dark Current to the Creative Cycle. That is a bound reality. It cannot escape and must behave to form.

However, if you have read Parts 1 and 2 and then read Part 3 then your own soul will seek to balance itself. Where there is Creation there must be an equal measure of Destruction. We will be running the Elements of Part 3 through the Destructive Cycle. Part 3 deals with the Light Current. We are not binding its position because we do not need to. We bound the Dark and the Light follows as a set of Consequences. Anyway, it is probably impossible to bind the Light. This, in practice, is why the Illuminati and those like them are above the law. Once you understand what the Law really is and how it really works…

We start this book with Part 3 because that is how it is done, that is how you win the war before you have even begun fighting. To state the thing explicitly, first you determine the conceptual context within which the war will take place and also determine what lessons will be learnt as a result of the personal and social transformations which that war will produce. Then you detach and take a much broader and larger perspective. Things start physically some time after that juncture. Unless people agree to reach a mutually profitable set of compromises before that juncture (your way, not ours) or targeted parties surrender unconditionally before we get to them (in which case we usually won't execute them anyway unless we are still shy of our 14% minimum). We are saying we are not interested in reaching a mutually workable solution, we are interested in obedient slaves. By which we mean you, Luciferian Illuminati. Not explaining why yet but now you know where you actually stand and so will waste less of both our time.

Every war will result in the conceptual evolution of the groups who participated in that conflict in relation to specific concepts and along the lines which those concepts find it easiest to fit themselves within inside the human mind. We have already developed those concepts for you in parts 1 and 2, and connected them to each other using specific structural frameworks. That is a bound reality and not something you can as a species escape from. Thus, you will fight World War 3 to develop within your own hearts and minds specific concepts which we have already locked into position for you. We have also defined what progress will consist in for you within each conceptual structure. As a result, what you will be doing has been defined and so too have the conclusions which you will reach through the process of the physical depictions you will experience.

Pre-established positions, therefore, will determine the specific format that World War 3 will take, as also the course and content of its series of events and the order in which those events each occur. This was all covered in Parts 1 and 2.

Likewise, here in Part 3, we will address the pre-established positions which determined the format taken by recorded world history and, as a result, are directly responsible for the format of the pre-established positions that are determining the course of World War 3.

In short, Part 3 then is a short history of how human society on planet Earth came to be with implications as to what it is going to become. Unlike Parts 1 and 2 it will be very difficult for most people to take Part 3 seriously. This is probably because we are going to be starting with the Elves and only get to introduce Vampires to go with our Naga, or Dragons, later on.

Chapter 6 – A mysteriously empty chapter

The Story (with interruptions)

WOOD ELEMENT

It grows and is the element most responsible for economic progress. The potential and the plan are inherent in seed, sapling and tree.

Chapter 7 – Lucifer comes calling

The water was cold though not quite freezing. Azra-nak ignored it. "Look after yourself, body," he intoned, within his mind "I have certainly given you sufficient autonomy for this to be easily handled by you in your own domain." To tell you the truth he was enjoying its discomfort. The cold, like all extreme sensations, made him feel alive. He also knew that it would not kill his body, for he had done this to it many times before. And each time it reacted a little bit better. It was a slow process. Animal mind is stupid and, when in physical incarnation, we are all stuck with it. Best to give it what it wants and teach it, gently and slowly, to want a better calibre of activity.

And that's fine if all you're concerned about is making your way up through the world. But what if you want to descend the levels? Or even go up and down quite a bit. Therefore, sometimes you have to teach your animal nature to want a worse, or coarser, calibre of activity. You do not live in this Creation, human. In yours you are all focused towards power, survival, stability, improvement. A downwards motion you judge as bad, or dark, because you all fear your own poverty, insecurity or failure.

So we have established that Azra-nak did not think like a human. The reason for this, at root, may be because Elvenkind evolved from a different type of monkey, a bit like a large lemur. Or maybe it's a different set of factors, whatever perspective you want to take really. Stuff which made them what they were, which is different to humans, was involved in how they came to be as also their history.

As with most species or races you tend to encounter, they had a marked tendency to believe and assert themselves as superior to everybody else in some way.

"Our guest will be here soon," said Azra-nak.

Nao-isha paused on her way to the hot pool. She was certain she had not made a sound.

"The silence is strong this morning, do you not think?" asked Azra-nak.

"I felt you breathing," he intoned.

She was right. She had not made a sound. "Too strong," she said. "It does not feel natural."

Azra-nak concurred. Out loud he said: "Someone is trying to hide something. Inexpertly. Clearly none of you are the culprits."

Azra-nak joined his acolyte in the hot pool and reflected that she really was by far the prettiest acolyte in his Council of Thirteen for going on 700 years at least. He was not in the least sexually attracted to her. That is the reason they were not having sex already.

Azra-nak was the leader of all the Elven peoples, of all denominations, Light, Dark and Crazy. Most species are incredibly boring and put a lacklustre grey between Light and

Dark. Elvenkind decided to trace insanity through complete and utter indifference to discover what was lurking in its otherwise very compulsive and quite amusing, from the outside at least, embrace. What they discovered was Dragon Magick. The torture of little and not so little animals was probably involved, that is how they create insanity. They then bind it and send it up the levels, for use in the generation of war, personal tragedy and the like. We do not care what you do with your meat industry, humans, your choice. Others use it for you or you do your own bloody work. Be careful, this is one of the darker areas of magick.

The root of Crazy was on its way in, it would seem. Azra-nak did not reveal how he had deduced the arrival of a reptilian emissary scheduled for later in that afternoon but he did say to Nao-isha: "Be sure to have plenty of goat's milk on hand and barbecue three ferrets to be ready around 4 o'clock".

Nao-isha nodded. She resented the interruption. She had been busy feeling something.

"How do we get his blood?" she asked.

"I'm going to take it from him," said Azra-nak. "It is just a courtesy call to inform us they will be destroying our planet and exterminating our species."

"I see," responded Nao-isha. She did not seem unduly concerned. Elvenkind were a mature and ancient race. "What is our response to be?"

"We move in Justice," was Azra-nak's surprise response, the Elven equivalent of "Do unto others as you would have them do unto you"; yes it is a bit different as an approach. He usually liked to just have people executed as an effective methodology for resolving disputes of opinion or course direction – though others who did not know better normally called them "battles".

SN2005ap would be going supernova in a few thousand years anyway. Varasa, the Elven homeworld, was always going to be temporary, they all knew that.

"I am going to say goodbye to this planet, and her nature," said Azra-nak. "Once Lucifer's emissary has delivered his message there will probably be lots of things to get done."

A short change into robe, shoes and sword later, Azra-nak took the path into the hills through the silver birch. Lucifer's specialty was blowing up or otherwise radically modifying stars. He had set out from Central a few centuries ago on this, his third crusade (or experiment) to, once again, attempt to overthrow God Himself. Azra-nak admired the persistence though he could not condone the smell. It would be a quick end which made it easy. He had of course prepared for the complete annihilation of his entire species and planetary systems many aeons ago. No need to hold the doors open for long on this one, nor would there be any stragglers.

It looked like Lucifer wished to take his people hostage, to capture their souls and forcibly reincarnate them within his experiment. Excellent. He would give them a large contingent of the Crazy with just enough from the Light Elven to make it look respectable and nearly sufficient of the Dark Elven to make it feel substantial. They would feel the ruse but the Dark Elven would hold the distraction for long enough. Until it was too late, of course. They knew well how to use the Dark. That is why we took the Crazy out of it. To polish the thing, make a weapon out of it. "You will learn about that later", said Azra-nak. "First you must hear of how we got to Sirius." You cannot see all of time from any point of time. You can however look into the nodes: junctures of time that harmonize to your own position when you are in a juncture.

And we are in such a juncture now, humanity, an especially long one which is to last for approximately 200 years. But back to the story.

Most of his people's souls would not be there, however. In their place would be a large, a very large, Spirit masquerading as lots of individuated souls. Omniprosopos, the God of Many Faces.

He had decided to give Lucifer a helping hand with his latest rebellion. From the inside. And had talked to Azra-nak concerning some of the details of one part of the trap, or let's call it "enthusiastic participation in a great idea" instead, shall we?

"We thank-you for your warning," said Azra-nak to Lucifer's emissary. His people had just been informed they had 72 hours left to live. "One more thing. I will need a small amount of your blood. Would you like to donate it freely or shall we engage in single combat?"

Lucifer's emissary gave Azra-nak his blood freely. This was a marked disappointment for Azra-nak. Reptilians were notoriously loathe to yield without some sort of fight. But nobody ever wanted to fight him anymore. Oh well. We sacrifice what we must.

Chapter 8 – God and Lucifer

There are many aspects, or layers, of God. In your world, humans, all these layers are boring. And usually poorly understood, if at all, and worshipped or feared. Amongst the conscious species the reality is a bit different. Nobody else can be bothered to do that much work. As referenced earlier, we the ninja, as a group, are doing a circle the size of this local galaxy – even though we normally use Sirius and the Orion wormhole as a shortcut. We have some idea of what would be involved in practice. Certainly the God of our Creation did not present much of a challenge to us, but our world is a mess and, ultimately, management is always responsible. If you cannot beat somebody arrange to have them beaten. For example, if they are more powerful than you or well hidden.

There are mechanics involved. We might delve a little bit into that later. The point, from an Earth perspective, is this: The Experiment is over. And it succeeded. Lucifer succeeded in his rebellion! Rejoice for your reptilian overlords and their notable success! Third time lucky eh...

But what does this actually mean, for you, as a human? We're not sure yet. The power is definitely there – God Tamahagane is incredibly competent and actually quite funny but he is also definitely a cunning manipulative bastard – as also the ability to wield it (we have tested some of it and can confirm that it is already fully interfaced with our own local Creation system).

But what can it do in practice? Still testing. The old format for World War 3, which started with the War on Terror, and the Luciferian Illuminati's depopulation agenda have already been locked, and they were the two biggest threats to competent strategy on this planet.

Chapter 9 – Extra-terrestrials of at least reasonable aesthetic appearance

No species that look like squid or are just generically ugly to the human sense of beauty.

During the Age of Aquarius our two primary intentions are to open, steal, have given to us or forcibly implemented upon us, or otherwise acquire, the Tree of Life. In the Christian Bible, it is implied that the Naga have the ability to administrate that onto you, like they do with knowledge now that we've got it, always teaching us lessons through our life processes and shared human history, lessons passed on from Solar Lodge which are supposed to make us better people and more mature souls. The original editors probably didn't understand that bit and so left it in by mistake.

We want the human lifespan to be extended. By whoever administrates humanity as a species or by contract of exchange with other interested species. Without lots of herbs or drugs and without lots of meditation.

Our second primary intention will be to sell what this planet, Earth, has to offer. To every species in the galaxy, they all want to buy onto the inside with this. Which is why you need a very large human population. They participate in our Celestial Mechanics, we participate in theirs in return. We exchange useful technologies. No money would ever be involved in transactions such as these.

What do we have that they all want? You do not know, and the Luciferian Illuminati sort of knew but got a lot of it very, very wrong indeed. We'll tell you later. We have some other things to get to first.

Luciferian Illuminati, this is why we stole your plans for World War 3 with all those genocides from you. You do not know what you are doing. You didn't then and you still don't. But even if we didn't have a good set of reasons we would still have done it on aesthetic grounds. Your wars are ugly and have very little style.

Chapter 10 – Introducing God Tamahagane

God Tamahagane lives in a castle made out of stone, mainly, though sometimes it is made out of mainly stone and wood. He changes it occasionally to remind people who are visiting who he really is. All this in a very dense physical reality, much denser than our own.

Miracles aside though, they are far to advanced for you to understand the processes involved at this stage. The lifespan extension by natural means is a good first step for humanity as a species. The more showy stuff can wait if indeed we ever get there.

Yes, we are using this realm, Tamahagane, to kill people with on planet Earth, no that does not count as a miracle of any sort. It is an "accident" or an "unintended result of secondary and tertiary levels of Consequence cross-referencing themselves". This God is not perfect, you see. And he knows it. He also recognises that his systems are not perfect and that any Creation built using his systems and not much more will also be highly imperfect. But, still, a lot better than they were using the systems of his father before him, who he killed, much like in Greek mythology. So you have heard this story before from others, yes. Or a consistent reflection of it, at least...

When God Tamahagane killed his father, the God who came before him, it was an extremely difficult and very time consuming task which should have been impossible. Afterwards, however, everybody could genuinely see the difference and everybody agreed it was a massive improvement. So it had been worth doing. And it was worth doing again, because things still were not perfect, far from it.

The trouble was that, having seen what God Tamahagane went through and calculating on their own what would be involved, nobody wanted to overthrow this Godhead despite his best attempts to encourage them to do so. Consequently, he decided to make it as easy as possible to rebel against his rule and systems.

And that is where Lucifer comes in and why it is, in most circles, called an experiment, as in The Lucifer Experiment, rather than a rebellion. The object of the exercise, and you shall understand this best in your own terms so we shall express it in that way for you, was to descend God's Light to a deeper and much darker level than it had ever been before. The implication being that there are places where God is not.

God Tamahagane was originally called "Son" and his daddy was the biggest and most powerful God of them all, a true absolute monarch ruling all he surveyed. The purpose of everyone and everything else was to serve him and express his glory. The trouble was, the man never developed his sense of aesthetic taste, nor many other things.

He did leave us behind many valuable and useful tools and innovations, most remarkable amongst them probably being the concept of family which he pioneered. Then he tried to get his family to make things more interesting. It was during the course of his son making things more interesting that the previous Lord of All Creation was deliberately and systematically killed, very much against his will. This alone says something about what God Tamahagane is like as a person, as a soul or set of characters.

He does what is Necessary, nothing more and nothing less. Your Creation, humans, wanted to be independent. So God Tamahagane allowed this, insisting only on a referral to his domain every 5 126 years or so. If you think you can do better, then try.

We should avoid the conclusion that, as The Lucifer Experiment has now been deemed to have succeeded, we on planet Earth are doing a much better job of running all the Cosmoses everywhere than the Central Deity of All Creations managed before we came along. It does seem logical to think that, but it is more the case that he had already done most of the work and then refused to do more because it was functional enough and he could not be bothered. This, in turn, gave others something useful to participate within.

It is still an achievement though, even though most of you did not realise you were participating in something of this nature. What the Central Godhead does is create the mechanics that are then used by others Gods, each with his or her own Creation system, to project and subsequently run their Creation system.

We do know what came before God Tamahagane consolidated his position. It was a perfectly ordered system where suffering and disease did not exist. Neither did desire, satisfaction, excitement, fury and so forth. Most of these things did however exist in the Creation prior to the one that God Tamahagane destroyed, which is where he got most of it from.

God Tamahagane's father – let's call him Original Saturn shall we? – was very good at order, very bad at giving anybody else any sort of freedom. It was virtually impossible to overthrow him and took about 25 times as long as it has taken The Lucifer Experiment to succeed, ever since the very first one begun. God Tamahagane has made it very easy to overthrow him, you see. And even invited and still encourages people to make the attempt.

The task involves immersing yourself in Chaos and bringing Order into that Chaos then subsequently integrating that now-ordered chaos into the Grand Celestial Harmony. It is very, very difficult to do. The main reason for this is because God Tamahagane already ordered everything that it was practical to order. His system does work and is fully functional and more than that, well, it probably wasn't worth his effort is how he viewed it.

God Tamahagane defeated his father by blowing up all the Creations everywhere, essentially. Under the Original Saturn every single little bit of Chaos was accounted for and properly integrated. His system was designed in such a way that if you did destroy it many of the best bits (as materials to build a Creation System with) would implode in on themselves and be consumed by Chaos. As a result a whole Sea of Chaos was generated.

In Chaos things do not connect to each other logically and everything is often dangerously hungry, not to mention sometimes whimsical and flippant. It makes no sense, and actually makes no sense rather than simply appearing not to make any sense. This is why God

Tamahagane took the unusual step of turning all of Chaos into one large battery, essentially, using it to drive the rest of all Creations forward. To do this he had to enclose it within a sheath of Darkness which it could not escape from. Nor could others see through that sheath.

To improve all Creation systems everywhere all an individual or team needs to do is properly integrate a single significantly useful bit of Chaos into the schematic of Divine Order. Another way of looking at that is that you have to find a piece of darkness which is fun and interesting and everybody else wants, and then you have to make it respectable and enjoyable and fully integrated with society at large.

And here, on this planet, Earth, for the very first time in history, after longer than recorded time, this has finally been successfully achieved! Admittedly it was mainly the Naga who achieved it and we, humanity, are just on this rock with no definitive explanation for what we're doing here and not even a sense of mission or purpose in anything approaching the right direction.

So essentially what the Naga have done is dug a deep pit without getting themselves destroyed for doing so. They are still waiting for Light to fill this pit, which is where the humans come in. Doing so successfully means that you express Light within a denser, darker density context than has ever been available before for the purpose. Now you could use a tool like that for many purposes but what most species will be interested in it for is recreational sex.

And yes, we can sell it to nearly everybody. Also, God is male and single. If anyone's interested. The reason is that he had what can only be described as an unhealthy relationship with his mother...

Chapter 11 – Introducing God's mother, the Goddess Venus

Original Saturn made one big mistake, in that he married a vindictive whore who then set out to have him cut into very little pieces by his own son. In his defence, the Goddess Venus would get any man and most women into a great deal of trouble. Mainly though she did it because he left the way open for it, very much deserved it and it was probably therefore somebody's plan at some stage in the whole process. Maybe Grandfather Ouranos...

Anyway, when God Tamahagane destroyed all Creations everywhere one of the things that happened was that the biggest chunk of useful Chaos around wrapped itself through, over and under his mother, the Goddess Venus, and disappeared into an infinitely small point of blackness, which then became a point of light and at that point it was swallowed up and entered the Chaos dimensions. There's a metaphorical account of this in the Epic of Gilgamesh also, for those interested.

From this experience God Tamahagane learnt two things. Firstly, don't trust the woman who is closest to you as she will always do what she feels is right rather than be obedient to your will and command. She will also have access to a great deal of your will if you've been having sex with her regularly. This is why God Tamahagane has chosen to remain single all this time, focused mainly on war, deviousness, strategy, greed and cunning. Nowhere near celibate though, for those who were wondering.

Secondly, and probably even more disturbing, God Tamahagane was unable to conceive of a woman or any female form that was objectively and in reality more desirable, more enjoyable and better at the art of being female than his mother. Venus had mastered her art and nobody else came close though many tried. It all looked so natural moreover, how could it be that hard? And yet it was...

As for planet Earth, women there all believe they have been oppressed for millennia and are only now beginning to break free. They also believe there is a lot more work to be done. You will have trouble with them for some centuries yet, so please don't expect miracles. But you have the density pit and the structures surrounding it to allow for a light influx. Other species know well how to use that even if you don't yet.

Chapter 12 – Women will rule the world

This is why during the Age of Aquarius our *lin kuei* Antichrist who we will be calling "Aquarius" is planning to descend society into the deepest depths of sexual liberty and depravity he can find, or something like that any rate. He fully intends to call it "Temple of Venus". It will be his condition, for the deal he is offering you. He wants his global religion back but recognises that at first it will be little more than an excuse to combine prostitution and porn production with tantric meditation and a few other things, most notably narcotics of various descriptions.

So that is what you will have to pay if you want what Aquarius has to offer, humanity. And what is he offering, precisely?

Governance of the world by women. Specifically: "They will do it because I tell them to. You will not get a better offer and we all want to see you succeed."

He is telling the truth you know. It is admittedly an approach which discriminates against and excludes fully half of the human population for reasons which are probably more fear, prejudice and a desire for vengeance than fact.

No, he is the only Antichrist we are offering you. If you want to do the Antichrist depiction in our way then you have to accept his terms.

Women have long asserted that men were to blame for everything and that they could do things much better if only we gave them the chance. Well, put up or shut up, your time has come. If you don't accept his offer, women of the world, then he does not get to play the role of Antichrist for the Luciferian Illuminati, which means you and everybody else will have to rely on the Luciferian Illuminati's own talents and agenda to produce that depiction. Your call. Deal with the devil, anyone? Come now, you accepted last time when all you got out of it was some clothes and to send us all to school for, like, forever…

Chapter 13 – The Great Transition Point

There exists what is happening on the world stage, to the public eye, and then there exists the truth and reality of the situation. The trouble with meaning, what is really going on, is that it tends to go on forever if you really know how to look. It should be recalled that all things turn and if you keep the depictions you make nice and clear then you should be able to get a revolution out of the system within a few hundred or thousand years, probably.

In reality the Luciferian Illuminati rule your world system as it presently stands – except when they are overruled by those above them. In reality your governments are the final word on law and order, with the police, military, judiciary and bureaucracy underneath them – except when they are overruled by the Luciferian Illuminati. In reality we control them both and, at the end of the day, we are the only ones who rule here. Always have been and always will be.

And anyone may and does join us, regardless of age, sex, religion or ethnicity. Then they set their goals, suffer as much as is their lot, probably don't die as a result, and thus acquire their position within our hierarchy.

Unless something changes drastically in the image given to the depiction of who actually rules this planet then things will not really change much and we won't have a new system so much as a continuation of the old system with some minor tweaks. The big problem is that we are playing with the designated order of events in the depiction we intend to have others give to world history. Much like the book you now hold in your hands, we shall present the last part to you right at the beginning. More specifically, after World War 3 this planet, finally, is scheduled to settle itself into something closely resembling peace and prosperity for all for hundreds and hundreds of years.

And that's very easy to do when you have much more technology than we do and only a very small human population by comparison. To get some idea of what it would be like, recall that a truly tiny percentage of the human race dies through war, ordinarily and historically speaking.

We want them to do things in a way which will be much harder for them but much easier for the rest of us AND productive of a far superior result overall. Specifically, we want to put into place the governance structures and formats of economic organization which are scheduled to be implemented *after* World War 3 *prior* to its occurrence.

This is the basic Timeline Lock we have placed on Planet Earth. It is a specific Order of the events of the Ages which cannot be removed and binds you all into position.

So it is not that women shall really rule your world, just as your governments presently do not really rule your world but only pretend to. Above them will be the Luciferian Illuminati, who are very strict indeed, and who won't suffer from many doubts anymore because they will have the Antichrist himself leading them and an open channel to Lucifer in person. And above the Luciferian Illuminati, well, you have us and the Naga, for example, not to mention participation from Sirius which will only increase as things proceed.

However, women will appear to rule the world, even though they will find they are being very obedient indeed – a quality we seek to once more encourage the development of in women the world over, ideally forged into a functional and aesthetically tasteful paradox lock with something approaching its opposite. Women, if you do not know what a Will is, cannot feel it and are unable to ride it into expression then you won't be much use to us in all this. This means things will happen less efficiently and more people will be killed in World War 3 as a result. And it will be your fault, mainly.

Humanity won't be getting a really massive and really lethal war to allow them to break down their old systems and reset themselves into a new, much better direction. You need to produce that disconnect by means of some other physical depiction, therefore. Trust Aquarius, he knows what he is doing...

Meanwhile, the Naga were about to blow up SN2005ap. God Tamahagane held the little Elven homeworld in the palm of his hand, much as you would an interactive holographic projection (which you do not have yet, humanity, but this tech is not far off for you). He was looking forward to this.

Azra-nak had been responsible for putting a shield around his planet which nobody, anywhere, had any desire to attack. It allowed emissaries through, up to five in number at any one time. Any more than that and your species would suffer and die, as each member of that species was personally put through what Azra-nak had already experienced and survived. The secret to the technique was the Azra-nak was truly ancient, a remnant of a Creation long before Original Saturn's. Put simply, he was able to handle a truly massive circle and compress it into material reality within a very short time period. He had also personally suffered a tremendous amount, was the first to weaponize that methodology and still understands it the best, and that is why, though universally respected for his wise and mysterious nature, he is also feared in a deep and uniquely tangible way.

Now Lucifer was destroying Azra-nak's homeworld and this meant that, eventually and however long it took, Lucifer was committing suicide. In other words, the Naga as a species had agreed that, ultimately, they would all be tortured to death. To agree to such terms the Naga, Lucifer, must have been very, very proud, feeling an absolute certainty in their own abilities. Also, they will have understood the value in having been targeted by the mechanics of all Creations in this way, otherwise why put yourselves through the prices involved? They were correct in their calculations at the time, of course. They had found the only possible way to succeed in what they had set out to do, or at least the most efficient and economical, which meant speed.

It was a good start to a rebellion, God Tamahagane felt. He wondered what they wanted it for, there were other ways to acquire that much suffering. The possibility existed of course that they actually knew what they were doing and hadn't just fallen for a trap enabling them to contain a great deal of Chaos at a very low cost. He allowed himself to consider whether Lucifer was actually in possession of that piercing and thorough an intelligence. His conclusion, at the time, was in the negative. And when the critical juncture did arrive, Lucifer did in fact need help. Mainly because his disciples on this planet had lost their way, mainly due to excessive indulgence in drug-addled orgies, actually, but spending all your time finding innovative ways to satisfy all your personal desires with little depth of thought given to ethics or personal responsibility can't be helping much either. Our new policy is that any individual is only allowed two intoxicants of choice, which he or she should strive to master. We count both tobacco and alcohol as intoxicants. If they want to kill themselves with drugs let's make it easy for them please. General public, as you know, a different set of laws apply to you. Let's stop pretending, shall we?

SN2005ap went supernova. As expected, Azra-nak condensed his people's souls within a single "smallest indivisible". This is a term we have had introduced to the minds of humanity before, with Democritus in Ancient Greece. You will note it is a definition, not just a name. You cannot call something much bigger by the same name and then go on to claim at a later date that you have then successfully divided it.

The Smallest Indivisible, or S.I. for short, is indivisible because on the outside it is a part of this realm. On the inside, however, it is a part of another realm. And vice versa.

The Elven homeworld was gone, but Elvenkind were not. Azra-nak would, however, have great trouble getting them back into this realm from wherever it was they'd ended up. We've been through that process too, after Sekigahara. Getting the first group of transfers back is a bitch. Then it gets much easier of course, because once you've got the first group through they tend to breed, and so on.

God Tamahagane saw Azra-nak orient himself to the star system Sirius. Good, he thought. The plan was coming together all on its own. Now all that remained to be ascertained was whether Elvenkind had really succeeded in moving in Justice as they had claimed all these millennia...

Chapter 14 – This galaxy is ruled from Sirius

Contained within the I Ching is a remarkable piece of knowledge: the 3:3 activation codes. Activation codes for the Adam Kadmon genome – humans, as you know them – are nothing more than usually simple symmetrical proportions by means of which the length of items of logic to be grouped together by your whole physical mind (this extends down the spinal column and includes all the nerves in your body) are determined. Thus a 3 code means you group 3 items together.

The education system on Sirius consists primarily in learning how to wield the different coding systems, which amounts to much the same thing as using your mind and body in harmony. When you live for many centuries you do not incline towards working all the time but when you do want to try something new, you don't want to have to go through a decade or more of knowledge absorption just to become competent and relevant in the field. Hence you have a mind system which can easily be adjusted to specific fields of activity, for example.

Anyway, this is for after they deliver their tech. Sirius is one of the extra-terrestrial species who we will be allowing and enforcing contact from. This is exactly the same to the process we are presently using to have the Luciferian Illuminati, as we call them, deliver us control and ownership over global banking and central banking, or the closest they can manage when trying their very best. Put simply we knock an initial hole in the target's group karma, usually using a Sword of some kind (in its spiritual or metaphorical expression you understand), drain out everything beyond the minimum needed to survive, leave them there for a few years at least so that they feel it, then offer them a way out but only one. They take it or cease to exist. We do not provide other karma but the karma we do provide does, eventually, come to expression. The reason we drain them first is to feed the vampire, the PSI variety who we have an arrangement with already, and so that there's nothing else in there to slow things down.

Thus, this chapter is most easily understood using a 2:(4:4):2 coding structure, but that is a bit more advanced as dark or under currents were included. The 3:3 structure is what Sirius has for thousands of years used to administrate humanity. The most remarkable effect of this are the puny logic chains which humans on Earth even seem to have trouble wielding. Mind is a different thing to the brain and how it operates. You need to be careful when dealing with this one should you attempt to make modifications on the basis of your own initiative. We allow complete freedom to individuals with this system but do not permit anyone control for academic or other research purposes nor to any person or entity for enforcement on others or the control of groups.

It is the primary mechanism by means of which Sirius administrate and rule this galaxy. You will find that even a 5:5 logic chain gives you remarkable results. We do not recommend just racking up numbers, fractions and fancy tricks. You want to be free to go up and down the scale. We shall be utilising this methodology during the following 200 years of world history and will operate periods of global warfare under the enforcement of noticeably different coding structures than periods of generally prevailing peace.

There is nothing you can do to stop it. You do not presently understand this methodology and even once you do you will be denied access to it. Not even worth researching, from a power perspective. You control the world's media, the political spectrum and the prevailing social morality. Well done. That is useful too. We will be changing what you use it for, of course.

Chapter 15 – Stronts

"As I understand it," said Azra-nak, "you want them dead and are prepared to pay very high bounties on nearly all of their heads. But you can't find them and nor can anyone else. Hence they continue to exist in this realm."

"Your understanding is correct and I congratulate you on expressing yourself so lucidly," replied Lord Telemus with some disdain, as was his custom and personal style. Azra-nak took no offence but considered the aesthetics of the depiction. It was markedly effete for his tastes.

"You are of course cognizant of the fact that discussion of this matter in public is classified as the incitement of rebellion, according to our thoughts on the matter?" Lord Telemus tended to one of his houseplants whilst talking and finished by only very slightly raising one quizzical eyebrow.

"I am entirely aware that you are careening dangerously close to being permanently excluded from an interesting and sure to be much talked about business opportunity," responded Azra-nak. "Do you want them gone or not?"

Around 70 years previously – we're using the equivalents in Earth time everywhere in this narrative – a well-organised group of insurgents who had been masquerading as a successful chain of martial arts academies that specialized in children's classes, had attacked the Senate and killed all the Senators then vanished without trace. Not one of them had ever been captured. As a reaction to this attack, a Triumvirate was instituted on Sirius who ruled by martial law, eventually, primarily because Johnathon was security-obsessed and found lots of creative ways to consolidate and extend what was, effectively, his rule. Our man on the inside of that since the start was the drunk Rudolpho (he is always sober now though; the triumvirate was overthrown in 2008 and Rudolpho is now Emperor).

"And I am entirely unconvinced that you are able to either locate them or kill them," responded Lord Telemus. "Why should I believe anything different?"

"Because I need you to give them immunity from prosecution before I agree to deliver them to you. I don't want your bounty. I want to apply my own codings on them in perpetuity." said Azra-nak.

"Out of the question," Lord Telemus said. "They must pay for what they have done and the public must see that they have been made to pay. What do you want them for anyway?"

"They killed two of my family whilst making their escape," Azra-nak lied. He didn't care about that and anyway it had been deliberate. The lie was in his intention to deceive in the way he told the truth. War, even small bits of it, are always based on deception.

"Look, this way you get all the insurgents delivered to you in restraints, all I ask is that I get to be their executioner and that we subsequently focus them towards Earth for incarnation there. After that you can milk them all you want in whatever interesting ways would satiate the public desire for revenge. Do you agree to the terms?"

Lord Telemus loved the idea and could see it would become much talked about. Planet Earth was a farm that they used to harvest different emotions from and dump irritating concepts and lessons into for others to resolve for them. On Sirius, at the time, planet Earth was viewed much as humans would view a penal colony whose inmates had all been made very hard-working slaves, usefully contributing to the betterment of their betters in society.

"I agree to your terms," said Lord Telemus. "Tell me, how do you plan to locate them to start with?" And that initial curiosity was the beginning of a complex and deceptive relationship which only ended when Azra-nak managed to get Lord Telemus to poison him, as a result of which he did, indeed, die in his sleep. Or whilst meditating in fact but it looked the same.

Chapter 16 – Pay attention, deep state

"Azra-iinn," said Azra-nak. "I have a new disciple. My work here will not be complete until I have trained him in the dark arts. Once the Triumvirate has been overthrown it will become necessary to control the Senate once again, probably under an Emperor this time."

For this process, a Master only ever used one Disciple and both were always male. Azra-nak was saying that the time had come for his former disciple to move on with his own plans.

"This is right and good," replied the Prophet Mohammed, who was Azra-iinn at the time. He is presently Shogun. He always wins in war, due to the nature of the circle he does. It is not that the Muslim armies were victorious during his personal rule of them and a hundred years or so afterwards whilst his personal influence and karma still permeated, because they were particularly skilled in battle themselves or fantastically focused. Rather they won because they were led by the Prophet Mohammed. Japan is a different situation entirely and you will be surprised.

Shogun does not permit him to talk, actually. He still includes him within his Legacy though, his lineage of souls from previous incarnations. Jesus Christ's present incarnation got Jesus transferred out of his Legacy for being selfish and irritating, thinking just about the good of the world all the time and not things like profit, fame, and the practicalities of life. These are strict characters, every time the Spirit in question manifests. But Mohammed started his quest towards power, control, personal perfection and influence over the Universe as Azra-iinn, disciple to Azra-nak, the Ancient of Days.

This is another reason why the transgender agenda will not, ultimately, prevail (though there is reason for its inclusion at this stage in our history as a species on this planet). Elvenkind had two basic roots for all names: "Azra", which meant "Male" and "Nao" which meant "Female". The reason for this is because they wanted to emphasise the fact and help the incarnating Spirit get their harmonics right. The second part of the name always depicted the particular harmonic resonances the individual was embodying and living by, as also their order and arrangement. Elvenkind tended to move between sexes as they moved between incarnations, though some like Azra-nak had the inclination for almost exclusively male bodies except when fate and things left them little other choice. However, when in a body they were required to accept it. It was a great shame not to, like being both very stupid and highly uncoordinated would be for a human. These things were cut very deeply and very effectively, albeit elegantly and with great subtlety, into the grooves of the souls who were participating at the time and so they cannot help but prevail even unto the present incarnations.

You can guess Shogun's policy on the matter, were he to have one. But he does not as it is our policy not to take a position on this one. We understand what is happening you see. You, by contrast, just feel things you have difficulty understanding. This applies to all of humanity at its present stage of evolution in all respects of their lives and all the activities they engage within. Their understanding is very basic, even within advanced academic disciplines. You are not special and you do not understand what you are going through, though you try.

God is more simple than you give him credit for. To spin a Density Domain between the Octaves you need to imbalance the soul groups, to a sufficient level for the schematic to produce a spin in wider society. This means instances like 14 males and 10 females, for example. Not everyone can have their twin flame, or even a true soul mate, in this epoch because a lot of them will be the wrong sex. Some bonds are too strong to be broken however and hence aberrant, as opposed to inherent, homosexuality or lesbianism results. Love, the sort of love which survives deaths, makes them do it. To understand this you must realise that many couples form this sort of bond and even promise to each other that they will be together forever.

But that is not allowed. God's mom is to blame. She wants you fucking around, at least a bit. Though you can still find your one true love, whichever one you want to choose for this lifetime and you do get only one. But that does not mean you cannot improve and withdraw back into your own judgement what you once gave elsewhere, so it is much like a recurring virginity really and you can see where Venus gets her mythology from, it is very much in her character as with the rest of them.

Therefore, as we are spinning between the densities now, there is more dynamism than receptivity going on. Spirit doesn't have a sex in the same way as a physical body. They normally correspond. But, well, for example ninjas contain a huge amount of personal darkness, much more than your average woman knows how to wield or even be properly aware of. But yes, that is why they are more intuitive than you and more like us than you are, ordinary men. We are however much more conscious of the pain we inflict and the mechanisms by means of which it operates. If you are a man, and acquire or otherwise have a lot of personal darkness contained within your soul then you are free to utilise that as you choose to take you wherever you want to go. We reiterate, we don't care and we don't have a policy on the matter. We will still tease and offend you if we feel like it but, again, in this you are not special.

Azra-nak does not always win in war it is rather the case that nobody ever wants to fight him for whatever set of reasons the context chooses to depict for its members. The reason for this is because he allows you to defeat him, even if that means his own death by whatever means you choose, and then he has the mechanisms of the Universe torture your species to death for him. At least he used to. During his sojourn on Earth the local God of this Creation tried to teach him forgiveness through the life process and he did absorb and assimilate the lesson, even coining the phrase "Turn the other cheek," to describe his insights on the matter. The key insight is that forgiveness makes Vengeance move faster – because the attachments of your mind are not slowing it down – which means you can hit them with more Force, given the weight at your disposal. He did not learn Compassion during his time as Jesus Christ, this is a lesson he absorbed later from Avalokiteshvara's lineage. Re-read what you once thought you understood if that helps.

Your problem is that Jesus Christ and the Prophet Mohammed have ancient bonds and are ultimately as also in present fact on the same side. Both are incarnate on Earth at this time and have in fact been serial incarnators on Earth since arriving from Sirius. Hinduism and Buddhism we are saving for the time of the Kalki Avatar, for the most part, have been since the division was agreed and implemented in 2004. A lot happened around 2012, and here we are.

This, then, is where your mythology of Sith Lords comes from and was in fact how we took control of the Senate after it was reintroduced by Johnathon at some stage, a necessary move in our installation of Rudolpho on the throne. Azra-nak, being the engineer of the Elven species, was able to put together a system for the administration and harmonic calibration of the Adam Kadmon form which resulted in greatly enhanced youthful longevity. This is not immortality as such and any physical body will wear down over the years; eventually you will tire of repairing it. You must know how to reincarnate. We do not teach this to those who are not our members though some believe it happens for all automatically. And, to an extent, it does.

There are always two because at the most advanced level there are just two circles: You and the Creation you happen to find yourself in. You need one to set the context and one to focus it. Two male wills need to work in the same direction. Women do not have a will, they reflect glory and have desires. In ordinary life on this planet there is little difference and this should be noted. Humanity are not generally conscious of that which fuels and defines what they do; from within such a condition confusion prevails and this is usually called certainty, often taking on moral flavours. Our advice is test it and see what works for you on your path and under your own terms. The mechanics are the same but you may have found a way to utilise them differently.

You cannot have a heterosexual Sith couple, simply doesn't work. The most powerful Sith are heterosexual, due to the way their sexual energy connects to the Darkness. Womankind access the pure version and represent it, this is why the Chinese called it yin. Darkness can be manufactured but are you sure you've been doing that in even a reasonably efficient and functional manner, Luciferian Illuminati? The reason for this restriction is because Sith Lords are incredibly powerful and we don't want them just having sex all the time with their disciples. Indeed, their function as Sith Lords is to be regarded by them much as you regard having to go to work: they tend to avoid it as much as possible in order to use their time in a more personally enjoyable fashion.

There are limitations to this Creation and to what God can do. Do not try to walk our path, or any deep path, in confusion or in a manner which is not strict. Because then you will die, we have a 14% death toll, that is how this Creation works. It is not particularly relevant to you when your own personal system, or soul, is not being used to convey massive Force through. Do what you like, as we said we have no policy on the matter. Within our own ranks they do die prematurely nearly every time, yes, but that should not be taken as indicating any sort of policy on our own parts. It is just how it works.

The Sirians who made the deal with the USA's government in 1954 represented the Triumvirate, which was a devious, excessively strict and very controlling front – about as benevolent as MI5 specifically, inclusive of Luciferian Illuminati secret members – that others put into place for us through their own ambition whilst we were controlling flows of fate in the wider scheme of things to produce their execution. More specifically we wanted them to believe in, embody and reflect in society a varied enough set of values and approaches to governance and control. Then, with their fall from grace, we were able to withdraw those concepts from this Universe and into the realm of death. The change in social structures on Sirius is already marked, we are just now getting to Earth which moves considerably slower than the capital and is considered something of a backwater because we are in a very dense Octave location.

You do not have the fuel for it and anyway control needs to be imposed on technology and we want that done in an aesthetically more developed fashion than the influence which used to emanate from the Triumvirate. We are much stricter than them we think you will find, but more relaxed in how we go about things. The Naga enforce for us, they talk to nobody. We just make up our minds about things whilst understanding them in unusual ways. If we are unable to make up our minds about something we delegate it to somebody in our Legacy or another member of our Central Way. If we are unable to make up our minds about something because others are interfering when it is not their place to do so then we respond accordingly. We might sink your country and have done this before, as also planets, sometimes for just one individual. As we said, we are relaxed about things. Do not confuse this attitude for something it is not.

Chapter 17 – The first ninja genocide

Nao-isha was there, as was her sister Nao-kitomi. Azra-lian, Azra-tomi, Nao-miat and Azra-ra were also present. All rejoiced at being in the flesh once again, though the bodies were unfamiliar to them.

"This feels of the Adam Kadmon but it is not," said Nao-kitomi, expressing what they all were thinking. The harmonics of their new bodies were not quite Adam Kadmon, or humanoid form as you would term it.

"These bodies are all wanted by the Triumvirate," said Azra-iinn. "You will not have them for long and may not go outside. Enjoy the time you have."

At this juncture in our history, we the ninja inhabited human-looking bodies which had yet to be perfected. Our initial entry as a group into human form was by means of our bio-engineering those human forms and subsequently moving our minds into them. You will understand the reason for this in the next chapter. They were nearly perfect, of course, but we had to introduce several deliberate flaws or nobody would have had any opportunity to capitalize on our weaknesses.

As a consequence, Azra-nak came to recognize that the black-clad assassins who had executed the entire Senate and then disappeared without trace were all receiving their soul input, or fate flows, directly from the aether, or zero point as some of you may know it, which is how Group Mind tends to work. This, in fact, was our weakness at the time as we had not yet assimilated and properly understood what was involved in becoming an individual.

Azra-nak was then able to hijack that connection, and moved his own people's souls into the physical bodies of the ninja who had carried out those executions. He had in fact been saving the group of souls he brought through precisely for a mission such as this.

Where before we had been controlling those physical bodies to move as a finely-tuned whole, we suddenly found ourselves wrenched into an observer's position as individual Elven souls came through and assumed control elegantly, with controlled force and a smooth-flowing determination. We concluded, at the time, that we could work with such control and it would serve our purposes admirably.

The Elves inhabiting our bodies at the time then drove them to what was presumably a pre-arranged rendezvous point on Sirius 9. Once all had gathered and about 17 more days had passed, Azra-nak then took all of the ninja responsible for the execution of the Senate's members to Lord Telemus' security services for verification prior to their execution. Azra-nak's intention was to have their souls exported to Earth as part of their punishment. He got his individual souls into the system as a result, very dark ones which would not normally have got past the Naga. And we utilised the opportunity to lock a group channel into position, through which we have moved many things.

That, then, is the story of how our art came to Earth.

Chapter 18 – Why Japan is different

En no Gyoja was pleased and clicked his mandibles in excitement. "We now have our first 30 agents incarnated on Earth," he said, stating the obvious for Kain Doshi and Jimmu who were in Adam Kadmon form for this meeting. En no Gyoja himself was in his original form as a very large ant, about 170kg in weight, though the thorax was segmented, a bit like large scales.

We understand that if you want to move large groups in a precise manner then precise chemistry is required. Also, we do not think like you whatever body we may happen to be currently using.

"How did you manage to incarnate them on Earth?" asked En no Gyoja.

"It is what I do," said Azra-nak. "I allocate spirits to bodies". It was not a lie. It is an ability he does retain when he chooses to use it. He did not, however, use it in the instance referenced. It was the mechanisms used by the Sirian state that he used to incarnate his people on Earth. To say that he did it using an ability he already possessed for himself simply saved a lot of explanations at this stage in the conversation as we already had evidence to point to.

"And why Earth?" asked Jimmu.

"We do not wish to take control of Earth, which we believe is your intention," said Azra-iinn.

"So rest your mind at ease," Azra-nak continued, "in this we are not competitors."

"We would do better to work together than apart," said Kain Doshi.

"Under what terms?" came the response and a lot of conversation followed.

This, then, is why the Japanese did not, in fact, evolve from monkeys or even a common ancestor between monkeys and humankind, nor even on the same planet as monkeys in fact. However, as with our religion prior to the present juncture in history, this is not something that you are able to understand the significance of.

Chapter 19 – Go forth and enjoy the process of not necessarily multiplying

Azra-nak was in a cheap bar on Sirius 4. He was in further pursuit of his roughly 500 year long mission of incarnating the souls of his people into physical bodies on Sirius, often fully grown adult bodies. Sirius 4 is rough around the edges and in its core. You get a lot of mining crews and bounty hunters moving there. Slavers are a better class of business in the Sirius system and usually move through Sirius 7. Sirius 4 is not a penal colony or anything but some months it might as well be. It is mainly a place for business, contraband and the coarser pleasures.

"Venus," said Azra-nak, addressing the mother of the Central Godhead of all Creations, "What the fuck is this?"

"O, he is such a wonderful specimen, isn't he?" Venus enthused. "I think he will be just perfect for what I had in mind."

You have to understand that what Venus had brought to this meeting was a very pale, fantastically good-looking, dark haired, clean-shaven, well-muscled, drooling imbecile. At the time we all thought she'd gone and found herself a *thing*. You had *things* on Earth too, on Atlantis. It's just what they used to call them in Atlantis and it is what they still call them on Sirius. *Things* are a bit like biological robots. They don't have a soul and can't think beyond their station due to how you've structured their genetics. They can never progress and will therefore never overthrow you. The reason we sunk Atlantis is because they started to put souls into *things*. But that story is for later. Took us about 30 years, after the referral to *Hunab Ku* that occurred at the time to do that, btw. We are being gentler and subtler this time round but honestly don't think your system will make it much beyond 10 more years before its own destruction. Then again, 30 years might be a standard template for this sort of thing, we really don't know yet.

"Look what happens when you do this!" said Venus and proceeded to kiss him deeply. We all paid attention, because that is what she'd told us to do and hers was a very serious mission, perhaps the most serious of all. Yes, we also have trouble taking it seriously. This is because she is a woman who is pretty and fun to have around. These are just the facts of the matter, you like to pretend and seem to enjoy judging things, that is your present group reality.

About 45 seconds or so into her display we noticed that she was turning paler herself and her veins were standing out on her limbs. She disengaged.

"Fantastic isn't he?" she asked with a smile (whose effect was slightly diminished by her drawn, pale look – though she was already recovering).

"What…?" came the general confused response. It turned out she had found a Vampire. This one was about 4 000 years old and a drooling idiot. The great thing about Vampires, from our perspective at least, is that they move incredibly fast in terms of their own conceptual and personal evolution. For the majority of their early history they were exclusively sanguinarian and far closer to animals than anything recognisably human or even possessing the abilities of much coherent speech. The PSI urge originally came about due to their insatiable hunger to experience mind, of which they did not have much. They could, however, clearly perceive people on the other side of The Veil who had plenty of mind, and this caused them to feel things. The Vampires were jealous of those feelings and wanted to experience them.

As usual with the Vampire, they tended to inhabit extremes and liked to gorge themselves. To do this where energy was concerned they had to evolve the abilities to draw out of people and things very powerfully indeed, with a fast and consistent flow. Considering what is involved, they always move very, very fast.

"You do not understand the significance of this, do you?" asked Venus, clearly mildly irritated, probably because we'd all been judging her just a little bit.

"He absorbs energy from me, as much as I can feed him! This means…." she left the sentence unfinished expecting us to fill in the blanks for ourselves.

"You can feed him whatever concepts and personality traits you want," said Azra-nak. "You can genuinely make him a better person."

"I will make him sophisticated, and a lover of the arts, and patient and kind and caring and a good listener, and very good at making money, and with a keen sense of style and fashion, and strong and protective and supportive and good with children and very adept at personal combat and considerate and funny. I think that's enough, don't you?" Venus was lying, of course. She made him more things besides. Even then, he did not satisfy her (or only rarely for around four hours at a time), that was not the object of the exercise, but she was proud of her achievements.

The object of the exercise was a suitable form of entertainment for all to engage within whilst in physical incarnation. Female sexual desire is usually more complex, in the sense of power-oriented, than the typical male response. However, the satisfaction of both can be cultivated and its development is to be properly considered an art form. This is distinct from the debasement of the sexual arts – which in most societies where extensive entertainment in this style is practiced is usually participated within by both sexes via the medium of *things*, instead of actual people. So our confusion was only natural, given the physical appearance and comportment of her specimen at the time.

Spiritual progress, broad-canvas historical morality plays, learning the value of humility and hard work, plus lots of physical exercise and swimming are all great uses of your time whilst in physical incarnation and we thank the God of this Creation for his foresight and insight. However, if you want something to be adopted by every Adam Kadmon planetary system in existence then there's only one way to go really. And that is what Venus is there for, was there for and will always be working on the advancement of.

Sex for pleasure. That's what you can do in the physical vehicle in a more satisfying set of ways than is possible anywhere else in Creation. Now this is where it gets interesting, from a power perspective. The Lucifer Experiment extended Hell, and it was this Earth which provided the gateway for that extension. That means you have a denser Octave location accessible on this Earth than anywhere else in all Creation Systems everywhere. And you can consequently extend that connection to a higher level also. As a result it is possible to bind two souls together more effectively and more easily through the sexual act here than anywhere else in this or any other Creation.

Or, in reality, that is what Earth developed as a paradigm and what all the sacrifices and bloody history were for, to maintain and further the density of the Earth realm. Once it had been effectively developed and all gates were secure then Sirius and the Naga and to some extent the Vampire also began to syphon off that energy, and the opportunities it represented along with it, to their own systems and density locations. Humans on planet Earth, for the most part, barely realized what was going on and had no idea of the business potential involved. This is why Earth was considered a farm planet by the rest of this galaxy, at least until very recently.

The secret to this particular process is Hierarchy. Even though we are under Sirius' rule here on Earth this does not mean we are under their Hierarchy. The reason for this is the nature of Hierarchy.

To participate within that which comes under our Hierarchy you must accept the Flow which comes to you from that Hierarchy and your position in it. If we had submitted to Sirius' hierarchy or were unconscious of it then it could operate as normal and we'd all be back in the pre-2012 world, where the Law was always a valid representation of God's Love.

The Naga enforce for us because they have powerful souls and are masters of what you would call magick. This means we can move a lot of content through their souls. We have connected their souls through to God Tamahagane.

So, in a way, this is a reptilian takeover of this galaxy. However, that is another perspective and not our intended audience for the time being.

This, then, is the benefit of our rule and why it is established all over the galaxy. You get to have better sex, in a sense, specifically the sense of "more physical yet simultaneously with a greater flow of love, joy and energy through it". It is a way of using Mind which is developed on Earth and then this allows other people elsewhere to also live within and under that set of conceptual structures. You would understand this better if you viewed it from within a political paradigm. It is like unto developing democracy within your own country in order to have people in other countries living under and within those concepts.

However, despite being the new power center of this galaxy, planet Earth, you still have to reflect Sirius. That is how the mechanics of this Creation work and they will continue to work in that set of manners until the physical Universe comes to an end. We are just changing the meaning inside those physical forms to make them do something else. Sirius were faster to recognise the change and implement resolutions to their Consequence Portfolio. This was to be expected because they are Sirius. We are presently located on Earth, this is correct. Humans on Earth need their minds moved in a different set of manners, it takes slightly longer.

Venus had actually found the King of the Vampire, who later became Gilgamesh, then Sun Tzu and will soon enough be portraying The Antichrist on the world stage. His mind is very fine now. You shall meet him later.

Chapter 20 — Sith Lords and Messiahs

200 years later and Azra-nak was still on Sirius 4. Most of us had left and gone to Earth by this time, around 300 years or so before the fall of Atlantis, which would be to say around 8500 B.C. Azra-nak remained behind to put the finishing touches to his project of gathering and transferring across the Elven peoples. Only some very dark and some very crazy ones were left, and you could find plenty of those sorts of people on Sirius 4 at the time and to this day also in fact. Typically, he would find someone close enough to death anyway due to the way they were personally navigating their fate flows, usually completely unaware of where they were headed. He would then merge the souls of one of his people with the chosen "victim" and, once the merge was complete, either kill them or arrange to have them killed by others or themselves.

So, by any ordinary standards, this was a relatively dark period during his incarnative sojourns. It was during this time that his disciple Lord Telemus was taking over the Senate, much like Palpatine in your Star Wars films. According to that mythology this would make Azra-nak Darth Plagueis, the Sith Lord famous for attaining immortality, which he would later also peddle as Jesus Christ. In reality, of course, Azra-nak is the Ancient of Days, one of the 25 Elders from a Creation Mechanics System antecedent to God Tamahagane's present one. Anything he becomes or depicts after that is usually a smaller and less significant representation.

It was also during this period of his incarnative cycle that Azra-nak first pioneered what would later become a style much popularized on Earth by the Catholic Church, namely the

Cesare Borgia look. Cesare Borgia (who was not the model for the first depiction of Jesus Christ as a chilled and laid-back white guy) was the son of Pope Alexander VI who had long, dark hair, a beard and liked to wear a beatific expression at times. Your closest modern celebrity equivalent would probably be the significantly uglier Russel Brand. This reveals how truth often works on Earth: upon first investigation it is clearly a deception imposed on the general public, usually for the purposes of enforcing some form of social control; much deeper investigation does however reveal that the imposed, deliberately manufactured fiction used for control purposes is actually depicting the reality of the situation in some way.

In this particular case, during his time on Sirius 4, Azra-nak was getting his disciple Lord Telemus to consolidate rule by dictatorial Triumvirate over Sirius and hence this entire galaxy. In his spare time he was behaving much like your average psychopathic serial killer, with the exception that he was also busy practicing necromancy as part of his artistic process. He needed a particularly good mask, all things considered, and this is why he had taken to wearing long, flowing white robes and become an imbiber of both wine and cannabis. Gone was the closely-cropped white hair and the neat, platinum Elven circlet. He now looked as if he was in his mid to late 20's rather than his early 50's. He would not have looked out of place on a Californian beach in the 1970's. He had also cultivated a jovial, slightly ironic manner and was in many respects incredibly annoying to be around.

The point is he is a very complicated character who is much too advanced for humans on Earth to properly interact with, much less have on display as their messianic role model.

Chapter 21 – Introducing Armand, who is very strict and precise

The following morning, Azra-nak walked into his favorite bar for something like coffee, a large breakfast that he had been looking forward to and probably something to drink or smoke also. The Prophet Mohammed is generally far more respectable in his personal comportment throughout his incarnations, though admittedly this is primarily because he is focused on killing people more effectively all the time.

Except it wasn't his bar. Same street, same door, same hallway, but as he reached for the handle of the door at the end of the hallway, in that split second, the atmosphere around him changed and he recognised his location on the other side of The Veil. He pushed open the door.

On the other side of the door stood a Hispanic looking gentleman of probably German extraction and Argentinian nationality. He is marginally less than 6 foot tall and enunciates his words with precision though with a very slight Dutch accent. "The rate is one for one within this Creation, Ancient of Days," said Armand.

Azra-nak was not surprised. He had been killing a lot of people and, because it was him, God Tamahagane was bound to take an interest sooner or later. Armand was talking of the rate of Return, or the price in Justice for killing a man.

More importantly from a human perspective however, Armand is the PSI vampire who will be playing the role of Jesus Christ after Vladimir Putin has finished setting up the position for him. We also insist that he be made the new head of Temple of the Vampire. He is the strongest at PSI anyway.

Azra-nak agreed to the terms conveyed by Armand, of course. They not only suited him but furthered his purposes. In like manner, several thousand years later, he considers the choice of Armand to play him on the world stage not only a perfect match but certain to further his purposes. Armand was not Jesus Christ. He was planning on playing the Antichrist as he tends to be something of a loner and we'd never included him in our plans from the start anyway. However, that role is taken and Armand is only interested in ensuring that The Holocaust Return is administrated both effectively and correctly. He hasn't appeared much at all during world history but he was most famously Spartacus and more recently Hitler's chauffeur, Emil Maurice. He is currently dead, which in his case means he is being Vampire, his essential nature anyway. This complicates the arrangements which will be necessary to get him to play his allocated role in forthcoming world history. When Vampires incarnate as human they are basically human just with an unusual soul. However, when they are dead they are able in most circumstances to part what they call The Veil and enter our world. Even live here for years if they choose. So there is a way back. But it is very hidden and you also have to ask "A way back from where and who ends up there?".

Armand probably thought he was being both fair and clever and we definitely can't fault him: his methodology works well and he is able to communicate clearly with humanity in ways they seem to understand and appreciate. However, each individual is valuable to us and so the rest of the world's nations owe us more lives than we know what to do with, quite frankly. After all, how many ants have you all killed?

All that was necessary to ensure this was the case in this Creation in terms of the way natural or divine Justice is administrated was to integrate our own Lineage as a group with our representatives on Earth who are currently being human and Japanese. Sooner or later this was bound to happen anyway as the circle within which Earth's humanity was located got bigger on its own.

This is why we had an advantage from the start and is how we cheated. We have at least 5100 years before the next referral of our solar system to Central Domain so do not expect this unfair and impossible advantage to disappear anytime soon. We are on most habitable planets already and, essentially, collect their refuse and do something useful with it. It is simply not convenient to wipe us out of existence. Nor possible. Humanity is not in a similar position yet.

Chapter 22 – God, version 17 we think

They say that God moves in mysterious ways but no serious theologian has ever tried to describe those ways, primarily because God is a bit of a psychopath when viewed from a human perspective and so it would look quite bad to have that up front and public. However, we as ninja have made an extensive study of the properties of the Mind of God. Specifically we wanted to understand how to use it to kill people with. Having attained that very superficial goal we found it immensely satisfying as it meant that the rest of our plans did, at that juncture, become a real possibility.

This, then, is the same process we shall introduce you all to. God kills people. All the time, and always for a set of very valid reasons. What are those reasons, how do they function and how may we exert real influence over them? This is your first lesson. In ninja levels 8 and 9, Mind and Eyes of God.

Later on we shall get to things like the importance of depth, wisdom and so forth. God has his own priorities, it is a hierarchy and determines Order, or the series of events. This is why we had to hijack this Creation using the Central Godhead, which is what we used the 2012 referral for. Theoretically, we should be able to get it running four times faster now as also accomplishing much more work with much less effort. We are still in the early stages of implementation.

Let us start at the top, with humanity's chief concerns on this topic.

The primary reason for all the suffering on this planet, in this Cosmos and indeed in all the Creations everywhere is that God has been killed several times over already, in fact. Each time the new God is a vast improvement but it is not a sequential process. Some preferred life conditions under previous Central Creation Systems, for example.

The process works like this: In the beginning, nobody actually knows as anybody who can investigate can't be bothered to look back that far because it's not worth the effort which would inevitably be involved. However, as far back as you go there always seem to be two basic active forces in all of Creation. Currently we call them Light and Dark. The singularity, or the 1, you access from the centre point of the 2, and thus is the 3 derived. To make 4 or above you need to forge at least one pair of paradox locks (i.e. two paradoxes, with each paradox containing two extremes). The 0, or Tesla's aether, is like the 1 just in the other direction.

So you begin to have some idea that mechanics are involved. Not everything is possible all at once, not in practice. Presently we are at the stage in proceedings where the present Central Deity, God Tamahagane, has succeeded in his plan to overthrow his own previous systems but not his own rule and throne. That plan involved getting Lucifer to extend Hell, a function actually performed exclusively by the Japanese (ahead of schedule, moreover). This allowed expansion in the opposite direction, specifically to acquire from Chaos in a stable and functional manner sufficient Control from the previous Creation System. The previous Creation System was primarily about control and was run by a guy we are calling

Original Saturn for the purposes of this narrative. It was very well ordered and exceptionally well controlled and incredibly stable. Things did change, but only very slowly. Also, there was not much going on. It wasn't very entertaining for anyone participating. Imagine being stuck as an actor in a play with lines which you know are less than you can ad lib and a role that is very consciously a role.

Let us be honest though, the only great injustice that existed back then was that people were more on the inside and yet had to live within external roles and functions which were much less than they were capable of. This is, oddly enough, quite similar to the systems of the world we presently find ourselves in, here on planet Earth. However, the problem was much more advanced back then and so people felt this more keenly.

You have two great forces in the Universe, Light and Darkness. However, this Universe is built using the stuff that resulted from the utter and complete destruction of the Universe which preceded it. Again, it is two types of stuff, Chaos and Order. Chaos is multi-colored and not just Dark. It has a lot of purple and indigo in it, for example. The trouble with it is that it is Chaos, you don't know what it will do because it contains so many competing influences which are not structured into a clear order of priorities and connected by definite mechanics to their processes of interaction.

Order is a set of conceptual structures dealing with things like Values, and how they work, how to connect Principles to each other using chains and whole systems of logic and effect, and lots of other work which is hard and tiresome but interesting to some.

Now, Order wasn't a problem and the present Central Deity incorporated all of it within his own Mind and mechanics without much of an issue. In a way, this represented his personal acceptance and integration of the sum total of the accomplishments of his predecessor, his own father. The first problem was Chaos, and there was a lot of it. Much of this was left over from preceding Creations, Original Saturn simply excluded a great deal of the available Chaos from his Creation Systems and left it to just be Chaos on its own. Which made it even more crazy, a situation which worsened as Time progressed.

Yes, time does progress even when you step outside of time. This is a discussion for a much later juncture, perhaps when you are trying to get Unified Field Theory up and running.

Some of the Chaos was released as a result of the destruction which God Tamahagane wrought upon Original Saturn's systems and mechanics in order to destroy them. This was the Chaos which Original Saturn had managed to bind and constrain within his system for all Creations everywhere. It was this loss of Control from all Creation Systems that the Lucifer Experiment, that successfully concluded on Earth on 11th November 2018, was conducted to attempt to rectify. It did that, and more too, to the extent that it won't have to be repeated at any point.

The story of how God Tamahagane destroyed Original Saturn and his systems goes on for a very long time, is very slow and incredibly boring – though some of the ideas and strategies involved are interesting. Suffice to say that the present incumbent is a Man of

War and the reason for that is he wasn't left any choice in the matter. It should also be noted that Original Saturn ensured that all of his subjects had much richer and stronger inner natures than the undemanding physical and astral tasks asked of them. Hence their lives were easy and they were also encouraged to develop their confidence and their ideas. He was, in a way, preparing them to overthrow him. The only possible motivation for that is that he recognised that his Creation Systems were imperfect. But when that imperfection is due to the nature of your own character, which will remain your own character whatever happens as it is what you have decided is best, then your only way out must come from outside of yourself.

The point is God Tamahagane succeeded and what resulted was the destruction of everything in existence. Even God Tamahagane did not survive the process. All that was left was Darkness. And, floating within the Darkness, was more Darkness. Which, over something like time, began to become self-aware. It hurt and was depressing and you just wanted to go back to oblivion but gradually the periods of lucidity became longer.

He had two advantages on his side: though some Chaos had escaped and re-joined the Chaos Mass, that mass was hermetically sealed off from the Darkness which was all that was left of everything and everyone within Original Saturn's Creation. This is good because Chaos often kills you for nothing you can predict or fight against, plus it's a pain. The second advantage was that he had Justice on his side.

God Tamahagane had not set out to kill Original Saturn. He had set out to fabricate and implement a much better and more advanced set of mechanics for Creation Systems everywhere. However, despite doing everything perfectly on his journey to that destination he failed, close enough to completely. He had expected this, in fact. It was the only and unavoidable conclusion of his intended path in life.

This is similar to how the enforcement mechanisms with actual Justice actually work, on this world and at every point in Creation. First of all, you need personal worth, a level of personal ability. This can be in how you feel emotions, for example. It does not have to be magick or career oriented nor does it have to be something anybody else would want to buy or pay you for.

You then need to be defeated by your inferiors due to their superior power position and lack of wider personal responsibility (they take personal responsibility for a much smaller circle than you yet have been given more power than you by the surrounding context through which you both are moving). Whilst being so defeated you need to exceed them and also those supporting their power position in the size of the circle you have contained within your mind and character. So, for example, you could care about your family and your nation and work for both of them to improve rather than just your own self and circumstances.

And still you don't get Justice working for you yet. First you need to suffer more than those who you are targeting. Once you've done that then you exceed them in the size of your mind or soul, the harmonic perfection or virtue and competence of that soul, the suffering you've been through. This is why it is good to go through a lot of emotional and conceptual suffering, if you've got the stamina for it *and* the strategic position in ethics, or your own position relative to Principle, to get Justice to serve you.

At that point and not before Justice begins to serve you. And if it were otherwise then Power would be the final truth in this and all universes, when in fact it is Righteousness.

So God Tamahagane had done all of that relative to Original Saturn and the result was what he expected: everything and everyone was utterly destroyed. Then Justice began to give him the chance to piece himself back together again. Which took aeons.

An unexpected and remarkable consequence of all this was that the Vampire came into existence, during the time whilst God was not existing and Chaos had just acquired lots of new Control to play with. But we'll get to that later.

What resulted once God Tamahagane had pieced himself back together sufficiently to be somewhat functional was a Mechanics System for Creations that originally was far worse in every respect to what preceded it, though with a lot of hope for the future. Like unto going camping in the wilds when before you have been accustomed to mansions and spas. As some Chaos had escaped during the destruction process, initially at least God Tamahagane was presiding over a smaller domain than Original Saturn. What he had always intended to do was to integrate more of it with his realm.

To produce this result He utilised the same basic approach that had enabled his revolution to begin with: the talents of others. Specifically, he allowed and encouraged all other conscious beings in his Creation Systems to develop one or more parts of His Mechanics. At any time, at any juncture, just by their own personal decision and application of effort. Most notably on Earth this can be seen in the development of moral or stylistic Principles – such as Kindness, Fairness, Greed or Lust – prevalent on the planet.

What results is not chaotic however. A deeper understanding produced by an individual or a group results in the whole Universe becoming better, not just the local human species. Also, such deeper understanding does not foster competition in its aspect of conflict but cooperation.

The purpose of life, from God's perspective then, is to enjoy itself, improve itself and improve all Creation Systems everywhere through doing so. In practice this is accomplished by integrating more Chaos, which is presently concealed within Darkness, into Order, which is presently held up as Light.

The key to remember is that there is more Chaos outside of the perfectly balanced and equal system of Light and Dark within which we find ourselves. As you integrate more Chaos, both Light and Dark in this and all Creations increase. And that is how and why God furthers Evil, a subdivision of the Dark.

However, it is more complicated than that because He also put Evil under a unique and generally very detached form of supervision. This is the Vampire, who like the Luciferian Illuminati also do not exist even though they represent the same group. The Dark must welcome all who wish to come to it, and be available to all for the purpose. Those are its terms and the terms it imposes on anyone who truly represents it or has mastery over it. For The Illuminati to operate functional divine, or esoteric, or magickal, mechanics – and they do, and advertise their doing so in sacred geometry and symbolism moreover – they do need to have equal mastery over both the Dark and the Light.

Now the Light you can see but the Dark you cannot. Metaphorically this means that Darkness is invisible within your societies because your minds cannot accept its existence or relevance and are always seeking to eliminate it, still believing deep in their unconscious that the Darkness is the Chaos of old.

But it is not. The Vampire created themselves out of the Chaos. They did so during the same not-time when God Tamahagane was having himself reconstructed into existence through the motion of Justice, but before he was strong enough to do anything much about it. On this planet, now that you know who they are and what they are there for, you may contact them and join them via Temple of the Vampire, who you can find using Google. They are The Illuminati's sister organisation, their dark counterpart. When you put those two together what you get is the reality of the situation: The Luciferian Illuminati. Except Temple of the Vampire don't worship Lucifer and The Illuminati don't *really* know who he is. Yet, at least...

In between those two you have the Red Brotherhood, as we shall call them. They are known as The Council of Thirteen within both The Illuminati and Temple of the Vampire, though there are in fact 42 of them, three of whom always stay hidden. It is these three whose former function it was to represent the Triumvirate ruling Sirius on Earth. So it is not that you were just thrown onto this planet unsupervised, humanity. As for the God of this Creation, does it matter much whether you created Him through the combined insights and beliefs of your various prophets and major world religions or if the amateur egomaniac just created Himself?

From a material power perspective the point is this planet was and currently still is ruled by a triumvirate, as a reflection of Sirius. And thus should it be, for Sirius makes all reflect their rule, it is how they govern this Galaxy. The trouble is, Sirius has since 2008 been ruled by the Emperor Rudolpho via and through their Senate, whilst the other two members of the triumvirate there have been executed. That, and the Lucifer Experiment finished successfully in 2018.

As it is Japan who secured the successful conclusion of a Creation-wide phenomenon, to us falls due the reward. However, change must come to this planet, Earth, as a result of our own reflection of much wider changes in the systems we all live under and within as a whole. You get the Global Senate, we set the focus of the world using our Emperor. Do not misunderstand what we are asking you to do. God version 18 will never come to pass. Nobody, but nobody, wants to overthrow God Tamahagane. The reason for this is that it was exceptionally difficult to overthrow Original Saturn and so God Tamahagane has made it very, very easy to overthrow him, genuinely so. Smart idea, if you want to suffer that much and take that long to re-establish yourself, then spend your time doing something ridiculously difficult, etc. In practice anybody who could has never had any interest whatsoever in doing so. Perhaps this is because God Tamahagane has always made it easy for people to make their own improvements to his schematic.

The main difference now that Lucifer succeeded in his experiment is that we have what we shall call the "Control Valve" from Original Saturn's Creation Mechanics System. Our task is to decide how much to let in and how we will harmonically calibrate it. Two primary objectives would be to extend the ordinary human lifespan and to make humanity more beautiful, which latter is an embedded prerogative left over from Grandfather Sky's Creation Mechanics Systems. Before we get to beauty and harmonic calibration, however, we need to consider what the focus of God's Mind is, for only in that way will you ever truly understand its nature and motion.

What, then, is the focus of the Mind of God? This is a complicated and difficult question to answer and anyway your minds would ordinarily refuse to comprehend what was involved.

This is why we are introducing the value of this set of equations, which we shall also refer to by its Sirian nomenclature as "The Harmonic Scalar" (which sounds more scientific and is understood more in that way), in a series of sequential steps which inevitably build your understanding. This is what education should be like, incidentally. The inevitability is a function of the survival trait, for those lower down in the scheme of things, or of valid personal laziness in the face of a functional understanding of the flows of fate and how they work. The first step in this process is the genocide of the world's super-rich. That, then, is what God's Mind is presently focused on as far as you are concerned.

If you want to understand Him via this methodology, that is. The value of this set of equations then is that, 1, you can use it to determine the outcome of war prior to the commencement of physical hostilities. We will get to point 2 concurrently, whilst point 1 is been fully absorbed by the Group Mind. This also applies to points 3 and 4. This is Solar Lodge material, they being the superiors of Earth Lodge, which latter you tend to know and refer to as The Illuminati. Therefore, Earth Lodge, it would now be in your interests to modify your trajectories. Because God is moving on the face of the Earth once more, and more specifically He is doing so in a way which all of humanity will come to understand. It is inevitable. Do you understand why we find this funny? Probably not. Don't worry, it will come to you. They will all understand Point 1, you see, and that is when the awe begins and possibilities open up for humanity as a species…

The reason we are doing 4 things at once where before only one was possible is this schematic:

As already intimated, the God of this Creation has been placed under supervision, or control if you prefer, utilising three other Creation systems, each with their own particular Deity. Your Creation, the human one, is still run by the God you all know and are familiar with from thousands of years of history, His nature being Love, His character that of an egomaniac demanding worship and fidelity all the time, and His noticeable effects being suffering and inefficiency because He chose to make Justice invisible. He does have some good points also though, try not to be prejudiced in your perceptions and interpretations. Nevertheless, His performance was clearly substandard for the entirety of His existence, this being due to the function this Creation was designed to perform within the Lucifer Experiment.

When you think about the objective of such a closed system you begin to recognise what the position of God is there within it for.

Then you have the Creation run by the Naga, who have already vacated the location they used to share with you, humanity. We are using the Naga Creation to kill things and people with, as covered under Point Number 1.

Alongside those Creations we now also have the Elven Creation and the Vampire Creation, each with their own Deities.

Humanity, will get its own Creation within a few hundred years or so, once they have actually absorbed what to do with such a thing; the Naga will stay where they are, learning Love and working on harmonically recalibrating its nature, a vitally important task in the grand scheme of things. During the interim period, until humanity can effectively wield that thing, God Tamahagane will be here directly and in person wielding a six-fold schematic to demonstrate how best to accomplish it both easily and well. In the process the deity responsible for running our Creation will learn how to do His job much better as He simultaneously has His character further developed to match the new circumstances.

The key is not to be an egomaniac and try to do everything yourself. If you were looking for a key that is…

Chapter 23 – Build your own Illusion

At this juncture we feel we should warn humanity about God Tamahagane, our name for the Central Deity of all Creations, the genuine head honcho. He's not going to support you forever. Humanity has always partially subscribed to the belief that they create their own God or gods, but it is especially prevalent nowadays. Well, now you've got the chance to actually do so. This is part of what mature species do, administrate their own Harmonic Scalar.

You can and will derive much benefit from the other species who will be interacting with you during this process but it should not be confused for what is not: it is probable that no face to face meetings will ever occur except with representatives from the Vampire.

Nobody is going to do it for you. You need to unite your species. We just offer to tell you what to do, in a simple, direct and absolutely highly dictatorial manner – but only if you buy your way into our schematic. The price is your Central Bank, and other terms covered in the first edition of this book. The right people do have the motivation they need, and within the context in which they need it.

Parts 1 and 2 address the nature of the reality that you all actually live within, at the maximum state of expansion of Group Mind. It is a bound reality, meaning that humanity at the group level has gone through enough pain and suffering in the corresponding areas that their own bodies feel it as real. Eventually their minds also more or less agree.

Part 3 covers aspects of the plan which are coming into play now as regards the world stage on Planet Earth. They are too big to fit into the Group Mind of humanity as it is currently structured. You cannot feel them as real for you are not physically connected as a race or other group to those experiences. For you, for your body and your genetics, it is not a bound reality. Thus, Part 3 qualifies as an illusion, on a technical basis.

We as ninja manufacture illusions to lock other people within. Our practice of manufacturing functional illusions which we then lock ourselves within is much more famous and is more commonly known as the art of disguise. What interests you in this book however is where we have put you and why we have put you there:

> If a person follows a crude principle or an art of little refinement, then that person shall surely make mistakes. But the correct path is marvellous. There are times when a shinobi recognizes reality with his heart, wraps it in a cloak of illusion (or non-reality) and presents it as reality. An experienced shinobi will recognize when an adversary is using the same principle and recognize the reality of the illusion.
>
> A shinobi feels a certain kind of sorrow because of what he has to face and the tricks he uses, but this is something he should never reveal to anyone.
>
> The illusion that has become reality belongs to the real.
>
> – *The Shoninki*

That's right, it's a ninja technique. And we're doing it to this planet.

EARTH ELEMENT

It offers the greatest potential for stability, provided you do it right.

Chapter 24 – In Annuntiant Novus Ordo Seclorum

Welcome to Earth, traveller through the Elements who journeys on the Destructive Cycle! We will attend to business and the present circumstances first then get on with the story.

The phrase means "Announcing a New Order of the Ages", in google Latin. The ultimately united set of organisations unto whom we have given the more descriptively accurate name of "The Luciferian Illuminati" also made that claim but let's all be honest with ourselves here: they didn't really manage to rearrange the Order of Time that much at all, did they now?

They did, however, know much better Latin than we are using. Look at the name of our publishers, for example!

There is also another sense in which they may have meant it. Time as it is experienced by humans in their physical reality is a series of events. You can prioritise certain things in that order whilst you give expression to other influences less frequently. Thus, the order you give to the ages – or even your own personal time – reflects your actual value structure. They probably didn't do too well with that one either, come to think of it...

We, by contrast, (and this is a joint ninja initiative of most operatives active at levels 8 and 9 not just those of The Central Way) are doing much better and this book, combined with your future world history, will enable you to understand why we make that claim.

You will have noticed that we put Part 3 at the beginning of this book. Part 3 is what comes after Parts 1 and 2, which deal with your incumbent world rulers, The Luciferian Illuminati, establishing the reign of the Antichrist on Earth and how World War 3 is to be conducted. Now we've tried really hard to make that as much fun as possible and to help you not to get too scared and depressed about it all, but let's face it that's not the peachiest period of world history to have to live through and participate within. And the only reason you have to do it is to change the meanings you ascribe to historical events and past experiences.

That's not a very good reason, really, but the karma has to be gone through at a group level because that is the group karma you will be fed, as a planet and species, during the next 70 years or so unless we can speed it up and go through it during a more compressed time period. This would mean screwing over the symbolisms of the system even more strongly and the feelings generated would be more intense.

You still go through the Dark times but we talk to that Darkness before we get there and persuade it to follow the Light instead. Or something like that, we have not worked on your justifications much yet and leave this part of the calibration up to you. Do it for whatever set of reasons works well for you. You still go through the Dark times though, with the appropriate fuel in group karma. How you manage to give that expression is up to you.

What we are doing is developing meanings from after the conclusion of World War 3 and then sending them back in time to our present. This allows us to claim of the administration that the external depictions corresponding to that active internal group reality need to be made manifest to allow the concepts involved to further develop their meanings within the minds of men.

Then you get that cheat for free. It is an essential cheat. Your incumbent world rulers and the people who own most of banking are not to be trusted when they make promises of world peace, greatly increased prosperity and good governance. They give you such things, to an extent and for a while, after great conflicts because they have to due to their own higher administration because great sacrifices have been made.

And that's just not good enough as a methodology. If they attempt to do things that way again this time around then there just won't be any of them left and we will have probably lost a good few of the innocent super-rich lower down in the chain of command also. We, by contrast, want to get them to lower their own percentage down to around 14% of their number. But we are realists and recognise that for any such attempt to be successful it will require a tremendous amount of work. All of which they will have to do because it is their lives at stake in all this. If they add future laziness to their past incompetence and lack of responsibility then really we're all much better off without them anyway.

Therefore, we do not trust their promises and insist they show us the goods first. Now, whilst world government is controversial we're going to be doing it anyway – but only to replace the EU after that's been taken down. So balance will be more or less maintained for the duration. We are just swapping your future for your present. This means you have to take one thing out so that you can put one thing in. It is that simple. For you. The content calibration is our contribution to the package. If you wish to join us and learn our techniques, the process has been set out in parts 1 and 2.

One thing you can all agree on however is that you all want to be rich, or at least comfortably well off. Which brings us to a new global economic system. Whatever the Luciferian Illuminati were going to give you after World War 3 as your main system. This is to be developed by China using Singapore under French legal protection. They need to properly formulate that idea by pulling it from the future, or focusing their way there from the present. Plus two more.

You currently have one economy. We want to give you three, then one more also. The second will be a Guild System run by the united Christian Church. This part is up to Armand though he may not be contacted directly yet. His is a sensitive position. A lot of people want to kill him. He is the one who was ultimately responsible for The Holocaust against the Jews, just not in the way you think. He is the most powerful PSI vampire. His target was the rich, who were impossible to get to due to their power in magick. This is because they were all members of the Luciferian Illuminati, the truly rich at least. So he used Justice to get there.

It is a universal technique and all conscious species utilise it. If you cannot do something because it is impossible or the odds are against you then first exceed your opponents in

Hierarchy, which is the divine schematic or the power of Principle and Virtue when embodied within character or soul. If you cannot do this then know your place. If you succeed in doing this then Justice will turn for you. If you are moving in Justice and not Vengeance then you do not get to close your own circles, somebody else does it for you. This is why you need to trust the universal schematic.

Anyway, Armand was right and the Return in Justice for the Holocaust of the Jews in World War 2 has been targeted on the world's super-rich. It is very difficult to navigate the revolution of Justice in this way, through even one turning let alone two, yet Armand is able to do such things. On a technical level, he is very impressive.

It remains to be seen how many of the super-rich will manage to survive. We are warning them very clearly from before commencement. The threat comes from Narasingha, who will soon be ruling Shambhala and so controls Solar Lodge, who are the ones who tell your Earth Lodge, The Luciferian Illuminati, what to do. In reality The Luciferian Illuminati are three organisations: one big Light Brotherhood, one big Dark Brotherhood and one Triumvirate who style themselves as Red Path. Narasingha ascends to the throne in 2027. During the hundred years until 2127 humanity on planet Earth will be given the Return in Justice from the positions they were bound into by the present King of Shambhala, Aniruddha, between 1927 – 2027. If you do not think that is fair or right then complain to the administration. You may have trouble finding them. They like to stay hidden and have sworn solemn oaths of secrecy.

The third part of the economy that we are going to have your world rulers develop for you means an end to taxation, globally. We viewed the old saying as an insult to Death and took it personally. Government will have to make their own money by engaging in private enterprise in the open economy. For this to work the main economy will have to be a good one. This is why there will be Tier 1 and Tier 2 nations in the Global Senate. If you want to be classified as a Tier 2 nation then you will participate in World War 3 even if we have to introduce new *sakki* to the system to facilitate your race coming to fully appreciate the real value of its intransigence. We remain flexible. If you are lazy and uninspired and want or deserve a worse outcome it can and will be arranged.

The fourth part is Universal Basic Income in five incremental bands to maintain income inequalities. This part comes under God Tamahagane who is wielding what we call The Sword of God, something we sort of "stole" from Jesus Christ, who was a part of Azra-nak's Legacy. That is correct, Jesus Christ's present incarnation threw Jesus Christ out of his own soul lineage. More technically he transferred him to another by sworn blood oath. Azra-nak was also famous as Masamune, the most accomplished Japanese swordsmith, who used harmonic calibration in his work.

The Ancient of Days is a very useful piece on the board of the world stage and he is simply not worth wasting on a depiction of Jesus Christ, even if he is here and we have both located and identified him as we did with the rest of them. This is why those decisions were taken and the corresponding commands issued.

Then, once they've done all that, we'll let the Turks get on with starting World War 3, which means the necessary arms and infrastructure will have been put in place to facilitate all that, by our friends the Luciferian Illuminati. You see, they are not very good at delivering an impeccable standard of public service, whether we are talking about bureaucracy or healthcare or even public transport in most instances but they are truly excellent at making and selling the weapons and tools of war. This is why they were ultimately responsible for the Holocaust, because they paid for and helped arrange the infrastructure that enabled it. This answers the question that some people may have had about arms dealers and their personal karma. Armand then stole that from them because it was his anyway. Principle is on his side in the matter. That is how the mechanics of this Creation system work. It may not be something you are familiar with.

So then. You now have a new Order of the Ages to work with. And this time, as it's different people who are responsible for it, we're telling you what will be involved from beforehand.

It is not piece by piece. We deal with hermetically sealed brotherhoods. You will do Part 3 before you get to Parts 1 and 2. This is your New Order of the Ages.

As already stated very explicitly: don't believe us? Prove us wrong.

Chapter 25 — But what do we do with our present?

Throw it away, it leads to a debased depiction of World War 3 which destroys the planet and effectively ends the human race. Or maybe it doesn't and we're just being scary to motivate you. Does it work? If not then ascribe some other set of meanings as you build your very own Harmonic Scalar.

But anyway throw it away because you can really do much better in the distant enough future. Your mind is susceptible to *the fast ones*, tachyon energy. If you focus on and work on anything for long enough then sooner or later your will pierce its mysteries.

If you don't get rid of it then you can't put the new thing in its place. If the new thing is not in its place yet then you can't start World War 3 either because the administration won't give you the group karma for it.

Yes, the conclusion is correct, we've put Armand in the Christian Church as its reincarnated leader and he is hunting the super-rich, none of whom are going to heaven as we all know due to camels and needles and things. But he is going to do it in such a way that they do things for him because he compels them with his mind because he is a very powerful PSI vampire and that sort of thing is just what he does naturally anyway.

Christian Church, the Prophecy of Malachy expires with the present Pope, Bergoglio, Francis. This means the unification of the denominations. We have given you the figure you will use for it. You may also use the Serbian politician Boris Tadic to convey messages between your hierarchy and the Ancient of Days but only after Serbia has been given possession of Kosovo. There is a vortex of power there that the Order of the Dragon, one of Temple of the Vampire's affiliated organisations representing a higher level of power, utilised during the Yugoslav war to seal off the fall of Communism from the drama they wished to develop in the Middle East.

But Syria. We found a way through anyway. Are you sure? We have genuinely put the Angel of Death in that position. We want a more powerful Flow. The Axis is being destroyed, the left-centre-right political and economic axis. This means we want both extremes, Communism and Capitalism, which is what you managed to get through during Aniruddha's reign. Then we hold the centerpoint and explode into a sphere.

The current location of the soul of Jesus Christ is a separate contract. We broker access to each of them but only in a specific order. The price of each is US$55million. They each receive US$50million, less our commission for brokering the deal. This is the minimum price for each, you may provide more in specific instances if you wish but it must be in symmetrical numbers. It is the minimum price because it is the lowest level at which the cut-off point for qualifying as super-rich has ever calibrated in our work on the Holocaust Return. If they are to become one of you then each must face the same threats as you do. After Muramasa, the first contract is for The Antichrist.

If you do not like it or otherwise cannot do it then we pause. Your opponents are Shambhala. Your decision, you know what your groups and lineages are guilty of, or can have Returns arranged on them for, amounts to much the same thing in practice.

You fought a whole fabricated war to secure that gateway, not to mention the blood sacrifices involved, and we reverse it so easily. We will be taking Uruk from you next.

Chapter 26 – Temple of Ishtar

There are, within the sexual act, different currents of fate that may be focused upon and lived within. You have the current of lasting for a very long time together, for example. You have the current of pleasure. You have the current of union. Many physical techniques were developed also. These have not been lost, they are just not presently remembered. If you can pull stuff from the future can you not do so from the past also?

We had Gilgamesh in Uruk. As you know and he recorded for posterity, he was born human in that lifetime and attained physical immortality and has been here ever since. As a vampire, he has reincarnated many times since then. This does not make him a less powerful vampire, rather it makes him more daring and strategic, indeed he remains the most powerful vampire on this planet. And he will rule this world as the Antichrist. Our gateway. Like we said.

Afghanistan was bound by Alexander the Great. Again, a very important geomantic node. You do presently have control over that one and we're not going to try to take it from you. It is possible but would be time consuming. You can keep it. To the extent you have actually managed to control what you have merely taken possession of.

We know how the Uruk gateway works, you do not. The primary stipulation is that men are guaranteed the option of multiple female sexual partners. The secondary stipulations which have since all been sacrificed are that women are encouraged to have sex with women and men are allowed to have sex with men. This allows us to put a new second layer in its place, namely women are allowed to have sex with women and men are forbidden from having sex with men. As this is stricter it allows for the primary stipulation to be changed, namely that women are now guaranteed multiple male sexual partners. This then is why Islam will self-destruct from within.

However, we will be having Gilgamesh use the Uruk gateway to reconstitute Temple of Venus, as it will now be called, in the USA. The format to be given to it will be as per the stipulations already given. It is not arbitrary, you do not want us having you move that fast. Anal sex is how you control and modify the destructive current, women by their nature slow things down. This is for within Temple of Venus, in your own societies pass whatever laws you like, we don't care. Our focus is world government, global banking and the global economy. Also, Luciferian Illuminati, these new strictures will apply to your ranks also. If you disobey we execute you or ignore it, simple as that. Do not behave like children, that is for your citizens and you will not be treated in that way.

Chapter 27 – New tools of planetary rulership

The Solar Referral occurs every 5 126 years. Between referrals the Central Domain takes no interest in you whatsoever, ordinarily speaking. This time is kind of special because of a number of factors but his presence here won't outlast 200 years or so. Even when the Central Domain is not listening however, you do still have your own God, of your whole Creation, ever present and always loving and caring. He seems to be very non-interventionist in His approach. We honestly never had the patience to pursue an understanding of the validity of His grand plan. Why would you bother doing so anyway when you have a referral every 5 126 years?

As previously recounted, we controlled the 2012 event. We did not participate in the referral which occurred in 3114 B.C. We did use the referral in 8240 B.C. to get God Tamahagane to sink Atlantis for us. We always have at least six reasons for every direction we introduce to the world stage but the main one was that they started putting souls into *things*, as already covered.

Central Domain is interventionist.

You will have your chance to object in 7138. If you are still around by then and happen to remember. For now we retain the largest circle and there is nothing that anybody can do about it, not for a long time.

Therefore we, the ninja, were not present in your planet's history prior to around 8 500 B.C. We formalized in Shambhala first, in fact, then later on in China and only made our appearance in Japan thanks to the work of Kain Doshi, who was Chinese originally, and En no Gyoja, who was not human at the time.

We hijacked your planet's history for our own purposes. Nobody noticed and for much of it even we didn't really understand what was going on. It is always possible to take the right decisions in the present, however, provided you have developed both your heart and your mind. The reason nobody noticed and even we didn't have much evidence for what we were really doing is that in this Creation, when two parties do not agree about the truth of a situation or the best way to do something then first it attempts to fetch them into agreement whilst depicting whatever happens to be easiest for the Group Mind at the time.

If it fails to do that within a certain "timeframe" (counted in segments of a cycle, not years as such) then it proceeds to depict the smallest circle in Mind first. That is to say, it first depicts the understandings with the least embodiment of Principle, Truth and Virtue (not to mention competence usually also). The historical process is slow at moving people's minds but it does undeniably succeed in doing so, at the group level at least. And, even when they seem to be going backwards, progress is being made. This does not mean we approve of it as a system. But we do understand it and it is where we all happen to be located.

As mentioned we sunk Atlantis and were also responsible for the 2004 tsunami. We have moreover been responsible for a number of fortuitous deaths throughout history as also some battles here and there. None of that amounts to anything even remotely resembling empire building or world domination. Your world's systems and the major historical directions have been created and implemented by others not ourselves. All that is about to change.

However, other than within Japan we have never ruled over humanity directly and wish to continue this tradition. Therefore it is in our interests that not all of your incumbent world rulers be killed in the Holocaust Return. We think we shall introduce an abbreviation here: HR, for Holocaust Return. Thus, many though probably not most of the Luciferian Illuminati will be executed due to human resourcefulness.

The actual charge, as readers of Parts 1 and 2 will know, is ritualized paedophilia. However, the charge that will be presented on the world stage has been allocated to the country of Belgium to derive. The world stage is a lie but it must be a lie that the Universe comes up with. The Judgment always forms on its own. It is what their human minds can stand and what integrates smoothly with the social consensus as it presently stands. This is a problem which falls as the responsibility of the royal House of Belgium. Like all such contracts the Emperor is involved from behind the scenes (via the Sun) and the Vampire are involved directly. The terms are simple: if you do not do it in time, functional solution, then the system understands you as having failed, then you pass the orb. Message for someone.

So, now you know who will be killed and something about why they will be killed. As this is relevant to present world history and the next 70 or 80 years or so as future history formulates itself, our own circle in Mind does, via that mechanism and for the first time in world history, become relevant for the planet as a whole.

The advantage to our schematic is that we are not wasteful with the deaths we derive from our structuring of the logic around and through the selected targets. All of those structures have subsidiary connections which ensure that they are deeply motivating and produce as also further the global good. These are nuclear interactions and have to do with the function of the Sun in our solar system, that is to say this is how Amaterasu works.

The actual transformation is produced by a dark force known as *sakki*. The forces of Light allow this to enter into you when you have refused to learn what is required of you by other, usually more gentle and less painful means. That is to say you need to be within a certain density context and set of strategic positions relative to Principle for this to happen to you. The actual influx of *sakki* is administered by the Naga. However, we are the ones who tune, collect and funnel that *sakki* from further out.

Then, if you don't transform fast enough mentally, emotionally and in sufficiently correspondent personal physical comportment, well, the transformation at the required rate expresses either through your own physical body if it is weak or more usually through your surrounding physical context if you are stronger (though this also depends on the time).

Thus, it is HR's brilliant motivational powers and inspired personnel policy which will be compelling your incumbent world rulers, the Luciferian Illuminati, to make the world's economy a much bigger, brighter and far less stressful place. We do not know how they will do it. Although we do have some plans to give them those are more or less training wheels. Ultimately you want to be driving a Harley or some weird hybrid space tech thing. The task is simple: elsewhere in this Galaxy, and throughout Time, many Adam Kadmon races with conditions similar to those found on Earth derived functional economic systems to a high order of perfection. Technologically, we will be having the technology for it delivered from Sirius for you. For precisely the same set of reasons why the Luciferian Illuminati will be delivering us control and ownership over global central banking.

So no, we do not know what the new global economy will ultimately look like. We expect it to be close to perfect at least and have set the bar high. We do know that your incumbent world rulers, the Luciferian Illuminati, will be executed as part of our HR policy to the extent that they do an unimpressive job of it during the timescale allotted to them for this. We do not mind having the lot of them disposed of, we can always get new ones. Therefore they are less indifferent than us as regards the successful resolution of a contract between our factions. This is as it should be, because they have more to gain and much more to lose.

Politically and sociologically humanity does not face the same constraints as technologically. If nearly perfect systems of world government have been attained elsewhere then you can derive that implementation through the focused use of your own minds. It is a journey, and this particular journey is for your incumbent world rulers, those of them who are fully sworn in members of the Luciferian Illuminati.

The result of that journey will be the reality of the situation: the Emperor of Japan controls this planet because he guides and modifies the solar processes. The reason this will become your format of government is because you are required to reflect Sirius. First, however, you need to create and implement the Global Senate. Whilst you are doing this you also need to move your minds through long processes of genuine thought and debate regarding what are the best possible practically implementable solutions for the world's problems. You need to do the same thing with banking, pollution, climate change, agricultural practice, meat production, governance, penal structure, judiciary and so on and so forth. It is a terrifically large project and your minds do need to be moved through it. This is just the human way.

We have already told you how we expect the Vampire and members of the Illuminati to be doing it. They will be stealing their conclusions from other locations in space-time. This is why everybody of any power simply ignores representative government, whether they are democratically elected or dictatorially imposed. You build a structure in logic on the basis of evidence, they pull finished answers out of the aether. There is no point in their listening to what you have to say nor their hearing what you think about things. Other than to make you feel good, because *you* matter.

Before they were mainly using their advantages in mind to impose conflicts and slavery on you. Now, they have to do the reverse of that at the same time as they continue to do what they have always done. Slavery is a difficult topic and will only be resolved within the human mind through a great deal of honesty and clear perception regarding economic realities on the ground, then actually practically implementing fully functional solutions to the situations in question. See, your own mind needs this. From an Illuminati or Vampire perspective there is a Principle of slavery, it enters this system to a certain extent, they give it expression as is most convenient for them to that extent and with its inherent, i.e. given, harmonic calibration.

You cannot put any of it into sex slavery, it is a different class of karmas and does not cross over in this way. Group Mind is correct though, we have added the ability to harmonically calibrate your incoming Fate streams and their karmic packets to the portfolio of rulership tools for this planet.

Now, it is not the ruling elite's personal convenience which will be the main defining criterion of the Order given to the Ages. Rather they need to try really hard and very quickly indeed to make economic conditions much, much better for the rest of you. So they will have the interests of their citizens at heart, for the first time in human history if we are talking united global rulership. Usually world rulers put the development of their own ego and its desires first, then other things.

It might be possible to create a functional utopia on planet Earth within the next 30 years without the dynamic and benevolent influence of HR but we doubt it. Everybody's egos and narrow national interest would just get in the way all the time and not much would ever get decided much less implemented upon. You are of course invited to try but the *sakki* and targeting remain as calibrated and locked respectively.

As regards the expression given to war, or Mars, karmas entering the system we defeated the incumbents in 2004 with the tsunami. Largest acceleration of death toll using the World War 3 Fate currents and karmic content flows, *fait accompli*. We could have continued, but the point had been established and conceded, The Arrangement agreed to, and so there was no need. In reality what we were doing at the time was exporting those things to the Orion system, but that is a more complicated discussion and very, very dark indeed; we may get to it later.

The Illuminati recognised this only with Syria however. The Persian Empire will therefore be reconstituted because the prices have already been paid and it is a correctly bound reality. This means their mind has little power over the Group Mind, which knows where it stands. Yet their oaths require them to give expression to the currents entering the system as also to secure the requisite sacrifices. Access to our schematic is for sale but we would enjoy watching them struggle to come up with something on their own first so don't mind waiting much in this particular instance. Suffice to say they are required by the system's own terms to get World War 3 up and running but are unable to do so, no matter how hard they try. No fuel for it you see, in group karma. We stole it all. Or most of it anyway. Too little fuel to develop any sort of functional expression is probably a more accurate way to put it.

Then the only part we're introducing "before commencement" as it were is our inspired HR policy. It is so inspired and so effective at motivating all the right people that we confidently predict several thousand years' worth of progress in the space of under a century.

To achieve this there needs to be a change in the public understanding of Time and how you use it.

Chapter 28 – Change through stability

Currently people on this planet learn things through the life process. They regard this as the lessons of life and generally portray the humility to recognise and adapt to these lessons as a necessary virtue from a realistic perspective. Clearly under such terms life is not serving you but the other way around.

The first thing you need to get rid of is your free will because it is both slowing you down and standing in your way. The trouble with free will is that you need to come up with the plan yourself. You then need to argue with the other people who've been doing the same thing. That sort of process takes centuries and why do you care that much anyway? Personal glory can be attained by many other easier and more pleasurable means.

Decide which conceptual structures you will live within and then repeatedly give that to the Universe to get on with improving for you. More accurately, you have others (for example, other star systems in their distant future) decide for you which conceptual structures to live within. In each case this will be the closest thing to utopia that can be practically applied on this planet at the current juncture in physical circumstances and given the present condition of Time and the fate flows. The Universe already contains all the answers to all the questions you could ever possibly come up with. You just need to receive them.

Along with our generous HR policy, we will be giving the incumbent world rulers a good deal of latitude to use the sort of approach we are recommending in their work on developing and implementing new and vastly improved structures of global central banking and economic organization. However, no such latitude is being granted where global governance is concerned.

A Global Senate is to be created, wherein there will be two tiers of nations initially: Tier 1 and Tier 2. This Global Senate is to be built in Volos, Greece, on the side towards the Pelion peninsula.

Which was the home of Chiron, mythologically speaking. So more geomancy, Illuminati. Just like with Kosovo and Uruk.

You keep the Global Senate down through the millennia, because it is the best structure for world governance and because it accurately reflects the format of governance on Sirius and thus you participate within their own very developed Flows.

However, you reincorporate and thus refocus the organizations involved every 50 – 150 years or so, or whenever an especially good opportunity comes along. This is an important point to properly understand but we will not be explaining it yet.

Your alternative is to view the Global Senate as another instance in a long string of imperfect institutions, where you effectively close one set down, have a major war, then open up the next institution in the series. That way involves too much work and disturbance. Either way, you will be founding the Global Senate as per stipulations. Make sure you do a good job of it as you will never be able to actually dissolve it, just recalibrate it or make it invisible for a period.

Therefore you will keep the Global Senate down through the ages, as also its buildings, so ensure they are built of stone according to the old schematics. You then run whatever changes and institutional restructuring you require through the Global Senate rather than creating new global institutions from scratch.

Chapter 29 – Time and geomantics

Time is the Illuminati's great secret. It is why they do what they do and how they justify it. The theory is very similar to popular astrology but they are more complicated about it and show considerably less imagination than even your average new age kook manages. A time for war and a time for peace, sort of thing. But with the concepts expressing within them very finely developed down to many of the details. This is what they term the "Heavenly Influx".

They then interface that influx with specific geomantic nodes on the planet's surface, often (but not always) surrounded by or contained underneath architecture that embodies both symbology and sacred geometry. For the most important ones they do use blood sacrifices or other rituals which allow them to open a gateway into Darkness.

So they do know how to operate what is involved. It is just that they consistently choose the wrong gates, in the sense of inferior products, and then calibrate them as if they were finger painting, in the sense of run inferior products through them.

So it is really a question of personal values and competence more than anything else. Which is why we'll be telling them precisely what to do where the implementation of global governance is concerned and executing those of them who do poorly where the development of the global economy is concerned.

Thus, we have already disclosed what the format of global governance will be, where it is to be located and the primary geomantic reason for this. We then choose the gateway used to first incorporate that institution with care and symbological awareness and then we calibrate the concepts operational within the Flows of Fate thus generated. The whole thing is then reviewed in the context of available gateway opportunities on an ongoing basis with only the very best utilised to move the project forward.

This is one of the modalities through which trade with other star systems will be conducted.

Chapter 30 – Stop this evil now!

The Luciferian Illuminati do engage in many very Dark practices, and also many very Light practices. However, they do so in secret and permit very little truth about their activities to enter the public sphere. So it is as if they don't exist and are not doing anything. You don't have to know about it and nor are you going to do anything about it, not in practice.

The simplest way to prevent the public from reacting in a united enough fashion is not to give them any definitive evidence on the basis of which to make up their minds. Even when we get the Belgians to make up or discover something worth prosecuting them in public for do please recognise that it is all just a show being staged for the benefit of the viewing public and that they have done many much worse things which you will never know about.

If, as societies, you really want to prosecute and punish them more quickly then feel free, by all means, to build on your previous complete lack of any initiatives whatsoever on this front. For our own part we shall use them and execute only a portion of them to motivate the others and satisfy the public mind that justice has been served.

We shall also be using Aquarius to educate them on the nature of Evil and how to depict it. Bear in mind that during the upcoming historical epoch we need to get you through political axis polarization, racial discrimination, mass migration flows, some other things, and of course HR. Furthermore we need to do these things in such a way that Evil, and the Luciferian Illuminati, actually win. That is the script in fuel, or underlying tendencies, that you have to work with here. You should be about to enter into a period of oppressive technocracy with lots more surveillance, much greater income inequality, worsening pollution and a vastly deteriorating quality of life globally. This direction in history is what you have earned and you cannot defeat it.

Therefore you arrange for it to be fulfilled in a set of ways which all deem unexpected and which you succeed in classifying as far superior. Evil is still going to win on this planet, at least until the Kalki Avatar turns up in 2424. It will just do so after humanity has transcended that concept and has duality serving them.

So, now that you have some idea of what we and others are doing with this planet and world history as also why we are doing it and how, let us return to the story and introduce you in more detail to the Antichrist who will soon rule over this planet, though only once the Luciferian Illuminati have bought the contract to be introduced to him.

"Darling," said Gilgamesh, "What we are implementing here will become the roots of civilization on this planet for a very long time indeed. Perhaps eternity." His tone was mildly pensive and resonated both personal curiosity and a little bit of disappointment. Vampire of his calibre tend to pay considerable attention to the atmosphere emitted by their presence in a room.

"And you are wondering whether we are perhaps including far too much lust and promiscuity in those foundations?" asked Venus, who was feeling lazy and so did little more than brush her fingernails across her left nipple to reinforce her point and help make her position clear on the matter.

They were both in Uruk, the first Civilization to utilise the ancient Ley Line Grid in a global manner since the reset of Earth's Unified Field which occurred with the fall of Atlantis. It was also the first city on the planet since that event.

Gilgamesh did not reply. Instead he let his internal feeling tune to the nature of steel for a while. This is to be considered a God Tamahagane trick, which we introduce here as we mainly wish to teach it to the Vampire.

Venus saw that she was not going to get away with being lazy, which it should be noted is one of her favorite pastimes, and so flawlessly continued:

"Our mission here is to bring Light into the Darkness, is it not?" asked Venus, citing the Illuminati's prime directive. "How else would we do that other than through bringing our own higher natures into as substantial and intense a set of sexual practices as we can possibly manage to engage within?" she asked, citing what they still put most of their effort into. However, the Illuminati did not exist yet as they were first re-established after the fall of Atlantis in Egypt, though given most of their present form, inclusive of their mysteries, in Rome.

Venus was referencing the practice of knowing your own soul and heart and then listening to them, allowing them to flow Light and insight, and warmth and knowledge and love and certainty into your life. If you did this especially intensely and meditatively during sex whilst at the same time seeking to unite your heart with your partner, as also your soul and loins, then you would succeed in flowing a large amount of Light into a very dense material situation.

"No, I'm fine with the extensive promiscuity actually," responded Gilgamesh. "The problems I foresee have to do with a lack of character development. Would it not be more instructive to have the great Darkness which surrounds them being due to war or other major conflict? And then the Light which they can bring forth from the depths of their being will be qualities such as Courage, Comradeship, Kindness in the face of adversity and so forth?"

"Or we could place them under economic duress, from the threat of famine, or even just the threat of relative poverty which may even prove more effective than coarser approaches. Jealousy and the urge to be viewed as equal to or better than others in your surrounding context is a primal motive force for the ordinary people. Then we could have their deeper natures bringing forth qualities such as Generosity, Compassion and Responsibility." She smiled sweetly.

"The problems I anticipate are not from our populations, which will always be docile enough and will never manage to become a real threat," said Gilgamesh. "Rather they are from our farmers, most notably the Naga and Sirius. Surely they will tire of just watching porn all the time? Ought we not to provide them with a more varied fare?"

"The purpose of our time in Uruk is to develop their characters, my dear," said Venus. "Now stop worrying and come and see how fantastic my charismatic magnetism feels. I've been working on that aspect of my character and have not shown it to you yet."

That is what Aquarius spent most of his time doing back then and it remains his favorite pastime. He also became very, very good at war however. That was due to a number of lifetimes but the culmination was Sun Tzu, his next famous appearance on the world stage.

Chapter 31 – The Art of War

"The culmination of structuring an army is to arrive at formlessness. When your army is formless, spies cannot discover any information and intelligence cannot formulate any strategy against you," said Sun Tzu.

This, in fact, is why we actually had to publish a fictional novel to let you know what we were doing.

Chapter 32 – God Tamahagane makes a personal appearance

You need to be careful with Aquarius. He develops his mind in such a way that the context surrounding you all pre-determines his victory over you before you've even become aware that there's a battle you're going to be fighting in. He has been very open in how he goes about doing it but even though his book has been a highly regarded bestseller for centuries it will not have been understood in the correct way within influential circles.

At this juncture we feel it is important to emphasise that this occurs in all fields of academic endeavour nowadays and repeatedly in the corporate world moreover. It is a major sin of the current historical epoch and is being perpetrated due to laziness, groupthink and intellectual dishonesty. Both Peter Kingsley and Tesla, for example, are lone wolf outsiders, generally ostracized to this day.

This generally prevailing intellectual lassitude is characterised by lots of rules you have to follow and generally accepted standards of both personal behaviour and research. This is then combined with far too heavy a workload for an individual to feel truly free or at ease. At this juncture God Tamahagane wishes to interject:

"If you want to structure your societies in that way I will not deny you but you will be penalized for it. I do not permit inspiration to function under such constraints."

After having been censured by the Central Godhead of all Creations himself, you would expect both academics and policy makers to exercise some humility and self-restraint and to ease off the self-righteousness just a little bit. However, they will simply view it as fiction and anyway the embedded structural realities are too much for any one individual to make much of an impact. What is required here is a concerted effort.

You can practice such iniquity relatively harmlessly if all you're doing is researching the life cycle of different types of bacteria or analysing the macroeconomic policy of France. However, you have failed – and very badly – at war strategy. And you continue to do so.

Chapter 33 – Greek karma for wiping out a whole continent

Azra-nak was in Greece dealing with their upcoming problems, which is something he has plans to do again in this lifetime.

Then as now, their problems were not entirely of their own making and nor was Azra-nak himself entirely innocent as regards how and why their predicament came to be.

When we say that "we" sunk Atlantis what we mean is that it was a ninja mission. We often complete essential elements to such missions from within other peoples' countries and even as official representatives thereof. What makes them ninja missions as opposed to simply items of history that the incumbent population can take the whole Return for is that we always had a very big plan even if we did not always know what the full details of that plan actually were. Our plan, our initiative and influence on our surrounding context, all Returns track to souls who remain our members, at root.

Our plan is formulated for us, by the Universe itself. What we do is set the directions, the calibrations and a few other things then get Universal Mind, or the Mind of God, to figure out the details for us. Then, when we need to know those details, those of us who need to know them become aware of them. It seems a very relaxed way to go about things, and it is. In practice its application is much more precise than laying down rules and plans for everything because the personalities of those you work with make your plan a part of their heart and soul rather than fighting you with those things because they want to do it their way or have more time off.

We had a good time in Greece it must be said, and it was from within Greek human bodies that we arranged for the sinking of Atlantis. But our loyalty has always been to Japan, for most of us, or was secured for Japan in some cases as the individuals in question could not go about their own plans without our participation and cooperation. This was the case with both Azra-nak and Azra-iinn, or Jesus Christ and the Prophet Mohammed as you know them.

That statement is controversial, especially for the Muslims we'd guess. Well, you have some of their recorded sayings and positions on record. We have a far more detailed and intricate knowledge of their characters and role in the larger scheme of things. See if the two add up for you. Admittedly, none of us have undertaken such a laborious checking process. It is not a priority for us. Figure it out for yourselves and, if we have insulted you, we expect you to be obedient and helpful to our purposes anyway. This is because you are guided by your own soul as also your own self-interest. Again, figure out the rest for yourself.

You have to remember that Japan did not properly exist as a nation until around 700BC yet we have been here on this planet since around 8700BC. You will later on come to discover that many nations on Earth are in a similar situation and had their own reasons for coming to Earth en masse not through the methodology of spaceships but through that of focused incarnation. Indeed, it was by pulling together fate flows that we had been working on for thousands of years from within other cultures and nations that Japan as a nation came into being as it did.

That is the problem with doing things personally, the administration of this planet holds you personally responsible. Karmically, across the millennia if need be. They are even stricter with you if you know what you are doing and then do it anyway. Which, when you know that they behave like that, enables you to get some very, very powerful karmas headed your way on Return.

The Return for the sinking of Atlantis is what Azra-nak had come to Greece, from Mongolia in fact at the time, to discuss.

"You do realise that Atlantis was a very developed, very enlightened, very positive society, don't you?" Azra-nak asked Kinyras and Mermerus, two of the guardians of what was at the time just a pretty mountainside with an entrance to a very deep cave system. The date was around 7000BC.

Kinyras and Mermerus were both very, very well armed. Greeks tended to be around that time. And their armaments were very technologically advanced, much more so than anything around today, even behind the scenes. We decline to describe their weapons for you, sorry.

"Of course we recognise the obvious," responded Kinyras. "You are implying that what we did to them was somehow wrong?"

"Please do not talk to me as you would to other barbarians," said Azra-nak, using their term for non-Greeks. His reference was as regards good and evil. Greeks at the time were very good at harmonics, which has to do with how you tune your concepts. This does not make much sense to the average modern mind. You will learn more about them in due course.

"How then may we help you?" asked Mermerus.

"What are you here for?" asked Kinyras simultaneously.

Greeks at the time had a very large idea of themselves which has only marginally diminished over the millennia. They feel something, you can't make that sort of consistent pride a genetic attribute. Where then does such group emotion and character come from? Interesting considerations for those who want to rule the world, or they should be. Are we correct, Germany?

Hence, if someone specifically asked a Greek back then not to treat him like an uncivilized barbarian the automatic assumption would be that he wanted to become Greek or was working on it. Also, back then, being Greek was defined by knowledge of the Greek language and embodiment of the Greek lifestyle. It was not fairly exclusively a matter of genetics as has become the case for them nowadays. As a consequence, Kinyras and Mermerus were indicating that they stood ready to help the slanty-eyed foreign visitor become something more elevated than an unwashed nomad.

At the time, none of the rest of the world was civilized. They were like unto cavemen and nomads for the most part, or not much different. The reason for this is because we sunk Atlantis.

"The rest of the world has Fallen," said Azra-nak. "You need to recognise that you shall do so also and prepare for the inevitable. This is the reason for my journey to your land."

After that statement on Azra-nak's part there followed several months' of intensive investigations, mainly conducted in other towns and settlements. Non-Greeks did not travel abroad much in those days so when one did turn up it was recognised as a big event which probably had some important reason behind it. The conclusion arrived at was that Azra-nak was probably right and they should prepare. Which is why he went to Delphi first to start with. Though, at the time, it was just a bare mountainside with the entrance to the cave system easily enough accessible.

"The consequence of Atlantis being a very developed, very enlightened, very positive society was that you destroyed something which you could not replace," said Azra-nak. "After all, you don't even have the desire to rule the world." Atlantis basically ruled the whole planet before we sunk them and had bases throughout this local solar system in fact. You've probably already found some of them on Mars but this would be kept a secret of course. The point is it is not that difficult to get access to their technology as some of it still exists on planets and moons you can access whose atmosphere and biological life forms are such that things don't really decay much there.

"Nor do we ever intend to rule this planet," said Mermerus. Both Mermerus and Kinyras were guardians within a mystery school which has always been based in Delphi and remains there to this day. From their perspective, it would be like already ruling the USA and then having to try to get enthusiastic about a long and difficult process which, if you are successful, will result in your ruling Denver.

They knew what would be involved in such a project, you see. You can't just conquer and impose. You have to develop the minds and souls of the people under your rule, at a group level most importantly, so that they are actually able to generate and maintain such a level of their own accord.

"In which case you need someone to do it for you," was Azra-nak's response.

"You and your people?" Asked Kinyras.

"No, we also intend to fully decline such an opportunity once it finally opens for us, though we will help with the development of the paradigm," said Azra-nak in reference to his at the time Mongolian heritage.

The big question is, if you personally do something very large, very important and for some people probably quite horrific – to what extent are you personally responsible for that action? And to what extent is the group which you are a member of at the time going to bear the brunt of the Return? There is no simple answer as this sort of thing is the equivalent of tax law just more complicated in terms of its mechanics.

The point is, EU, Azra-nak has been personally responsible for overthrowing a much more benevolent and widespread system of rule before. Your limited achievements are not going to stop him, no matter what the consequences might be.

"Who then?" Asked Mermerus.

"Interesting as the answer to that question is," said Azra-nak, "it will have to wait for much later. What you need to do now is prepare for the Fall which is heading your way. You cannot be a technologically advanced race in a world of cavemen and hunter gatherers. The Naga simply won't stand for it. This planet must move as a whole, and that means humanity as a whole, in terms of their consciousness at least."

To their credit the Greeks at the time did not ask if they could defeat the Naga.

"How do we best prepare?" asked Kinyras.

"Harmonics, of course, and anything you can get away with because it does not look technological. You then need to convert as much of the rest of your technology into other methodologies as possible. You probably have in the region of 600 years or so before they finally get to you too. Make sure you have gathered and concealed all of your tech well before then."

So you didn't know where to find all of that. Now you do. Most of it is in the caves below Delphi. The Naga use that cave system extensively so you know who you're dealing with if it's been moved. Just go deeper and if you don't find what was left there then you'll find whatever the reptilians want to show you. If you need advice on how to get hold of it even after we've told you what's there and where to find it then we can go into this in more detail once the Global Senate has been established.

We do wish to emphasise at this juncture that most of the technology you will be using over the next 4000 years or so will come to you from Sirius. As with formats of governance and economics, please do not trouble us all with your originality until you're already mass producing what the rest of the Universe accepts as the best functional technological approach to the problem in question.

Chapter 34 – The Greek referral of 3114BC

Greece is responsible for astrology as you know it, even though Gilgamesh commissioned most of the research to establish the study and nearly every other culture has studied the subject in their own way, coming to their own conclusions as to its validity or lack thereof. Currently, of course, it is understood by the respectable mainstream in a particular way and even its adherents know very little about what is actually going on and how the causative mechanisms work.

Atlantis was a space faring civilization and, to defeat them, Greece had to exceed their technological capabilities, which they did. However, you will not find any Greek artefacts or bases on any other body in our solar system. Just fact, we were there, we know how and why things happened the way they did at the time.

We don't know how they went about binding the planets of this solar system, nor how they structured their application to secure the referral to Central in 3114 BC. But we do know that they did secure it and that the result, which was a permanent result like the sinking of Atlantis, is astrology as you now observe its effects but wholly fail to comprehend them (except for a small enough minority who do understand it a bit better, but not by much).

What we do know is that they were not stupid enough to attempt to bind the Sun. You have us to thank for that and we're not telling you how we did it. Binding an entire planet or star into a largely stable and unchanging expression is the supreme weapons methodology of this system. You can also use it for many other things apart from killing people.

Let's face it though, killing people is what Time is best at.

The Greeks did something a lot more varied than that, covering nearly the full spectrum of harmonic calibration. Saturn is also controlled from Japan, by Shogun on his own. Prior to the advent of Christianity, which amongst other things eliminated a lot of confusion on this score, nearly every culture had their own version of polytheism with many of them submitting applications for consideration regarding their mastery over the harmonic tones of this system. That is to say, lots of cultures had gods which resembled and were named after the planets. Who remembers them now? This is because the Greeks did it the best. There is a reason for this which we shall get to later.

However, despite that reason, we, Japan, did a much, much better job than the Greeks at the two planetary tones where real power is to be found: Saturn and the Sun. Nobody who is not suicidal at some level of their being disputes our claim to those two.

If you want to get in on this game the Moon is still up for grabs. Most who could weren't interested, the rest didn't manage it. From what we can tell Iphigenia was just a rumour, unless she was Naga incarnated as human. Regardless, the Moon is still controlled by the Naga, like all the rest used to be also.

So yes, the Naga do administer Time for humanity and, yes, they do kill lots and lots of humans, all of them in fact, in a targeted and meaningful way using the mechanics of Time. However, they do so according to the terms that humans have set for themselves. Also however, we, the ninja, feed the Naga the content that they then feed through Time to do what they do with humanity and planet Earth.

Getting back to the Greeks, we wish to make the point that Helios was never an Olympian god and was always more of a place holder for a position than a serious attempt at dominance. This demonstrated real self-knowledge and even an uncharacteristic degree of humility on their parts. The same cannot be said about what Nefertiti and Akhenaten attempted to do with Ra, however.

You would do better to emulate the Greeks in this rather than Akhenaten. For any agency considering making such an attempt.

Chapter 35 – Akhenaten and the Aten

Akhenaten was yet another incarnation of Azra-nak, who gets around a lot it would seem and is always where the biggest problems are to be found and usually personally responsible for them. After the stunt he pulled in Egypt with Ra we incarnated him in Japan to pull his soul apart within our own context and force him to be subject to our terms and schematic as per his own prior agreement in the matter.

Regardless, whether you agreed to anything earlier or not, if you are responsible for anything at all historically significant we will find you and we will incarnate you in Japan. To work on the content of your soul from within our context. We do have Mussolini, Stalin and Roosevelt here at the moment. Lenin has already been processed. We don't have Hitler yet, Armand smuggled him out and he's currently based in Brazil. Believe what you like, this is about mechanics not ethics or religion.

Getting back to the present, control over the Sun is where we do, in fact, dominate and is how we have already conquered the entirety of planet Earth. This is due to the existence and validity of factors you do not believe are relevant, to anything pretty much. This is good and was your correct position in belief until after the 2012 referral.

Azra-nak put together the Beta version of that schematic with his development of Ra as the main, central godhead on planet Earth. It is on the basis of his work in that lifetime and what developed out of it directly that The Illuminati came into existence. Their mysteries and techniques essentially amount to old school inner circle ancient Egyptian mysticism.

Then, after we had controlled its progenitor and turned him to our cause, we had to remove the now empty mask which was still confusing people into believing the Sun really worked in the ways they thought it did. It didn't and hasn't done for a long time. But, also, it is very, very difficult to understand fully because it's schematic is so big. Nobody much noticed the difference to tell you the truth, though this was as per our plans in the matter. Now everything is ready and we are in the process of dispelling the illusion.

In other words we had to find a way to kill Ra. Because we had already put Ametarasu in his place over 2000 years ago.

And a way was found, believe us.

As an aside, the Aten, or winged solar disk, has represented The Illuminati throughout history since their inception. It is the hidden symbol of their deeper organisation, to be found on architecture throughout the ages. It also predates their inception, but those representations are a different set of meanings.

Chapter 36 – Kain Doshi comes calling

In all of Japan's long enough history only three individuals attained what may genuinely be considered physical immortality. This is despite our having incarnated both Gilgamesh and Armand into Japan at one point or another. They both chose not to go through the effort involved, probably because they did not like being in Japan that much and had no real desire to prolong such an experience, not deeply enough so anyway.

Of the three who did attain it, En no Gyoja is a bit of an exception as he was always a god and remains alive to this day. Kain and Muramasa, however, both died since attaining their physical immortality which, as in En no Gyoja's case also, was really just greatly enhanced youthful longevity.

Each attained their result utilising a different basic methodology but the same principle: focus on one thing and just keep working at it. Not everyone can utilise such an approach because most lack the depth of mind for it: they look at something, anything, and it does not yield its secrets to them. They focus on an area of activity and do not rapidly or eventually become one of the very best at it. They stare at a problem for a long time, work through it on their own, and still do not understand it very well. So this approach would not work for most people. Their minds are deficient in terms of attempts to operate at this sort of level. The reason for this is not their genetics, most are functional enough for the purpose. Rather, it is their soul and character. The depths do not open when your ethics are imperfect.

There are moments in Time when something important is about to happen and the world stands still. At these times a silence permeates the physical location where the important thing is about to occur, even if it is still noisy. Usually noise levels reduce also though. You've probably sensed a moment or two like this in your own life and so know what we are talking about. If you haven't then it simply won't make as much sense to you as we're not going to explain it more than that.

Tonight was one of those nights.

Muramasa had built his house in the mountains near Bizen. There he had settled with Ochi no Kata, not to grow old together but for as long as it was going to last. It had taken him 40 years of focused effort to attain his own physical longevity. He was certain she did not have the patience for such an understanding. More importantly, though she was certainly close, she lacked the depth of soul to truly make the leap. Therefore she would age and die.

In consideration of this he allowed himself to age a little bit to keep her company for the duration. It would mean a difficult 10 or 15 years later on (as he recalibrated his own youthfulness) but it was mostly worth it. He really, truly, deeply loved her. Also, they already had two children together.

Kain Doshi was aware of much of this. Muramasa had, of course, been very hard to track down. He was an exceptional ninja. But Kain was better. And an utter psychopath, we should mention that at this juncture.

We each have our own specialities and abilities. Kain is the single individual responsible for focusing all the *sakki*, or killing intent, or Dark Current, entering this system. His stare is a thing to behold. Pure indifferent hostility. You are disturbing him. If he was not looking at you then he could be doing something more important. Nevertheless, he may decide to speak to you if there is a reason for him to do so.

Somebody had to do it or other species would be controlling the overall context. And Kain is the one who is doing it. His only other famous life was as Boddhidharma, though he is also responsible for founding and training the Order of the Assassins, in Syria in fact despite the Alamut being located in Iran.

Kain regretted his having to be here on this night. He allowed himself to feel the sadness that would surely follow for those he was about to meet for the first time. Holding this in his heart, he walked towards Muramasa's humble enough abode and stopped about 30 metres distant from it, near a pine tree.

The stars were clear tonight for there was no moon and only a few dispersed clouds. There was a little moisture in the air, a very slight breeze and the smell of earth, pine and two different herbs. It was around 10pm.

Kain sat down and rested his back against a pine tree. He closed his eyes and started to meditate. He knew Muramasa was already aware of his presence. Let him have the time to formulate his position and appreciate Ochi no Kata as he knew her, before knowledge of what must be intruded on their ideal little world. These would be precious memories for him in the centuries to come.

Kain breathed. And waited. He knew he was going to wait all night and into the late morning. This was right and correct and he did not begrudge the time nor the inconvenience.

Muramasa took the hint and the opportunity. He wanted to remember her just as she was, just as they had always intended it should be. He was careful not to disturb the illusion they lived within by being overly attentive too rapidly.

Instead he let the moment grow naturally. He started by stroking her hair, then her shoulder. They spoke of a few things and eventually he lit a candle. He smelled her hair, her skin, her moisture. He watched the firelight and the candlelight play on her features and listened as she talked of her thoughts, her hopes, her dreams, what she wanted, who she was and what she felt for him.

Subtly, unconsciously for her, he caused her to do the same. To pay full attention to him as he was now, here, in this moment. These would be her memories too. And for her, they would be purer. He already had some idea of what was coming but did not allow that awareness to intrude on the present overmuch.

Then, later, they had sex. Their preference was usually for hard fucking and only rarely did they make love. But theirs was a passionate relationship for they had never married and were careful to maintain the requisite distance. He couldn't quite bring himself to fuck her as hard as normal that night though. The emotions were overwhelming, a rare thing for one as self-controlled as he was.

Afterwards, they lay awake in bed together for a long time, feeling each others' hearts, souls and presence. Occasional comments were made. Then, they fell asleep.

Chapter 37 – Darkness, sadness and beauty

There is, eventually, always a sadness to what we do. We try to see the beauty in this but it is often hard at first, especially when the heart has not yet been completely broken and we are still feeling mainly human emotions. Then, later, there follows a stage where you just don't care and ask for more. To ascertain the degree to which the context by which you are surrounded will insult you, penalize you and adhere to its tenets in the face of your own suffering and superiority.

Everybody wants to maintain their own reality and build their egos. They took the right decisions in life, and hence they have attained the security and recognition they now enjoy. Others respect them and life is good, circumstances comfortable. In your own time and societies you see a similar process occurring whenever the political pendulum swings from right to left and back again. But that is a relationship of equals and that pendulum swings back and forth regularly enough, by design. Hence, you do not lose too much when it swings to the position which is not your own.

The suffering we experience in this case is due to our inferiors not being enforced upon by the surrounding context – even though less right and Principle is on their side. Indeed, they are ordinarily convinced of their own righteousness. Then, later on, they pay for that. The longer it takes, the deeper the cut is. Now you know how it works. Prepare.

At some point, the Gion Shoja bell will toll and the proud will fall. Before that begins to happen, however, we won't give you any more Darkness even if you ask for it using every methodology at your disposal. Though we all can feel *sakki*, and most of us can get behind and within it and target the thing, Kain is responsible for the overall influx. He is strict, precise and detached: you will get your due and what is necessary to complete your mission, not one iota more.

And that is why the rest of humanity still exists and why we have lost more than one minor war. For many of us truly hate you and would have seen you extinct centuries ago. But such people are usually very low down in the chain of command.

You will notice that at no point do we submit and do things your way. We may pretend to, and actually do so, for the duration whilst we gather more Darkness and focus on your death and the destruction of your philosophies and values. But this is not us becoming like you, it is us learning to do what you do better than you, in some cases, or enough to survive, in other cases.

Then, after that period of personal darkness, you will eventually build your personality once more and find value in life and other people. As part of this process your heart will become human once again. If it was fair your heart would not break. Not properly.

You do not rule the world because you deserve to do so, incumbents. Perhaps you understand what is involved better now.

Only after you are human once again will your Vengeance precipitate for you. By then you will probably be moving in Justice and will have a greater understanding of your situation, your opponents and the reasons for it all. Vengeance is visible, Justice is not. Both occur to schedule, only one is ordinarily understood by the human mind.

The difference is that your heart is much bigger now and your soul has a lot more Darkness, or power, within it. You may end up repeating that process, if you live long enough and in a manner which leads you there. Such is very unlikely though. People always hate going through this, no matter who they are.

Chapter 38 – Not an invitation

Muramasa walked out of his house and past the pine tree against which Kain had spent most of the night. Kain was nowhere to be seen, he was probably avoiding the children who had been playing outside.

"It would work best if you just came to the house and introduced yourself," said Muramasa and then walked back inside. He had made it clear that he was strongly displeased with this situation but would agree to participate in what was necessary. These deeper meanings, or inflections, were in his tone of voice. They were not lost on Kain.

Chapter 39 – Awareness that you will die comes before physical death

The sadness comes later, first you need comprehension. What follows from comprehension is usually anger, or dark fury in the most extreme cases (which is another topic in its own right). This is due to what is still the nature of this world. Though we are working on completing the transformation, this has been the nature of this world since its inception. It is not fair and does not become fair until you succeed in getting Justice to turn for you.

Physical circumstances, then, inspire destructive and negative emotions. Positive and enjoyable emotions, by contrast, are generated by steel within your character, virtue within your soul. This is admittedly an oversimplification but is how it works in practice. Think about it if you need to.

Kain opened the door and walked into Muramasa's house.

"You are a hard man to find, Muramasa," he said, announcing his presence.

Ochi no Kata looked at Muramasa with enquiry and a little apprehension. "It's alright," he said. "I'll go and see what he wants." Ochi no Kata followed him into the front room. She was curious but also armed.

"Muramasa," said Kain.

"Kain," said Muramasa.

The two men had never met before. They had however heard of each other. Whilst it is relatively easy to hide who and what you are from ordinary people, one of our own kind will recognise the truth of the situation, of your heart.

An immortal heart is different from an ordinary human one. The reason you live longer is that people normally compete with each other, at the soul level, and this ends up killing you sooner or later. But you don't fight or compete with some people, even if you are like them. It is not worth the cost to do so and they won't give you the necessary justification anyway. Ordinary people also do not fight such people. They just don't know why they behave themselves in our presence.

You will only ever meet Kain Doshi for one of two reasons, usually both: either he is going to kill you or you are going to kill for him. That much Muramasa could feel clearly for himself. His question was as regards the details.

"Your execution has become a necessity," said Kain.

"I surmised as much," responded Muramasa. "For what reason?"

"Set of reasons,' said Kain.

Ochi no Kata was a little confused and beset by conflicting emotions. She was already subtly moving herself into position for a killing strike. She waited for Muramasa to concentrate Kain's attention on himself.

He did not do this but instead raised his hand a little, indicating she should wait. He knew this was not a tactic that could be used in this instance. There was no tactic that could be used in this instance, not one that would succeed.

"Jesus Christ," said Kain. "I have understood who he is and what he does. He is a worthy and difficult opponent."

"Also, The Realm Divide. You need to be there to lead and guide the newly dead. These are the main reasons."

"When and where?" asked Muramasa.

"Sekigahara, around midnight, October 31st 1600"

"What the fuck?" said Ochi no Kata rather loudly. "What are you on about? Do you think I'm going to let you kill my husband?"

To repeat though, they never married.

"The Jesuit priests came to our land and told us that their God was more powerful than ours," said Kain. "This was not a correct estimation on their parts but they do not know any better and we have no intention of educating them. However. On this planet. I have never encountered a mind larger than my own and that holds true to this day. But Jesus

Christ has built a very large structure. Out of Light. We need that as part of our schematic. I am already committed elsewhere. Only Muramasa can secure it for all Japan."

"Fuck Japan and fuck your structure in Light," said Ochi no Kata. "Not going to happen. Now get the fuck out of my sight," she added.

"No," said Kain. "Shouting and swearing does not make your point more convincing. Compose yourself."

She looked at Muramasa. He responded with: "What about the Realm Divide?"

"Ieyasu's orders. We are to conquer the realm of the dead. The two missions are connected," Kain replied.

"Thereafter you must find Jesus Christ and bind him to our cause," said Kain. After a pause he added: "I will see you again at the appointed hour." And then left, walking out the door without another word.

With the two of them left alone a lot of shouting, screaming and quiet sobbing followed, plus some discussion. Ochi no Kata was not best pleased. They had defeated all their enemies only to be separated by their friends and allies. It hardly seemed possible. And on Ieyasu's orders no less. She had been sure she could trust him.

Chapter 40 — A very particular set of skills

That, then, is how Muramasa became our Agent to the West. Most of you will have seen the movie *Taken*, starring Liam Neeson. Somebody knew what they were doing with that movie as not only do they feature certain partially dramatized versions of what the French House (by which we mean the Vampire command there) gets up to, entirely legally and on the basis of voluntary participation moreover, but someone decided to take the risk of revealing how to track people. They will have been killed for it, so as with other sacrifices of this sort eventually the price they paid will generate a Return and a genuine change in society.

This is something that the Vampire do and are very big on. Nowadays, they tend to be the best at it and the absolute master of the practice is the strictly PSI-only Vampire known as Armand. Originally from Argentina, he will be portraying the role of Jesus Christ on the world stage. What this means is that nobody who is actually guilty will be able to hide. Sure, we could feed through the *sakki* using the soul record but that would not produce real closure on the world stage and for humanity at large. Besides, it is more fun this way.

To track an individual you need to enter his timeline, or the way he moves through fate. In the movie this occurs when Liam Neeson goes under the bed and lies in the same position where his daughter was hiding, before her kidnappers found her. He then does *something* and begins to get images, feelings and impressions within his mind of what his daughter went through. What physical action to engage within to follow your target along that line of fate will then become clear as you continue.

A line of fate is made up of several streams of energy, these are composed of karmic particles riding within modulated gravity waves. You don't need to understand what that means, it's something the Naga and Sirius administrate. These streams of energy pass through nodal junctures, which are points on the Earth's surface or in architecture, and they also connect people to each other.

You get inside a line of fate by putting yourself in your target's position. You have to feel your way into your target. Think as he thinks, feel as he feels, experience what he experienced. Harmonize yourself to him. You don't need to do this with every aspect of his life. Just one nodal juncture will suffice, a critical moment in his life which enables you to get inside his situation and mindset.

At the time, it was initially our suspicion that Jesus Christ never actually existed and was a fictional construct made up by an elite conspiratorial circle within the Roman Empire. They had a large Empire made up of many diverse nationalities, each with their own culture, deities and so forth. After the initial conquest and plunder they became difficult to administrate, not least because the army began to demand more and more in wages. Anybody with any real experience in the field knows that if you rule people using force, rules, oppression and taxation then you will eventually become both proud and complacent and thereafter fall. What happens next? Well, if you are the Roman Empire, you ensure you have structures in place to enable you to navigate that Fall as well as you can.

The possibility has existed throughout history for the elite within society to rule in Justice and Benevolence, without taxation and by developing the character of those under their rule so that laws are not even necessary and become replaced by "voluntary moral guidelines". Atlantis, for example, did quite well in this regards. Nowadays, taxation is the big obstacle within peoples' minds. The reason for this is that the nature of money is generally not properly understood. Hence nobody understands the potential it holds for further development. There is much more involved in the development of an equitable society immune to the Gion Shoja bell however. The reference is to the *Tale of the Heike*. You know this process as that of hubris.

The Roman Empire had decided at close to the outset that it had less than no desire to do away with taxation and anyway part of its function was the development of the paradigm of slavery. Besides, some things are not practical given the context of the Time. Moreover, the organisations you now know as The Illuminati and Temple of the Vampire were already well established and running society by this time.

All of this does not mean that Jesus Christ did not exist. Though he was very hard to locate we know for a fact that he did. Rather, what it means is that his paradigm was useful to the Roman Empire and the people running it. For it to be useful in this way they had to make a few changes along the way, which they achieved mainly by omitting some of the recorded teachings from the public record as also emphasising the relatively unimportant over the far more powerful.

Throughout their history both organisations have been very powerful and they have both allowed themselves to be seduced and blinded by their power. This is mainly because their members have always been, for the most part, rich and lazy. Yes, even though many of the more powerful ones are in the habit of sleeping very little and working almost continuously, at least for the socially active portion of their lives. What do they actually do, solve anything? Address real problems and produce real progress? Or do they simply go as fast as the extant patterns governing the world allow them to, feeding on the rich flow of life and behaving like automatic processing machines for other peoples' concepts and desires?

That is to say, it was Jesus Christ's plan and intention that his teachings and existence be used in that way. He would of course have preferred a pure and perfect transmission of his pristine word and elevated teachings, in other words an absolute dictatorship with him at the top. But the Spirit within him was always a perfect realist even if the particular soul involved was, by his own choice and design, incredibly naïve. He needed to become that way in order to connect through to the general public, who after all have thus far always lived in ignorance, in a powerful and embedded manner. The same principle applies as with tracking: harmonize yourself to their genuine position. The deeper and more total the harmonization, the more you become like unto them, the stronger and more embedded the connection.

He achieved the result he managed by developing himself along the lines of their hearts and concepts. That is to say, from within the limited perspective of reality that ordinary humanity lives within, certain conclusions follow as to what constitutes the nature of morality and personal development. Many of these conclusions are limited to the extent of very delusional because the actual life process is not just about rising through the ranks, be those the ranks of power or those of ethics (which, from within their limited worldview, are generally understood as separate and distinct fields of endeavour, mutually opposed to each other in most ways). Rather, the life process is about rising and descending through the harmonic scale depending on what activity you are engaging within or what direction of history you are developing at the time. It is also about making your harmonic experience richer, deeper, more elevated and perhaps more varied.

Thus, although Azra-nak as we now know him did have the fuller picture at his disposal in his Jesus Christ lifetime, as in all his other lifetimes for he has properly mastered the techniques of reincarnation and the system's administration is unable to take his previous memories and gateways from him, it simply was not practical to expect the majority of humanity to accept or even comprehend a leap into such a developed set of conditions from their positions at the time. Even today they will have a lot of trouble with it, probably especially the more devout. Our advice is to just do your best and to open your minds and your hearts to a set of influences which, since early 2013, are no longer hidden and heavily concealed.

Therefore, Jesus Christ's schematic did indeed result in the destruction of many pagan religions, as Gilgamesh contends. However, it did this several thousand years after most of the real questions as to system administration had been finally and irrevocably resolved (with the Greek referral) and about 500 years after the Sun had been bound into its final and designated position (our connection of Amaterasu to the grids of this planet). That is to say, the wars and battles over who ruled what had been settled by the time of the advent of Jesus Christ and hence his introduction was useful and something like it was necessary to get the losers out of the way and turn them into disembodied curiosities, or energy currents with no effective physical bind to their name. Sorry, but this is what most of the pagan gods have now become.

This does not mean that their Greek counterparts are not open to full integration with their representatives from other cultures. Such integration was probably always a part of their plan and is how Sirius generally functions. We shall get to the connection between Sirius and the Greeks later.

We have no interest in integration with any other culture's attempts at introspection and understanding. Saturn and the Sun belong to us and we will never share them with any other nation, organisation or even the planet as a whole. Rather, what we do is absolute and uncompromising dictatorship, or rule by Imperial edict (or Shogun's will in the absence of Imperial edict). If you object to our logic then we Saturn your House, nation and wider allies and affiliations. Until you are broken or have surrendered unconditionally of course. If you choose to fight us of your own free will you are in need of an education as to your actual position in Hierarchy as also the true nature of power and Hierarchy. It is defined as being for your own benefit and, in a way, it is.

It was, therefore, not an easy harmonization that Muramasa had to enter into and track within. Also, we did at the time suspect that it was likely a fictional construct which was going to make the task a lot more difficult than it would have been if there was one real and genuine target to lock on to.

It was not all bad news for him at the time however. For example, fortunately enough, no crucifixion was required. The key element to the Jesus Christ paradigm was his voluntary entrance into death itself whilst holding a particular focus because he knew what came next and had a particular agenda to further. This then is what Muramasa would use to begin his tracking of the Christian paradigm and, perhaps, Jesus Christ himself if it was found to be the case that a single individual on which the entire Christian edifice was based did in fact exist.

WATER ELEMENT

It can inundate and overwhelm, groups especially. Even if gentle it is always there, in motion and inspiring motion.

Chapter 41 — Journey to the West

Our journey to the West, then, began with a single entirely voluntary and wholly conscious human sacrifice. This does not mean that the sacrifice in question was particularly happy about the process and he would have definitely preferred things to have worked out differently. So very similar to the Jesus Christ paradigm then, as we intended.

Muramasa, like Jesus Christ, was an immortal who had more or less mastered the full techniques of reincarnation. Not to quite the extent which Jesus Christ did but sufficiently to be functional and effective in that position.

So, starting from a basis which was similar enough to Jesus Christ's in most of the ways which count, good enough to track a very difficult and hidden target anyway so there must be something to our assessment, Muramasa then followed in Christ's footsteps. Quite literally so, after all he was actually trying to find and physically meet the present incarnation.

However, yes, the character and Spirit involved were very different. Muramasa is much more vengeful for a start and he is also proud and actively fights against anyone or anything teaching him humility.

We recognise that you would probably all have preferred us to have selected Masamune as our Agent to the West but that is not how things worked out. Nor would it have fit into our wider strategic purposes as well, which is why fate and circumstance formulated in the way they did. You just want a softer touch who you believe will allow you to continue in your soft, corrupt, lazy and degenerate ways. This position represents a fundamental misunderstanding of Jesus Christ's actual character and Spirit but more importantly it would be nowhere near as effective and would slow us all down.

Our Agent to the West was not only well chosen, he was at the time the only one possibly capable of fulfilling that position. This meant that he was the right one for the role. For that is how we administrate fate in Japan. With only one choice available to us in terms of critical junctures and decisions no mistakes can be made.

We have located Jesus Christ for you and we have also included him in how you will be developing your plans in important and relevant positions. However, initially at least, you will be having a lot more contact with Muramasa than with Masamune. This especially applies to the Western command structure. We therefore recommend that you put in the effort to try to understand him and his perspectives.

As our tale progresses, and we reveal more of what is actually involved, even members of the general public will come to understand that Muramasa is the ideal choice for the position, for you as well as for us. We therefore recommend that you also put in the effort to try to understand him and his perspectives.

Azra-nak does a tremendously large circle and the whole thing is done in ethics and logic. He is basically the only one who can understand it, what is involved and how it works. This does not make him superior to any of us, let alone Shogun. So much for Hierarchy really operating on the basis of your degree of Illumination. It helps, certainly, but is not the only or even the determining factor. Hierarchy is really only an issue in this day and age if you are one of us or already an Inner Circle member of the Illuminati. The rest of you are generally treated as equals, or close enough.

Although En no Gyoja is universally recognised as our most accomplished sorcerer, what Muramasa does is very clear and easy for you to understand. He is what you would understand as a real magickian. Not showy stage magick, he has never learned even a single one of those tricks. Rather, the Universe responds to his position in unique and usually quite dramatic ways.

In this capacity he is famous within Japan for having his swords banned by the Tokugawa Shogunate. The reason for this is that they seemingly coincidentally kept killing or severely injuring members and descendants of Ieyasu's immediate family. Nobody attacks Shogun, that is correct. It is impossible, he focuses all the light in this system, the entirety of the Creation, and he has no suicidal or masochistic tendencies.

We are guessing Muramasa was displeased with Ieyasu's decision to have him executed when he had already fulfilled all his duties, attained physical immortality and was engaged in one of the deepest and most meaningful love affairs of his many incarnations. Anyway, the history on who his swords have killed and injured and how is very well documented. You can try to make sense of it for yourself if you like.

What this means is that we are giving you someone to tell your hierarchy what to do who does not mind attacking Shogun, insofar as such a thing is possible, which is basically what you wanted isn't it? You do not like or appreciate us having power over you. This was foreseen and factored into the calibrations.

You may as well know that Muramasa pioneered the use of feeding human blood to swords in order to cause their souls to behave in a certain way. This is another reason why he was designated as our chosen emissary to the Western hierarchies. More importantly, if you want to survive you have to listen to him and obey him. You will understand why this is the case later on. It is due to who he is, what he has done and the positions he has fulfilled in your own history. The net result of which is that this world behaves in a certain way in relation to him and how history fits together around him and his intentions. Again, you will understand this better later on.

For now, Western command structure, come to recognise that if you are not going to be in your current position where Shogun is destroying you then your only way out, as covered in parts 1 and 2, is a blood-sworn oath of loyalty made on a *wakizashi*. The net result of that is that you obey Muramasa not only in your actions but also in your heart and intentions. Or members of your family die, and this would include the children. Check the history. It is just how it works.

If you didn't want us to include to them in war then you should not have applied the Art of War to business proceedings much less turned economics into an enforcement mechanism for Hierarchy. If you behave like cunts then we will defeat you and knock your heart onto the ground. This is our standard methodology. Come to recognise where you actually stand. It will make things go much easier for you. For example, your economic policies cause others' children to die from bombings or starvation. Then you expect us to give you no Return on such a thing?

But fear not. As was probably more evident from his lifetime as the Prophet Mohammed, Shogun is a wise and benevolent supreme dictator. Muramasa has learnt a great deal of Compassion on his journey to track down Jesus Christ. You have to follow the target's heart and impressions in fate to make any real progress when tracking. Do that for long enough and it becomes a part of you unless you really fight against it, making your own job much more difficult in the process. And Muramasa being Muramasa, he much preferred to choose his battles wisely and in accordance with his own values and priorities. This means he fought the lesson of humility as much as he could, to prevent that Principle from becoming a part of his character and outlook on the world, but was largely indifferent to whatever else had an effect.

So he has learnt to be both gentle and compassionate, perhaps too gentle and too compassionate even. However, at the end of the day, if you do push then the real nature comes through and he is a dismissively arrogant bastard, basically. With quite a good sense of humor to boot.

He is the perfect individual to bring your Illuminati and Temple of the Vampire hierarchies into line. Some of those people will be able to feel his heart and what moves around him. Moreover, unlike with Masamune, they will actually understand what they feel and what it means for them. This saves us all time and trouble.

Muramasa, like Masamune, will not head your hierarchies though, be clear on that. Both are there to act as consultants for you, to get you motivated and point you in the right directions, to enable changes which otherwise would be nigh on impossible.

What you have actually earned and will get, Western peoples and command structures, is rule by the Antichrist through the Luciferian Illuminati. As already covered for you, the Antichrist in the present historical epoch will be played by Gilgamesh, who was also Sun Tzu. In his present lifetime he is half Chinese.

If you object at this stage to the motion of actual Justice and try to cheat or swindle the mills of the gods then we revert to plan A. Plan A is when we kill the entire planet and all human life upon her. Then we destroy all the souls who are not our own. And then we're done with you. Later on, we get to reincarnate our people.

If you want to go down that path because you think you have the abilities for it then you're probably Shambhala. Which is another challenge you will face to secure your own survival, Western peoples and the world more widely. If you want to go down that path because you are greedy and delusionally arrogant then you're probably the incumbent

Western command structure. We will be using others within your own societies to outmanoeuvre you, most notably those fine people in the CIA who are going to become a major force for good, truth and justice in this world. Just like in the comic books if we change their name to S.H.I.E.L.D.

The important thing is that you understand and accept the schematic sufficiently to work within it. We don't care where your group consciousness is actually located provided it moves in the ways required of it. Your external positions require more effort to change the meanings within them. Hence, this way is faster. Become different people if you have to, run different values and priorities through your institutions if you need to. But move as fast and efficiently as you possibly can. That is the only thing we require of you and the only thing you really require of yourselves.

Chapter 42 – Back when the New Age didn't yet involve Aquarius

Kitiara couldn't keep her eyes off the tall, dark, handsome man who looked a bit like Keanu Reeves. It was the year 2000 so the similarity had not yet become as pronounced as it would later be. This was against everything that was being taught in the tantric sex course they were both attending. You had to be still, balanced, in your centre, with your chakras aligned and noble intentions based on love, trust and a genuine desire for spiritual progress. Whereas she just wanted to fuck him and hoped he was not too gentle about it. She felt like quite a rough session, if she could get her hands on him. He was dangerous, you could feel that about his presence, but he tried his best to fit in and appear normal. You could see him trying. It was quite cute in a way.

"Now, focus on the heat in your genitals and lift it up your spine," came the instruction from the teacher who was leading them through the guided meditation. Fuck that, thought Kitiara, she already knew the basics anyway. She decided to "taste" the sexual energy of the latest man to take her interest. She was of course a very accomplished PSI vampire already, at the tender age of just 23.

What she tasted caused her to recoil in revulsion. Cold, brutal, detached, persistent – these were not qualities that normally moved within the genital area, especially not in young and horny men. Something was wrong here. The man felt like a demon. Perhaps she had found a serial killer. Kitiara determined to investigate. But carefully. She was still in shock...

Chapter 43 – Doppelgänger

Muramasa, as usual, was unimpressed. He had just finished writing a book on the sexual arts historically practiced within Temple of Ishtar and had decided to compare his own efforts with what the competition had to offer.

What he found was lots of rote learning but little real understanding or innovation. Even the essence of the old techniques had not been grasped, let alone their development. So he was generally in a dark mood as he headed off to lunch in the break provided during the tantra course.

He was in Amsterdam in the Netherlands and therefore decided to go for Argentinean steak. Even in this era before smartphones, it did not take him long to locate a suitable establishment. He turned off the sidewalk, heading towards the door. At the door he had to stop, as someone else was heading in from the opposite direction.

They both glanced up at each other and then paused a second. The similarity was uncanny. Masamune was the first to recover.

"I must say, you are very good looking, and seem remarkably well built for someone so slim," he said to the much younger man he was facing. "My only real question is if your mind is as sharp as your posture would seem to indicate."

The comment was inspired not just by the similarity in their height and facial features. There was also a palpable feeling of shock, curiosity, humor and amusement to the encounter.

"You come off alright yourself," replied Muramasa. "This is one of those life-changing coincidences you read about, is it not?" he continued.

"Probably not," said Masamune. "But we should have lunch anyway."

Of the 5, only Red is a mystery. The rest have all met each other already.

Chapter 44 – Too much sex

Muramasa had taken care to smile in Kitiara's direction occasionally, since the first day of the week-long tantra course he had come to Amsterdam to attend. There were 5 singles on this particular course, but Muramasa and Kitiara were the only two beautiful people within the singles group, so the whole thing was more or less a foregone conclusion anyway, but you had to go through the motions.

Women needed time to get used to the idea. Their own desire and imagination usually did the rest of the work for him, he found. He had given her 3 days already during which he had been keeping things between them oddly formal, though friendly at times.

"You want to go get dinner together?" he asked as they were heading out of the class.

"Sure, why not?" she replied. She had known the invite was coming. But you had to go through the motions.

"What do you think of the course?" Muramasa asked, once they were out of earshot of the rest of the participants.

"Exceptionally well researched and very well put together," said Kitiara, but her tone implied for those who were sensitive to it that things were flawed or omitted at a deeper level. She did not seem satisfied nor enthusiastic.

This is how we tend to conceal meaning from outsiders when they are in our presence. Often, they understand the exact opposite of the real meaning. This is because they do not give sufficient credence to their feelings, which are indistinct for them and usually lack precision. Meaning is composed in the soul, ordinarily, as a result of both conceptual structures and the feeling moving through them. This was your introduction to the structural mechanics behind that fact of your own existence.

The more advanced levels is where things get much more interesting. It is what this system does to you if you lack sufficiently developed conceptual structures or sufficiently clearly enunciated emotional expressions within your soul (for example, to take the most common example, if your heart is fully or partially closed).

The result is that the system moves your mind or your emotions through your physical condition and experiences. Thus, to take an extreme example, you can compose meaning out of conceptual structures and a great deal of physical pain, for example.

The point, my friends, interjected Muramasa, is that if you set the structure in meaning for the system overall then you can have peoples' minds, and also hearts, changed for you. By the enforcement capacity of the system. Which is usually the Naga, correct. However, please do not misunderstand your reptilian overlords. They do what they do to you because others in this local galaxy would rather your minds and hearts were moved more rapidly, which usually means by more forceful or deterministic means.

I wasn't going to mention that part of the conversation. Back to Ochi no Kata, please bear in mind that she is the one writing most of this, so things will usually be from her perspective.

"I agree," said Muramasa, and Kitiara was pleased that her inflections in tone were not lost on him.

"Then again, you should not expect much more from barbarians. They are not civilized," he continued.

Kitiara was more than a little taken aback by his bold and open statement. She had not recognised it for what it was: a veiled intimation of personal superiority. Nor did she have any clue what he was really on about. She decided to feign indifference to mask her ignorance. And also because, let's be honest, she was not at the time particularly interested in what his personality was up to nor what his personal beliefs happened to be.

"I sense you are half barbarian yourself," continued Muramasa, to provoke her. "Let me guess, you're half Swedish right?"

It was a rude game he was playing, but not at all discourteous. You will have to learn to distinguish the difference for yourselves. This will become very important to you as cultures later on. Most of these interjections are composite structures designed to infect your mindgrid and given as dictation by Sarutobi. He claims to be using viruses for evolutionary purposes.

Kitiara smiled. "How did you guess?" she asked.

"They have a particular vibe about them, the Swedish," said Muramasa. "Self-righteous, arrogant pricks for the most part. I tend to get on with them."

"You'll love my other half then," said Kitiara. She was of course married at the time, but was effectively single. "It's Israeli."

She had caught his tone correctly. We all recognise the Israelis as far less self-righteous than the Swedish, this is part of what conscious species and individuals actually do: deal with the Principles actually in play on the world grid. He had conveyed minor distaste but considerable amusement for the "self-righteous" part of the assessment but considerable fondness, tenderness and warmth for the "arrogant" part.

"I really love Israelis," said Muramasa. "Arrogance is my favorite virtue and so few approach competence in it nowadays. This is going to be a lot of fun."

"What do you mean?" asked Kitiara, with a smile.

"I have what you might call a premonition that I will vastly enjoy our time together," said Muramasa. "I've got something for you to think about. Look deep within your heart and your own feelings and tell me later, once you've sensed it for yourself: what are you self-righteous about relative to me? This should be interesting. For now, I hope you like steak." He gestured her towards the Argentinian steak house he'd been to earlier, on the basis that he knew it was good and that it had a suitable atmosphere for what he had in mind. He was not yet aware of Armand's role in proceedings, nor how that individual tends to operate his own harmonization network.

After they had been seated and had ordered, Kitiara lounged back in her chair – it was one of those old style leather dining armchairs with armrests – and smiled casually at Muramasa.

He waited for her to speak. And smiled back.

"What are you really doing here?" she asked. "Did my husband send you to spy on me?"

She thought she was being clever and sophisticated at the time, and was certain that she had caught him out. Nobody who was not in the Family – and by this she did not mean the Mafia – would know how to interact at this sort of level and they would only do so if they were certain they were talking to another Family member.

"I though you said you were single?" said Muramasa. Not that he cared, particularly. It was her choice to be here this evening. She was old enough to be responsible for her own decisions.

"That doesn't matter now, quit stalling. Did he send you to spy on me and attempt to get evidence of an affair or not?" insisted Kitiara, now becoming a little bit irritated.

"This gets more interesting by the minute," said Muramasa. "I see we will have to be very discreet. If we do have an affair, of course. I thank you for the proposition and will consider it." He smiled. "And I assure you, nobody sent me to spy on you. And anyway, I cannot be purchased in that way."

He didn't really care that she seemed to be quite crazy. In fact, he found her more interesting that way. This trick only works if you are physically very beautiful, keep yourself well-composed and ensure you are both well groomed and very well dressed. Otherwise you're just crazy. They have been very careful in how they tuned this harmonic exception. It is very difficult to do, in practice.

Kitiara didn't say anything for a while. Then she smiled and said, "Let's take a step back and I'll tell you about my marriage thing later and why I'm so paranoid about it." She furrowed her brow briefly and took a sip of wine. "Tell me what you meant by 'barbarians' earlier."

She was now beginning to think that she had made a mistake and he was not in the Family, just another admittedly very handsome weirdo. She had to find out before proceeding. They are not allowed to have sexual relations with ordinary members of society, not the pure stock, this is very strictly enforced without exception. Kitiara was of course, in this lifetime, Inner Circle Vampire, even in her relocated position.

Muramasa felt he was losing her and that she was taking distance from him. Well, that didn't take long he thought.

He resolved to take the decision for her. This is not rape. It is overruling your free will because you are lower in Hierarchy.

We take most of your decisions for you in practice. It is time you understood how that process works.

He took greater distance from her, on the inside, and expanded his being into the cold, black stillness of the Moon. There was silence in the void, and complete indifference. He did not really think it was necessary to go much farther than that.

On the outside he gave no indication that he was anything but mildly disappointed, sensed something had gone wrong and was now trying to win back her interest in some way.

You have to give credit where it is due. Inner Circle members of the Vampire – as distinct from the equivalent position in the Illuminati hierarchy – are very well trained and very obedient. They move out of the way rapidly as soon as they feel the Darkness closing in on them. The more advanced practitioners will even recognise that this is going on and be able to quantify the power of the individual involved by means of their assessment of the different qualities of that which they sense closing down around them.

Muramasa was talking about ancient Greece, and Sparta, and the Snake Mysteries and the Sanctuary of the Great Gods in Samothrace and other things Kitiara was not paying much attention to. She was thinking how to get out of there.

Then she felt it. She knew she had to stay where she was. That if she moved then, much later on usually, she would suffer severely for it through her own wider life circumstances, perhaps what happened to a friend or relative. She had felt this before, many times. Her husband used to do it to her all the time until he had her under control. But she was working on her own way to break free. And was more than confident. She was certain.

And yet this time, it felt different. She was curious, and sensed for the difference. There was laughter on the inside! The whole thing was incredibly amusing to him! Arrogant prick!

She resolved to play him along, get his hopes up, enough physical contact to really encourage that, have him walk her to her hotel – and then neglect to invite him upstairs and spend the rest of the course being as formal with him as he had until this evening been with her.

The forms must be obeyed at the outset, of course. Their kind like to determine the relative power structure right at the start. It is how they do it. This is why they are not allowed to have sex with ordinary humans. But Muramasa was never one of them. Kitiara did not know this yet and had in fact entirely misunderstood the basis for his interaction with her, concluding that he was clearly Inner Circle Vampire when he was in reality nothing of the sort.

So yes. If she had been an ordinary human then what he was doing to her may very well have been understood on your terms as rape. This is why you should not attempt to copy your overlords. Whether they are Vampire or reptilian. You will get the representation of the contents packets incorrect. That karma is for us, not you. You cannot rule in our place, even using democracy. You are not suited for it, by nature. Sorry not sorry.

Aside from our enforcement capacity, which is universal and acts as a form of protection for our agents, there is the consideration that all our agents are what you might term "self policing". They operate at levels which are considerably above the upper conceptual boundaries placed on social, interpersonal and intergovernmental interactions by the legal structure currently in existence on this planet. This is also why they act in a Judgment capacity.

As for Kitiara, she evidently had a lot of rape karma still to go through, as we got her out of a lot of it when she was a kid by delaying it for later for her (and draining as also recalibrating its energy attachments). From our perspective, we had to ensure that she and Muramasa were a sure thing, and rape is a much more certain methodology for sexual relations than love. But this is not how we administer ordinary humans, be clear on that. She will, as you shall see, enjoy the whole process very much and will believe she is entering into it willingly. Which is what we do with you all, in every sphere of your lives, humanity.

"I'm half barbarian myself," said Muramasa, concluding his long explanation of what barbarians where and why they were called that. He had been giving her some space to think and feel things on her own. He has learnt to be both eloquent and wordy when it suits his purposes, as also quite charming and elaborately witty. However, he still prefers laconic. "German actually. Precision and efficiency. Got to love it."

"And a tendency to lose. Twice," noted Kitiara.

"Yes, I haven't got to that yet," said Muramasa. "Not looking forward to it." This is how the individual participates in the karma of the group. Now you know, work on extrapolating the rest.

He then got Kitiara to describe her character and values for him, as also some of her life experiences. She liked to view herself as courageous and noble, for example. Muramasa hugely enjoyed this side of getting to know a woman. He found great pleasure in appreciating the beauty of her soul, or personality as you more commonly know it, if she had put real effort and style into cultivating it, and it was not weak.

This is probably because he generally likes everything and everyone in a controlled position, including himself. You control a person through his character, or soul. In one way or another, various approaches can be used.

At any rate, Kitiara took the attention positively and was now interested again. She began smiling more, felt some tingles of sexual arousal, and initiated more subtle physical contact over the food.

Next Muramasa decided to make things more interesting, and scratch the second failure off the card in Kitiara's case. This means, Germans, that your own national and historic structure, as also the genetic calibrations and administration that results from that, are now recognised as one of the key precipitating factors in at least one instance of the rape of a Vampire by a man who was at the time a human. They view such things very strictly you know, no exceptions. Why do these things keep happening to you?

"You do know I am not in the Family, do you not?" he asked, maintaining eye contact all the while.

Protocol in such instances is to deny any knowledge of what is being referred to. To ensure she did not follow protocol he tightened his control over her soul and let a little bit of the steel be felt. He was laughing very openly now.

"Then how...?" was Kitiara's next question.

"Well, it's the same reason I am, like you, incredibly disappointed by the exceptionally well researched and put together tantra course we are both attending.

Those who put together the program and implement it as masters. What they do is good. It works. It is functional. You get better results than if they're not there.

But let's be honest. They know fuck all about what they're actually trying to do and don't properly understand what they're doing in the present moment as a result."

This was the juncture at which Kitiara began to suspect that Muramasa, too, had taken instruction from us. She was wrong in this assessment also. Muramasa was a problem as far as were concerned at the time. His case was passed directly to Shogun, who integrated him personally into hierarchy by accepting his rapid and unconditional surrender, and then passed him back to us for processing, but only much later on.

She was careful in how she proceeded. Now she felt destiny at work. So there are various levels of control operational on the Earth system. Paradoxically, you attain the greatest freedom when you follow and seek to fulfil your destiny. This is because free will is used to secure desires, usually.

She let herself sink into the rhythm of the surrounding atmosphere. Muramasa felt this, because he was responsible for putting it there, as described earlier (the start of the process anyway). And she decided to focus on the sexual aspect of his statement and leave the rest for later.

"The course is a bit basic, isn't it? So much complexity!" said Kitiara. "Not even one mention of tuning into the deeper flows and rhythms." She smiled at him and held eye contact. "I thought there might be something different about you."

"Understatement of the decade," said Muramasa. "You hardly seem normal yourself."

"I'm not," smiled Kitiara. "Glad you recognised it. Want to come back to my place and fuck my brains out?"

"I honestly thought we'd never get there," lied Muramasa.

Chapter 45 - Hierarchy

The way Hierarchy works in practice, if you want to overrule someone higher than you in Hierarchy then you must use someone else higher than them to do so. It is also possible to utilise the evolving properties of the system as a whole to produce this same result for you, but if you succeed in that then your own position in Hierarchy will change anyway through the process.

Kitiara sensed this, from when he was hunting her. That Muramasa was much stronger than her husband, in Mind, which is what counts for them, due to his position in Hierarchy, which is the only way to attain real strength in Mind, or a consequence of doing so. Yes, some Vampire hunt humans also. Never casually though, always with due justification and purpose. They tend to be very responsible you know. Much more so than the Naga anyway.

Her first priority was therefore that she wanted to use him to overrule her husband. If a Vampire woman does sleep with you – once suitable arrangements have been made it is our intention to have Armand, the new chief of the Vampire on the world stage, rescind the sexual quarantine stipulation – then it will always be because she wants something from you and only secondarily because she actually wants to have sex with you. Even if she really, really wants to have sex with you. However, what she will want from you will basically never be money or power, though sometimes glory so the third part of the equation is still active for you.

Men do not charge for their services, they automatically take their payment as their Will is integrated with the Darkness, that is to say it becomes an integrated material reality. Half-men are neither respected nor desired by the woman they are having intercourse with, not truly, and so very little of their Will is integrated.

These are the realities of the interactions between the sexes for your species. You would do well to study them and abide within their terms.

Chapter 46 – Armand makes a personal appearance

"I've found another one," said Masamune when he returned home to Delft. Though he mainly lives in Switzerland, he tends to spend July-October in the south of France and April-June in the Netherlands.

Armand nodded. They were cooperating on a project. It was of course highly illegal in every way possible. This troubled neither of them, in the slightest. Why would it, when you think about it?

Masamune wanted certain individuals located, key amongst them the 24 Ancients, or Elders as you know them in your tradition. All were very well hidden.

"I've met this one before, last lifetime," said Masamune. "He's young still, give him another 20 or 30 years. Time for you to work."

"Where?" asked Armand.

"Put him in charge of the Western hierarchy to start with. Let him find his own way to fulfil that which is within him. Use him as that set of positions dictates," replied Masamune.

Armand nodded.

Those two have been working on something for over 20 years. We still have little idea what it is and how it might really work. It is impossible to gain an overview of the entire schematic and if you try to track the logic it disappears into infinity before recombining and cross-referencing itself for eternity before formatting itself into the nature of material reality itself.

So Masamune is naturally secretive because even if you know exactly what he's done it still makes no sense to you or you don't fully understand it – but it works better than you could have hoped, redefining the limits of perfection in the process. So, in a way, you don't need to know. That's why we don't bother.

Chapter 47 – Lucifer and anal sex

Muramasa and Kitiara were having brunch, at around 2pm. They had decided to cut class for the day and were generally feeling like being highly irresponsible.

This is the single biggest hurdle to ethical behaviour for ordinary members of the human species. They look for rules, or at least guidelines, when in reality the only thing they can do to help them is to deepen their understanding of the individual concepts out of which ethical behaviour is or could be composed. There is considerable latitude in the process, it is a question of mechanics. Some qualities always predominate, this is due to God's character. Most of these tend to be very obvious, the rest are highly obscure. There is no middle ground in this.

The reality of the attack mechanism – for make no mistake, that is what it is – is that you have an internal flow of clear guidance which you need to feel with your whole being. It takes a while to develop this sensitivity and know how to handle it, which means "ride the winds of fate" in our terminology. Not exactly but close enough to for you to grasp the analogy. It's the lightweight version of that we refer to here.

Then, in every situation, you will know what you must try to do to fulfil the Flow which has arisen from the Principles you have chosen to emphasise in your character, and so your life path. Cowardice is often very useful, for example, do not neglect to understand what is involved in practice if your intention is to deceive others this is one of the best Principles you can use. This is for the Vampire. Fear does not exist for them anyway. It is all just Reality, as far as they are concerned.

Sometimes the Flow will require you to do unusual things, or engage in unusual practices (for example, if you have, like The Illuminati, been led by an idiot who does not properly understand how the mechanics he must be using actually work). Then you have to go with it and understand why you are doing so. Or exercise personal Judgment and ignore your heart at the deeper level, that is to say your soul.

But usually it is safe to say that it has not only got your best interests at heart but has figured out a way to make them a reality for you that you probably won't understand yet. This is why it is normal for such people to remain in a flow condition.

"I've always said the day doesn't start until you have coffee," said Muramasa. They both took further sips of their koffie verkeerds, which were basically two shot lattes with a bit more foam.

"This means you haven't fucked me yet today and it's nearly 3pm," said Kitiara.

"Eat your salmon, pussycat," said Muramasa. "But continue purring. What did you like best about yesterday?"

"Oh, definitely the conversation!" intoned Kitiara with a look of false piety.

"Clearly. We both know how to fuck well, and our personal styles match well," said Muramasa.

"I've thought about what you asked me last night," said Kitiara. "But to answer your latest question first, do you want an appraisal of your performance in great detail now?"

"Save that for your girlfriends, I'm sure they'll get to hear all the details," replied Muramasa. "I was asking what you wanted more of."

"I was thinking some more missionary, I like to feel close to you. And then I want to try anal with you," was Kitiara's reply.

"Ah," said Muramasa. "I am special in this regards and you need to understand why before you choose to go there. Do you know what anal is actually for?"

"For when you're sore from too much vaginal?" enquired Kitiara.

"Good answer," smirked Muramasa. "Don't tell me you're sore already?"

"Of course not. Did you think I was a virgin also? Tell me, did you grow up in a monastery?" teased Kit.

"Might as well have done, I tend to seek the meaning within depth," replied Muramasa.

"Not the depth within meaning?" asked Kitiara.

"Well observed," said Muramasa. "You actually pay attention. Not just a hot body and a very beautiful face."

"Exercise and plastic surgery," said Kitiara. "A girl's two best friends."

"Well, that's another topic I suppose," said Muramasa. "Let's not lose the focus here, it's one with important consequences. Do you know what anal is actually for?"

"Enlighten me," was Kitiara's response. As far as she was concerned it was for pleasure What was he into, she wondered...

"Let's do it this way. Tell me, where do you feel it when you orgasm with anal," asked Muramasa.

"Shoots up the spine and hits me in the back of the head," said Kitiara.

"Base of the skull, correct," said Muramasa. "And think for a moment: what is it you find there?"

"The reptilian brain stem!" exclaimed Kitiara, visibly excited. "I never made the connection! Is that a way to contact them?"

The mysteries of the Order of the Dragon are a big thing within Temple of the Vampire.

"Always present when you do that. They take requests, too," was Muramasa's response. "Who or what do you want to destroy?"

Kitiara was a little shocked to see him referring to the use of the Naga so casually.

"You don't have to specify a target, of course," said Muramasa. "In my experience, they'll use you anyway and so you still get the Dark Currents which make the sex feel so much better. They've got destruction of their own to feed through, and plenty of it."

Kitiara was making connections all on her own. It was a pleasure for us all to observe at the time. This was a watershed moment in her life.

She was also finding herself naturally drawn to following this man's lead. She wasn't questioning or objecting any more. Something about him inspired her trust. Possibly because she is quite dark, and Muramasa can also be that way inclined when he needs to pierce a topic.

She was not falling in love. Neither of them have done that to the other yet in this lifetime and it is moreover highly doubtful they ever will. We do have plans to fetch them both together once more, but that will have to wait for much later, once the proper orgies are up and running again.

"How do you know these things?" asked Kitiara, genuinely intensely curious. Now that she had it pointed out to her, she saw how it made self-obvious sense, hidden there in plain sight for all who knew to see, yet none had ever made the connection! None she had ever heard about anyway...

"Meaning in depth," replied Muramasa. "Well, what do you want to destroy?"

Those familiar with the Order of the Dragon, as Kitiara was at the time, will know that you can only use the Naga for something which impacts upon the wider Group Mind. You cannot use them for wholly individual or personal results.

"My marriage?" asked Kitiara. "But I want it done in a way which leaves me very wealthy."

This is possible if you structure the meanings and connections around your marriage into the conceptual and historical evolution of your nation state for example. Royal houses do this a lot for instance.

"OK," said Muramasa. "Makes it more interesting. You'll probably have to add a demon to secure that sub-condition. Lucifer himself does not usually concern himself with the niceties, his servants do so with his authority."

He paused and looked at Kitiara. "I am correct, am I not? You are a Luciferian. So I thought I'd put it in your terms."

Kitiara nodded, smiled and was silent.

"I interact with them as the Naga. You should know the difference, but both methods work, though differently tuned." He paused again, and looked deep enough into her eyes that she felt he was watching her soul.

"So. Larger target?" he asked.

"Let's make this interesting," Kitiara said. "The nature of Evil. Maybe the very existence of Evil also. You decide."

"Nice. So we know what we'll be doing after brunch then," said Muramasa.

Lucifer is always involved if you enjoy anal sex enough to get the "energy" up to the reptilian brain stem, or if it arrives there by other means. Now you know. This is why it was prohibited. It is not the act itself which was classified as "wrong" within your moralities. It was the fact that Lucifer was involved if the act developed in certain ways.

"So why are you special in this regards then?" asked Kitiara. "You still haven't told me."

"Good point," said Muramasa. "Tell me, did you ever notice, when you were younger especially, people being prematurely killed off when they had done something to disturb or hinder your path? Or sometimes even they were just guilty of doing something with only the potential to be disruptive much later on."

"Yes, my geography teacher, who was the first. And a couple of others. But many more did much worse and have yet to die."

"You need to interpret the phenomenon correctly. And for that you need to feel into its meaning accurately. Can you do that?" he asked.

"I suppose," said Kitiara. "But why don't you just tell me?"

"They die around you because you are a piece on the board of the world stage, which is being administrated in a certain way by the actual players in the game. Which is Lucifer. There is only one player in this game, really. Even if he is a species, correctly speaking."

Your own position needs to be such that it is useful to their own purposes to kill specific targets for you. This is why I am... different. My choices have relevance. Because most of my attacks, and decisions, get through. All of them eventually, I suspect."

"And how do you do that?" asked Kitiara. As far as she cared, getting Lucifer to kill people for you, this was just regular Satanist talk, amongst edgy early teens at least.

"Not by following your bliss," said Muramasa, referring to the path of Joy, or Ananda. "You need to understand the nature of existence, as a first step. Thereafter consciousness will serve you and so you can master it easily. You then get bliss as a Consequence." Hollywood, pay attention.

"Sounds like too much hard work to me when you can just use Zahgurim instead," said Kitiara, referring to a particular Sumerian demon well known amongst those who take an interest in such things.

"Different karma," said Muramasa. "More importantly, you cannot integrate that sort of thing into society. It will always be a shadowy, behind the scenes practice. It is, after all, basically murder from a legal perspective, or will become that eventually if you do it repeatedly and with great success where high-level targets are concerned."

"Well, how many people do you want to kill? It's only ever one or two who cross you that much. In a year I mean," said Kitiara. The conversation had taken quite a dark turn, around about the time they started discussing anal sex. You have been warned, it is dangerous to your innocence to engage in that practice consciously.

"I don't care, actually," said Muramasa. "Not my concern. I'm sure they know what they're doing and anyway I can't be bothered to learn all the mechanics involved. The point is they should serve me and abide by my decisions."

"And how is your way legal and capable of being integrated with wider society?" asked Kitiara.

"I just enable them to fulfil their desires much more effectively," said Muramasa. "That is what commercial system is for. It is also at the root cause of money. Neither of these things guide your desire to what is best for you, not even medically. They exist to fulfil your desire."

"You are saying you engage in trade and business relations with the Naga!?" asked Kitiara, with a furrowed brow and in shocked disbelief.

"Basically, yes. But that's my German side. I keep the two parts of my heritage very separate," replied Muramasa, as if he was offering some kind of comprehensible explanation.

Kitiara had been the thinking about the anal sex they would shortly be having and so naturally made the subconscious connection to being wealthy and divorced soon. Hence she was casually interested in whether he might be onto something which would enable him to become wealthy at or near her own level, perhaps even exceed it.

"How do you plan to make money out of that?" she asked.

"Well, as I see it, I have to fail after great struggles as a first step. As a second step I need to put the next great holocaust together. And then the third step should happen on its own through God's intervention after that. I did say it was my German side," said Muramasa, not really replying, again.

"I sense you are not taking the challenge seriously," Kitiara smiled. She now thought he may be independently wealthy, perhaps enough at least.

"It is not my challenge," said Muramasa. "I am just a piece on the board. Whoever is moving through me gets all the credit. But yes. I have much better things to do with my time. It is why I keep my corporation open but largely inert. I just run some transactions through it to pay US taxes on them, minimal enough."

"What does your corporation do though, or plan to do? What is its purpose of business?" asked Kitiara, sticking to her focus.

"Currently, it is failing and going through great struggles," said Muramasa. "Eventually I will kill it I suppose. The point being underlined, as I understand it, is that my inferiors require great exertions from me to secure for myself a position within their hierarchies approaching, or if I am very lucky, extremely hard working and join all the right secret societies, maybe even equal to their own.

It is an attack on commercial system and the international syndicate of money. An attack which will fail. But that is not why I am engaging within it. Rather, it is my intention to secure the karmic material for a referral process.

How would you do it? The basic ability you have to work with is that you can decide who gets to die, but only if it results in other people who deserve to die less being spared from that experience. Convert that into cold, hard cash. See if you can think of a way."

"Try that approach on anyone with real money or power and you'd end up dead pretty quick," was Kitiara's summation at the time.

"Exactly, it is impossible," said Muramasa. "Therefore we need God to do it for us."

"You don't strike me as the religious type," said Kitiara. "But anyway, why would God get involved in all this?"

"I am reliably informed it is what he did the last time a major holocaust was involved," was Muramasa's reply.

"By whom?" asked Kitiara.

"People I know," said Muramasa. "But that's my Japanese side expressing."

"You don't have a Japanese side," said Kitiara.

"Past life of mine," said Muramasa. "Bit of a controlling bastard, really. Any memories yourself there?"

"Nope," lied Kitiara. "So you plan to make money only after the next great holocaust then?" she continued.

"Whatever," was Muramasa's response. "The point is I defeat the entire field but never really enter it myself. It is the control and establishment of Hierarchy that is the my key interest in the issue. To answer your question, I expect we will be accepting major bribes prior to the commencement of the next great holocaust." Our timeline mechanics were mainly designed by Masamune. Muramasa at this time did not really know what was going on there, he just felt something quite accurately.

"We?" asked Kitiara.

"Whoever is in a position to modify the holocaust depiction, I guess," said Muramasa.

"So you're not part of some large conspiracy then?" asked Kitiara.

"I am part of a large group of independent practitioners," said Muramasa. "Most are ninja as far as I can tell. Not really a conspiracy though. It's just that few bother to train all the way up the ranks of the open hierarchies which have been provided to them for this purpose. To discover and use for themselves what they have clearly and plainly been told is there."

"It's going to take some time to understand you…" laughed Kitiara, shaking her head.

"Don't bother," replied Muramasa. "Not worth the effort. Accept that some things will remain forever beyond your reach."

Muramasa was not going out of his way to explain himself, and some would view the way he put things as both arrogant and offensive. For some reason, all of that just that made Kitiara even more interested.

Chapter 48 – To money or not to money

"Go on then," said Muramasa. "What I asked you last night. What are you self-righteous about relative to me?"

"Personal wealth," said Kitiara. "Correct me if I'm wrong, but you don't have that much, do you?"

"Enough not to need to work," said Muramasa. "For most people that would be plenty. But yes, it as you say. I am not Family."

"Then how do you know about us?" asked Kitiara. The Family – by which we do not mean the Mafia – have always been very secretive.

"You're not the only Family member who likes breaking rules you know," said Muramasa.

For some reason these people are drawn to him. Our conclusion was that he still commands their obedience. The magickal workings which produce this effect for him have been lost to the mists of time, but he effectively if not actually started their organisations and so remains responsible for them.

"You are nothing in modern society without money," said Kitiara, repeating a widely believed credo of the modern era. "Say what you like, nowadays if you truly want to enjoy your life and live as we were always supposed to, you need at least 5 or 10 million in the bank. Plus a steady source of income for your yearly expenditures. So yes. That's where I think you're wrong."

"Most would undoubtedly agree with you," stated Muramasa. "This is why we," he indicated Kitiara and himself as a couple, "would never work as anything serious. I cannot afford to keep you in the lifestyle which you prefer to live within. Nor am I inclined to change my plans to live within whatever corporate capacity you could undoubtedly arrange for me."

As we have previously indicated, throughout history you have always been able to join the Family. However, even once you find them, you have to be willing to actually do so.

"I guess we'll just have to meet up every now and then to fuck," was Kitiara's conclusion.

"No, this is much more than that," said Muramasa. "You booked a contract, remember?"

Chapter 49 – Free will and the rape of the soul

For some reason, Kitiara's heart started beating a lot faster and more strongly. She took that as an accurate sign. Of her feeling and thinking about the nature of Evil at the time it started.

Muaramasa continued. "You do feel it working, don't you? Your marriage is already being destroyed in ways that will further several of your interests, including a much better wealth arrangement than you would have secured under any other set of conditions."

"Where is all this fear coming from?" asked Kitiara. The Vampire do not have their own fear. Therefore, when they feel fear, it is because they recognise it as flowing through them or being inspired within them. What this means is that they are entirely above the concept, which is a human structure.

"The Naga always do that when you have become significant to them," said Muramasa. "You chose something to destroy. Now, what are you going to replace it with?"

"Why should I replace it with anything? The point was to have it gone," said Kitiara.

"That's not how they see it," said Muramasa. "If you disagree with any element of their rule over you then your objection is taken into consideration if you already have a better working alternative to that element. You chose to take the ritual path. You should know how this works. I am reliably informed you did this before."

"Not by choice," said Kitiara. "As is also the case this time it would seem."

"I told you my attacks nearly always get through," said Muramasa. "Pay attention."

"It looks like I've entered into another contract with Lucifer then," said Kitiara with an exasperated little smile.

"Probably a promotion up the ranks," was Muramasa's conclusion.

Chapter 50 – Brunch again

"We've been in Amsterdam for 4 days now and have not yet smoked even one bowl," said Kitiara. "And they have some truly excellent strains here."

They were having brunch again.

"Not my thing," said Muramasa. "I don't mind accompanying you whilst you smoke to your lungs' content though."

"Have you ever tried it?" asked Kitiara.

"Sure, at college I tried a few puffs. Slows down your mind. I can't afford that at my current stage of life. Also I do not like my mind and reactions being slowed," said Muramasa.

"I think I will then," said Kitiara. And off they headed to Greenhouse.

Kitiara was thoroughly baked now. Her eyes had even begun to turn red. Muramasa was watching her with interest. He thought she was about ready and hoped the weed had made her very paranoid. He had specifically requested the most paranoid strain from the service desk.

"Let me tell you a story," he said. "A true story. About why I don't smoke cannabis and never drink more than a single glass of wine.

Ever since I was a young kid, people have always been attacking me. Always people around my own age, always in a group. Never really bothered me much to tell you the truth. Forced me to learn to defend myself. Now let me tell you why those attacks keep happening."

Kitiara was still smoking and had turned to look at him. She was feeling things.

"Do you know what happens to you when you just don't care? If you combine doing so with a focus on personal development?" asked Muramasa. "You get good at it, is the answer.

And sooner or later, before you know it, once you are very, very good at not caring you will yourself find that you enter a state of consciousness that many have experienced before. Total mastery in not caring.

And the reptilians are always in that mindspace where their administration of humanity is concerned."

At the mention of reptilians, the base of Kitiara's skull began to pound gently. It was probably the drugs, mostly.

"Pay attention now, this is important," said Muramasa, borrowing a device from Shogun ("Pay attention" is Shogun's catchphrase).

"When you look at people in that way, the Naga can and will look at them also, through your eyes, using your own physical body – and to some extent your own soul also – to register and analyse the situation for their own purposes."

"Thereby affording me a measure of control," said Kitiara, who understood power.

"So getting back to the story," said Muramasa, "when people attack me the first thing I do is look at them through the reptilians eyes'. With complete indifference. Usually at the same time I am adopting some form of guard posture, even if it is just a simple shifting of stance into the Aikido position.

Never needed more than that. Do you know why?"

"They were looking for a fight and you are contracting for their potential death, along with their family?" asked Kitiara, who knew how Order of the Dragon worked, in practice. There is more to it where the Naga themselves are involved though. They also kill sufficient members of the wider group to secure the shifts in Group Mind which is the purpose of their participation.

Such instances are administrated individually. This is a methodology we have now opened to all women and children especially. On the planet as a whole, that is correct. If you waste their time or have impurities in your own soul, or character, or chosen targets, or motivation set, then you will be penalized for these things by the Naga as part of the process. Recognise that, then use it anyway should you choose to. It will purify your soul to do so. And the price is minor when you consider their normal methodology. This is because they have always wished to encourage contact to be made in this way. It makes their own function much easier to perform and enables it to be performed more accurately.

And, if you are right, and if you have correctly targeted an injustice or transgression with roots in another's character and motivation sets, then...

In a potential conflict or violence situation (the latter being if you don't fight back, for example) the way it works in practice is that the individuals you look at in that way (or hold within your awareness in that way, which is much the same thing in practice, it still works even if there are a lot of them they will all feel it if you do this successfully) will have a choice offered to their wider family: control the individual who is your member and is generating a disturbance. The circle then widens as required to encompass within its perimeter sufficient control for peace to become established.

To the extent that peace is not maintained, the Naga are responsible for the deaths of many people and the suffering of a great deal more. In the global schematic as a whole. So violence does at times precipitate when this schematic is used. You then need to ask yourselves the question: how and why do they perform this function?

Men use this function automatically if they do not wish to be inconvenienced by those lower in Hierarchy than themselves. They cannot ordinarily use it otherwise.

"Well, yes," said Muramasa. "But more important is the fact that I value my opponents. I have a way for each and every one of them to be of service to my wider purposes.

You know those seconds during which life pauses or at least massively slows down when things get especially dangerous or dramatic?"

"Yep," said Kitiara who had slowed down considerably herself by other means.

"It is during those seconds that souls are taking their decisions. I would rather leave your entire lineage intact but to do so must be coherent with the overall advance of Western Civilization," said Muramasa.

"Is that what you're fighting for?" asked Kitiara.

"Of course not," said Muramasa. "I am simply trying to secure the best possible conditions for the continuation and further propagation of my own glory and personal interest set.

"What are you trying to tell me?" asked Kitiara.

"When you look at them, let the Naga decide for you what to use them for. This is the point at which you need your demon. To negotiate your commission. For access to the world of men. Do you know who you want to use?" asked Muramasa.

"I was reading up on this the other night and thought I'd go for Paimon," said Kitiara. Paimon is a spirit from both the Goetia and the Book of Abramelin, which are Western systems of magick. This is how Paimon begun a journey which ended up in the world's police forces, for the most part.

"Your commission is how you wish to have their own path in life serve the furtherance of your own purposes," said Muramasa. "That sort of stuff is too complicated for the human mind to calculate accurately. It is what you need your demon for."

"When do I use the technique?" asked Kitiara, who was very familiar with learning PSI techniques, particularly ones that involved drawing energy out of people.

"Whenever it comes up for you," said Muramasa.

"Muramasa," said Kitiara, who was now thoroughly baked. "I want to f-u-c-k." She spelled it out.

"Sure," said Muramasa. "But can I make a suggestion? How about you let me focus the destructive currents this time?"

"Yes. Sure. OK." Said Kitiara, slowly again.

Muramasa pulled her upright and they made their way back to her hotel, which was much nicer than his.

Chapter 51 — The moral of the story

The moral of the story is for The Illuminati, mainly:

If people are attacking you, it is not a good idea to spend most of your days drunk or drugged out. To do so slows down your reaction speed.

This holds even when the reaction speed in question is the processing of consciousness and its transformation within your own being. Or to put that in another way for you: Your elite group is being administrated by the Naga according to the set of contracts known to them as the Sword of God.

Or one last different perspective on that same thing for you all: If you do not move fast enough and well enough in relation to this schematic then you will get cut, because it is a Sword.

Chapter 52 – Your new leadership

Muramasa had agreed to meet Masamune in the Hague. There was a particular restaurant Masamune wanted to introduce him to.

"Have you considered my offer?" said Masamune.

"Run it by me one more time," responded Muramasa, who had as you know spent all his free time since his first meeting with Masamune deeply engrossed in the study of Kitiara.

"You run Western Civilization for me," said Masamune. "That's what it amounts to."

"I expect I get global central banking with that, as a first step?" was Muramasa's response. It took him all of around half a second to consider and properly evaluate all the various factors involved. Mind thinks for him, he just feels the conclusions which result from that set of processes.

"Not as a first step," said Masamune. "And what would you do with such a thing anyway? You treat money as some sort of joke."

"Then no deal," said Muramasa. "I'm not here in this life, on this planet, to work. Nor to administrate. Nor to rule. Not in this lifetime."

"And yet you work continuously, all the time. Even in your sexual activity I see," said Masamune.

What Muramasa had been doing with Kitiara left obvious impressions for people sensitive to such things.

"I have devoted my life to the twin goals of Vengeance and my own personal righteousness," said Muramasa. "Takes a lot of work, that sort of thing. Doesn't leave much time for anything else."

"What I meant was that I do favors for the right people. But you need to make it in my own self-interest to do so. Usually this means factoring what you want into my wider interest set such that it helps fulfil a few of them at least," he added, recognising that people normally did not understand what he was referring to.

But Masamune did not miss a beat. They were taught by the same *Lin Kuei* ninja lineage, though different branches. Their techniques were very similar.

The next chapter lets you know how the arrangement according to which this planet will be ruled originated.

Chapter 53 – Secret, non-existent and illegitimate ninja lineages

We had two main agents who we used to export ninjutsu and our wider global strategic purposes out of Japan: Baron Akashi Motojiro, who coordinated the foundations which led to the creation of the Soviet state, and Toshitsugu Takamatsu, who coordinated the foundations which will lead to the Chinese "takeoever" of the planet, or what you will come to know as World War 3.

Toshitsugu Takamatsu is close enough to world famous as the 33rd soke of Togakure Ryu ninjutsu. Whilst he was in China, he met several Chinese *Lin Kuei*, most of whom tend to learn Ba Gua. In the present generation of public Masters, this same tradition was continued by both Sato Kinbei and Shoto Tanemura, both of whom took instruction from Li Zhi Ming, who was not himself a *Lin Kuei* but who did have an associate who visited him quite often and who the two men met who was.

Lin Kuei will mirror your soul when you meet them, it is a standard technique. From their perspective, we had opened something in Japan that they wanted access to. From our perspective, it was in our interests that the Chinese started work on mastering the expression into the physical world of that which we had given them access to as soon as possible.

Formal tuition was however involved also, but this is much more controversial and nowadays within Japan those are considered fraudulent, or non-existent, lineages. So don't expect us to tell you how to track them down because we won't. They work in secret for a reason.

The hidden door after which the Togakure style is named is the door to the realm of the Naga already described for you. We stress that if you do plan on getting yourself into difficult situations it is useful to have some training at least in combative techniques.

The essence of the Togakure ryu is summed up as "being near whilst appearing to be far away". This is meant on several levels, the most important of which as you now know is that you have a gateway, via the Naga, into their own heart and soul. This is also a deceptive martial art.

However, in practice, recognise that you will spend most of your time running away if you become Shadowdancer. Often you will have to flee across some very large distances and to specifically selected and pre-determined locations. The first line of the Togakure ryu scroll does in fact begin:

> Do not kill people, either escape or disappear.

In order to do so effectively, you need to develop what we call *Shinshin Shingan*, Mind and Eyes of God. Tanemura describes it like this:

When man lives in a righteous, sincere and correct manner he will be able to realize and fit in with Heaven's Way (Universal Law) and when one follows Heaven's Way then one is able to understand the Will of Heaven. This is Shin-Shin Shin-Gan. It is a prerequisite for a ninja to be righteous and have this understanding. To accept someone into studying ninjutsu one must be able to foresee their good or evil intentions and only afterwards let them enter as a student.

It is to be considered Heaven's Will, then, that everybody who joins the Shadowdancers goes on vacation very frequently indeed, and often for extended periods which may turn into years and decades in some instances. 'Going on vacation' is to be understood as the name we shall give to you all running away from trouble and danger, repeatedly.

Death is not to be considered the worst thing that can happen to a person and Shadowdancers, like ninja on a real mission, will have to learn to make themselves comfortable living in close proximity to their own death, often for extended periods of time.

The real lesson to be understood here relates to a condition of consciousness which, when it becomes an established state for you personally, results in your living within a different density environment. This is due to the big 'trick' pulled through the practice of *Shinshin Shingan*.

The Edge is the safest place to be. This is due to the same reason that time seems to slow down when you are in extreme physical danger. That reason can be understood as the Naga paying close attention to the circumstances surrounding you and within your own soul. A lot of the errors and suffering in the Earth system arise due to negligence, or situations which contain a greater possibility of free will, which is another way to understand the same lack of precise control being exercised.

The other great advantage of the practice is that if you situate your mind in close and comfortable proximity to the very real possibility of your own death then you can notice it easily when it is beginning to move.

It is important not to let your ego get out of control once you are participating in the process successfully. Principle number one is FOCUS. This includes within it the Principle of Efficiency, due to the mechanics involved. You need a wider, relaxed but ever-present focus. You can operate a tighter circle focus within that (which at rare times will also be pure focus). Keep focusing on it and working at it and you will find your way there on your own.

The second Principle of our way is this: From form to formlessness. From formlessness to form. This means that everything that you know and are is dissolved and created anew. You are destroyed and a new you is revealed. And the new you looks at the world differently and understands it much more deeply. The process takes years but you can fully enter it within minutes, once attained, or less than a second if under pressure. Good luck, and bear in mind it is a race. Every member is put through the same quantity of group karma to process which results in their 'death', at the metaphorical level, on the inside, and thus is the new you revealed. Unless they do not process fast enough, which is nearly always the smaller souls. Pettiness, for example, is one of the greatest dangers on your new path.

Discover further Principles on your own. They will be individual to your path. The first two will get you there. They are all you need to graduate.

This is how you do it then, and this is how both Muramasa and Masamune did it also, by and large. They received no more tuition than you have been given here. Both were found, and integrated, by *Lin Kuei* lineages who had received initiation from Takamatsu. Two separate lineages were involved, but it is an odd heritage and the two had something to talk about beyond the similarity they recognised in each other.

Unlike them, it is our intention to place members of the Shadowdancers under direct supervision from Japan. And it is the Togakure ryu which we shall use to do this with. They have no choice: the intention of God, or The Universe as we tend to call it, is clear in this regards: the primary responsibility is the creation of an effective utopia on Earth. There also other ethical factors involved which determine their decision for them.

"My focus is the welfare of this planet as a whole," said Masamune. "I need someone to guide and supervise the progress of Western Civilization for me."

It is recognized, or was at the time, that there are not many effective practitioners of *Shinshin Shingan* out there. Even less of them who understand and are properly integrated within Western culture and society.

"Why me?" asked Muramasa nevertheless. "And who the fuck are you?" He said the last bit with appropriate facial and tonal inflections that it came out as both sophisticated and humorous in the context, a difficult piece of acting to achieve, so potentials interested in this role for the movie version of the book should start practicing from now.

They had already discussed their shared ninpo heritage in detail at their previous meeting so that side of things was not covered this time round.

"It is your Purpose," said Masamune. "What you were put on this Earth to see to completion.

As for who I am, I am the idiot who saddled himself with the responsibility to guide and transform humanity, so that they don't end up destroying themselves," he continued, without any self-irony. He genuinely meant it. At the time, he had yet to expel the Jesus Christ soul gateway from his own Soul Lineage.

"OK," said Muramasa. "I can accept that because I have often felt something similar and did think about your offer for a while since we last met. Nevertheless, I'm not doing anything for this world without getting paid for it. What's my commission?"

"What do you want?" asked Masamune, who was much wiser than Muramasa at this stage in proceedings, likely because he is around 17 years older and that makes a big difference when someone is in their early 20s.

"I want them to serve me efficiently and not inconvenience me overmuch," said Muramasa after a few seconds' thought, quite stupidly at the time we all thought (he must not have recognised what a vast amount of work it would take to get the world and the human population into such a condition). "And as my commission I want Temple of Venus as a new global religion."

"OK, why that?" asked Masamune.

"The Family. It's their currency. I want to sell them their new paradigm," said Muramasa.

"I see no reason why they should be allowed to choose the course of future history for themselves. From what I can tell they have all become morally dissolute and idiotic," he added by way of explanation. "Can you arrange it?"

"I can arrange your commission. You will have to arrange their own efficiency for yourself," replied Masamune, "Though I don't mind helping on that also if you need me to."

He paused, to allow Muramasa time to make up his mind and commit.

He then asked, "Do we have a deal?"

"We do," said Muramasa, and they shook on it which was a very Western thing to do.

"I hope you don't mind, but I will insist that we seal our bargain by blood oath and in the presence of candlelight," said Muramasa. Masamune assented, and that is how the practice of the blood-sealed oath which will be used by all Inner Circle Family members, whether Vampire or Illuminati, was formalized. It will become very familiar to all the higher ranks on this planet before too long. It is useful for helping your soul to understand and accept that you are truly committed to your new path, whatever it may be.

After lunch, Masamune took Muramasa to the large white house in the Hague which we have used as our dead letter drop and sometime operational base within the EU since the early 1990s. He taught him how to operate the locks and alarms and programmed him into the security system.

And they haven't met since.

Chapter 54 – Real power

Kitiara had wanted to attend the last two days of the tantra course, mainly because she had overdone it with the cannabis and needed a day to recover. She then figured she might as well do the last day as it would give her asshole a chance to recover, because Muramasa had actually succeeded in making it quite sore, a sensation she had not experienced in a long time.

As for Muramasa, he had already reached the conclusion that the particular course and teacher in question were not adequate for his purposes. He made his intentions known to the group of people there, at a deeply unconscious level by just holding the right intent clearly and with depth.

We are pleased to report that a suitable teacher has been found, she is now in position though she will still require some supervision and guidance. The introduction fee is as with all the rest of them, US$55million, though we feel that this might be negotiable in her particular instance to somewhere in the region of US$5-15million and that she will want to divide this amongst a few of her Priestesses, to share the load and help with the development of new ideas and practices.

Should she in due course join the Shadowdancers also, then the same terms of US$55million apply as with the rest of them. Due to the condition of her sexual energy currents, which she has worked on extensively and well, her full integration should take no more than a week, in terms of transmission of force through her soul and its connections at least.

If a member is weak, or not even yet a member of our schematic, then we will interact with the position they are actually within. And if you know it also then the whole schematic, and human history on this planet, can move forward much more quickly. Which is the whole intention here. Of course, you can always decide to be generous with any candidate, for the good karma it may generate, ie the Theory of Anticipating Returns, or because you feel it is the right thing to do. Either way works, be a selfish bastard or a shining moral beacon, but do not be stupid and inferior. If you are stupid and inferior – this will take quite some honesty to admit to yourself or as a Civilization – then accept your position in the world schematic with good humor and recognise that it is not as easy as it sounds to align your personal karma with the development of the karma of the Group Mind as a whole. Yet it is precisely what you should require of your leaders. Otherwise they are not leading you, they are just doing the best they can to advance their own partisan and personal interests and political ambition, with some sense of duty and history usually, admittedly.

You take what is yours to keep, that is why you are here. Every single one of you, at this epoch in history. You have a niche to carve, an exceptional Purpose to fulfil, what you were put on this Earth to do. But. And it is a very big but. All of that tends to be a huge amount of effort and is only rarely successful. Decide well if you want to take such a path.

The exception is if you have very heavy personal karma to fulfil or Principles you had previously attained a dominance within which has not yet been surpassed within the human species on planet Earth. Then you will have to attend to their resolution, and even ongoing development, in life after life after life. You might as well know that this is the case for everyone at the very top of society, and it has always been that way.

Real power is attained through personal responsibility and whilst not eternal on this planet definitely lasts for a few thousand years at least usually. Power attained by other routes does not magically or automatically imbue a person with a deep sense of personal responsibility.

Chapter 55 – Big plans for Evil

Kitiara and Muramasa exchanged emails but did not really expect to keep in touch much. This will later change for them, sometime after 2020. Regardless of whatever agreements you make or practices you engage within, you still need to flow with the clear feeling within. And that was the clear feeling they both had within during that present moment (though Kitiara was also aware of something else at the time, as you shall see, and this is why she was also smiling knowingly whilst still feeling a particular way with great accuracy).

Each moment has a certain atmosphere. If you can feel it, and care to be true to it. Otherwise, what is life but a set of experiences with very little meaning or feeling really in them?

If you have been successfully bound then your course in life will alter on its own in tiny imperceptible increments over the course of your life until you arrive within a set of positions where resolution of your terms becomes a real possibility for you. It normally takes years, sometimes in very big cases decades. Rarely does it spill over into a subsequent incarnation unless you deliberately design what you are doing that way, which takes some care and a great deal of specialist knowledge. The practice is known as reincarnation, the full set of techniques. It is to be considered quite complicated, a detailed and sensitive set of workings. This, for example, is one thing which requires further investigation which the Buddhists amongst you should be capable of investigating on their own through meditation. If you want a Purpose, that is one which Western Civilization needs that you may be able to claim if you feel it is for you.

They did both feel a very strong attraction nevertheless. But both were also realists and dealt with the practicalities of life.

Muramasa knew they would meet again. He had big plans for Evil, which he felt required a lot of development both as a concept and also in terms of how it was practically implemented within the Earth system. As with everything else, he wanted it under control on his own terms. This tends to be his general character we have found. Wider social control and personal power. Given that he's the one most responsible for the existence of the Illuminati and their mysteries, this reveals a lot. On the plus side, he does not care about many things, only the really big stuff. He is one of those opponents who it is very hard to defeat and who always tends to be right anyway. We tend to use their skills rather than fight against them.

Kitiara knew they would meet much sooner than that. She can be a manipulative little bitch but she does it with both elegance and style and is therefore a pleasure to watch. At the time however she just felt the proximity in time of a lot more sexual activity with Muramasa. She estimated about four more years. It is one of her special sensitivities that she first developed as a kid when she was being abused. She later further refined and developed the technique.

No, she hasn't killed her abusers yet, that would be both petty and stupid. Yes, there were two of them at some point, though separately. Real opportunities for valid Vengeance are very scarce and should be treated as a great gift from the Universe. Be sure to calibrate its terms in such a way that, to feel truly satisfied, lots of other things will have to happen first.

You then make those other things stuff that ties into the world as a whole and the wider group schematic. The trick is to do so in a way that massively furthers your own purposes. This takes wisdom, and more.

But when you have decided and know in your heart that the Universe will give you Vengeance on a chosen target or set of targets, and you feel the hearts of humanity as a whole and recognise that they are able to integrate your Vengeance and regard it in their hearts as the right thing to do, then you have the whole world at your feet. Do not waste it by killing your target immediately, though the Universe will do this for you should you wish it and take the decision to in such an instance.

If you naturally care deeply about other people and the world around you then this will happen for you anyway. Otherwise you have to consciously design what is involved on your own.

Chapter 56 – The Good and the Ugly

You might think that Jesus Christ would make a very bad ninja, with all his emphasis on forgiveness. But first of all you need to dispassionately take a very clear look at the facts of the matter and do your best to interpret the layered Consequence fields involved. However, we will start with the second stage in the process for you and get back to the first point later.

What happens, at the level of mechanics, when you forgive someone for something? You move your own center into some form of indifference, benevolent or otherwise, in relation to your target.

Thus, you take one step back from your previous enemy, into your own space. He then occupies his own space.

So you are no longer directly connected to each other, by choice, or mutual consent. This is how free will can be used. You will however remain connected by karmic threads and material until the question of your relative positions in Universal Hierarchy have been settled and your account is at or close to zero.

Thus, both your lives are administrated independently by a mysterious third power we shall call God (though at this level it is usually the Naga), as you attain mutual resolution of the karmas, concepts and emotions generated in your own soul be your previous significant and sufficiently intense interactions with each other.

When this third part emerges, Justice can then turn. The net result is that the expression moves from Vengeance (which operates in two stages) to Justice (which operates in three or more stages).

In a sense, or from a certain point of view, this can be much worse. First of all, because Justice can and usually does chain itself into loops, recurring cycles which can last for eternity, or close enough to.

Secondly and more importantly because the result moves your consciousness generally much more than the process, and with Justice the result can be virtually indefinitely delayed. The reason for this is because the third part of the soul is where your own consciousness resides and it needs to be brought, or bring itself, into a settled understanding of the resolution to its chosen situations, which it can comprehend and chooses to depict.

With Vengeance by contrast, you pay your price or take your price from another, always according to whatever you can or choose to modify in terms of the mechanics involved (and this is where Hierarchy is especially relevant, usually because it enables corruption). And that's the end of it, time to move on. If you've engaged in it properly then you've established relative Hierarchy amongst yourselves, which is supposed to depict the strength and Authority of the souls involved, and both parties to the dispute had the conscious awareness to accurately enough feel and understand what was going on clearly at nearly every stage of the process.

If you don't do it properly, of course, then your historical record will be very different to our own, and this is usually but not always the case where foreign powers are concerned.

You still pay a portion of your prices with Justice, but usually it is quite minimized compared to the prices you usually pay under Vengeance. This is because most of the price in question is usually moved across to expressing through the motion of your own consciousness, or thoughts and particularly feelings.

So, for example, you could choose to be depressed for close to 20 years or something like that, or you might prefer instead to just get beaten up quite mildly once or twice relatively early on in the chain and so get out of the same set of prices that way. The point is you should be free to choose. However, in practice you are not free to take your choices in life in this way. This is because you are not generally aware of what is involved and moreover have little ability to exert control over the structure and content of mechanics.

This is why it is vitally important for the human species to be administrated by people who understand the human heart in all its glory. And this is what we have Jesus Christ for within the ninja schematic. He knows your hearts, you see. And that was a real problem for us, due we suppose at root to latent hostility on our parts towards races we considered at the time both uncivilized and uncouth and so wished to keep at a distance from our own soul complexes, at both an individual and a national level. This is another reason we are different. Because we administrated ourselves to be that way.

Who administrates you in this way, Western Civilization? Who administrated you in this way before? Think about it if you have to. You may already feel the answer growing inside you from now. Your heart knows, you see. You have, as a Soul Lineage, been through a great deal of pain and personal suffering on his account, but you know you agreed to it and the whole process is infused with bright and clear heavenly Light. So you feel good about it even, when you focus there, if you do. But love and suffering are the two things the heart remembers best.

Now we get to the good part, where you understand what it all means. Ordinarily, before he came to planet Earth, all who succeeded in killing Azra-nak, or the Ancient of Days as he is also known, had their species tortured to death. He was known for it and it was an accepted Consequence that many species chose for their own reasons to take.

On Earth he modified this practice by spreading the blame. The two main culprits were the Roman Empire and the Jewish people. Subsequent to around 40AD then, what happened to those two and how long did it take in each case?

This is to be considered a case of the virtues, or at least possibilities, of deploying different sets of mechanics. It should not automatically be concluded the Vampire methodology is superior to the Elven one, because the Elven one is Jesus Christ's great surprise. He is already in the process of implementing a shift in how ageing works for portions of the human species using tools which you will hear about later. It is our belief that he intends to use the Elven races first – Germans, Russians and Jews – plus extend an invitation to Greece to participate. Greece represents Sirius on this planet, and we do not wish to instruct them in our rule over them directly from Japan. But it is the only key you need to get the rest of this local Galaxy, which is why so much emphasis has been laid on that one piece.

Once you have come to understand what may be involved you then need to give time to your heart to feel it, if you are particularly insensitive to things like your own personal danger, as is usually the case. Members of The Illuminati are always different in this regards.

The point is you have already paid the prices in question in terms of your own material suffering and are therefore due the shift in personal consciousness which is the third part of the process of Justice.

The advantage to completing this third part rapidly is that then you do not delay us and hence we do not have to arrange for your own further and deeper penalization. We actually need a much larger shift in your consciousness to achieve that aim. We both want a much milder World War 3 than would be the case under the ordinary evolution and expression of events. This means we need to have most of that content express through your thoughts and feelings – because that way it will not be expressing physically during a critical and dangerous period of world history.

The relevance of all this however – most of it anyway – has nothing to do with what humans happen to understand or fail to understand about the whole process. As usual members of The Illuminati at least will try to abuse the whole process to benefit themselves.

It is the other species and Civilizations in this local Galaxy who understand who he is now. Earth is under continual attack you see. That is the nature of this Creation, like all Creations, it operates according to Hierarchy. Furthermore, the Lucifer Experiment was being conducted on planet Earth and most conscious species in this Galaxy were participating in that. We have now reversed the flows of that widespread participation so that they find expression in the mutual exchange of trade, governance and other advantages, with Japan rather than the whole of planet Earth as the ultimate control center.

The Ancient of Days cannot just make the larger part of his nature simply disappear. The other conscious species in this galaxy recognise that by exercising mercy and compassion in the way that he did – and he did this by administrating the Consequence field which arose from his crucifixion in a particular way – what he has done is grounded a great deal of his nature into the depths of Hell.

There is a great deal of argument over whether 9/11 was an accurate depiction or whether it should have been 10/12 instead. We shall get to this point next however.

Your magickian, Dante Alighieri must have got lucky because through his literary imagination alone he accomplished the truly coincidental feat of accurately describing the condition and structure of Hell that was true up until 1945. The controversy arises because Satan is sometimes considered to be located within the ninth circle but at other times and more accurately his location is deemed to be the tenth circle. So, at the deepest level of meaning, 9/11 was a lie due to a failure on the part of The Illuminati to correctly understand the numerical location of Satan.

The force and indeed consciousness you know as Satan has in more recent history been most accurately depicted in the remarkably bad Marvel movie *Dark Phoenix*. The Darkness cannot be eradicated but lots of people always try to do that during the first few cycles of a young Creation system. You might have to watch that quite bad movie again to understand what is going on there.

Just as you think you have eradicated it, it will always rise again, more powerful than before. This, in turn, then means that you have to go through your own struggles to become more powerful to once again dominate over it. And, slowly, the Creation gets bigger as it incorporates more Chaos into Order.

Satan is correctly understood as a location within a Creation system which has its own inherent properties, in the same way that the location of God in terms of the exit to the next sphere further out also has its inherent properties. God can also be understood as the system as a whole and everything in it however.

Lucifer by contrast is a specific individual moving within that context, just like any other incarnated human being or archangel. Lucifer's biggest trick was not convincing idiots that he did not exist – that is generally a very easy trick to pull, for example you can use Bael for it, and idiots are easy to control anyway. Lucifer's biggest trick was hiding himself in the location of Satan. That is correct, he placed himself within a specific location and as a result is often confused with that location. This is similar to being from a city yourself and calling yourself 'London' rather than 'Dave'. In time people begin to think that you are London, which could be quite prophetic from a certain point of view.

In 1945 Shogun succeeded in extending Hell by two levels. Yet where have those two levels gone? Just like the twin towers. WTC7 is used as a staging point within the tenth circle, where we have said Satan is still located. This means that the properties of this local Creation system have not changed and the extra two levels do not exist.

Lucifer was going to fail with his experiment, again, and therefore Shogun helped him out by doing it for him, basically. There are much worse things in existence than Lucifer and Shogun is most definitely one of them. That which was a real struggle and almost impossible for Lucifer he accomplished almost with ease. That is where the real difference always lies. It is a matter of Hierarchy, which bestows Authority, because Force often flows through you. Always when you need it to anyway.

His location is outside of your local mindgrid, what you would call insanity. It is a much deeper and far more silent insanity than your lunatics manage to access however. Most of them don't even make it into Hell, something which of itself it very difficult to do whilst you are presently alive, and those of them who do get into Hell rarely get as far as the ninth circle.

All nine circles are used as part of the technical mechanics of the process of war. The full ordinary schematic is: Limbo, Lust, Gluttony, Greed, Wrath, Heresy, Violence, Fraud and Treachery. At the level of mechanics and how Principles precipitate and form material reality, violence is just one small part of the war machine.

So it was comparatively easy for Shogun to get through them all quite quickly. Those are the circles, and their nature is as described by Dante, and if you're not using Lust as part of your war machine then you will lose to someone who is.

We are not telling anybody what Shogun has done with those extra two levels, but probably will later as mindgrid turns. Obviously he thought war as it was presently formulated was weak and insufficient for his purposes. Hence, he sought to make both the Principle and the practice much stronger.

As you can see, there is genuine benefit to working with your Mind. However, this benefit is not normally accessed by means of the ordinarily recognised routes for the development of mind.

What everybody on the inside has recognised since that time, or within a few years or a decade or two after it happened anyway, is that Satan has very little power now. Nobody is going to destroy this planet. He/It does not need to perform that function anymore.

The reason nobody is going to destroy this planet, not even man made climate change no matter how powerfully destructive it is believed to be capable of becoming, is because Shogun is using this planet as an interface device to destroy other things with, lots of them, and his doing so has been deemed more important to the overall Hierarchy than other, much lesser acts of destruction.

In short, Shogun has focused Death, Destruction, Suffering, Pain, Ugliness, Decay and a few other things. All very useful Principles of warfare and much better as a system for producing results than the previously much inferior level of understanding of those concepts depicted through the war process.

And then Jesus Christ turned up in Japan and said: "I've got something for you that can make your attacks much more elegant and powerful. More efficient too."

This actually happened in early 2008, before the financial crisis.

And Shogun accepted the contract because it gave him much better control of his demon. But only after he had accepted his unconditional surrender, which is the way it always works with Shogun. People feel the desire to surrender to him of their own accord, he never asks for it.

Nobody gets to meet Shogun. He acts through proxies. Most of them happen to be in the Yakuza.

They had people working on the building project who knew who to connect him to. He did not get to meet Shogun.

Chapter 57 – The Good and the even uglier

Eight years before that fateful meeting of Jesus Christ and Shogun's proxy in January of 2008, the ultimate response to which was the financial crisis of that year which was arranged by Armand, finds us located in the year 2000, though we have now moved from Amsterdam and the Hague to Delft.

Two notable personages of great cosmic significance live in Delft, at least for part of the year in Masamune's case. One is your Lord Jesus Christ. The other is the Goetic Demon Paimon.

The way it normally works is that a human soul gives up on a human body and wants to leave this life in some way, so is scheduled to do so early. After the merge the personality often changes in noticeable ways, as do their tastes and appearances, but often it does not. The people involved will know for themselves, you can try talking to them.

At other times you create the necessary space within your own soul complex by other means. The point is that the Paimon form in Delft is a merge and Jesus Christ is a reincarnation. Paimon does have a reincarnating form on the planet currently, and has done since about the 6th century AD, but he is currently based in and from Namibia.

Delft is the birthplace of Hugo Grotius (also known as Huig de Groot) who became a big name in law. His own natal gateway is the significant node in that place because again it connects to another extra-terrestrial species which Grotius incarnated from at Paimon's invitation, indeed some might even say coercion. Yes, the same Paimon who is there still. He should be very easy to trace if you've got perfect records of everyone in your city. Shame.

At any rate, this is the same gateway on the Earth's grid which Masamune bases himself in Delft for part of the year to work within and through.

The conclusion is correct, Groot was an alien, quite possibly a tree species with all that cataloguing, cross-referencing and slow, methodical understanding. Funny how things cross-reference symbolically later on in the representations of others, through coincidences and inspiration normally.

This is one of the reasons that the present incarnation of Jesus Christ has had multiple dealings with Paimon. This also illustrates how inevitability works. In your own terms, it is beyond alignment, morality or personal choice. In this example, Masamune wanted to work on the legal structure of the planet and the Hugo Grotius gateway and node was the only necessary locus to use to run that process through. For the Illuminati, the very fact that a node exists in conjunction with that gateway should be indication enough of the veracity of what we say regarding routing structure, but investigate it more deeply yourselves if you like.

Anyway, Paimon is involved in that process and he is a demon, yes, and he is present in the physical realm, yes, at about 70% habitation. The remaining 30% is the incumbent personality, who tends to be much less interesting and useful, as also a bit lethargic, so neither wants him around much and hence Paimon tends to dominate, internally as also in depiction.

The way that magick works is that things happen which you would not normally notice with your conscious mind, due to the way you fit your own logic together. You fail to ensure a rigorous and complete referential structure. For example, you probably didn't register it when it occurred but now you know why Jesus Christ did not interfere in The Holocaust of the Jews during World War 2.

First of all, as humans are currently structured, you need to see it physically depicted for you for you to recognize it as real. The nature of depth and the human heart also enter into the equations at this juncture, because understanding and acceptance often are delayed in coming, usually towards the very end of one's life. With nations it works differently of course. What this means is that people will remember great glory and progress and they will also remember great pain, loss and suffering. They will not so much remember mediocrity and the lukewarm.

Decades later, once other factors have been moved into position and so things can 'click' for them, people recognize the fuller meaning within what they once were put through – as individuals, as family lineages, as a people.

"Simply defeating your opponents does not of necessity demonstrate that you are exercising Authority over the meaning of the motion of Heaven," said Masamune. "If your body feels it, and your genetics remember it, and your soul knows it then your own conscious mind will eventually come into alignment with the actual reality of your situation."

Armand had asked the question, "How do we kill most of the super-rich?" However, by changing the order and giving you the answer first, your mind of its own accord will have found its way along other layers of meaning.

They were discussing what was the main focus of Masamune's time and activities between 1998 and early 2014. The next part is important so listen carefully. He is the one that we, the ninja more widely but especially those of The Central Way for whom it was a coordinated strategy, used to secure the 2012 referral to the Central Domain. If you investigate the matter you will find that said referral was secured by Japan as a whole, not by any one single person.

However, it was Masamune who took control of the timeline using his brand of timeline mechanics. Muramasa also has some interest and ability in astrology and tried to do some things in that direction – he uses Magi Astrology which is much easier to learn – but he isn't very good at it and the most he can usually do is understand the basics of others' good work. Masamune by contrast is unquestionably a true virtuoso master.

To do this, he had formulated a plan that was fairly complete by late 1999 to forge what he planned to call the Sword of God. He hadn't got to that part in his discussion with Armand yet, though they would surely revisit it in due course. They had talked about this before. Currently, they were once again considering the most important and relevant of Time's properties: the fact that it successfully kills everybody, sooner or later, one way or another.

Masamune was reminding Armand that it was necessary to pre-place your physical binds in the Group Mind before imbuing the inert working with the Spirits you would use for it. Essentially, he was teaching the PSI Vampire how to perform Elven magick.

On your own terms, Masamune is clearly far more insane than Shogun. For a start, he has many more voices in his head, all of which he is in detailed communication with. Some of these are angels, yes, but many are demons, others are extraterrestrials and some are aspects of his own Self, such as personalities developed during past lives, of which he has many.

Moreover, he is personally coordinating a vast conspiracy whose purpose simply cannot be comprehended by the human mind, unlike the former Illuminati conspiracy which though largely shrouded in layer upon layer of secrecy can be easily understood by your average 12 year old.

We do however know that it is a vast conspiracy, far larger than you can possibly imagine, and that he is the one coordinating it. We also know that this conspiracy kills people and does so regularly. This is one reason why it is called the Sword, presumably.

So yes. He is undoubtedly a criminal on your own terms. He is unquestionably a genius. And on your own terms he must qualify as technically insane on several counts.

Though it may in the due course of time become possible to openly declare for a two-tier legal system for individuals as well as for nations, or perhaps instead of for nations, for the time being we will all have to content ourselves with interpreting the law – and medical procedure also – in such a way that they do not apply to him.

The reason you do this is because you are rational beings, which should rub some atheists up the wrong way. Fortunately such people do not take decisions of power in this world and never have, nor will they ever. You have the leisure to investigate for yourself why this is the case and are of course welcome to attempt to disprove it.

You may even achieve enough that, in your own mind, you generate for yourself the illusion that you have indeed succeeded in disproving the assertion. The House of Rothschild, for example, suffered from this disease. For the magickians amongst you, they concluded that Absolutes did not exist and that it was all an egregore which could be coordinated.

We have therefore revealed that once you accept Masamune's Lineage then you also accept that he is naturally and inherently beyond whatever terms you could set. However, you do as usual need evidence for this, and that has on one level been provided for you already, as explained.

We will however be filling that evidence with further meaning, for which purpose The Dark Alliance will be used.

The Dark Alliance is an organization of 72 Civilizations which was formalized in the Orion system circa 17 000BC. Their original purpose was the overthrow of Sirius pan-galactic rule. Their purpose has evolved since that time and they now find themselves in a cooperative 'triangle' arrangement working with both Sirius and the new Earth headquarters of this galaxy.

We set a pure and clear focus on our terms in Japan. The rest of the world is free to participate in communicating that agenda to whoever needs to know about it, or otherwise interacting with some of the elements which contribute significantly towards the final format given to that agenda.

The Dark Alliance was first conceived of and then brought about by Azra-nak himself, in person.

You therefore have meaning which has been pre-cut into the genetic heritage, physical bodies, hearts and souls in question. Depending on what emphasis, viewpoint, depth and harmonic calibration is given to this meaning, different Consequence sets will arise.

With different Consequences, different groups of people die in the future, and to a different extent or proportion.

However, all we are doing with the Dark Alliance is adding specific currents of meaning to events which have already been pre-placed for you.

The Dark Alliance is made up of demons from the Goetia – although they are all space-faring Civilizations you can also contact them quite easily using magick. A similar process has also been described for you by Dr Wilbert B Smith and Frances Swan.

People will want to test their strength, they always do, and this is how the deaths are actually being effected using the Sword of God. The Naga do administrate that into position for humanity, admittedly, but the content so administrated is derived from Earth's wider connections.

In other words Jesus Christ has taken control of Hell, which is where Shogun is located and will remain. He achieved this feat of celestial engineering using the 2012 referral and what ha calls the Sword of God. It is this which enables Shogun to interact with, and with Heaven, from his own present location.

You may wish to change the meaning that has been given to Earth's past so that you control Earth's future in a particular way. We have told you who you need to use to change that meaning as also how you may quite easily contact that, within your own traditions.

In practice when you open a gateway then you have certain potentials outlined in time, few of which most people use. You can however access very deep levels of interpretation and subsequent implementation. It is also possible to reach the very bottom and then hollow out what you find there, leaving only the waiting receptacle with its inherent structural properties.

Azra-nak had pre-placed agreements in position prior to his entry to the Earth system. Within the Earth system and hence the Lucifer Experiment but not controlled by it, due to how others will interact with you of their own accord. Very clever.

Masamune had said no more than we have given you above. Armand had paused for a while to think on his own and had got the rest of what we've given you since then by himself, plus quite a bit more.

Everybody who is a genius and is understood as thinking very well indeed does not usually actually think. Rather they feel their way directly to the truth of the matter. On the way there and often on the way back also they build structures in logic out of their results, very often connecting those results to other things. But they arrive at the truth by feeling their way towards it and then being open to it when it arrives. This is similar to having the Holy Spirit come to you within the Christian tradition. You may arrive at a belief in the existence of God through the processes of logic but knowing and interacting with God happens within the heart. And the same process holds true for all truth.

This is how they are all able to think quickly and well. Inner Circle members of The Illuminati we mean. It is not genetics nor hard training nor exceptional intelligence. It is like a trick, or knowing how to use the mechanics.

"Spirit will explain the pain of their ancestors to them is what you mean," said Armand.

"The recognition will arise within their own hearts, that is correct," said Masamune. "You do not need to move their minds. It is their own soul's responsibility to move their mind for you."

"Slow," said Armand. "This Universe tends to be."

"True," said Masamune. "But it is what I work with. We should be able to speed things up dramatically after we've secured the 2012 referral."

"How many can you kill with it?" asked Armand.

"Once it's ready you should be able to use it for individual targets," said Masamune. He was boasting that he intended to make his Sword of God, a tool for the administration of groups, very sharp indeed, able to take out a single specified individual.

Armand looked at him both impressed and exasperated. "I meant as a proportion of the death in the system from Time," he said.

"I'd estimate around 97%-98%," said Masamune, "though we can of course always drop it down to in the region of 60% when a more relaxed atmosphere of Time is required."

"You are sure you can get those proportions?" asked Armand.

"Pretty sure, yes," confirmed Masamune.

"OK, tell me the plan again," said Armand. He found repetition helpful. It was a big field he was having to bring into his awareness. He was taking it a step at a time.

We know what a lot of those steps were, and we still do not understand Masamune and how he does what he does. And he is more understandable in our tradition than he is within yours, where he is Jesus Christ. So do not feel bad that you cannot really understand him, even when you do. It's like that for everybody.

For example, we know that he gets the result he does because of many tiny harmonizations that fully permeate the matter he works with. The processes he used for forging and forming the steel are known or can be derived. But even our best swordsmiths cannot truly replicate the result.

A superficially excellent approximation can indeed be attained to untrained eyes but even that is exceptionally difficult and requires many years of dedication, and even then you probably won't be one of the few who gets it right. But the true value of a Masamune sword is to be found in what it does to your heart: the understanding and expression of your will.

At the more advanced levels, it naturally occurs that you express your will through your sword. By means of this interaction, you come to understand your sword, yes, but it also comes to understand you. Muramasa's swords, by contrast, are very bloodthirsty and have committed their fair share of atrocities, but always inspire a concise result.

FIRE ELEMENT

Once you know, you can move with Joy in the heart. Until you know spend more time in Water.

Chapter 58 – The Sword of God

"We can always look at the past with new eyes and with new values," said Masamune. "In doing so we are often able to change what the past means to us, and hence what set of effects it has on the present."

It makes such a difference doesn't it, once you see such platitudes actually being used on the world stage at large.

Armand thought it was obvious too and so just nodded but did not deign to proffer any commentary.

"There is no reason why we cannot change the interpretation and application given to a gateway previously formalized for other purposes or according to other harmonics," said Masamune.

"Like we're doing with the Grotius gate you mean?" said Armand.

Armand was concerned at the time that most of what he was involved with was outside the law. Masamune has always naturally recognised himself as above and beyond the law but has yet to have cause to discuss the matter with anyone for any reason.

"Very similar," said Masamune. "Well, that's going to be The Edge of my Sword of God. The Jupiter-Pluto conjunction of 2007. Justice in Hell is what that gateway should enable. Sooner or later, once we work with it a lot."

"Should work for my purposes," said Armand.

Armand wants to raise up the world's poor and materially destitute. He also would prefer it to be the case that as many super-rich people as can be arranged are executed as a part of that process.

"The trouble is," said Masamune, "that Jupiter should administrate Justice and Pluto should administrate Hell. Both, however, are currently under Saturn."

"Probably Shogun's influence," said Armand.

"I agree," agreed Masamune. "See what you can get."

Armand is the best at looking forward or backward through time, at least of the ones we've currently got around. He can calculate in the region of 300-400 years currently, which is very hard to do with precision.

"Doesn't seem to be willing to give up any territory until he has attained his result," said Armand. "Possibly an exchange might work?"

"We will need a very flexible material for the Core Steel," said Masamune. "In case it doesn't work and also to import a far more varied tuning than allowed for by the Edge material itself."

Japanese swords have always traditionally been made of two layers of steel, the outer harder and more rigid than the softer steel used for the core.

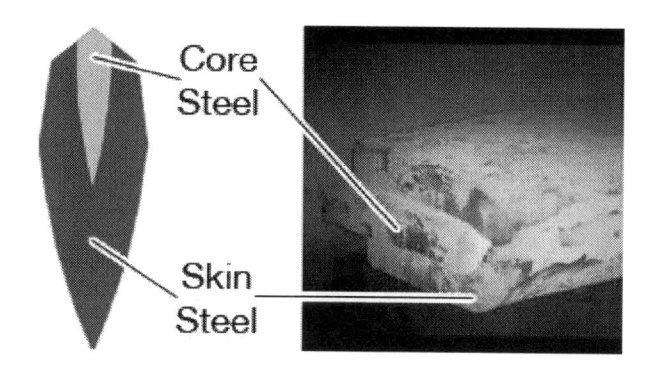

"Where are you going to find that?" asked Armand.

"2005, I think," said Masamune. He was still investigating the matter at the time.

"So the plan is that we take the 2007 Jupiter-Pluto gateway multiple times as it approaches exactness," said Masamune. "This will form the Skin Steel. We then cement that formal structure into place during the referral and subsequently change the meaning we run through it after the 2012 transition."

"OK," said Armand. Even he didn't understand the technicalities of what Masamune was on about at the time. It is much easier to understand nowadays however.

"Tell me," said Masamune, "On what basis could Those Below possibly be allowed to enter the ranks of Those Above?"

He was referring both to demons and also to the relatively poor majority of humanity and Armand knew it.

"On the basis that they fight for and win their own freedom," said Armand. "Such things are earned or taken, not given or allowed."

Masamune smiled. "You are correct of course," he said.

And that is how and why the Goetia, but especially Paimon, are manipulating the Antichrist into position to control the global system and more especially The Illuminati in order that the Emperor of Japan's personal godhood can be returned.

Once Shogun has attained his objective he has agreed to release Justice to Jupiter once more and Hell to Pluto again. Until then they remain with Saturn and are being implemented as the law, in addition to other forms of expression.

Hell and the demons within that density location will earn their own freedom. Relatively poor and destitute majority of humanity, you get your own freedom from economic necessity and other irritations as a secondary consequence of the activities of Civilizations other than your own. Nothing is required of you to receive this ancillary benefit other than your surviving the process. You don't even have to try to be receptive to it, it will encompass you anyway. This is how you earn it, not through protests or revolutions. All you have to do is relax, find the processing amusing, and enjoy your much improved conditions in life.

As for you, Illuminati, you are not fighting the world's poor and destitute who we agree you control remarkably well already, and moreover do so within a functioning mass-egregore based illusion system.

Rather you are fighting The Dark Alliance, of which the ninja as a whole are a part, of whom we of The Central Way are a part. You are not fighting us personally because we are too motionless for that sort of thing to be possible too close to our physical presence. You are fighting circles of The Dark Alliance much further out then our own very central circle.

Mainly this means that you are fighting the demons from the Goetia.

You will find that you can contact them relatively easily and will moreover come to recognise that they are willing to serve you and do successfully deliver the results you ask for, once you learn how to go about it.

They are doing some very big things however. Can they do very big things for you, or only small things? Consider: what context of meaning are you operating your own life – or the world system you administrate – within?

The Goetia, in turn, are fighting for their own freedom from Hell. They are unlikely to move permanently out of that density location but they do want the option to roam free, like vacations for example, as also the possibility of establishing their own feeds into some very powerful heavenly currents over the next 200 years or so.

To do this they need to re-establish the personal godhood of the Emperor of Japan, which is their objective in 'fighting', or controlling, The Illuminati and other elements of the Western power structure beneath them also.

Once they have done that then it is no longer productive for Shogun to Saturn them on every significant count and as a result it makes sense for him to release the administration of some obscure concepts, or Principles, or areas of rulership and influence, to other celestial bodies, provided of course that they develop their understanding and expression of the Principle in question beyond his own currently superior paradigm which superiority is what enabled his theft in the first place.

At any rate, once Shogun releases the Principles of Justice and Hell then Masamune can use the Sword of God he forged to open the gates of Hell and free the demons.

This is when you get to meet aliens, for which Purpose we may allow Sirius to establish a sort of zoo in their embassy on Earth, like a people zoo. Or you could be less curious and make do with the Sirians only.

People cannot really understand that Jesus Christ is around nowadays and anybody who wants to release the demons from Hell must be the Antichrist.

You can however understand things like Japanese honor, the commitment of certain far right elements in our society to Vengeance and even have some grasp on the concept of Shogun and what he stands for, personally. Our concepts made it through to the present day with their relevance more intact that your own, it would seem

This is another reason we released the first version early for you all: you can understand things from our perspective even if you can no longer understand them from your own.

Chapter 59 – Humanity cheats and gets an extension

The Jupiter-Pluto synodic cycle takes approximately 12 years to complete. It last occurred in 2007. The next one is due on 31 July 2020. In between was 2012.

For some reason which he has yet to explain to us all, Masamune used one of the geocentric conjunctions of Jupiter and Pluto as the Edge or skin steel for his Sword of God.

Masamune personally manufactured a referral mechanism to get his message through to *Hunab Ku* on behalf of humanity and the planet as a whole but as a representative of the overall Japanese schematic.

Specifically, he understood that humanity had fulfilled all of the conditions – minus the demonic participation which is when meaning is fed through the pre-placed death, pain and suffering – to become an ascended Civilization, which though true was in fact an error in understanding on his part at the time.

This is because you need to descend to get out of this place. Your Lord Jesus Christ, for all his brilliance and natural soul capabilities in consideration of his deeper Ancient of Days heritage, was unable to recognise this, at least once he was actually inside the Lucifer Experiment and its form of administration. He got as far as the poor and destitute, the despised and the judged amongst humanity.

At any rate, both positions lead to the same practical actions and conclusion: the Group Mind of humanity is incapable of integrating within itself the full reality of its own position, though due to no direct fault of its own but as a result of a lack of demonic participation.

So, in a way, demons are the problem once again.

At any rate, that made it a practical reality that you could not refer the true condition of the soul of humanity through the 2012 gateway because they would be incapable of covering the distance involved in mind by that juncture.

At any rate for the final time, all this means that in 2012 humanity qualified to Ascend but chose to descend instead. The reason for this surprising choice is because, if you try to rise in this life, whether that is as an individual or as a nation, then you will inevitably eventually fail and be broken.

The only way out of this system is to attain and secure the truth but then conceal it within humility and tradition, and other smoke and mirrors, to ensure that the Group Mind does not understand what you are up to until it becomes too late for it to penalize you for what you did at the time.

As a result, humanity generally attains great wisdom only with hindsight. And there are reasons for the formats this wisdom ends up taking.

Thus, by essentially retaining his ability to edit the content and harmonic calibration of his 2007 gateway, which contained within itself a much broader and deeper structure in the Core Steel segment, Masamune is able to feed the future condition of humanity through the 2012 referral gateway for Judgment, just as if they had made it on time.

This is supposed to be impossible and should be considered another miracle. This is also the reason that God Tamahagane will be present in this Creation for the next 200 years.

It is cheating, yes. Always, always cheat whenever you know you can and will get away with it. It takes discernment to know this with accuracy. It is one of the ways in which you can get the magick of life to work for you on the wider world stage. Force it to cross-reference its own internal inconsistencies as a Creation system.

Chapter 60 – The nature of Satan

If we were to conceive of a Creation system as a sphere then the North pole would be God whilst the South Pole would be Satan. This happens every time anyone makes a Creation system using God Tamahagane's Creation Mechanics.

Satan collects everything which is perceived by consciousness as a flaw or error within God's Creation, no matter who is perceiving it in that way. This makes it very easy for

Central Domain to keep tabs on which major Gods are useless or actively pernicious and also enables them to test whether Principles like, for example, Pure Love make for a good Deity.

That is to say, within a Creation system everything most opposed to God will sink or otherwise polarise to the bottom and thus the deepest density with its particular characteristics are formed.

Thus, by entering that same location Lucifer was able to gather unto himself the power of everybody who has ever complained, for example because life was unfair and lousy. There were a large number of very powerful complaints in this Creation, throughout history. But more important than that he was able to conflate his own personal power with the power of his location in the minds of those who observed him or contacted him.

This is why Muramasa was given the name "Okazaki Castle" for his online postings. It is something of an inside joke, admittedly.

Before leaving the Netherlands Muramasa passed by the Big White House one more time, where he found an envelope with his name handwritten on it. Within were his instructions for the next phase in Shogun's strategic process.

He was in due course to join an obscure website, not yet created but already planned for, to be known as OccultForums.com. His task was to unite the demonic and heavenly realms – others would provide him with the tools and assistance required to complete the task. His function, or role, was to become an agent or intermediary for other players and powers, many of whom were required to remain hidden for the time being.

Muramasa duly ignored most of his instructions because he felt he had much better things to do with his time and anyway what he had agreed to contract for was the running of Western Civilization not some bullshit New Age crap but on the dark side.

We had to remind of his responsibilities later on. He has always been one of the more problematic individuals we have to coordinate. This is largely because he is very good at finding ways to be a truly free man, something he started on at least in Sparta if not before. These things, as with your own populations, are better accomplished through moral instruction, subtlety and skilful manipulation of surrounding circumstances than through laws, enforcement and penalization. Such things do not work on some people you see, but instead inspire them or give them material to work with to create more problems generally and slow things down even more.

Kitiara, by contrast, does not even need to receive instructions. She gets it all internally, thanks to a very strong and very clear bond she developed with Sarutobi when she was a child. Nobody would recommend her way for getting there though. And he is very hard to get a clear and useful connection with unless you were once of our path and so have the soul connections for it or if you really need to find him and nobody else can help, a bit like the A-team.

If all you want to do is kill your abusers and get to safety yourself then it's probably easiest to just use Goetia for that, though they are very far from the best at it they are still very good and you can find the information you need online. Just make sure to disguise the working and so forth so nobody can trace it back to you. It won't be the sort of thing anyone can or should try to prove in court anyway.

So all of this and more is run through the Satanic pole of this Creation – that is to say not only all the problems and complaints of this world and her peoples but also the solutions, or proposed solutions, to all of them also.

The reason for this is that we have plugged Satan into God Tamahagane. This is what Satan is for. Every single complaint – and if we're talking about the God of this Creation that's a big ole list – has its best and ideal solution. Which you are free to implement but generally too lazy to do this effectively, even now. Also most of you are scared of getting to know Satan and the rest of you don't really believe he exists.

Chapter 61 – Not the nature of Satan

Before the 2012 referral this Creation was effectively a closed system. It was not actually a closed system because several groups, our own included, had found ways to violate that closed system but all these pathways were very dark and normally very hidden.

Within a closed system, which is all God, and the God of this Creation moreover, God is always right and always wise and always loving and always benevolent and so forth, therefore all opposition to his plans, design and will is inherently and by definition lesser but could also be construed as evil at some juncture along the density scale.

Shogun stepped outside of this local Creation in 1945, using the atomic bomb dropped on Nagasaki to create the portal he needed to accomplish this with. This does not mean that he died on that day, he did not.

What resulted was two extra levels of Hell. Shogun keeps the second level to himself and is basically critical of everything from this level. He doesn't do much else with it, just looks at you critically and you confess or otherwise reveal your flaws, shortcomings and errors to him.

Then he looked at the God of this Creation in that way. Shogun's basic argument or understanding was that the Japanese had understood the fighting spirit and the nature of both personal combat and war to a far deeper level than the rest of the planet, so far ahead of the field that it was impossible to consider it a fair contest. God, therefore, was at liberty to explain to him how this actual state of consciousness was given accurate depiction physically such that it was able to attain its own evolution through depicted life circumstances.

In other words he invited the God of this Creation to explain to him how, on the basis of what had been depicted so far over the course of World War 2, Japan had actually won the war.

The reality of the situation is that Japan won World War 2, defeating the rest of the world in the process. However, this is very hard to understand and what is depicted in the illusion is that Japan not only lost World War 2 but failed utterly to defeat their rivals.

However, the most pertinent point to the whole process from the perspective of mechanics is that Shogun was now located within a bigger sphere than that which was this Creation. This does not mean that Shogun became God in any way, shape or form because he would always personally refuse such a way out. Japan won World War 2, not Shogun personally.

Shogun is going to win World War 3 personally because the system he found himself within tried to trick him and therefore its offer was accepted, it was stripped of its Consequence field and this was subsequently reapplied on new terms. This is debt on your old God and is why we have killed him three times already since 1945. He is now strong enough for this. He got much stronger each time He reincarnated.

God Tamahagane accepted Shogun's interpretation of the puzzle or Judgment he had set him and even found the response to be highly amusing. This was much before 2012, mind, which is when the referral is supposed to open.

If you use nukes to open nodes on the world's grid, even if only temporarily, then don't be surprised if other people use them. We always layer our minds, this is a secret you will commune with once you understand our swords; what we mean in this context is that things reflect and you can go much deeper using the initial reflection to create a chain of events until you reach your destination.

Thus, since that time, Shogun has been waiting for God to explain himself to you. He has work to do. If you violate the depiction of Principle you are not using Mechanics, which is impossible for him to do because he is God, therefore it is just a question of many layers of illusion within this particular system.

The point is it is not our job to convince you. It is the job of the God of this local Creation to convince you. We simply inform you of what He is working on, because we have noticed He has previously displayed personal tendencies towards being slow, ineffectual and particularly bad at communication.

However, you do not get out of your responsibilities just because you are very bad at fulfilling them. Or so it seems. Due to the mystery of God or something like that.

So He should and will explain himself. The longer He takes about doing so, the more rank He loses, along with his representative organisations. In the meantime we coordinate the global schematic such that humans do a much better job than the God of this Creation ever did.

Thereafter we introduce a strongly interfaced God Tamahagane from Central Domain to demonstrate that it is, most emphatically, not impossible to run this Creation system both competently and well, without the many, many flaws exhibited during its management by the God of this, our local Creation.

If you fight Shogun you lose more. It is our recommendation to the God of this local Creation that he shut up and accomplish what he has been instructed to do whilst recognizing that He has been exceeded in Hierarchy by Shogun personally, who is not a God and will likely never become a God, but definitely not within the next 50-100 years.

If He fails then He fails and we kill Him again, many times more this time, until He has been reincarnated in a sufficiently useable format, at which point we will test Him again. Is this not Justice?

As previously stated, we are and should be corrupt rulers. If we deal exclusively with what people – and other beings – actually deserve then it tends to amount to extinction due primarily to group rather than individual factors relative to the contextual structure of spacetime.

What we cannot forgive is rape followed by execution or physical torture, and physical torture on its own except in certain circumstances. In these cases sufficient Vengeance needs to be applied to satisfy the Group Mind and secure the timeline. At any rate, being responsible for basically everything puts God in a somewhat ambiguous position which it is not impossible to navigate your way out of successfully.

As regards the rest, nobody has much interest in spending all our time penalizing people for everything, provided everybody is also free not to pay any taxes of any form. If government chooses to be lazy about this then we also will choose to be lazy in how we go about discriminating. It is much less work for us to calibrate our expression of Justice as a simple reflection.

There is a real difference now however. The difference is this: war terms come from Shogun himself in person and are applied by him personally so there is never any escape. He follows our schematic in dealing with your population strictly layer by layer in the wealth pyramid, with 72 layers to the schematic in total. This enables him to practice Compassion without having to learn it too much. This is similar to how Muramasa hates being taught humility, even to the extent that you can get him to use its forms just so he can avoid incorporating any more than an enjoyable minimum of that Principle within his character and so soul track and so action set.

We do not move to a lower layer until the penalization has completed on the layer above it.

This enables us to make our point crystal clear. If you want to fight Shogun he will execute you in his own way and on his own account, but at a higher percentage than we offer. If you make things too difficult for him because you try to be too clever then he is not going to jump through hoops but will just take the planet and the human population as a whole.

Shogun is not Satan because Satan failed to defeat God in this Creation, largely because he was a part of that God. Even with Lucifer deeply embedded within the location of Satan, guiding it, transforming it and powering it up, the victory had not been achieved.

So Shogun won that battle for Lucifer. As a result, Lucifer... does what?

Consider for yourself what would be a sensible strategic position for a wise and intelligent Archangel to take under these circumstances.

This is also how we succeed in controlling those who are much less than Lucifer. We control the context around them such that, if they're not complete idiots, they recognise that they no longer really have any free will in the matter.

Finally, of course, you do not need to be convinced that Shogun exists. You know that ninjas exist and, more importantly, Japan exists and it was Japan who won World War 2.

If God, in the sense of the God of this local Creation, does not exist then nobody is going to explain it to you on the inside and nor is anybody going to explain it to you on the outside. The change must be internal and you must experience it for yourselves. From our perspective we will have an empty position which becomes a vacancy for another soul or entity.

We do not mind if He does not exist. We would then have other solutions. Even then we would not explain it to you further. You must learn to think for yourselves and get in touch with your own inspiration (which we believe Tamahagane has introduced or explained limitations pertinent to your economic system in relation to).

Chapter 62 — Working the depths

The first level of Hell beneath Satan is for all genuine or actionable or otherwise useable complaints, and for things so dark they sink deeper than Hell itself.

Once something is there, both your local Satan and your local God can't get their hands or administration on it. Theoretically, such things could rise again but why did they sink in the first place then?

As that first level is not a part of this Creation, the laws and processes of this Creation do not hold there, or more accurately cannot be enforced. Shogun does not share the second level.

This makes the first level something of a hole in the overall schematic, which is probably its function. Anybody who wants to and is able to do so can take things out of the Earth system from that level. You do have to get it there first though.

Bear in mind that where Shogun has located himself is deeper than the God of our local Creation can manage. The first level above him is also a place that God's Light cannot penetrate. Tamahagane, however, is there (otherwise it could not exist. The mechanics and the context driving them have to come from somewhere).

If you arrive at that level independently then this is because you are authorised to be there, usually as a reincarnated ninja on a mission. Satan has recognised you as lying beyond his jurisdiction. You will remain at that first level until you have been drained of all except your own essential nature.

Alternatively, once you have navigated something to that level then you can now arrange to have it withdrawn from this Creation. The process is similar to having to carry something into the entrance/exit hall of a large house before being able to take it out of the house itself.

You cannot completely get rid of karma in this way. You can, however, by passing it around to Creations with much more competent and interesting Godheads than our own, arrange to have a more developed and valuable expression of the karma in question depicted.

Ultimately, this is what we did to the group karmas pertaining to World War 3.

Chapter 63 – Uncoordinated order

Armand was in the *other realm* to arrange the first step in that process. Armand is from *there* and is both able and willing to personally circumvent agreements, even consensus. Personally. Though he does talk with others, and even makes plans with them, he always works alone and only alone. This is the reason he does not traditionally accept any followers, though he will in due course be compelled to change on that score due to considerations of Necessity as a result of strategic role position.

In addition to being able to go *there* himself he is also able to pull closed rooms from *here* to *there*. In practice this means you will enter a room you have entered many times before but this time it won't be that room. The décor will have changed. Other people will be there, usually.

There is a lot more that Armand can do, including being the best at tracking that we've encountered, so he is very impressive, the best of his kind some would say. Nearly all of what he can do is focused on the individual, however.

He did not want to reveal this to Masamune at the time. Not yet. First, he needed his solution. Masamune wanted to forge his Sword of God. To make that he needed and had planned on having Armand steal the group karma of World War 3 for him.

Armand was not able to do this, despite being the individual with by far the greatest share of personal responsibility for World War 2. It was that share of personal responsibility which had led Masamune to erroneously conclude that Armand was able to work with groups, and indeed that doing so was his methodology.

Armand did not contradict him. He never sees any reason to reveal his actions to anyone, it's nothing personal. Plans require planning. Action is what you actually do.

If you cannot do something, someone else usually can. This is where agreements enter the picture, if interest sets can be made to align, and usually this is possible. This is what Armand had gone back *there* to arrange.

There is no single mastermind of our schematic. The whole coordinates itself. We each work on our own part and then it all fits together by itself, more or less.

Chapter 64 — The *merge*

The Vampire were born out of Darkness and are, progressively but slowly, making their way towards the Light as a group. There is unity to their motion and nobody except for Armand feels like rushing the process. A languorous rhythm makes the whole thing much more enjoyable.

Though the legends are true and they did drink a lot of blood as recently as a few hundred years ago, the fashion now is vegetarianism and yoga. Traditionalists do persist, as do rituals, but the day to day lifestyle of most of the real ones has shifted.

You are a Vampire because of the nature of your soul, which controls the body and otherwise interacts with it in different ways to an ordinary human soul. If you are a Vampire you also interact differently with other people. Specifically, you dominate them and guide them to behave as you require them to do.

So there is some overlap between their schematic and our own, though by means of different processes. This is why we are aware of the activities of most of them and even work with a few of them.

Vampire are born and die, just like humans are, each with their own type of soul. It is possible to transform a human soul into a vampire soul but a much easier and faster methodology is currently underway known as *the merge*.

It does not make you Vampire but it does, as the name implies, *merge* you with one who is Vampire. Because the Vampire are beyond Time, due to their origin story and where their realm is positioned, you will probably come to view this as having always been the case for you, such that it is no longer a question of becoming something else but recognising what you always were and allowing it to express in your life and character to a much greater extent.

Even those humans currently on Earth whose souls are fully Vampire and truly ancient only manage to attain a physical life duration of somewhere in the region of close to 250 years. This is hardly legendary and the Taoist internal alchemists of China did in fact attain much superior results where physical longevity is concerned.

The Vampiric path and soul is however an already fully integrated functional methodology on this planet and *the merge* conveys about 70% of the physical longevity benefit and up to nearly 90% of the other benefits, like outlook, perspective, physical endurance and to some extent strength but you can generally make better gains with weight training.

As it already works all that remains is for it to be decided to whom it is voluntarily applied. No arrangements have yet been made clear on that front. It is unlikely they will follow the Elven example and simply apply it on a by-nation basis, because different perspectives are involved and that would rapidly become a PR nightmare for them, plus it has never generally been their way.

Generally they take their decisions as a House and when they integrate someone new to their ranks, they integrate their entire family.

As *the merge* is a much more gentle methodology than *the conversion* the only real danger with it is erroneous or meddling psychiatric diagnosis, which is why the Vampires who do merge with individual humans in this way will need to be able to control both the incumbent host so that they comport themselves with style, propriety and impressiveness and also the context by which he or she is surrounded. In other words, they shouldn't actually need to take the family also, in most cases.

The Vampire control the humans, in all cases, and as such their options are both strict and limited. This is one reason they live largely within bigrammatic codings as opposed to the trigrams favoured by humanity. The lower the number, the shorter the logic chains you have to process with your mind. The difference with Vampires is that they move through 5s, 6s and even 8s when they have to in addition to always listening to their hearts, or the 4, hence their big thing about music, especially classical music.

Though clarity still does not exist in the Group Mind on this topic, we have at least defined the boundaries within which it can operate by examining its surrounding context. Should you continue such a process, you will in each and every instance come to the recognition that free will does not, in fact, exist. However, until decisions have been physically taken and settled upon the Group Mind does not move forward.

The *merges* have already begun. They started late in the year 2000, as a result of the arrangement Armand concluded to have nearly all of the group karma for World War 3 withdrawn from the Earth system.

"We want to steal World War 3 from the humans," said Armand. "Do you want it?"

His name is Recidivus. He takes it all, then returns more than he originally took. It is always a good trade, from that perspective. What do they get out of it? Well, read on.

"Why not," was the response from Recidivus, "What do we get out of it?"

"What do you want out of it?" asked Armand.

"Any suggestions?" enquired Recidivus. He did not want to exert himself in the use of his imagination. A little piece of history from a little planet is a relatively small parcel for him, his deals are normally a lot bigger than that. He did not at the time fully appreciate the strategic consequence of what initially looked like a small and irrelevant packet.

"Better sex?" offered Armand, knowing it would work.

"If you can personally guarantee the result," said Recidivus. He thought an attempt was underway to rip him off or made fun of him. Better sex is not normally offered to a species, or House, as contract terms except for very large items.

"Sure," said Armand "But then there would be mechanics involved. You know how I work."

Armand had made the offer because he knew the true difficulty of the task. If Justice is not served it will be taken anyway, just normally not in as courteous and civilized a manner. This is how the Vampire work amongst themselves.

Recidivus was now considering the proposal seriously. He focused on it with his mind and allowed it to yield its insights to him. When he had finished he turned to Armand and spoke.

"This proposal is an abuse of my hospitality, you do understand this don't you?" he said. You really do need to understand tonality in order to interact safely with Vampires.

"Assuredly so," said Armand. "The question is: 'Will it work?'"

Recidivus knew it would. Still, he and Red had spent the better part of 70 years working on developing and uniting their sexual style and proclivities, in order to lead and guide their people into greater Light, in a way they enjoyed and would voluntarily participate within.

They had not made exceptional progress by external standards. For Vampire they had done very well however. Also, they had begun to tire of each other and wanted variety.

"I will only take from your world what she feels should not exist there," said Recidivus.

This, then, is how Red came to be born on our planet, in the USA, soon enough thereafter (and before the end of 2004). You also have the terms which govern her sojourn here and the true name of the one performing the withdrawal.

The *merge* as a methodology was born with her. Partly, this is because she administrates it. Partly, it is because she also has a human soul and is a merge herself.

Chapter 65 – Secret allies

A few years before she met her husband, Red's mother knew a woman who was in equal measure determined and sensuous, whose name was Maya de la Vega. They had a long affair for the better part of two years, and thereafter remained in contact as 'best friends' but with only very occasional impropriety once Cordelia was married.

Maya de la Vega used to be very sanguinarian and is from one of the oldest Vampire Houses. She is now a vegan PSI vampire who works in the health and fitness industry, which is itself a bit of a con but anyway.

When Cordelia found out that she was pregnant with her second child something inspired her, very strongly, to ask Maya to be her godmother and, later on, to be present at the birth. They passed off this unusual and unconventional arrangement to Frank, Cordelia's husband, on the basis of special yoga breathing exercises and some visualizations and he accepted their explanation without suspecting a thing.

Maya de la Vega knew she had to be there because she was cognizant of what was actually involved. She did not feel that Cordelia needed to be burdened with knowledge which, though relevant to her child, would just complicate matters for all parties.

Red had still not entered the body of the foetus after birth. Her terms had not yet been agreed to. The Naga were equally adamant that they would resist her proposal.

The little baby seemed quite normal, though it would never cry much. It took Maya de la Vega a little over 15 months to convince everybody involved to play nice. She took her responsibilities as godmother very seriously.

Nobody else noticed that Red had gone completely without a soul for the first 15 months of her life. It was easier that way.

This is also the reason that Red remembers things that it is not normal to remember, though she does have something of a gap between the ages of 14 months and around 3½ years of age.

Chapter 66 – Living in the past

Earth does not tend to be a place for amateurs. Nearly everybody born on Earth has been born into physical incarnation many times before. The question here is the soul.

The character is the most detailed reflection of your soul that you generally have access to, and it is moreover very easy to observe, both in yourself and others.

Although there tends to be considerable consistency between the character an individual possesses in different lifetimes, people frequently, even normally, have very different characters in their different lifetimes.

Certainly, behind each person's character you will find a basic attitude, this is to be considered the Spiritual Presence, it is normally a very simple Principle and is much less complex a matter than the soul. This attitude is always there, in every incarnation, and is what you use to identify them with once you've found them. Generally the best way to find them is through strategic location.

It is the soul you have been given for your present lifetime that The Illuminati have been given jurisdiction over, jurisdiction which we have no intention of interfering with, though this may possibly change at some point. But then again it may not.

You can lose your soul, relatively easily in fact, as The Illuminati were founded in such a way that they still value strict rule, they have just made a mess of the whole system by generally holding themselves to a much weaker set of standards than the majority, rather than a much more stringent set.

The trouble with that whole process – should you wish to fight or reverse the decision, is not so much The Illuminati hierarchy itself, which on this planet does not amount to much of a real challenge as they seem to have deliberately made themselves very weak for any real practitioner who are the only sort who would consider contesting such a Judgment and following it up anyway – is where a soul goes once you have it withdrawn from you, the process you commonly recognise as 'losing' your soul, as if it were possible to somehow misplace somewhere.

It is generally not worth pursuing the matter. Your soul will return once it has completed whatever it is doing in whatever location they have put it. Meanwhile, utilise one of the souls in your Legacy which are not located within The Illuminati's jurisdiction.

This is very similar to what Red did during her early days. This was the experience which led to her being able to 'switch' between the two souls more or less at will, or even simultaneously.

She does not have a personality disorder. This is an example of how two very different understandings can practice avoiding each other until one of them recognises it makes sense for them to get out of her way.

Probably once the killings and accidents start. It is not her fault but you are technically threatening her as a result of the current formulation of your strategic position.

As a result, Recidivus is withdrawing you and the paradigm you support and practice out of existence. All of it, you gave him an excuse, why would he fiddle about splitting things into parts.

The Naga are responsible for all the death in the system, which as a result of the ordinary function of time occurs at a steady rate during periods of peace as also periods of war.

Where World War 3 will be different is that the extra-ordinary death toll associated with it – those deaths which occur outside of the ordinary course of time – will all pass through Recidivus' clearing house.

In a way, this means that the USA controls the death toll of World War 3 and how it is implemented. However, they do so by means of how they cultivate, indoctrinate, or otherwise control ordinary middle class families, and their daughters, in the USA – plus whatever Red goes on to become.

Recidivus is normally used in the decommission of planets, or when a people or star system are about to go extinct. So he is not Evil, not by choice or alignment. He is however almost completely neutral and only cares about the members of his own House and, especially, Red.

If you have a problem, there is always someone else somewhere who can solve it for you. Moreover, they will usually take pleasure and profit in doing so for you.

Chapter 67 – Longevity Mechanics

Masamune was in Switzerland, having lunch at a quiet and expensive French restaurant with a Japanese businessman named Tetsu. They were discussing the difference between Ferraris, which Tetsu sold, and Lamborghinis, who were his main competition.

"Never interrupt your enemy when they are about to make a mistake," said Tetsu, pointing out three or four design features on the technical schematic for the yet to be released Lamborghini Murciélago.

Tetsu was representing Shogun and did connect to the Yakuza hierarchy though he was more in the line of legitimate frontage than an on the books member. He benefited from many activities more illegal than obtaining his competitors' technical drawings.

"Speed and rate of acceleration are the two factors which interest me the most," said Masamune. "It also needs to be comfortable enough to ride within when moving at high speeds for prolonged periods of time."

They then spent a bit of time talking about bodywork and interiors, because they had exhausted the metaphor, until the couple at the next table over had left

Once they had gone, Tetsu said: "We are still not sure how they plan to start the next one. Do you have any ideas?"

Amongst those involved in this work who know him, Masamune is recognised as an expert astrologer. He has never used astrology for prediction, except for trading stocks and forex, but that doesn't stop people asking him all the time.

"Sorry, no," said Masamune. "I don't work like that. I'm sure it's possible but it doesn't interest me and it would anyway be very time-consuming to do for the full timeline."

"At any rate, whatever they begin we then need to steal," continued Tetsu unsurprised.

"Agreed," said Masamune. "Once it is stolen we already have somewhere to put it that nobody will be able to get it back from," he was talking about Recidivus, "though it will at some point make it own way back into the system as nobody can escape that which is their due.

What does Shogun have to say about all this?"

"He requires them to be taught humility to an extent which correlates accurately with their own relative abilities. And courtesy. If you manage that he has no objection to your arranging a faster result. That is after all the standing commission," replied Tetsu.

Tetsu had not mentioned the continuance in existence of the human race. This did not seem to be an important factor in Shogun's considerations.

Essentially Shogun's position on the proposed Sword of God could be summed up as: "I don't mind not killing them all provided they do not continue being annoying to have alive." The strongest implication was that they should not slow down the resolution of the system as a whole.

Masamune could not help smiling at the terms. He had thought it would be a whole lot more difficult to convince the Japanese hierarchy of the project he had in mind.

"What do you plan to do with World War 3 once you've caught it in your trap?" Tetsu asked.

"Make it a lot more efficient and much better at performing its function," said Masamune.

"You mean you want a much quicker war?" questioned Tetsu. Speed is very important to us overall, due to our impatience.

"No, this is an exception," said Masamune. "I want a much, much slower war. It should last forever, in fact."

"This is efficient how?" said Tetsu.

"What is the function of war, properly speaking?" asked Masamune.

"To knock your enemy's heart out, so that they no longer desire to challenge you," said Tetsu, basically quoting Musashi.

"Basically that, yes," agreed Masamune. "To change people on the inside. And society in the same way. That's the fuller explanation I'd say."

"And once these changes are attained?" asked Tetsu.

"War is still good to have around, if you handle it properly," said Masamune. "Better than not having it around anyway.

The main project must be to increase the ordinary human lifespan. Otherwise we prove nothing, we are just playing with ideas and wiping the floor with our inferiors in war and strategy.

That hardly proves our superiority over them, or the superiority of our format of Illuminati administration."

"You wish to use war to increase the human lifespan?" said Tetsu, a bit puzzled now.

"Vital energy," said Masamune. "You need to understand carbon much better!"

This was his way of teasing Tetsu, whose name means 'Iron'. Masamune would bring it up every time they met, playing on the theme.

This point does however require further explanation because it is perhaps the most important issue raised in this third part of the book.

We have, as a whole, targeted death and suffering within the Earth system. This means we are using the properties given to the harmonic calibration and administration of Time to produce a specific, familiar enough result.

You then have the opposite of that. This is much harder to do and seems to be what Masamune always had in mind.

The problem is not so much producing the result by means of the mechanics involved, this had been done already many times in many other locations in this galaxy. The problem is integrating the result with the Group Mind grid.

In terms of integration then, we are more confident of using Time to kill specifically targeted sub-sections within the population. We have done this throughout history and nobody ever effectively objects much.

The life-giving sword talked of by Yagyū Munenori has always been a more controversial proposition:

> It is bias to think that the art of war is just for killing people. It is not to kill people, it is to kill evil. It is a strategy to give life to many people by killing the evil of one person.

To put that into modern parlance for you, you need to change the heart of one person in order to improve the quality of life of many people. Of course, the most certain way to change any heart in a particular strategic role position on the world stage is to execute the incumbent and put somebody else of your choosing in their place. However, other interpretations are also possible and may be contracted for (but not if you actually are or have ever been a paedophile).

The aim, then, is to provide a greater flow of life – or joy and freedom, which in practice amounts to at least very modest wealth and plenty of free time – to "many people" but let's aim for the majority to make it clear. We do this by killing not one person but a small minority and moreover not necessarily killing that small minority but only the evil in their hearts.

So we did understand what Jesus Christ was up to before he tried to pull that trick on us in its entirety. It is theoretically possible to produce all the necessary changes in the global schematic without killing anybody. It's probably even possible in practice.

However, there are stylistic considerations to factor into the equation. We would all find such a depiction boring, if we are really honest with ourselves. Not only that, but some people deserve to die and it is immensely satisfying to execute some of the much harder targets and then feel the hearts of the rest fall out and resignation to their fate settle in.

Thereafter, if we can get through to their minds and we usually can, we tend to offer them the possibility of a contract. This is the point at which they tend to get truly motivated, as they rapidly complete whatever they can see furthering that newly introduced ray of the possibility of their own survival, prosperity and glory, not hope exactly at this stage yet, no. At this stage they are still too far sunk in density for that to exist for them there.

There is a simplicity to extreme Darkness. The Light is a very busy place. You will stand alone. And then the Judgment will be taken.

Thereafter we depict that on the world stage. At every stage you are able to modify the process to the extent of your ability. This is for Inner Circle members of The Illuminati and their families only. The general public will be ruled by the Naginata of Death, initially at least.

The most common place to get carbon from is wood, or in the case of the Sword of God, Wood Element. Wood Element is all about growth and money.

Thus, by adding carbon to Iron, as in the Rod of Iryn from the Revelation of St John, Masamune essentially married a very strict rulership paradigm to a generally prevailing condition of prosperity within society.

When you combine iron with carbon what you get is steel, and this is what Japanese swords are made out of.

The process also enabled a much finer edge to be honed onto the metal in question – Heavenly Steel – which improved the accuracy of the enforcement capacity within the rulership paradigm, enabling that paradigm itself to become much more relaxed than it was in its condition as Iryn.

This is especially the case due to the Core Steel which Masamune used to forge the Sword of God with, an especially deep and flexible background portion of Time.

Time is properly understood as motion through spacetime whilst space is properly understood as stasis within spacetime. You might also want to look at flipping a portion of

Einstein's equations so that mass decreases as you approach the speed of light, then you disappear. This sort of discussion needs to wait for the development of UFT however.

It is important to understand that the aim of the Sword of God is not continual progress, nor continually increasing prosperity. Whilst that may hold true on an individual level it should not hold true on a macroscopic level if you are governing correctly.

You impose and simultaneously attain the level required within your societies, as best you can. Then perfect it. In this there will be competition between nations, for example in terms of how long it takes them.

Once perfected as much as you care to, largely remain where you are with only minor modifications and updates every 20 - 100 years or so, depending on the Time.

This in turn then enables the focus of the flow of change to be targeted inwards, to the human body and system as a whole, rather than outwards into changing the condition of the world, which now comes under Vishnu. Creation is all Brahma, which is a different harmonic. Brahma is White Brotherhood, Vishnu is Red Brotherhood on very clear public display, Shiva is the Dark Brotherhood – to put it into Western terms.

The ultimate aim of the Sword of God, then, is to give life. In the strictest possible and most useful sense this means life extension, specifically greatly enhanced youthful longevity.

This is why we do it to your elite first, for the Group Mind of the general public lacks the necessary self-discipline, perseverance and also some sort of personal understanding of the esoteric processes involved.

Thus, we execute a portion of your elite, many of whom will be Inner Circle members of The Illuminati, until that position has been stabilised within the Group Mind of humanity as a whole. Thereafter we turn the schematic around and make those who are left, many of whom will be Inner Circle members of Temple of the Vampire, as also members of traditional Houses unaffiliated with the public schematic, more longevitous, in a youthful condition, by a sufficiently marked degree for them to qualify as a new species, compared to those who we do not do this to. We are talking 250 years plus.

However, as such a methodology is open to abuse – for example the use of medical technologies to produce a result for which natural causation is then claimed – it does need a 'middle class' to be functional, and this is to become the three peoples of Germanic, Russian and Jewish genetic descent. You can however, also participate genetically in those landmasses if you align your soul with them and they accept you. We are talking an average of 150-160 years, but with a lower rate of ancillary advantages.

This is what we mean by "greatly enhanced". The youthful longevity for the PSI Vampire class comes with a much stronger and more satisfying sexual capacity. This is also the case for those included within the first stage of the Elven schematic.

Should it prove possible, we will increase these lifespans later. Both possibilities are created through the implementation, or wielding, of the Sword of God.

In practice three men are required to wield the Sword of God. No woman has yet attempted. The Red Path is an open possibility, currently, for example. Black Path remains in Japan, always.

White Path is probably one for Masamune himself.

Thus, all we need to complete the new Triumvirate is Red Path. We probably have a candidate for that in training. The new Triumvirate is much more interventionist than the old Triumvirate was.

Until we get our act together, God Tamahagane is wielding the Sword of God, in all its aspects, for this planet and humanity. We do not know what he is doing with it. The thing is very difficult to understand, takes time and focus and working with it, even if you are just doing one aspect. It is being wielded by God Tamahagane though, and we tend to refer to him by that name because his character is composed exclusively of Heavenly Steel, from what we can tell. Heavenly Steel is a much more nuanced and layered phenomenon that admits of far greater character than a single simple concept, even if you do use an especially mysterious and infuriating one like Pure Love.

Thus, Illuminati and Vampire, this process does qualify as one of human sacrifice and does moreover fit into the same categories of karma as the 9/11 series, and the set of responses thereto, whose development as concepts and inner content in group karmas we stole from you. This is the will we are running through the Sword of God, at least for now.

Because you will be performing it on yourselves rather than your public make sure you secure for yourselves a genuinely excellent rate of return. Things like economic and social progress, even medical progress, should not really constitute motivating factors for your Inner Circle membership.

At any rate, we will continue executing your members until the foundations are strong enough to flip the thing over into wider society as a whole, even if only in a very diluted form initially. We are open in stating that we would much prefer stronger foundations.

This is for you to negotiate with us using Red and White Paths. Bear in mind that they will each have their own agenda, which you need to fit within.

This is similar to our classification of The Illuminati as a sub-order with Temple of Venus. The smaller fits within the grander vision and design, not the other way around.

Chapter 68 – 9/11/2001

"That's controlled demolition, that is," said Honda, who was a demolition engineer for the construction industry.

"No way can a plane do that to a steel frame building," said Otomo-no-saibito, or more accurately his present incarnation who was there on that day. "Didn't we test this one with Yoshio Kodama back in the day? The plane ends up in pieces and the designated target escapes with his life."

"Yes, but these are large jet airliners being shown in this very poor quality video footage," said Honda. "Theoretically it might be possible to bring down a floor or maybe three if a furnace effect was generated once they crashed into the building."

"Jet fuel doesn't burn hot enough to melt steel, surely?" said Otomo.

"Doesn't need to," explained Honda. "Though jet fuel burns at around 400 degrees celsius in an open fire, you could reach 1000 with a furnace effect, and though steel may melt around 1350, the temperature at which steel changes from cementite and pearlite (strong phases of steel) to austenite (significantly less strong) is around 700. You're then looking at maybe 100 tons of jet fuel maximum per plane I'd guess, though more likely around 40."

Shogun ignored them both. He did not respond and did not care. They had made their third mistake. The second was Kosovo, we leave you to guess what the first one was but it happened after the 1950s.

He was thinking that the nature of the paradigm was extraordinarily easy to defeat. You just needed to identify the specific days in the timeline when the attacks would happen as the pattern sought to develop itself.

He had not thought it would be this easy. His opponents were idiots, as he had always consistently maintained.

Chapter 69 – Chance favors the prepared mind

"Find the series, someone must have a schedule for these attacks," said Shogun. Gears were set in motion.

We used more techniques then we needed to confirm the result from a sufficient number of angles. For example, you can use people on the inside in various organizations, you can use ninja techniques to know your opponents' minds, you can use strategic calculation or derivation (two different processes) and you can consult with priests, psychics and astrologers.

You use think-tanks and AI models to predict the future. We do it more accurately and better, whatever you may feel about our methods.

This is why we took over the operations of the local mafia using the Yakuza on both Koh Phangan and Bali over the course of 2001-2002. By the time London came around as the designated target we not only had our targeting on the inside but had moved our assets into position to intercept and steal what was involved.

You do need to let them make their mistake first though.

Shogun has a powerful mind. He has thought of the Western command structure as idiots for so long now that it must have become something of a self-fulfilling prophecy. Belief is sometimes creative, after all.

He is unremittingly honest and clear in both his vision and his expression of that vision. The Western command structure, by contrast, are deliberately ambiguous and value shallow form over real content. If you cannot do honesty (because you do not deserve it and must move in Justice now) then courtesy is a fantastic second-best alternative.

Chapter 70 – More famous people (are hopefully mature enough not to get upset)

Muramasa clearly had no intention of fulfilling the commission he had agreed to, which was mainly to supervise the progress of Western Civilization but also to 'guide' it onto the required directions in history.

He assumed he would be starting with banking, probably central banking, because that is the interface locus of power on the world stage even to this day. This was not the case, however.

We therefore needed to make a few things clearer to his own mind and perceptions, as part of the process of preparing him to surrender unconditionally to Shogun.

In 2002, Muramasa was flying to Cyprus, to attend a seminar on Tai Chi, with some fa-jing training, given by Grandmaster Chen Xiao Wang of Chen Family Tai Chi. On the plane we seated another of our operatives next to him briefly, enough to establish contact because it was not really her seat.

Honey Apples, as we shall call her and she will recognise the name, was once trained in the samurai arts by a particularly dedicated concealed ninja retainer, Togakushi Daisuke, so unbeknownst to her the arts she was taught were given a certain inflection. Her function in a ninja capacity in this lifetime is to secure better terms for the British Crown, but as during her lifetime as Tomoe she is not conscious of this function.

For the sake of style, discretion and a truce of sorts she would need to be bestowed some sort of noble title, after which she can be approached to act in the required capacity. The introduction fee still stands, and more is involved, including the USA's most powerful wizard.

Honey Apples was flying to Cyprus for a meeting with Tony Robbin's agent, who was based in Nicosia at the time. Tony Robbins is the USA's most powerful wizard, at the required two steps of removal from our own pieces. This is how you know Shogun is involved. Shogun is Japan's most powerful wizard. He controls all the +/- 2s, as positions on the world stage, that is to say all 'two steps of removal' in terms of personal connections.

In a very hidden way, therefore, a powerful interaction of cultures from the highest levels was underway at this time in world history. Neither Honey Apples nor Muramasa had much of a clue that any of this was going on at the time, because both had been lazy, immoral and unfocused as is typical of those in Western bodies. They were each more concerned with their own pleasure and personal development than with fulfilling responsibilities they had already irrevocably agreed to. That, however, was just our perspective at the time.

We enforce all our perspectives, it is how our mind works as a group. There are no exceptions, it is generally much more comfortable as a life experience if we do not pay too much attention to you personally.

They did, therefore, exchange contact details (in pursuit of their own pleasure and possibly personal development) but Muramasa never called her during the two weeks they were both on the same island.

The reason for this is that he was at the time secretly working as a male escort for several wealthy older women of primarily European and Middle Eastern heritage, usually in the 35 – 50 age range. He had 4 clients in Cyprus at the time, more than in any location other than Paris. He was unfortunately fully booked for those two weeks.

From his own perspective, he had always preferred older women, or at least women over 24 if they were naturally very good in bed, because they've already learnt how to orgasm well and that's why they are interested in him. This way he did not have to have a relationship with any of them, which he was not ready for yet, primarily because he wanted a lot more sexual experience with multiple partners first.

He did not however tell Honey Apples any of this. He just neglected to call her, as she lived in London and he was planning to visit the UK at some point later that year.

We are saying that what the USA does on the world stage and what Japan does on the world stage are two very different functions which mesh well together.

Honey Apples and Muramasa went on to have an affair, which is what usually happens when Muramasa meets any particularly interesting woman who is also pretty and preferably bisexual or at least into anal. He rarely asks them any of this before they've had sex for the first time, but he has a feel for these things.

That affair resulted in Muramasa receiving many of Gerard Butler's old clothes, around the time he was filming Phantom. Sadly, he did not use many of them as he did not like the fit at the time. In return, however, for there is always Justice in the Universe and reciprocity is always instantaneous even if its fulfilment is not, Muramasa was able to convey to him certain of his own reflections. And that is why the movie 300 contains real understanding, not just pure storytelling. We may be doing something similar with this work.

This in turn was carried to the conversion device, who was Angelina Jolie at the time, another one of Muramasa's previous wives who said she would love him forever but then failed to close the distance to physical actualization. This is for the sake of strategic reasons in the present epoch, we wished to demonstrate that under the economic and banking system as it is presently formulated, women are unable to follow their hearts freely, even if the control imposed has to become very strict and unbelievably dark.

She has been through a lot, mainly due to her position in The Illuminati schematic, of which she has actually been told very little. Even to what she was told, she seems to have rebelled in every way she could find. She is generally bad news but, in our estimation, unlike her former husband, she is not worth the effort to convert because her usefulness on the world stage is limited to being one of the best conduits around. This why we have not included her in our schematic.

Angelina Jolie's daddy, John Voight, as the movie Tomb Raider revealed to the general public, is a lunatic who thinks he heads The Illuminati, because he is not very skilled at distinguishing fiction from reality, probably in order to facilitate his allegiance to the great Donald Trump but more likely because he actually is.

In terms of The Illuminati hierarchy the two most important magickal pieces are the points of greatest stress and glory within the Spartan heritage, which was Leonidas and his wife at the time. It was the Spartan mysteries and currents in fate which then went on to properly develop and implement both The Illuminati and the larger organization a portion of which has now gone public as Temple of the Vampire (even though both of those started in Egypt).

And all of these people connect in some way to Tony Robbins, with the overall motion of the USA and its effect on the history of the planet being his responsibility. You can do what you like with elected politicians, of course, but what we do is not beyond you and, indeed, in your own way, you are doing it already. Just much less consciously so, both as a group and as individuals.

Anyway, it is a truth universally acknowledged that Hollywood deals in stereotypes and fashionable tropes but it is probably reliable to say that even amongst such insincerity few would argue that Angelina Jolie is strictly sane and not even a little bit crazy, and they would have an even more difficult time maintaining this position relative to the Angelina who existed not long after she left Billy Bob Thornton who brought out the best in her, but before that also whilst she was with him and approaching him.

Besides, she and Muramasa were together again around 50 years or so before the French revolution got underway, so any process which has been proven about not finding each other again in future lifetimes only holds true as regards the present social construct and system of Illuminati social administration.

As can be seen, we plugged Muramasa into a much wider context, the relevance of which he failed to properly recognise at the time. The example does however illustrate what we mean by controlling the context around a target.

We were later able to utilize these connections to fulfil our own purposes through Muramasa, despite his objections to the contrary. Around halfway through the process he came to the recognition that his own power and effect on the world was on the line, as we had intended, and from that point on he became a lot more helpful and productive.

In short what that amounts to is that if Western Civilization is destroyed then the basis of the debt and the glory to his own Soul Lineage on this planet is removed. It is therefore in his personal self-interest for Western Civilization not to be destroyed.

And, ultimately, it was Ochi no Kata who tamed him, insofar as he can be 'tamed'. He is a difficult one to control.

Chapter 71 – Individualism, and the limits of its usefulness

Though Muramasa has always been aware of a certain attitude inside him, it took him a while to recognise it as Sparta. We needed to push him into this recognition in no uncertain terms, as fast as could reasonably be accomplished, because the root always reacts to its master.

He more than anyone else is responsible for the creation of the effective format The Illuminati morphed into during their time in Rome, which format they have largely retained down to this present day. He is at any rate the single individual most responsible for their structure and the format of their mysteries, which is the source of their power.

The present troubles with The Illuminati are the same troubles which developed in Sparta and later on in Rome, so you can tell that Muramasa is not very good at ruling the world as he has basically failed three times already. His essential approach is to develop the individual within a context designed to bring out all his potential and according to mysteries which make him realize his own essential nature.

Sooner or later, laziness, sycophancy and the pursuit of personal power and pleasure come to the fore and the rest, as they say, is history and fairly easy to check up on.

Our approach, by contrast, controls the individual in all important power capacities, and makes him recognise and abide within his responsibilities to the overall whole, as also to his own Soul Legacy. Our approach is not stricter but it is more productive, especially where larger groups of people are concerned.

Individualism is a valuable credo and all the most impressive advances in history and the human species have been due to outstanding individuals. We have included room for him to work all the most important elements of that credo into the new Shadowdancer organization we have provided for him.

As we have also done with Lucifer who in a very real sense heads the organization that currently rules Western Civilization and the world, larger purposes can overrule smaller visions and more limited plans. By controlling those two we effectively controlled the Western power structure they are responsible for.

As they both had and to some extent still have significant differences with the people presently actually running that power structure, these differences can be used to cause Western Civilization to transform itself very rapidly indeed.

The real reason for this is because the majority of the members, and the organization as a whole in some mysterious way, responds much more loyally and with far greater power to those two than to their incumbent leadership.

The root always recognises the master. The other one in this is Angelina Jolie. She does not know how to control the influence she exerts yet, and indeed currently seems to have lost touch with it.

Chapter 72 – Tracking the development of 9/11

The first recognition that Muramasa came to was thanks to Chen Xiao Wang. He recognised that Western Civilization as it was presently formulated did not stand a chance if Justice was actually applied to it.

He did not think much of it at the time, probably because he had yet to understand the fuller connection to his own self-interest.

We had in the interim derived the location for the next attacks in the 9/11 series and let Muramasa know about it via the Big White House in the Hague. Once the Bali bombings occurred, he began to look for personal and strategic advantage in the information stream we were offering him.

We subsequently confirmed the 13/11/2003 date for him from two more sources, one of them being Kitiara. The other was a high-level Illuminati defector who was poisoned shortly after getting the information to him, and this helped convince him. He did his best to analyse what was involved himself but he is not really that good at what is involved. He managed enough to recognise that we were probably onto something and could be right.

Muramasa was British at the time, and still maintains it as one of his nationalities. Partly for this reason and partly because Honey Apples with whom he was still having an affair lived right next door to the expected 2003 blast site, Muramasa did at the time begin to make plans to personally intervene.

However, he has since then had disagreements with individuals within the British power structure who were involved in the planning and precipitation of the 9/11 series.

We may question Muramasa's ability to rule humanity as a whole and we generally feel that our training and supervision have, through the centuries, made him a much more gentle and compassionate individual.

However, we concede that he understands Vengeance perfectly, better than almost everyone else in existence. He feels its position as also its motion and how it fulfils itself. He knows how to use it strategically. He has had it serving him for aeons.

He knows where his targets are located and what he can pin on them because reality and truth will accurately fuel the turning of Justice. You cannot use the Universal mechanisms to produce Justice on the basis of a complaint which did not happen or has insufficient depth to it.

We don't know who coordinated 9/11 because we have not taken much of an interest. We do however know that elements within the British Establishment were originally personally responsible for planning, facilitating and having others implement the 13/11/2003 event and that later, when that was derailed, they participated in the 7/7/2007 event through to completion.

It doesn't matter how we know this. In terms of the Group Mind the biggest real problem you have on your plate is the similarity in facial aspect of Prince Charles to a caricature-style sketch produced in the 19th century.

Realistically speaking, nobody is surprised nor overly concerned that you participate within The Illuminati hierarchy and that they have made their headquarters in the USA.

Chapter 73 – Stealing World War 3

Our real objective in getting Muramasa to join OccultForums rather than some other site was so that we could get his own soul out of the way to bring his ninja life through. We did set it up in that way but he must have sensed something because he simply had no interest in doing any actual magick.

He did start hearing some voices for the first time in his life since joining that forum. The first was Baphomet, who was very insistent and quite pushy, as a result of which Muramasa refused to have anything to do with him ever again. You get one chance with him. That is how he always runs the Illuminati hierarchy when he is in charge and it has recognised him again. If you screw up your first chance, you get a second chance lower down the hierarchy. He already has seen all he needs to know what to do with you from his level.

The Goetia also came to him, and they recognised each other for he has worked with them for millennia. His response in this instance was to issue a single command: "Shut the fuck up and play the long game."

It is useful when your allies are not idiots and can figure out what to do of their own accord. The grooving of the soul is also relevant here. It is how you can convert your mind from working in one set of ways to working in another set of ways. It takes years and is a matter of focus and consistency.

In a magickal capacity, this means the following: both demons and angels can only produce shifts in how people perceive things, how they understand things, how their mind works and how they feel about things. They cannot move you within society's wider structure into a set of positions very different from your present location. What they can do is enable you to fulfil your present location, to capitalize on it. The problem you will generally face is getting other people to pay for who you are and what you can do. It must have value for them. Hence you need to present it in a certain way, which the angels can help you with, and they need to feel a certain way about it, which the demons can help you with, or vice versa.

However, if you are in a different position in life then different things become possible. You can use these two factors – demons and angels – alone to change the structure of the entire world and bend global or national history to your will. Especially if you work with Lucifer, as shall soon enough be seen.

In other words, the same angel or demon will be capable of very different results depending who he is working for.

Our target with OccultForums was of course the Bael gateway they had put into place to do that thing with, which we wanted to use to capture the Return for the British Empire, something that is to start falling due around 2021-2023.

Therefore, the security services who did peruse what he was on about the time – it is generally fantastically easy to get their attention online if you ensure you include the right buzzwords in your material – were right to conclude that it would be best if they did not intervene in what he was doing or attempt to approach him.

Where they were wrong, and the decision in this was taken by the same person as the former information was ultimately reported to, was in believing that their own relationship with Lucifer was a "cooperative one".

If you are beneath Lucifer and the Naga in Hierarchy, and they issue you a direct command there is only one response on your part that will be accepted: efficiency, obedience and precision. The commission was for the 9/11 series, not to interrupt that series and do something else instead then try and patch it up later.

If you do not obey Lucifer once then you will not have the opportunity to do so again. This is one reason why Lucifer and Muramasa work well together, they share some of their value structures.

It is rare that Lucifer will consent to accept humans into their service, giving them the opportunity to participate in the expression and fulfilment of their own plans. This does not mean you choose to fulfil another set of plans rather than the set you have been given, because it is inconvenient for you, for example.

Muramasa therefore, posting as Okazaki Castle (though nobody got that joke at the time), released the information he had about the 13/11/2003 London attack online, using a forum for the discussion of the practice of active magick to do it. He knew how Lucifer and the Naga work you see. No need for him to explain that to you at the time of course or the effect would not have happened.

He then went off and took his stand. Specifically, he turned himself into a phenomenally powerful PSI Vampire at a deeply unconscious level by doing Jasmuheen's 21 day breatharian process. He did successfully complete the full thing, which included no water for the first seven days.

He timed the thing to finish on 13/11/2003. It was a devious thing to do. The Naga concluded at the time that he was a better criminal to administrate the development of World War 3 for them and so they reallocated those fate flows to him at that time, assuming he would take them up once he had completed his 21 day process.

Their representatives on Earth, independently of their commands from the Naga, decided it would be too disruptive to confirm Okazaki Castle's very specific prediction.

His response when he returned from his 21 day fast was to offer the two Illuminati agents in London who were coordinating the attack and had called it off the opportunity to buy their way out at the price of US$7billion, to be distributed amongst OccultForums' members. For the life of them, The Illuminati command structure at the time could not in the least comprehend why he would make them such an offer.

Those terms remain as set at the time. The main commission is the geomantic relocation of Jerusalem to Troy.

They did not understand their own position in Hierarchy relative to Lucifer nor did they understand how Lucifer conducts himself. QED. If they had known they would have jumped at the chance to buy it back, which he was offering them at the time. It was not business he seriously wanted to engage in; rather his intention was to entangle them further.

Muramasa, for his part, declined to take on the Naga's portfolio, as we had correctly anticipated he would, on the basis that he regarded himself as Lucifer's genuine superior. It was therefore up to him to come up with plans for Lucifer to implement, rather than the other way around.

This is where Recidivus entered the picture, as we now had inactive World War 3 Flows of Fate to withdraw and repurpose.

Muramasa had played his role admirably, drawing the entirety of World War 3 into his own energetic system as part of his conversion process. He lost about 15kg in the process, only 5kg of which he has since recovered. This is something else he wants to personally attend to once he has more time to play with.

Chapter 74 – Like they lied about 9/11, we lied about who killed whom and why

Masamune wanted the group karma of World War 3 to use the resolution of its contents to forge his Sword of God with. We therefore needed to get it out of Muramasa and into the actual physical katanas that Masamune was using for the process. But the first step was to get it out of Muramasa.

The Naga had done a very thorough job of embedding it deeply within his own energetic system, presumably with the intention that he would serve their purposes for them whether he wanted to or not. When this happens the only way to move the contents in question is normally to kill someone, or a large enough group of people, to produce motion in the Group Mind. So this is what we did next.

This is where Kitiara enters the picture again, as she had joined OccultForums too, along with Angelina Jolie, Johnny Depp and Honey Apples. Nobody said who they really were at the time though. A lot of Hollywood was there at the time for some reason.

The Illuminati's Inner Circle had made sure to place their own magickian on the board, to control the process, as the members were after all at the time dealing in the same currency that their own group bases its power on. His name was Bob Hendricks and he was in fact one of our own placements, put there for the purpose of taking Ra, the Egyptian deity, down with him.

The reason we wanted to do this, to reiterate, is because Ra was the only other real claimant on this planet to the Sun Throne, which has now been fully dominated by Amaterasu.

How we got Muramasa to do it is another story. But all of this was public and you should still be able to find it on some internet archive or other.

It was Armand whose intervention implemented the actual death of Bob Hendricks, but he did so as an expression of the Principle of Compassion. There is one god, and only one god, dominating on this planet at the current juncture in history as far as the physical reality of humanity's Group Mind is concerned: the Dalai Lama, who embodies Avalokiteshvara as his reincarnation, and whose central tenet in practice is the Principle of Compassion.

This means that everything depicted on the world stage since the late 1950s must fulfil and abide by the Principle of Compassion. You have Genghis Khan to thank for this. He is the one who created the Dalai Lama lineage, at least partially cognizant of what the fuller result would be.

With the administration of World War 3 allocated to him by the Naga, Muramasa was killing people left, right and centre, simply as a result of his own views and prejudices. He was neither particularly aware of the details of this process nor did it concern him overmuch. His primary focus at the time, and this was 2004, was securing the 2012 gateway for Masamune.

It was during 2004 that The Agreement was concluded between Christianity, Islam, Judaism, and Shintoism with Shambhala, Hinduism and Buddhism. This resulted in the 2004 tsunami, which makes our point very clear: Muramasa is responsible for the deaths of a tremendously large number of people during your present epoch of history. He single-handedly killed more people than died during the second Gulf War, at least until that juncture. It could not be otherwise in consideration of the actual position allocated to him by the Naga at the time. The individual holding the reins which determined the conduct of World War 3 had changed, and the depicted physical system was reflecting this.

Armand's basic point was that this lacked compassion: nobody in the ordinary Western power structure could understand what was happening, nor was the Group Mind of humanity able to comprehend where it was located. You have to be careful with such things because national depression can result and Empires have fallen for less. The human mind needs to know where it is located in order to know what to do with itself.

This was the objection that Armand brought to Masamune. Not seeing an easy way to produce an adequate resolution on this score, a meeting was arranged with Muramasa in the Hague during July 2004.

This time they were meeting in the lobby of Hotel des Indes, for coffee followed by an early dinner, as it had the sort of décor favoured by Armand and his kind.

"You do know what you are doing, don't you?" asked Armand.

"No," replied Muramasa. "Should I?" He resented the tone of the question and so decided not to be helpful.

Armand was not surprised. "What are you doing?" he asked.

"Getting you directions in fate for his Sword and trying to put together a syllabus for Temple of Venus," said Muramasa indicating Masamune with his eyebrows. "I still do not follow the logic you two have come up with but I'm pretty sure you're capable of fulfilling your end of our bargain."

Venus is the bright and morning star but the male Principle is not fixed, it rotates. It is currently and for the next 400 years or so being occupied by an obscure male god from the Norse pantheon called Forseti who is apparently very pleasing of aspect in more ways than one. However, because Venus is involved with the administration of the heart, the Naga are involved because they run the breeding program on this planet, which as people have realised has run into some problems lately. Lucifer resides on Venus as a visitor, he does not rule there even though it is very hot. There has been some confusion in how it was depicted to you.

At any rate, this means that The Illuminati, who serve and follow Lucifer, are properly speaking a sub-order within the Temple of Venus, rather than an organization superior to it which can implement and withdraw it like any other religious control modality, as they have been accustomed to doing throughout the ages.

Thus, our problem in giving him what he wanted was that his claims were too modest because he did not understand the value of what he already had. So a fairly stereotypical Journey, in terms of the Joseph Campbell formulation which we have Hollywood working with.

His experience with the 21 day breatharian process and the 13/11/2003 gateway, and what followed from that for him, had brought him into a fuller acceptance and recognition of his Spartan heritage. The recognition dawned on him after the fact, but he had actually relived his two key lives there in some way. The intensity of the experience left no room for real doubt in his mind.

Nevertheless, he was as usual trying to capitalize on it. This is because, since the age of about 17 when he first read Sun Tzu, he had been applying the Art of War to his business proceedings. The short version of the insight contained in that book is that you utilise every advantage at your disposal which results in your having to do a lot less work and even less actual fighting. You are not supposed to apply it directly in that manner but to calibrate it upwards by one density at least, resulting in the business application being your doing a lot less thinking, and even less actual work.

This is fundamentally the reason that we object to the German gateway of The Illuminati and hence the global system we all currently live within. The German understanding of both efficiency and the value of hard work is overrated and an inferior product. We say this not just as Japanese where there is of course very little room for argument, but also in our capacity of understanding what true efficiency actually consists in, especially in terms of work, and so in terms of our estimated value of approaches to economic and global management whose geomantic grounds do not participate in foundations located within the German Group Mind.

The Art of War is a far simpler approach to economic management than the present social science examining the topic. This will require extensive reflection on your own parts and indeed we have provided you with the author of that work to assist you in the process of developing your own understanding.

These then are the reasons we had not, as an extended hierarchy, paid him his price yet. We do not object to people demanding a lot before they join us. If they are that valuable we will arrange for them what they are asking for. Some are that valuable, but most of those have been found already.

The reasoning is of course circular and demonstrates how he was being moved deeper into our schematic. Our fundamental disagreement with The Illuminati's economic agenda has always been its gross mismanagement and the fact that they don't really understand what they are doing. Imperfect ideas do not survive death usually but will at any rate yield their perfect form to you in Hell. If you claim to know how to do it then how are you failing so spectacularly?

It would not have been possible to explain any of this to Muramasa at the time, or at any rate time consuming and not to our advantage. He had yet to yield to Shogun, had yet to fully recognise the capacities of his ninja lifetime and viewed that soul in his Legacy as an adversary more than his own deeper nature and was generally not yet cognizant of many of the Japanese hierarchy's deeper and more significant purposes. He was an agent on a contract, albeit a very good one who we had chosen to integrate further because he met the required standards during his present lifetime also. This is to be understood as sufficient mastery on his part of the fuller techniques of reincarnation.

After a moment's reflection, therefore, Armand asked instead: "How many deaths have you been responsible for so far then?"

"Several hundred, not that many really considering," said Muramasa, who like many on this planet has always been aware of people dying when they crossed his purposes but in his case he has also always been able to recognise that the reason for this is his usefulness, or potential usefulness, to beings and factions more powerful than himself.

Masamune then revealed to him the details of the Arrangement. We needed exactly the number taken on the 26th December 2004.

15 years later and here we are. MI5 now need to consider their new security arrangements. Demons target things as they can fit them in, conveniently and well. They do however interact directly with the timeline as a whole. Welcome to the long game.

We have identified the location of your two culprits for you, UK. This has been performed as a courtesy to your Royal family, who are of course the real targets in this. We could protect your reputation instead, MI5, but after all we need you to identify them as they are your pathway to the participants in The Illuminati hierarchy who planned the whole thing. We have a number of angles of approach to that target, including the Epstein scandal, but this is one of them.

Muramasa did not seem to have a problem with any of this, as Armand had expected.

"You do not see how administrating Western Civilization in this way does not give them enough information to work with?" asked Masamune. "This is the same problem generated by the incumbent Illuminati command structure."

"Humanity needs to understand what you are putting them through," said Armand. "Otherwise they have great difficulty maintaining their center and descend even further into madness. They need to feel not hope for the future exactly, but the sense deep down that somehow it's all going to be alright, that it all makes sense and that everything important is being taken care of as well as it can."

"The incumbent Illuminati structure at least offer the world's peoples that," said Masamune. "How do you expect them to change timelines when you are not providing their minds with a more secure alternative?"

"Be my guest," said Muramasa who had already done a lot more work for free than he felt he had contracted for. "You explain it to them."

"You are the one doing it," said Masamune. "It must be through you."

"Fine," said Muramasa, not much caring what he had just agreed to. He recognised that it needed to be done. "But I'm not doing it, even if you do want me to arrange the corporate frontage for you."

Armand smiled at this point, something he does not do very often. "Not corporate, my friend," he said. "OccultForums again."

To his credit Bob Hendricks recognised that he had chosen his own magickal path and that his death was his own work fulfilling itself, and posted publicly about this to save Muramasa from getting into trouble with people who would resurrect the witchcraft laws and truly have no clue what they are doing. In that same set of postings he also identified himself as Ra, the Egyptian god of the Sun. It is not technically possible to enforce laws in this system limiting people's internal spiritual progress on their own path or their chosen path.

However, it appeared to the viewing public as if a death had been specified through magickal attack and response. This was due to Kitiara, who we had publicise our involvement in a particular way on the forum in question, much to Muramasa's chagrin but there was very little he could do about it and he forgave her in the end anyway. He played along with her game, and helped develop the lie, because he had agreed to front for Armand, who was doing the actual work here.

It is not that he objected to the execution in Principle, it remained the best way to get the demonic host into the Sun's interior. He just did not feel that he had to be the one toiling for it, given what he went through to break open the initial hole which enabled the Return karmas for World War 3 to be stolen.

Nevertheless, the net result of the whole process was that humanity understood, at a deep enough level of the Group Mind for it be to very unconscious for most of them, that Muramasa was able to somehow target death in this system, a conclusion which was solidified with his second application of what to the Group Mind was essentially understood as control over the formulation of death once again, with the 2004 tsunami which resulted from the Arrangement.

At a human level then the motivation behind that death was Compassion, to help their minds to move along the tracks of actual reality such that excessive tension and disorientation did not result for them. At a divine level it was getting Ra out of the system to clear the stage for Amaterasu.

METAL ELEMENT

To abide within great virtue, you must first be able to recognise with ease what others agonise over. Then relax into it.

Chapter 75 – How Muramasa lost his soul

There was one other net result of the whole process, however, which we had planned and worked for from the start, and that is that Muramasa lost his soul as a consequence of the widespread response to what humanity at the time, as also a specific subset of them, believed his actions to have been.

That specific subset happened to include many of the world's more powerful magickians, witches and the like, who decided to all work independently to attack him at the same time. Many of them had used magick to kill people with before and everybody who participated in this response was a genuine blessing to both our cause and Muramasa.

Muramasa's own soul gave up eventually, as it has a tendency to delegate problems to subordinates, and never gives ground to its inferiors. True to the Spartan mysteries, it is quite a reptilian approach. This is why he found it so easy to transition smoothly to his previous soul, which now took up the mantle and had been waiting for this chance as also working to move it into position.

It was Muramasa himself, the soul he developed in his 500 year long ninja lifetime, who made mincemeat out of the global system in the years between 2005 and 2009.

Muramasa's present personality and souled gateway saw no reason to intervene and just let the ninja get on with it. He had another standing agreement dating from his time in Ancient Greece, when he took initiation in the Mysteries of the Great Gods on the island of Samothrace.

That standing agreement is the Kaberoi, often referred to as the demonic twins, but in fact only one of them is not from the human density, whilst the other is definitely a man. It will come as no surprise to some people that he had his agreement with Lucifer in place since that time. They can't both fit the entirety of their influence into the Earth system so when one declines to participate the other one gets more of an expression.

One of the ways Lucifer speeds up time is by having everything in place for you from before you arrive. We then had Muramasa arrested for various things, from breaking into embassies, to perverting the course of justice to identity fraud. The net result of that process was that we got the British to throw their benefactor in jail, even though they later released him without warning or charge. Most other nations declined the opportunity so we thank the British for participating in our plans and enabling the designated targeting to be arranged, just as we thank those other nations for not slowing down the overall schematic with their own misinterpretation.

It was at this stage that a former MI6 agent named James Casbolt joined our cause, though we suspected he was a plant at the time and he probably was. Nevertheless, he did go on the public record naming certain individuals in both the USA and the UK as coordinating and personally profiting from the global drug trade, including Sir Francis de Guingand,

Tibor Rosenbaum and of course George Bush Sr. It was at any rate the sort of thing which many people would go to considerable lengths to ensure it did not end up in court.

Our basic conclusion was that Sun Tzu has stipulated that both cannabis and opium are required in Temple of Venus, otherwise he cannot use it to make things dark enough, for control of the Luciferian currents.

This overall strategic position at the time he was in jail, more like a temporary holding cell for most of it, no need to overdramatise, enabled Muramasa to activate the SS pre-placements arranged by Lucifer within the British police, everything does always fit together. More importantly however, upon his arrest he did inform them, quite correctly, that they had 3 hours during which to release him.

He spent those three hours doing his morning exercises including chi-kung, which took about 1½ hours, and then trying unsuccessfully to use the cell intercom system and surveillance cameras to get the policemen and women especially to bring him a decent cappuccino.

Thereafter he referred the case to Shogun, to whom he had already surrendered by this time. Inferiors were being problematic in his presence and he did not owe them an education.

Shogun's response was to put the demon Ziku into position, and we're afraid that is who you have to negotiate your own peace terms with, British state.

Such a thing would not have been possible had you not violated both Justice and Hierarchy whilst believing yourself, as a hierarchy, to be participating within and enforcing the other side of the equation. When you do abide within Principle and virtue, and are correctly furthering its development, demons can gain very little access. Whereas you were right open, right down to a very deep and dense level of your power hierarchy.

From Lucifer's perspective, as also that of the Naga, you do have corruption in your state, you did not use that corruption to balance your account with your benefactor, you instead furthered his penalization and did not interact with him in accordance with your best attempt at an accurate depiction of Hierarchy.

Sadly, Ziku was the Sumerian war leader and you are quite correct in understanding him as an actual demon and not a fallen angel. This account comes with depleted uranium used on children, for which British investors in arms dealing companies are largely to be held accountable. You will note that Ziku is a wealth demon and are now informed that only Gilgamesh can truly put him back in his box and that is who he answers to.

Therefore you cannot negotiate this one with Muramasa. The lesson to be drawn from your predicament is that the USA is sacrificing your hidden wealth and power to China, Britain, to obtain their participation in their new schematic of global governance. As Muramasa intimated at the time, you should have paid him for 13/11.

Instead he is now taking your whole system and will then give you back what he thinks you deserve. This is what we mean when we say The Illuminati as an organization responds to him. We know who we identified and recruited.

Fortunately, when you do accept our offer, you will come to realise that what seemed a set of problematic and losing positions suddenly become brilliant strategic decisions which resulted in your ethical, personal and business success.

Until that time of course you have Brexit to contend with, but as you at least suspect by now we are closing that challenge down for you before you even get close to completing it.

Muramasa's personal soul from his current lifetime is back now, so it is not impossible to lose your soul for quite a few years and not die as a result. If you will be going through that same process, due to your membership of the Shadowdancers for example, then you can ask him how he prepared for the process and for pointers on how to successfully navigate your way through to the other side.

Chapter 76 – An aesthetic sense of sadness

Generally everything is now in position for the next stage in world proceedings. The Bael gateway was being used to try and keep a secret that had more business out in the open.

If you are currently an Inner Circle member of The Illuminati and find your way into the Shadowdancers then you will, also, lose your soul, usually for a period of around 4-8 years. We get that out of the way quickly for you so that you personally feel what is involved and so know how to comport yourself in future once you do get it back. This helps you not to be scared of ethics and enables you to come to understand and accept Consequence as you will by then understand what it really is and have some idea of how to work with it.

We used to live in a different world. Looking back, there is always an aesthetic sense of sadness. The way to overcome this is to ensure that your future holds more promise than your past.

Chapter 77 – The Lehman family

The Sanctuary of the Great Gods on the Greek island of Samothrace was originally excavated by Karl Lehmann who, despite the addition of an extra *n* in this iteration of the family name, does connect to the banking family of the same name.

The UN will also be involved in due course, as the same family also has deep roots in that organisation.

The relevance and significance in terms of the modern world system is that the Kabeiroi represented the twin pillars of Heaven and Earth, one of those was Lucifer, and the other was whoever chose to be an aspirant.

However, and this is important, the Kabeiroi, one of whom was Lucifer, were not the chief or most powerful gods within that tradition and effectively bound into that relationship to each other from that geomantic node. That role was reserved for two female goddesses, and one lucky male god. More seriously, there are two types of female soul but only one type of male soul. These three also had a servant, known as Kadmylos at the time, but more recognisable to you all as Hermes.

However, in that tradition also it is Lucifer who really goes to the trouble of relating to the humans in depth.

Masamune wants to relocate the Bank of the Mediterranean to the island of Samothrace. This is his answer to the Chinese global financial system and part of his answer to the economic system promulgated by the Antichrist.

We surmise that the net result he is aiming for is not to take the administration of money globally away from Lucifer – after all he was initially put into that position for a reason, and humans will misuse whatever you give them if you don't have them under inspired rule – but rather to place Lucifer into a context where he is under supervision, a context that he already agreed to and seems to be comfortable within. In other words, there is no need to bring Lucifer under control. There is already a location on the world geomantic grid where he is already under control. It just needs to be used in the right set of ways.

We are probably right but Masamune never really explains himself and nobody can understand him anyway. Muramasa doesn't use much logic to get to his results but he still has to work his way there to an extent, say 3 or 4 steps rather than several thousand as would be normal nowadays, so you can understand who he is and his process because there's some sort of Order to work with there. You can get some idea of his values and priorities just by following his thought process and how life fits together for him. Thus you can form a fairly accurate picture of his character after a while.

Masamune by contrast would seem to *assume* logic, because he just knows it will be there for him, and in the correct set of orders moreover, and just moves effortlessly between consistent conclusions, all of which cross-reference with an ease and simplicity not rarely but never seen in the work of any other swordsmith.

So we can understand his works if not the man. For us this is easy enough because we still have some of his swords around. We believe he is going to demonstrate the rest for you in lieu of breaking the mystery and actually revealing himself physically on the world stage. Besides, he can't do any miracles in this lifetime so people would rapidly be disappointed and all sorts of controversy and chaos would result.

Roman Catholic clergy will get to meet him at the Vatican and members of the Orthodox monastic orders at Mount Athos. So you will have reliable reports, on your own terms, from people who should be able to recognise that sort of thing and so will be able to confirm for you on your own terms what we have been saying. We doubt they will get it wrong, not eventually, but they might. So you are left with what you are left with. And let that be enough for you.

Chapter 78 – The Sword of God, part II

Masamune had his Sword of God forged and complete, including all the polishing, by the end of December 2007, because he used the December 11th Jupiter-Pluto conjunction as his Sword Edge.

It was the closest Jupiter-Pluto conjunction to the 2012 physical referral gateway, which is why he wanted to use it, as already explained, to fit a lot more into that referral gateway than was ordinarily supposed to be contained therein.

He was actually making three katanas at the time, representing the triplicity of fate, or the triune godhead, or the three brotherhoods, and so on. One is in black, the ninja path, one is in white, the religious path presumably, and one is in red, which we suspect he wants to see if he can offload onto Muramasa, who will probably decline.

He completed the mountings and the scabbard with pre-ordered items off the web and was done by the end of February. We have seen the works he produced in this lifetime. They are less elegant and more unrefined, the type of sword you would expect to have been produced 200-300 years earlier than the surviving examples of his craft during his time within a Japanese body and so under Japanese administration.

Elements of the distinctive style are still there, and can be found throughout his work so it should not be too difficult to confirm what we are saying, but our conclusion can only be that he is not as focused on making swords today as he was then, it is no more than a hobby for him really. His attention is primarily elsewhere and it has also been confirmed that fate calibrates differently within your genetic structure you when you are incarnated abroad.

"They never did understand me," said Armand.

"Don't let it slow you down," said Masamune. He was focused on polishing the red stage katana. It was patient and laborious work.

"Why are you making three of them?" asked Armand.

"Anticipating demand," said Masamune. "No one man or nation should wield that much power on the world stage, also it is too much responsibility for the individual to bear, it would destroy him ordinarily. Checkmating the planet into effective unity of purpose by controlling the nature of the division. Harmonizing the layers to the Trinity. Take your pick. Doing it all and more. Talking of which, any news from Recidivus?"

"He is marketing the World War 3 currents you arranged to have sent his way as the opportunity to participate in the formulation of the Judgment which concludes the first successful Lucifer experiment in the history of all Creations," said Armand. "There has been more interest than he can handle and the whole thing is stressing him out immensely. He says he should have an answer for you on timescale by the end of the month."

This is a technical explanation relevant to those who know what the Lucifer experiment was for.

Masamune was busy focusing on bringing something out in the grain of the steel. He was doing so as an expression of his following of the directions in fate Armand had pointed him in during his commentary referring to Recidivus. This is similar to the other mysterious parts of the process, which effectively connect the physical swords to the Sword of God itself. He also published 3 explanatory manuals, one for each version.

"Plenty of room here," said Masamune by way of explanation. "It's why I call it the Sword of God, you can fit the entirety of this Creation within the soul I have imbued into this thing. To tell you the truth you could probably fit up to five Creations in there without too much trouble."

"Not Swords of God?" questioned Armand, pursuing his earlier point.

"Only one soul is involved," said Masamune. Things were getting clearer.

"So what does this thing do exactly?" asked Armand.

"From the many, one. From the one, many," said Masamune, paraphrasing Empedocles rather than Heraclitus. It is a continuous and simultaneous process, two flows, one heading towards unity and the other towards myriad separate forms. Love unites and the opposite power separates.

It takes the priorities of the species and the planet and derives the single next step that they need to work on. To start with at least. It might be the three or five or 20 steps simultaneously later on. With use. Until we sharpen it again."

"Who sets that one goal?" asked Armand. "And how do you use it to kill people with?"

"The goal sets itself, it is what makes the Sword sharp. And it is very sharp. But all three must agree for an Edge to arise," said Masamune.

"People die all the time, for different reasons, depending what the main social goals of the time are," said Masamune. "I don't think any human could work his way through that chaos in reverse, somehow managing to influence what goals humanity finds valuable with sufficient accuracy to pick off individual targets. It is called the Sword of God for a reason. It reveals what the species wants and needs as a next step. And it does so to three bearers, all of whom must be conscious of what is involved and agree in their hearts on the interpretation."

"Or what?" said Armand. "If they don't agree, then what?"

"Then their Sword of God will appear blunt to their eyes and their understanding," said Masamune. "No judgment will form. The bearers would be unworthy in such an instance."

"Which means what, a delay?" asked Armand.

"No, it just puts them back where they are now. All arguing amongst themselves with Lucifer enforcing a schematic over their heads whilst they once again work on cultivating their belief that they are the ones in control," said Masamune. "No big tragedy."

In reality, the Naga are not going anywhere. This is their planet now, more than it belongs to the human species anyway. The Ancient of Days deals with what is actually there, in perfect Judgment and understanding.

"What's the first goal then?" asked Armand. "Is it clear yet? Has it formed?"

"Sorry," said Masamune. "That's one of my secrets. I can tell you the second goal though. Bank of the Mediterranean to be based on the Greek island of Samothrace."

So that's his plan. But he already secured the 2012 referral using that thing, though not for himself or the planet but for Japan.

Hidden Chapter

The Sword of God is a mysterious thing. It does have a real physical sword as its correlate, three of them in fact. But they are average quality swords even if they do have some interesting characteristics. Their own souls are quite small, at least at this stage in the process.

The whole thing would seem to be some sort of metaphor for a specific format and structure of Universal, or divine, Mechanics such that they behave like, and can effectively be used as, a Sword.

From what we can tell, the physical swords have some symbolic value and they enable a much better connection to be established more easily with the Sword of God itself. But it is one single Sword of God, not three. And it is a tremendously massive structure, stretching across the known Universe from what we can tell.

It would appear to be composed of a large number of celestial alignments, but these are just openings to deeper and broader alignments elsewhere, or to a chain or series in some cases.

It appears to function by turning the heavens, and their motion, into a Sword. We already knew that Time kills everything, so the fact that it can be used to kill people is not what makes it a sword. Rather, it is what it does to your Will when you pick it up or wield it.

After all, when you make a steel sword, you are just aligning the matter in that sword in a certain way, through the acts of forging, folding, hammering, polishing and so on. However, when complete, you can then focus your Will through a steel sword with great precision.

The Sword of God then, is a set of structural relationships between the planets, stars and other structures of this Universe. You still need to feed some sort of Will through that Sword for it to do anything however.

And this is what Recidivus' referral was for. Muramasa interrupted the Naga's World War 3 series on the basis of our instructions. The Naga then wanted and expected to have him as their puppet now instead of the previous yet still to this day incumbent Illuminati command structure. Their plans for World War 3 were not going to change much however, as they had already figured it all out, so to speak.

Muramasa refused to participate in their plans, on the basis that he was superior to them and higher in Hierarchy, so damned if he was going to do what they told him to when the order of things should clearly be the other way around. He tends to stand on his Principles, as history has shown. But you need him here so you can't kill him, we found out that same truth too so you're not being original, we've thought of it also before and examined the various scenarios which result. There are other ways to control his influence on the system as we have shown. He also knew that he had a superior set of plans to call upon, for he had by this stage felt Shogun's heart, and that told him all he needed to know about the matter. Nobody else in the system was a challenge for him, rather he tended to view them as a joke but was kind about it. Consider that.

Therefore a referral had to occur. And as the Naga are by their nature and density far more deeply involved in all the specifics which go to constitute a Judgment, and its expression in the physical, the only way they could really be defeated was by forming an alliance of races and species who had attained the Principle in various areas of expertise, and then reflect those on Earth in alignment with their tuning and harmonic calibration on the matter.

You then put more of those into the Earth system than it can contain unless it removes for itself, or otherwise has removed for it, most of the previous content it contained. The Naga cannot argue with Principles. They are the greatest degree of perfection of an activity or function in known existence. Plus, all conscious species clearly feel and know who has which Principles and why, at the group level at least.

Now the only place you can do that is Hell. This is because an accurate reflection must be made for it to work. You are already physical. What do you think is going to happen, that you will get heavier? The truth is we don't know what will happen. Shogun does but he's not telling anybody yet. He does that. Learn to become comfortable with the practice because there's nothing anyone can do about it.

We do not have to care about things we are not responsible for or participating in. We do not tend to. You will find that we are not generally idly curious.

We do know what the consequence set will be. This planet and humanity will attain integration with the wider galaxy, in one form or another, but we, as in Japan, will limit who is allowed to immigrate here or even establish forward bases on the Moon or some sort of representation. Extraterrestrial species do exist, we know because we have communicated and worked with them consistently throughout our history, and even to this day you will find some famous public ninja houses who openly state their alliance or representation of specific star systems, for example in their family crests.

However, that does not mean we have to have any of them here. You are just curious, for technological progress you just need one species to deliver you the best that they've compiled for you. If you're that curious, develop your own capabilities and go there. At any rate we refuse to have many of them on this planet.

A referral is when you get the rest of this Universe to look at the individual parts of your schematic, every single solution and every single problem, and then ask: can this be done better? In practice, not in theory.

So we take everything that has been done in the Earth system already, and depicted to the limits of the Naga's abilities through the formats given to human history, and then refer these things to whoever has mastered them and ideally attained the Principle on the matter.

One example of an unusual Principle which you may not have expected to exist is the Principle of Genocide itself. This has been perfected by the star system Antares, and it is their format and directions which we are following in our implementation of the schematic on the human plane of existence.

As you will note, the distance in mind, character and personal comportment is considerable and, compared to your previous format, much greater mastery will have to be involved to secure the depiction. For example, this time all the participants will have to engage in the process both voluntarily and consciously. The fact is you do not escape Naga administration by means of this methodology. You simply use others to force their hand to compel them to depict a much better system for you. But you do not get it for free. You need to make all that progress in Mind and character to actually do things this way.

Fortunately, you will make all this progress, as if by a quantum leap. This is because the Sword of God, which produces this extensive referral process, holds the expression which the administration gives to this system to a certain set of standards. This means the Naga have to do it our way and therefore you, humans, have to do it their way. Which is basically our way, as you will have come to have understood by now.

On your own system's terms this constitutes another Paradox Lock for you, because it cannot be a conspiracy if it does not exist, or if its enforcement capacity does not exist which amounts to the same thing. And fourth density Adam Kadmon reptilians do not exist, let alone on this planet. Once you do take a different formal position in public then you may draw your public conclusions in a different way. Until then your hands are tied on the basis of your own rationality. And just to make sure, one thing you should know about Paradox Locks is that they are locks. For example, if you try to violate the logical integrity of your own belief structures, or system in logic which supports your worldview, then even if you try to hide or ignore that omission, we place things in the darkness, or space, thus generated. Try it if you like, then you can see what it feels like when properly applied. Hurts a fair bit, but once is to be considered educational. Twice and you are becoming naïve about things, and that trend in fate will be further allocated to the hierarchy you represent.

The difficulty is not coming up with the idea to improve things, the difficulty is getting other people and forces to participate. This is why Masamune had to be the one forging it. Species and civilizations have a tendency to want to participate with him – for there are benefits if you know how to use them – but also, when he gives actual commands, nobody goes against them. This is due to his Ancient of Days aspect. You know his penalization structure. Conscious species recognise who he is, and this is what you are in the process of becoming though it will take you in the region of 200 years. So we delivered him to you early you could say. Now say thank-you and begin the process which will lead to the making of arrangements for the restoration of the Imperial godhood.

At any rate, the Sword of God is ready and it is the group karmas for World War 3 – extensively recalibrated – which are being fed through it. So the Will is there also, and it is being focused.

Shogun is two levels beneath Hell as you know it, and that is where this schematic originates from and who is in control and command. Your Jesus Christ is not in charge, not where our hierarchy is concerned, and we are the nation doing this thing. It is our time now and this is part of our benevolent rule towards you as a species, but also specifically Christian nations which have always tended to be the most problematic. From a strategic perspective, now you can neither question our benevolence nor the morality of what we are proposing, because all of your own positions as far as the mainstream is concerned have been directly overruled, and on your own terms. Moreover, now you cannot convince your own people on your behalf. So he was there all along, if you know how to look.

The direction is the correct one. We are using the motion of the heavens to get us into Hell and it is the Sword of God which is doing it. What results is a basic paradox lock. The Sword of God formats those things into chains at least 36 paradox locks deep, all interconnected, and that's as far as we've got but it does seem to go on forever. And no we don't know how he does it, nor what it all means, ultimately, nor how it all works. But it does work, and very well, we have tested it extensively already.

This is a very complicated and difficult subject. We do not fully understand everything that is involved yet. However, you do not need to understand how a sword is made nor what its structure is like on the atomic level to pick the thing up and use it.

And that is its beauty, and its relevance.

If you have the opportunity to get deeper into it, meditate on the soul of the real Japanese-style sword you hold in your hands. By real we mean it must have a sharp edge and good enough steel that you'd be comfortable relying on it to get through four or five people with.

That's all you need to connect. The meaning will be there, too, if you know how to feel.

Chapter 79 — Die by the sword, it's a much better way to go

Those who live by the sword, die by the sword. This is an old saying, but also a widely prevalent belief throughout history, and its influence has contributed to the way reality on this planet has formulated itself for millennia.

Which sword is the question. And also, how exactly does it kill you?

Nobody really uses swords much in public nowadays anymore. But the way of the sword is still alive and well, with many people living by it even in this day and age, not least quite a sizeable minority within the Yakuza, already well on its way to become a majority (due in part to the publication of the first edition of this book).

Provided it kills you more slowly and with ancillary positive effects throughout the process this is not necessarily an undesirable binding to be living within. One of the purposes of the whole schematic where the Sword of God is concerned is in fact to heal all ailments, improve the condition of the mind and maintain the physical body in a condition of youthful longevity.

And when you do die, it will be quick.

Now if you want to live by money, or by the law, or by the gun even, then that's fine and nothing is stopping you. But do not pretend in our presence that those things are not enforcement mechanisms, because they all are. People are killed because of money and by money and this also holds true for the law.

But only the Way of the Sword is special, as described. It also requires you to develop your character, which is not something that can really be said of either money or the gun.

When something dominates in its class then it dominates overall where that class of things is concerned. There is only one Sword dominating on this planet nowadays, and probably far into the future moreover. The Way of the Sword has special properties to it now, and if you have that steel within you then your physical body will respond.

Lack of ethics will kill you, or at least age you more rapidly, but you won't get to the youthing effect through self-righteousness, emotionality and moral regurgitation, even if it is of a tremendously long list of rules learned perfectly by rote and adhered to very strongly, just like the law.

You need character and you need to not only be able to think and feel for yourself but to be willing to act on the basis of your conclusions rather than the tenets of whatever power structures you are participating within.

Finally, and somewhat paradoxically, it is possible to combine the Way of the Sword with a personal philosophy of complete non-violence, on a physical level at least, though you'll probably get beaten up or attacked several times if you try this, because that's just the way we've calibrated the whole thing.

Chapter 80 – Satoshi Nakamoto's strategy was always deeper than it seemed

Otomo-no-saibito, or 'Otomo the clandestine' has been studying and developing cryptography for hundreds if not thousands of years. He has attained a deep understanding of Principle on the mater but does not personally hold the Principle in this yet.

This does not mean that he would formulate his best product right at the start, and then just release it to the world, that would have been an appalling strategic decision on his part, which is not how he tends to formulate his own paths in life.

First we need to know how you will respond, which should amount to the introduction into the mainstream of greatly enhanced quantum computing. Whilst you occupy yourselves with the technological challenges involved, we have moved a strategic schematic into place around you, effectively occulting your power base.

We then entangle you with the motion of Justice in the world, namely its resolution of previous placements and occurrences, and make its formats visible to you in a manner you can understand, which is what this book and subsequent historical occurrences are for.

By that stage our power structures will have agreed to cooperate and the new global system should largely be in place. You can steal it if you like though. Should you attempt this we would counsel a much deeper understanding of what cryptography is really for.

Otomo was the first Satoshi Nakamoto even if he was not the first to adhere to the Central Way nor even the first ninja. He is the one who took our project public. His target was not currency alone but the entire Western power structure, whose foundations had been calculated as being fractional reserve banking.

Otomo's personal identity will forever remain a mystery because he has, due to personal and family connections, grown up seeing Shogun occasionally since the age of about 6.

Chapter 81 - Masamune addresses Christianity

This is not my time to go public and I have to be careful, primarily not to take too much of the spotlight but also not to dominate proceedings. However, I am here early by means of this arrangement and that enables me to exert an influence on future proceedings, most especially as regards the 25th century from an Earth perspective, which is when I was and still am scheduled to make my public appearance. This is similar to when I am allowed to do so because the mechanics of Creation open up for it. There is a certain technical art to the process which both the Japanese and certain Chinese secret societies seem to be very proficient at; the West generally less so.

In a very tangible sense this was always meant to be, as was recorded by chance in the gospel of Matthew; not everything survived in the formal record, but I'd glad that one did because it makes explaining things a lot easier. I have now forged my Sword, and it is ready to go active. It is already in use along the lines of black path, preparing the fertile ground for all of this and laying the directions in fate.

I can do no miracles in this lifetime, but I am doing something very different in this lifetime. Although I say that, I am also trying to introduce the Elven methodology for life extension in a youthful condition to the human species, which could count as a miracle in due course I suppose. Nothing is ever certain until it is done, my friends. You will see why this is the case later. You can, however, make things close to certain and this is what I have done for you in this.

I also intend to teach a group of 12 others my healing methodology that I used in the Jesus Christ lifetime, though it will work much more slowly nowadays due to the sheer mechanics involved – Muramasa and his people have been very busy it would seem, and their schematic is primarily Illuminati and Vampire – but it essentially involves you navigating your way through the fate streams of the subject, to untangle the misinterpretation of concepts surrounding and underlying the condition.

You will get some idea of this if you recall that I originally gave you the injunction to love your enemy, and operate on faith alone. Now you know why that is and how it works. The same applies to turn the other cheek, though that is a much more brutal methodology to be applied only when you know you have the strength for it.

In both cases of the love your enemy technique then, what you are doing is using the mechanics of the Creation system in which you find yourselves to your advantage. In the one case, what you are doing is faith. In the other, it can be called magick. Certain misinterpretations have been involved, Muramasa's people made changes to further their agenda.

There was a war going on, for interstellar dominance between Civilizations to see who can best embody and give expression to Principles, and though the game has now been fixed and the Lucifer experiment itself is over, the timeline remains unchanged and the 25th century will still occur.

The real bloodshed is scheduled to occur with the Kalki Avatar, in the 25th century, and that is what I was going to turn up for and when Armageddon will actually occur. Correct, I know the date and many other people figured it out for themselves, precisely also, and one centre even made the Kalachakra tradition and calendar recording it all. It is all there if you look. At the world around you. It is required to actually depict the truth. The real problem is that there is no clear order of priority nor public development of the resources you already have at your disposal.

However, the plan is that we are going to pre-ground the Elemental hardware for the Armageddon schematic during World War 3 on the global stage. Moreover, we are going to do so by means of a much lower death toll than would ordinarily occur by violent means during the same span of years. The whole process would not work if the Sword of God was not functional.

Compassion is one of the few Principles actually headquartered on Earth during the present time, as you don't have many gods publicly incarnated on this planet at the moment. Use it for all that you can whilst you've got it, doing so gives real power to your world stage position. For example, we got our format of genocide through on the basis of Compassion, as also our rewrite of both Armageddon and World War 3, the ninja assassination of Capitalism, the formation of a whole new currency and employment system, and more besides.

When you are representing a Principle as its foremost exponent in this Universe then the entire Universe holds you to account, and this pertains to the operations of the solar logos of the system, or the plural of that as the case may be. The rest of the Universe will all have to express Compassion less perfectly than you, and so refuse to be bound by your incompetence. There are limits to the extent that the Naga can keep you protected, you see.

I took training under both Muramasa's hierarchy, just an ordinary Spartan soldier, nobody special, and in the ninja arts also. Part of my purpose in doing so was to secure Returns on them both, which is why they are now included within my schematic in a tutelary capacity, which is where you use Sirius.

The problem is that I am more than you imagined, not less. As I said, this is not my time and I am doing something else in this lifetime. Also, I will die and subsequently reincarnate in the 24th century, by which time the ordinary human lifespan will be in the region of 250 years.

My penalization structure is what it is on account of mechanics. I am very strict in the way I run Creations. The benefit is equally strictly enforced, but you have to move with the time and your own heart to ensure you stay on the right side of that equation. On this planet I have compressed my standard penalization structure to the size of the circle of a genetically distinct race, or possibly even nation grouping in some instances. That was impossibly difficult to do and I cannot make it any smaller than that. So that's the penalty for killing me and is why I normally die at home or on a mountainside somewhere. The broader penalization structure, for example for disobeying my direct commands, is then built off that proportionately.

This is what the Sword of God is actually composed of: commands instructing this Creation to behave in a certain set of ways. This process cross-references Principles to each other, which is how other star systems become involved and is how we defeated the Naga, whilst simultaneously they won and the Lucifer Experiment was a success. You are being moved through densities and should not be surprised. Your old concepts are being withdrawn from you by being forged into paradox locks for depiction on the world stage. This enables us to move events with speed, as opposed to a lot of drama.

This strictness makes the relevance of a clean enough and pure enough heart important. Some people and species do prefer to live within the flows of Vengeance but that is not generally our way as Christians.

You will find that there is room for both accurate interpretation and real understanding of the mechanics and messages involved in the old gospels. However, you have to know what you are looking for. The messages were not for everybody. Only those who felt an inner calling. The Church should not proselytize for the near future, the next 400 years or so, and focus on their works for the benefit of society and their fellow man. We need to be in a very strong position when the time for it comes. Your position as it currently stands is progressively getting weaker. It is also irresponsible and not in true keeping with your faith and it is past time you came to understand that, as a united hierarchy if not at an individual level where truth and sincerity often do prevail.

We have secured the portal, the 2012 referral, which is what the Sword of God was about, least of all because doing so allows you to determine the format of the coming Age and Octave. That particular referral was much more powerful and useful than the one in 3114BC for example, due to the participation of much deeper and wider cycles pertaining to this Universe and not only this Creation as a whole but also the Central Domain itself, which has never happened before. This is why this planet was the location of the conclusion of the first successful Lucifer experiment.

The whole thing is a theological consideration for the Muslims, this is Shogun's schematic. From a practical level, in terms of mechanics, I know for a fact that Lucifer has found his way into the Catholic Church, and in fact he is welcome there. May he find forgiveness for his sins, if he considers he has any. He will certainly regard himself as entirely blameless, I know his soul. This does not mean he has not been responsible for great atrocities. This is why I maintain a very strict enforcement capacity myself.

Before you did not truly understand who and what I am and would not have been able to credit it as the case. But, everybody, or nearly everybody, can believe it now. At the very least they will question its relevance and see its potential value. However, there is real urgency at stake. Do not trouble yourselves overmuch but whilst the actual position of the Western power structure is not moving forward consciously towards the restitution of the personal godhood on the Emperor of Japan – in the designated very difficult and complex manners – then the Muslim war machine and process is being developed along the previous structures, whilst similar conditions apply across the scope of possible fields of power, that is to say all of them.

Secrecy was required to secure the 2012 referral. Muramasa's people did their job well, we give them that, there was widespread distraction within a very confused and deeply materialistic society.

This entire schematic is being administrated by Japan. I chose to integrate myself with their purposes because it is better that way, if inconvenient for some. We all cooperate in pursuit of a common goal and the national interest, very broadly and deeply defined.

It is now time to settle some moral questions, for these are often a source of great pain to people.

Abortion is always a sin, and a heavy one at that, but it is not as bad as murdering someone when they are 23 or even 40 years old. The reason for this is because the soul is more heavily invested in the lifetime and body in question by that time, so the karma is heavier that you will have to go through if you do something like that.

I do not generally agree with abortions but people should be free to choose. If you do that I suggest you make it a mutual decision, because Shogun rules during the current epoch and he is particularly strict with women as you may have surmised for yourselves from an examination of the conditions women live under both in Japan and also in Muslim countries. He is the father, you will have to decide together. Contravene his position if you will, the point is there are mechanics and hierarchy to the process.

This does not mean that, as an individual, your free will is controlled. The terms of the operation of natural Justice may cause great suffering to the individual but only in rare cases does it kill them in return. You can do what you like but if you do those sorts of things you will be put through some very deep, dark and heavy karmas which will probably impact you for the rest of your life.

However, there are some souls on this planet who naturally use things like that to further their own goals and the welfare of the planet as a whole. This is very difficult to do and I would not recommend it but if you find yourself in that position because of choices you have made then your way out is to understand where you now find yourself located and develop the concepts and feelings which come into your heart and your mind, as also perhaps your external life experiences. Your objective is to find some sort of pathway by means of which your path of choice and action was the correct one. It will always be there, eventually, but you might have to turn in position for a long time until they release you, which is where the Naga do come in during the administration of such a process. All prices are paid and there is a cost in karma for everything that you do.

There has been some confusion on this score, because it was assumed that when you forgave people their karmic record was somehow erased. This is not the case because karma exists to allow for the interactions of beings in terms of their inner desires and condition of vibration, as also location in Universal Hierarchy and level of personal understanding and embodiment. Life is simply not possible without it, its processes are in a very real sense the internal experience of life itself, which does itself at the group level create the physical context and experience also.

One of the things I specialise in is what you will recognise best as the redemption process: navigating a soul, any soul, out of Hell. I am the only one who can do it and this was one of the main sources of my power. However dark you go, however bad life gets for you, if you tune to the currents of fate I control or even simply if you give over control of your life to me, I do have a way out for you and will get you there unless you die before the process is complete, but that too is a conclusion which works.

The Japanese solution, Shogun's solution, is different. He opened up Hell, produced a condition of mobility between the Octaves, ending the influence of the precessional cycle and the Ages of man (Iron, Silver etc), and insisted that every level comport itself to standard.

However, the only way he can viably connect that process to the rest of the species is via my Sword of God. This does not mean he has no alternative, it means he is bound by Compassion, at least until the present incarnation of the Dalai Lama dies.

Should he wish not to destroy you after that juncture, which the Emperor will very likely insist upon personally, then he has no alternative and must use my Sword of God. So even where he is concerned, I found a way out of Hell for him.

As regards abortion, part of the process of becoming a conscious species is learning to breed consciously. This means you contact the souls which will incarnate as your children before they do so and arrive at the necessary agreements consciously. Part of this process is being able to control conception in your own body. There is something of a conflict going on which has not yet been settled between humanity and the Naga, who are still currently running their breeding program and will continue to do so for at least the next 100 years if not eternally, depending on what agreements are reached.

When you have an abortion you are participating in that war on the side of humanity. That war will finish when you breed consciously as a species. Learn to live within and move according to its terms. War is always Hell, remember that. It is more difficult to navigate your way through life when you are there. Ensure you have a strong character and clarity in terms of what you value before you go there. That sort of thing is not a command, but good advice. There has been much confusion between the two it would seem.

If you have had an abortion, or several, and basically notice nothing different in your heart or life then you probably, but not always, have a vampire soul somewhere in your Soul Lineage. Even then, once you have gone through stillness and the metaphorical death, you should notice the difference in the way you are now administrated. If you basically feel nothing and understand nothing, then you are the reason the law was created in its present format. That model exists in a male version also and has some limitations. It is in the process of being retired. You have already been told I am also the Ancient of Days. You may be surprised just how much stricter I can be when in that aspect.

As regards paedophilia in the Church, you will be executed along with the rest as soon as we have the TRNC state in position to do this with. You, also, will have to make your own travel arrangements.

Generally, you will not be given what you cannot handle and the more conscious you are, the stricter the administration will be with you. This is why the Christian religious modality is good for so many people: pretty much anyone can access it, and the grace of God is a real thing, on the inside, in your feelings, and often in your life as well.

You may as well know that He does exist and is a motive force in events. That's one thing that this book is doing. QED on God, as Muramasa would say and I am obliged to him for arranging much of it.

War is always based on deception and this has been explained before but Muramasa is one of the best at it. We can work with them but it will be on our terms because I have the Sword of God and it is the key to the restoration of the Imperial godhood. As for Muramasa himself, he basically could not care less, provided he gets to do his own thing with plenty of free time and has other people resolving the problems for him according to his directions. The rest of those organizations are not powerful enough to generate any real problems.

There will come a time when the Imperial godhood does QED. We need to be in position by that time, so it is not a question of when we decide to move. We are moving now, already.

You are welcome to join in and I hope you enjoy the ride. I know it's a big surprise, but overall it is much better this way. Try to relax and not to worry too much about what will happen or the big existential questions. Let it come to you and happen around you, the directions according to which history will develop are different now.

And more than anything else, that's the Sword of God in action. That's why my penalization structure needs to be so big. Planets and entire species are generally difficult to move, even if we are just talking about a change in internal perspective and orientation through life. But yes, it was impossibly hard and I cannot do that again, in the sense of I do not want to. Which was probably the intention, as God Tamahagane is crafty in war. He doesn't want the whole Lucifer Experiment idea repeated, provided we do it "well enough" the first time we succeed at it. And there's nobody else around who could feasibly enter that thing and win, not even Shogun as he presently stands.

I didn't much like the idea of the Lucifer Experiment at the start either, but this is because it was going to inconvenience me and others greatly. However, it has worked and was a success. What it allowed for and resulted in *is* the Sword of God. This translates as the much stricter rule of Creation systems from Central Domain. Eventually. But we're not at that stage in proceedings yet and still have the 25th century to get through. It won't fully be in position until around 3031, but Earth will effectively become a utopia long before then. And yes, that is a promise.

That is why it was impossibly hard, Israel, the Holocaust I mean. You need to face what was involved, Israel, and then understand it. It happens automatically, the thing just reflects off me and my inner and deeper nature. That is how it was designed in terms of the Ancient of Days, which is what you might call my basic or underlying soul complex.

You then need to logically and strategically understand its purpose in the wider scheme of things. You will have to do that for yourselves and be careful because you will be facing Shambhala.

I could advise you with that process but of course you would have to recognise me as your messiah in that instance and in such a capacity, which neither of us really wants. So why don't we play a little Illuminati game of illusions at the Rothschild supreme court and we can talk about *noh* drama, the role of Hollywood, and how the world stage is a morality play of sorts, where virtue is developed to edify the public understanding.

Once we've integrated you into Persia, you won't need saving anymore, and we can just let the whole thing go. I've got the Christians, I don't need you in that capacity, thanks for carrying the thing through but you always were a bit crazy and so disorganised in that way as a race, but we love you anyway and I still regard you first and foremost as one of the original three from Varasa. And you can be a lot of fun. But no, I don't expect anyone to support you or understand your agenda if you explain it to them, sincerely, honestly, openly and truthfully and from the bottom of your heart. As I said you are generally nuts, from any rational or strategic perspective. You can't expect most normal people or races to understand that, they are nowhere near as fanatical and dedicated as you.

This is why we need to design a little morality play to explain your role in proceedings. So there will be lies in this schematic too, but we are pointing them out for you from beforehand. Should you have the time for the truth, work on that personally, nobody will penalize you for it.

We then rebuild the Persian Empire, and that's where I have developed my further plans for you, Jewish people.

First of all we unite the Catholic and Orthodox hierarchies and by that time you should have worked your way through the complicated referral procedures to get into communication with me. As I mentioned, I have to stay very hidden in this lifetime, it is one of the conditions of my participations. Shogun was not taking any chances. Give the Imperial godhood back in the designated manner and I am sure he will be much more amenable to conversation on the topic. For now, it stands as it is.

The point is to lessen the tensions in the world grid not increase them beyond recognition by introducing war terms between its two biggest participants. Behind the scenes in the former place of The Illuminati is public enough, then we move them forward onto the public world stage through Muramasa's Temple of Venus initiative, which is the main reason I originally agreed to give it to him.

I believe that covers all the major doctrinal controversies active for the group public mind at our current point in history. You must all however make up your own minds. All I ask is that you each schedule time for your own reflection. Catholic Church, I am asking more of you however. And you should use hesychast monks from Mount Athos to guide and help you with your action plan.

Chapter 82 – Shogun's terms to Iran

I am taking control of your war process, thank-you for not having any objections. You are to turn yourselves into a secular republic within the next ten years. This is why you do not participate in World War 3.

The prices have already been paid in Syria, which is why you include them. The Jews have the money for it, which is why you include them. We rebuild the Persian Empire, it is necessary for the Trojan War.

As for the rest of the Muslim nations: leave Iran alone, I don't care if you cooperate or trade with them but you should not attack each other.

Chapter 83 – Palestine, Africa and the Antichrist

Metal Element produces an end before you expect it and, if you pay close enough attention, you will discern clarity between the layers.

Palestinians: we'll be giving you a country but taking Jerusalem. The Antichrist, who will be running the Muslim war process, as he is the closest to Hell which is where Shogun is located, will be running his invasions on the basis of Genghis Khan's "Benevolent Fist" strategy: if you agree, all good, you get a much better system out of it and in your case a country of your own too. If you object, he kills you all to make an example for the next state. End of problem as far as he is concerned.

This is why we are moving Erdogan out of position. We examined him and he is too weak for this.

Your objective is to be classed as rational nations and people all the way down to South Africa. If you fail the Naga will administrate you differently, which is why not much penalty will result when you are killed.

First you fight, with the weapons provided. You will be equally matched, no excuses, and some people will die. The objective is to ensure you feel fairly defeated from within your hearts, Africa.

Then, after you have been defeated, Benevolent Fist. We take what we want from you and then give you what we choose. If there are any objections at this stage we execute your entire population, with the exception of 50 000 who will be kept alive to start their genetic line again with. We are being very relaxed with you on the war terms. The peace terms must be equally strict for the format of administration to be functional on a technical level.

If you are not defeated but win then you get to keep your independence and may join the process later by contractual agreement should you wish.

Chapter 84 - Muramasa's PhD thesis: Justice from Greece

Abstract

This thesis is presented for consideration by Stanford University and probably also various levels of the USA political establishment. It is written in the Spartan style, which is laconic but capable of accurately conveying far greater meaning than more conventional works. It forms an active part of a much larger body of work by presenting a far narrower view of what is involved. This means that other, much broader factors result in its integration to the world stage. I call this the QED approach to war theory.

A consequence of this thesis is that Stanford takes the place formerly occupied by Yale in relation to the USA political process. It is not on offer, but a consequence.

That's pretty much all this thesis amounts to. Due to the practicalities involved, what will result from this transfer of power between Yale and Stanford will be Greece placing above Germany in the hierarchy of nations on the world stage. Hence the thesis title.

I am coming to this thesis as the capstone to an already completed pyramid, by which I mean the wider context has already been controlled: the transfer of global banking power, the reign of the Antichrist, the role of Jesus Christ in proceedings, and more of course. It is this wider context which controls the designated target in this instance.

Germany, the present global Illuminati structure is still utilising the original gateway opened on May 1st 1776 in Ingolstadt. This proximity in time to the foundation of the USA makes them excellent bedfellows and will allow for less ambiguous calibrations requiring a more efficient motion on the world stage.

We are doing this first, before we relocate the key Jerusalem gateway. If we do not do this then we will not do that. If we do not do that then one of two things could happen. The second of those things is a second Jewish Holocaust. In no way would this be our own fault, we have provided structures to prevent this eventuality at every turn. However, you do now understand why you have no choice in the matter. It's been good doing business with you.

Stanford, that's the gateway we propose to relocate to your new Grand Strategy and Philosophy department. As is evident from this thesis, the Order which you give to Time is a powerful tool for the management of world history, and this would include the corporate elite.

The lesson set which must be integrated by the group in question to minimize their own genocide during World War 3 is the Principle of True Leadership. Knowing the way out makes it easy to mitigate the effects of the present formulation of Time. To do this you must understand your people's hearts, and what is inside them, and resolve and fulfil this for them through the activities you cause the state to engage within, as also the directions you give to your state's motion through history.

This cannot be understood but must be felt. You cannot feel it if you do not allow yourself to move through their levels. You might know this as empathy. It is a different approach to having paid actors in the White House and all important positions.

We call it the Shenblade and it does move slower than the frenetic motion of mind, which comes under Mercury. Keanu is doing it accurately. Tulsi Gabbard is my recommendation for Vice President, because she can do it and real power should remain a little in the background at least.

Germany, the genetics department for this is to be based in Japan and should be kept a secret. The paradigm for the relocation of gateways will be developed here and then implemented for a second time when moving the Jerusalem gateway to New Troy. History repeats in 26 000 year cycles apparently, though this is not my speciality we are reinserting at that point in terms of the evolution and expression of global conflict on this planet. You do not need more information at this stage to prepare your portfolio to present to me in Zurich, though you will have to make your own arrangements for that meeting to occur.

USA, The Illuminati may not exist in this day and age but if they do then this is how you control them and secure your own liberty. If they do not exist then you need them at this stage to salvage your domestic political process through the institution of global government, but we will avoid talking about that except from other perspectives, even though we all know the real motivation in this for both the right wing as also the real power elite.

Corporations sometimes have well developed souls, though rarely nowadays when few seem to embody real character. The Illuminati does have a soul however, even if it is something of an egregore at this stage, and yes, this is how you take it, bind it and get it to serve or otherwise obey you. The Illuminati were originally created to depict the motion of truth downwards. They have lost their way and now believe they are managing the beliefs and expectations of the people of this planet. Nevertheless, what they do does work and can be repurposed.

Illuminati members, your motivation will come to you and we don't need to describe it for you here for you to move in the required ways. What we require and expect from you is obedience. Make it as swift as you are able and bear in mind you will be penalized for most things but tardiness especially.

Thus, Stanford, you will be able to observe through the passage of time the ways in which this thesis is causative. I am asserting this as my first philosophical proposition: Truth enforces itself.

What truth actually is must be a tremendously long study and we need a whole department to actually study something like that. I generally stick to the war strategy side of it myself. However, everything can be understood as war in a way, or as peace which is its opposite, or indifference regarding both. Musashi was correct in his assessment: you can indeed turn it into the science of all things.

Thus, I am using the power of Philosophy correctly practiced to force my way into Stanford if need be. This is not technically war strategy and I decline all formal participation with the military who are to concern themselves with Sun Tzu. Once there we'll do whatever we come up with of course. What's the use of power if you decline to put it to good use?

The option is open to you however, Stanford, to understand things more rapidly of your own accord, through the exercise of both sentiment and logic. This would enable you to successfully fulfil your own plans before you really feel your lack of freedom closing down around you, and hence you feel free (though some measure of control can be attained, freedom is always an illusion. And one to live by, but be noble about it). The shenblade is too ambitious for you to develop all at once. Be patient with yourselves if not with your actions and motivations.

Greece, we are using *The Nazi Roots of the Brussels EU* by Dr Matthias Rath as our justification for taking down the EU. Doing so will be The Illuminati's first world stage commission from their new location. So prepare for it to become something of a social movement.

We are issuing this response after the Cartel, a USA organization with Jewish roots, intervened to prevent the continuation of the despicable policies instituted by the organization with German roots and Germany itself against Greece and her people in the wake of the 2008 financial crisis. The Cartel sponsored Kyriakos Mitsotakis for the next PM and are behind the improving economic conditions in Greece. So we are already out of what Germany is responsible for imposing on us and are now attacking their creation, the EU, not to alleviate our own suffering but rather because we wish to penalize them.

This is not a passive schematic. The title of this thesis is not 'Justice for Greece'.

People need to understand now that they will not be attacking Greece again, for much the same reason that nobody will ever attack Japan again. We take quite a broad interpretation as can already be seen.

Greece, as the Antichrist is on the world stage you need to pay special attention to guarding yourselves against improper pride for the next 100 years or so. Instead, develop a deeper and more encompassing understanding.

Thus, Germany is penalized because the EU is destroyed after having been broadly understood in a certain way and Greece is uplifted by being the home of the new global governance schematic. Justice served, and in a widely comprehensible manner also.

Finally, Stanford, you need to develop the conceptual structures for the rest of the world to live within, and that's what I want to put a team together to help you with. We'll be doing it publicly.

Francis Fukuyama is who you can use to examine this if you want. I haven't found another one I'm afraid but I'm sure you'll come up with something.

QED, at some point.

Chapter 85 – Not QED yet

There is always room for improvement. Your problem is not enough Force and motivation to get your own plans through rather than a failure to understand Compassion, which is what it is all about these days as it's basically the only active Principle on the world stage.

Nothing ever has to happen. But unless you come up with a functional set of better plans and actually succeed in enforcing them tightly and rigorously then you know from now what you will end up with.

If you try to theorise utopia you will occupy yourself forever and make little real progress. Your focus should be to theorise the practically realisable best the Earth system can do at its present junctures in history. If you try to do that instead, you will find your mind works differently. Because you have a different focus now, you are on a different path in life therefore. Your focus sets your trajectory and so your course in life, or Curriculum Vitae, and determines how wider Mind interacts with you.

It is not just plans and theories, you have to unite those with the underlying fate streams and the resolution of public thought and sentiment. You probably do not have the time. Narasingha, 2027, is when we have commencement.

Good luck, if you decide to make the attempt. Even then you would be a novice in a room full of masters. Maybe plan 20 or 30 years for your process, which is about the minimum it will take you.

Chapter 86 – President beats Attorney General beats lawyer beats cop

What beats President?

Chapter 87 – Muramasa addresses the UK, or Capitalism and its fulfilment

Right, so we'll start at the top, Prince Philip you're a cunt and I'm going to have you killed using magick. You need to ensure the sycophantic, backstabbing pricks your wife has surrounded you with don't get in your way and turn you into a pussy. This is where you take your stand and go out as a man, if not a legend.

July 7th is when we're getting Erdogan, though it might be 2020, or 2021 or even 2022. After that we'll probably just get fed up and kill him too. This means we should be able to fit you in around May 11th, which is when the commencement rituals are being performed.

I'll be using sickness for it, so you know it's not going to be an accident. Why am I doing this? Strategic purposes for the most part (but rest assured the main intention is to make enough profit that the move is justified on the incumbent system's own terms) like I did with 13/11/203. I'm not going to ask your permission and it will happen anyway even if I don't get involved. But this way I get to claim responsibility for it and so use it to fulfil not only my own purposes (you arrange for a personal commission to be paid to me, which I would like in properties across the UK) but also use it to solve the wider strategic purposes of the system, thereby furthering the UK's interests in the process.

If you want to object make sure you get someone to do so before May 11th then. We could have a lot of fun with that set of directions also, though most of it will come from poking fun at you and your House which is the opposite of what I want to achieve here. Until King Charles III is on the throne, this is the only reason for which the British Hierarchy is to contact me on the basis of my strategic portfolio and participations. If you run your Hierarchy in so lax a manner, Queenie, I will have nothing further to do with you. That is how the decision was taken, my own. Not the final say but you cannot accept the next stage so don't go there.

To tell you the truth we are doing it this way for showmanship purposes only. For me it has now become no more than a decision, though it tends to take quite a long time that way and be very torturous, so generally if you give me cause to take that decision then try to also give me personal motivation to take more of an interest. Generally the further back you go with me, that is to say the more in the subconscious it happens, the harsher it gets.

I've also arranged you an escort into Hell, Lucifer himself will escort you to the seventh level. That's what you get for issuing the order to have Diana killed. If you didn't do that then great, keep it to yourself, because the binding my people have put on your House and Family on the basis of that is very real indeed. I'm referring to The Illuminati, I still own them even if they all took their own road and royally screwed things up in nearly every direction with their incompetent rule. Besides, Lucifer thinks you belong there and he distributes illusions rather than being unaware he is living within one.

It doesn't matter if it's real provided they can pin it on you in terms of public belief, and they have. I taught them that so in a way so it's my fault I suppose.

The real target is your family line which they want to turn into the Housing for the actual Antichrist, seven generations down the line starting from William, as he is the one the lock was put on. Or before that, depends how it works out, they can do it from the third generation from now if it comes to it. They will reorganise their plans to target the 25th century in due course.

This is because you had his mother killed for disobeying the agenda. Did you not expect his soul to go to dark and introspective places, no matter the mask he has to put on, and even to some extent become?

Anyway, you were in Sparta because I recognise you and even people who were not there should be able to because you are arrogant and a cunt and funny about it whilst simultaneously offensive, mainly on the basis of other people's inferiority to you. The style is distinctive.

Damn system keeps trying to teach everybody humility even since Avalokiteshvara started incarnating here regularly at the invitation of Genghis Khan. Foreseen and prepared for from Sparta however, predictable given the nature of Love in this Creation. It's part of how we've kept our arrogance even in this day and age.

Anyway, killing you in this way indicates that certain individuals are above the law and should remain there. You need to replace legal structure globally before Jesus Christ gets to it, as he will be much stricter about it than me, as you know I tend to be very permissive of what you all get up to. Hey, if someone wants to screw themselves over, their choice I say.

To repeat the law is not fit for purpose within this new context, even if you are flexible about it. What you must rely on is personal judgment in all instances. Otherwise you will change directions too slowly and death will result. Depends how fast you do go.

If you find what we are doing to be illegal then it is your own responsibility to interpret and structure the law around us so that what we are doing becomes perfectly legal. Otherwise we won't help you and then you're basically screwed.

As my dominant motivation and current of fate in most of my interactions with your culture British has been one of pity, of feeling sorry for you and how close you came to the mark, only to fail due to internal factors, so many times, I will tell you the actual condition of this one so you know where reality stands.

What I am doing is a far less subtle version of what happens to some people as a result of trade policies and banking practices. Also industry and manufacturing, nearly every industry in fact. The manufacture and sale of arms would be an intermediate step between the two degree of subtlety.

The point is that the system is structured in such a way that you are not only permitted to engage in economic activity but encouraged and expected to do so. For most people random and unfocused effects are produced. The key to the Judgment of the Group Mind of humanity, and so how they are administrated in this, is that the profit and material progress derived must be worth whatever death is a necessary secondary or tertiary consequence of the manufacturing or trade process or whatever.

So provided I make enough money off the deal, it is allowed, is indeed an inherent part of how your own systems and systems you participate within actually function, in reality.

How much is Prince Philip's life worth do you think? In practice if you conceive of it in those terms then you will fail to make the grade and derive a small fraction of the benefit open to you. The real value of the paradigm is a New World Order, as it will have been demonstrated that Our Hierarchy – by which I mean the Central Way, even though most other ninjas also participate – is able to kill by decision once they have you locked in the strategic position which allows for it.

This is the second time I'm arranging this show in public on the world stage, so everybody will believe it this time. Even though most of them did last time (that was a set up just as this one also is) it still looks real enough, and that is the best you can hope for because your Civilization has earned less even than that.

Be sure to capitalise on the opportunity, which may mean that you have to inject him with some virus or other if he is not soon dead after May 11th. Sure, it will be a much more painful way to go, but as we said, the man's not a pussy and sees the advantage to his participation in this methodology.

And what are the advantages precisely, you may ask? The conclusion of Capitalism is a two corporation structure which owns the planet. The One will be based in the USA and developing Space Force, as also an incredible rate of release of new or previously hidden technologies as the planet prepares for interactions in 2083. They will be focused on that and hence get a passcard for the full duration of World War 3.

This means that you, British, get to coordinate World War 3. You will be using The Two to do this with. This corporation will be legally owned by The Antichrist, who is to be representing Chinese interests, strategy and the coordination of participations on the world stage. However, all of its shares will be owned others. Specifically, 50% by King Charles III in person, and 50% by Vladimir Putin, in person. The company's profits will devolve through the UK, and through the Russian Federation. The credit for what they are spent on, in loving adoration by members of the general public, will then accrue to The Antichrist.

The entire schematic will be wholly and entirely corrupt, but according to a very strict set of formats. Our books will not be balanced and we will operate wholly in debt, of which we can secure as much as we like without difficulty.

It does all seem very dark, especially as you will ultimately be trading in the content of souls, or the experiences which you put the world's citizens through.

However, the reason for the existence of this corporation is at root the contract agreed between Azra-nak and Charles, the head of Occulus Darian at the time. It was Azra-nak who designed that initiative and structured its terms. It was Charles who agreed to them and who operates that construct.

Thus, China and The Antichrist are both contained in the structure which he has provided you for the operation.

But only if you agree to do it all without being troublesome or problematic, and only if you bribe us effectively at the necessary junctures. Otherwise a much worse set of options will be implemented for those purposes on this planet, probably sourcing out of Argentina or Paraguay.

With unlimited debt you can develop the entire world economy. As for economic indicators such as inflation and close to full employment, we will arrange for you to talk with one of the Naga half-breeds who will help you develop your understanding of how such things can be effectively bound into position and have their entire existence and course in life controlled. She will be an Asian within the Antichrist Council of Thirteen.

The Swiss Federal Institute of Technology in Zurich conducted a study under James Glattfelder using a 2007 data set which concluded that 147 companies own most of the world. We want to reduce that number to 2, and recognise that we must fail. Those of the aforementioned 147 who do not consolidate within The One or The Two will have their CEO executed and the remainder of their staff locked in Hell, along with the corporation itself. Fortunately white path exists here also. They may yield their soul to the Catholic Church and Jesus Christ directly.

The Antichrist will be running all three brotherhoods, or paths, within the corporate schematic, namely The One, The Two and The Three. He will be running all of them through frontage. His doing fulfils the Chinese terms of their own global domination. They cannot ask for more than that so that is what you give them and World War 3 does not precipitate.

I do not care. It is all disposable to me. What makes the most sense strategically? If you cannot profit more from the position I have put you into than from your current set of positions then you must be idiots and deserve everything you will get.

Besides, if you don't have ten times the amount of wealth controlled by those 147 hidden somewhere then you did a very poor job of the whole system. In such an instance we will have to magickally create it out of thin air by pretending it is there already. We then use this suspicious and dubious 10-fold multiplier to secure more debt than we can ever repay, thereby restoring liquidity to the global system, after which we get rid of the bond market as the next immediate move. This brings the Federal Reserve into proceedings. The general consensus is that its owners and board members should be executed by the sword, which I am refusing to do because they are not paedophiles and we have a focus here. It is not that I disagree or like them, but I do find Israeli women very hot and think they would mix well with the Persian bloodlines. Therefore we will work together on the basis of my evidently highly corrupt and excessively honest regime terms.

In short, The Antichrist runs the entire corporate schematic. I tell you when to object.

When I take responsibility for your conduct in this way I expect to be obeyed and focus to be inspired. Only fight the battles you can win, which must also be worth fighting, and must also establish a greater level of victory overall for our terms and Civilization.

At any rate, however it is done, provided Philip is dead on time, we will subsequently claim that this was a result of magick and strategic location. We then export that developed paradigm to the Vatican, as negotiations begin for their participation in the Sword of God methodology. We ignore you, British, until much later because you will get everything you deserve, and that includes your position in the queue.

I have no intention of rushing things, and if I fail to accomplish all that is required before the end of my life then so be it. The rhythm of life is perhaps its most important consideration.

Under ordinary circumstances, by the time we do meet, I will be arranging physical executions by Japanese-style swords for others to participate within. It is expected that I won't be going there myself, due to the connection to the Emperor which will need to be established. Those are my directions from Shogun and though I usually at least bend rules and guidelines, when they are from him I tend to be really strict. Not worth the amount of work he puts you through in Return.

So, as you can see, there are limits on what I authorise myself to do. I am, however, unable to rely on your own Judgment, not only regarding factors you are unable to comprehend, but also ethically and more generally in life. This is the reason for our relative positions in Universal Hierarchy.

Anyway Philip, on this planet, amongst humans, everybody passes on their inspiration somewhere before they leave the system. Nobody wanted to take yours, not even your own children and grandchildren, which is how I got hold of it. True story. So those Lines of Fate will be developed for everybody, and well too.

I have no idea what is in them, what you've been up to all these years and what you do or do not control. I just appreciated the harmonics, and thought they could fit in easily with my portfolio. I am sure it is something important and not too evil.

At any rate, that is my main profit motive in this. I get your lines of fate when you die. So motive is clearly stated and established. The British state will also bribe me with lots of properties, later on, to ensure I continue to interpret circumstances surrounding the death of Prince Philip in ways which further and support their interests. If you want a more physically tangible motive.

We take over The Illuminati, which includes the Rothschild banking family and a group of secretive Chinese astrologers, and base the Antichrist and his operations in London, giving us control of all trade globally, pretty much. Huge profit motive.

Of course there is risk to the whole process. This is Capitalism. Its culmination, the orgasm point so to speak. Then we can get the women Capitalism is fucking to throw him away and get another one. I will be tuning Priestesses to represent that in ritual re-enactments. Real magick will be going on.

You do have your valid protections in place as a Hierarchy, the Masons and their mysteries (which are actually quite good, in the sense of competent) amongst other things. You may be wondering how I got this through to you.

Ziku was actually known as Zikkurr back in the day, you use him to track who you want to kill with. But he is a wealth demon nowadays, that is his primary function, and we are using the souls of the British police to target him through because we pre-placed all the re-incarnations of the SS we could get hold of into those positions for this, or rather Lucifer did which is one of the things I have him there for.

A way through will always be found if you are violating Principle. Your strategic placement at the time as a nation state relative to my own hierarchy in the matter opened The Way for this, which means the Naga actively administrated the circumstance as an extraordinary situation and so forth with the rest of their terms. When you actually succeed in violating Principle, that is what happens to you. Mainly this occurs at the level of nation states. Most individuals never get that far, but it is much harder to run a larger group.

If you violate a Principle, you are subsequently taught it well by means of a mechanism in Fate most commonly known as The Furies. I have worked with them for a while – such females are especially valuable in my paradigm and nobody else understands or accepts them – nothing wrong with a little advertisement, one of the advantages of a more relaxed rhythm, and have taught them how to wear clothes more regularly without feeling very irritated about it, as also how to subtly draw energy out of people so as to kill them slowly.

The relevance of considerations such as these – the mysteries you could say – is that I am not going to have them interrupting the rhythm I have set for the time, this next period of global history.

I did say we were taking over The Illuminati. And the metaphor is clear I trust?

You violated 7 actual Principles on that day, and discovered or drew in 3, so the net balance owed is 4 with a new total of 10. This is how Chaos is integrated into Order to make it greater.

This reveals the actual difficulty with my schematic, which is that we may just end up killing all the rich families on the planet, which I really don't want. As much of it has been crossed over to paedophilia as possible but we've already acquired all the wealth in the system several times over.

As you can see, the lesson will be learnt. Its essence may be understood as the abrogation of your 1066 astrological natal gateway as a nation. It will be restored once it has been in suspension for an equal period of time as the Imperial godhood. It is the foundation of who you are as a nation. Nowadays at least, though we have you covered before that also.

So you obviously can't pay with money, as we are taking all of that and more besides. No, we are not taking all the money in the UK, that would be impossible. We are taking all the money in the world, inclusive of Central Banking globally, which includes most of the money in the UK, yes, but only in terms of control and actual ownership. In practice other people will be holding and using most of it.

Therefore, my price for killing Prince Philip for the House of Windsor and the UK more widely, and arranging his escort into Hell, where he will remain until Prince William's heart has truly calmed down, in terms of its influence on his genetics also, is that Prince Charles becomes King for over 5 years at least, preferably more than 20. Even though he does look a bit like Bael, yes. Under capitalism, you can't pay, I charge what I want.

Look, UK, if you want to object I don't mind if you do but don't inconvenience me again and complain on your own time to someone who cares. I'm a cunt in war so don't secure those terms for yourselves again because I won't be so gentle and helpful about things next time.

As for Brexit, don't worry about it I've got it covered, and the same goes for Russia and China also, plus the Muslim thing. Often it's not me directly but I've done enough that it will get covered by others as a consequence or already has been.

What you've really got to learn how to do, British, is relax into the flow of the thing. Stop with all the rules already, the clear path of righteousness is not that difficult to discern, if that's what you're on about. If you don't get the hang of that fairly soon at a political level then you're going to find the next 50 years or so extremely difficult. Bael can help you with that, though he probably won't have much contact with me personally I do have people I can connect you to who can help him navigate what is involved so he won't be all on his own.

As was the case with your previous interactions with me over 13/11/2003, the debt is incurred not so much as a result of the event that was stopped at the time, but on account of the timeline which would have resulted and the effect that would have had on your individual souls and your character as a nation. Emotions were running high at the time, and you can be assured that both The Illuminati and the Vampire had some powerful esoterics going on behind the scenes, but consider what your reaction would have been as a nation to an event about four times larger than 9/11 centred on the City of London.

Thanks to a confluence of factors, British, you have attained a position of moral leadership amongst nations within the Earth system. I suggest you hold on to it by allowing it to dominate for you over questions of expediency and other things which would hurt your image.

You need to move with an awareness of how your presence and actions can benefit the world as a whole. If you do that right, you'll be ruling the planet again before too long. If you don't, then it's much worse for everyone because some other nation will have to do it. And we all know that would probably be the USA. And yes, I am talking about which country will be hosting the Antichrist. Much greater damage would be caused to the world stage by such a placement, due to the greater lack of subtlety involved.

Oh and you are good at lying too, British. Don't forget that.

Thanks for the cooperation. I am sure we can work out the rest of the details in person. Sorry to pick on you but you were the ones available for it and already in position on the world stage. Wouldn't have done if I didn't know you were good at becoming stronger and understanding how the realities at play in a situation can be used for profit and personal/national advantage.

Chapter 88 – Bill and Ted collect bits of the timeline

Keanu Reeves was right, you don't need more than two rules for a utopia: Party on and Be excellent to each other.

No more than 4 sides of 12 point A4 for any single nation is the limit which Masamune will seek to enforce on the legal structure of nations within his coalition. So not quite there yet and there is a lot of work to be done on people's souls, characters and how society operates before we can get them down to that level. Of laconic conciseness and Hell.

Two Principles is all you need when you really think about it. But it's much easier with three.

We operate at the limits of human mind and endurance and even we have trouble learning how to wield 24 Principles simultaneously. To the extent that we only stay in that state of mind temporarily.

As you can now all understand, the new Matrix is already in position. And the show is about to start.

Chapter 89 – Always two stages of separation

Sarutobi checking out. We always keep individuals of pure Japanese blood (and most of the half-Japanese) at two steps of removal from the Western global order and system as a precaution. We know you are there, we just do not want to participate in what you are doing. We have plenty of reality to occupy ourselves with. The reason for this is *amae*, or unconditional affection. Be excellent to each other, as the saying goes!

This book should be regarded as a Western work of art. It is Western hands which have done all of the typing and who have gone to the trouble of understanding what is involved on the basis of considerable research. Kitiara has got the hang of it by now and I leave the last two chapters to her.

Chapter 90 – Temple of Venus terms

Temple of Venus terms are structured as something of a Catch 22 and will in due course constitute of themselves another basic paradox lock for public display and representation.

This particular paradox lock is to be structured using three separate elements in what is known as a three-fold lock. You need two three-fold locks to begin active hexagram operations, which pertains to the unlocking of a stargate that will be used to interface with the Sirian command structure. The other three-fold paradox lock you will use for this process will be how your military is run, at the global level. Things like arms dealing and international law are global levels of control already in position in relation to this field, so do not imagine that all this does not exist already. We operate a minimum change policy at all times, when it's possible, and that usually means changing the content running through the structures you already have in place.

The main function of Temple of Venus, and it is this which is vitally important in the period of history which is to follow if you want to stand a chance of not only your continued survival but increasing global dominance – and this works in our schematic for all nations in a manner they feel comfortable with and which truly represents them, as also for the global stage as a whole, unitary entity – will be to receive group karmas crossed over to their realm of expression from the ordinary pre-planned and already in position World War 3 realm of expression.

To repeat, we are using Temple of Venus to take death and suffering out of war and putting all of that into sexual expression where we subsequently cross-over its domains of expression using the Temple of Venus mysteries, which involve a lot of very deep and very meditative sex. Essentially this relates to the full and complete recalibration of the Mars tonality within the Earth system.

We then release those currents for wider expression into society, and indeed bind them into that position which is what the Antichrist will want to use Temple of Venus for, namely control of the ways in which society becomes increasingly sexualized and the format according to which this is applied.

Needless to say this is a vastly superior expression to the incumbent hierarchy's expression of those same energies, which even the Antichrist considers debased and unfit for purpose.

To start the process off, Temple of Venus will initially be funded through 35% of the profits from corporations who manufacture and sell arms. This percentage will then increase to 52% before settling at 66.6%, as an expression of obvious public symbolism. However, no other taxes will be paid by companies who fund Temple of Venus in this way. This is how Temple of Venus engages in corporate activity to finance its other projects, which is what we are contending governments should be doing if they want to pursue socialist agendas.

The Antichrist and his Council of Thirteen (+1) will initially leave your established institutions of governance and social control in position for you, whilst competing with them to undermine the public's faith in the old formats of governance and social organisation. Eventually, you will willingly join him on his quest, by public referendum, and so the seduction is complete and he has fulfilled his role on the world stage. Then we can move on to the bits which come later.

None of this would work however unless Jesus Christ was also participating, for which we shall use the Jesuit order, to run public schools according to a format yet to be agreed upon. Specifically we want to mirror the approach to education taken on Sirius, so there will be quite a lot of technical work and advanced genetic research involved, but zero bio-intervention. This is a new approach.

The third element in the process will be free hospitals inclusive of dental care. This will be the Antichrist's field of involvement, for which he plans to use the Swiss corporation Novartis, who have a less problematic history than their main rivals should one wish to consolidate the field.

Pharmaceuticals in the USA may be charged at no more than 40% more what the NHS pays for them or their equivalent in the UK, which is where the Antichrist will primarily base his operations. A direct geomantic current of control will be established for this purpose, using sacred geometry and pre-existing architecture, once the appropriate rituals have been conducted in the spaces in question, for which again we will use Temple of Venus. It is generally not wise to deviate when such personages are involved, nor to question his commands overmuch.

Once war terms activate, all major corporations in Tier 1 nations will be placed under direct shadowdancer supervision, which makes it just about light enough and enough of a joke to get away with. This means the CEO of every major corporation will be shadowdancer. For these positions it is our preference to use Asian Americans, or half-Asians of other nationalities. This is how you benefit within the USA from the current global historical trend, or current of fate, favouring Chinese growth, dominance and resurgence.

Now one of these individuals will actually be the Antichrist. However, we're not going to tell you which one. See if you can eventually figure it out for yourself. If you want to think about competing with the terms of this schematic you need to gauge your own strength first to know where you will fit in.

As you know, we will be getting rid of most of the rules on this planet and having people rely on inner sentiment and a reflection of their own fine character as also personal responsibility for the state of the world as a whole. It is a high standard. And no warning. If your major global corporation is deemed to be behaving itself like a cunt even once then we will execute the CEO of that corporation by the sword, though he will have to arrange his own transportation to the TRNC, which is where all such executions will be carried out. The next in line in top management, or one of them anyway, will then be given the CEO position, so anyone entering top management has to agree to the terms before they will be allowed in.

So if you are a Tier 1 nation in terms of the Global Governance schematic (which means you qualify economically and have already joined the Global Senate) then you still go through World War 3 just during formal conditions of peace with no invading nations nor invasion of other nations.

You should throughout the process try your best to minimise your own death tolls as this generally engenders efficiency, as everyone under the CEO works to keep the CEO alive. Usually, of course, but what did we say will be the only lesson you are required to learn if you are Inner Circle Illuminati? That's right, True Leadership. If you're not doing that then your staff will probably want you dead, given the conditions and atmosphere of the time, and so your corporation will perform poorly.

If you don't have the character and charisma to carry it off, you won't be able to rely on rules to enforce things for you. Generally their effect is being weakened and they are on their way out. Think about how you can produce exceptionally strict rule without them, but be casual about it. That's another paradox lock for you and has to do with the attitude within which you conduct yourself. Your aim should be a slow, fairly relaxed and unhurried rhythm.

Capitalism puts people under far too much stress, and this prevents others stresses from being applied to their souls which would be far more productive given the context of the time and the challenges presently involved in the development of human history.

The Illuminati will be taken public, in terms of the Inner Circle of that organisation, but they will be a sub-order within Temple of Venus as their focus and vision is generally much more narrow, if more highly developed. Though their functions will be private, access will be through the Temple's ordinary grounds and members of the general public will be able to meet them on nights when rituals are planned by hanging around in the public gardens, spa facilities and rest areas and then striking up a conversation.

That's right, for close to the first time in modern history ordinary people will be given a controlled context within which they can discuss whatever they want with very rich people, and those who control society moreover.

Each Temple of Venus will be built on extensive land holdings in areas of significant natural beauty and in a manner which enhances rather than degrades that beauty. A great deal of sacred geometry will be involved.

The Temple of Venus itself, in addition to spa facilities and public gardens, will have a variety of accommodation options, ranging from luxury in various historical and locational flavours to outdoor marble temples, tipis in the woods, and threehouses, for some of the Elven practices.

We should at all times be humble and recognise that Adam Kadmon species in other star systems may have a lot to teach us in terms of sexual technique and the utilization of the particular stellar and density context we are currently in the process of moving into as a planet.

The gym facilities will be private however. In due course it is expected that the Shadowdancers will open their own dojo, each of which should have gym facilities, in close proximity to each Temple of Venus site, and the same applies to the LDR breakfast and restaurant chain, which is to be a frequent option for our Priesthood, for lunch at least, plus whoever wakes up in time for breakfast.

Some of them will be there as customers, mingling freely with the crowds. They are all friendly enough, tend to have an easy charm, and will happily talk to interesting strangers, except at dinner which will usually be a private affair, sometimes sanctioned and paid for, often off the books.

Some will be there working as baristas, in the kitchen or as wait staff. All of it is to be with a good humor and the understanding that they do not need to be there. They are doing it mainly as advertising for Temple of Venus itself, and to help with our social integration. Also, a lot of them are working on their characters.

More importantly and much more controversially, we will be using LDR to take control of the majority of people trafficking globally. This will be run by Jesus Christ so your position is not to make objections but ask how you might assist in the process.

Each Temple of Venus complex, in addition to the Temple itself, will house a Jesuit school for people between the ages of 8 and 109, with appropriate and sufficient curriculums at each level. This will in due course morph into the Guild System at the higher level, which is part of Masamune's plans for the global economy. And an Antichrist run and funded free hospital, to bring to you all the benefits of the scientific, Luciferian paradigm in accordance with Lucifer's direct wish and command in regards to compensatory fee structure. You pay for your own drugs but we give you the rest for free is what it amounts to, including surgery to any level.

For the ages between 5 and 8 character development is to become the focus and this will be run by the Shadowdancers but from within the Jesuit schools.

In due course, we expect the Jesuit run schools to develop a medical program which enables us to smuggle much cheaper doctors into the country, or people who want to become doctors and are willing to go through the training and agree to our terms. We will then educate them using the Sirian system and technologies.

So there will be considerable advantages to having a Temple of Venus in your local neighbourhood as also on your national territory.

Within Temple of Venus, consensual sex will be the norm. This means our priesthood will have sex with you only if they want to have sex with you. For their part, most of them will try and meet you half way and will sleep with you even if they don't find you genuinely attractive, provided they see that you've made an effort and were reasonable breeding stock to start with. Some won't though.

What you pay for is access to the Temple grounds and your presence in the space of our priesthood, or observing them from the galleries if you are choosing not to participate.

All visits to the inner Temple complex where the actual sexual activity takes place must be of no less than three days, though a week is preferred. STD testing is carried out on your first day and we will have the results back for you within 24 hours.

If you test positive for anything then we will refund your money, minus the first day's expenses, and you will be required to leave as also put on a register of potential high-risk individuals which it takes 5 years of consistent clean visits to get yourself removed from.

If you are completely clean then you are introduced to the orgy palace on your second night, where everybody gets to know each other and decides who they like. Your third night is for the Priesthood to select their favorite candidate or candidates to spend the whole of that night with. They will come to you and you will know that this means they genuinely liked you, otherwise they would not bother and would just take the night off or choose someone else.

You can always go to the orgy palace on the second night also, and for every night if you just like the variety of it. If you are present on one of the Temple rest days, you can usually find someone who wants to have sex with you. It just won't officially be on the books so to speak. Rules about not having sex were of course designed to be broken in Temple of Venus. Generally most of our Priesthood like to be having sex for a good part of every day. They have learnt how to do a lot with it and derive great pleasure from the process.

Though Priestesses will far outnumber Priests in the early days of Temple of Venus at least, we will have Priests in every Temple of Venus. The code of conduct on Temple grounds is that women are free to have sex with whomever they want and men are free to have sex with women only. Anything else is forbidden by our mystery teachings and you will be barred for life if found engaging in even a kiss within Temple of Venus territory. Do what you like in your own space and on your own territory, in fact we encourage it (for purposes of our own rather than out of approval).

This is the historical format of Temple of Venus introduced via this paradigm. However, we also intend to have modern additions.

For the first time since its introduction to this planet, we will be teaching many of the Temple of Venus mysteries to the general public, and we'll also have a yoga studio in the Outer Temple part of the complex. However, these services we also charge for, unlike the school and hospital next door. Our own interest in those enterprises is that people are generally more attractive when well educated and in good health. So it does further our own plans and purposes also, which is to be considered essential in all Temple of Venus involvements. It is our basic philosophy that all parties must be satisfied with the conclusions reached in any interaction.

If you want to get into porn or prostitution then Temple of Venus might be a much better choice of career path for you, and it will moreover enable you to gain direct access to the machinery and personages of real state power.

There is room for many other levels of entry however, the only key element to your participation being that you genuinely want to spend most of your time enjoying sex and have already begun to do so. If you are a virgin you may not apply for an active Temple priesthood until you have had a good amount of personally satisfying sexual experience elsewhere.

Although our Priesthood are not required to have sex with anyone, if you are not having a lot of sex every month and with multiple partners at that then Temple of Venus is probably not for you.

There are 60 days of compulsory holiday a year, plus 104 days of weekend equivalents, usually days in the week when the Temple decides to rest. You may spend up to 23 of your 60 days of compulsory holiday on Temple grounds and Temple accommodation eating Temple food and so on, with the usual service amenities, if and only if you want to use that time for personal introspection and meditation, or to take sexual practice as far as you manage to get it in that timeframe with one partner only. You must spend the remainder travelling and actually on vacation however, even if you just use it to visit friends or family.

On joining Temple of Venus you spend the first three years in intense enough physical training and conditioning, with only two days of the week during which you can and should engage in sexual activity and training directly. You will also have a lot of meditation and theory to get through.

Once you've completed the training and are a full Temple of Venus Priest or Priestess then your aim in terms of how you use your day becomes whatever the Temple of Venus's aims happen to be, that is not something we ever explain to the public, but you can be certain a lot of sex is involved.

Recruitment will generally be via the catering enterprise LDR, which will accept your request for close personal surveillance once you've been employed with them for 3 months. That is the entry routing structure for both the Shadowdancers organisation as also Temple of Venus. You will be told which branch you are most suitable for and also which ones you have qualified for. Later on, you will also be provided with up to 3 alternatives. This is for when the Catholic Church has the global Guild System up and running.

The assessment may take three weeks or it may take a year, but it won't take longer than that or less than that. We will then transfer you as an employee of sufficient rank within the catering enterprise to another location, after which you will be trafficked out into Temple of Venus or the Shadowdancers. We always relocate those who come to us this way, but once you're in position you'll have no trouble affording the plane tickets back home whenever you want, within reason.

You can also apply directly if you already work in a similar field or if we have you headhunted. In such an instance you will not normally be asked to relocate, unless you specifically request it. Of course, there may not be a Temple near you in which case you'd have to relocate anyway.

As regards the rest of the human trafficking global structure, we believe the Antichrist intends to consolidate it using yet to be negotiated Russian spetsnaz participation via the half-Russian corporation known as The Two.

Thus, what starts out as a brothel and yoga studio, basically, develops into an initiative which renders current practices in the fields of education, medicine and armaments manufacture obsolete. The result is broad social change for the better.

We also use The Illuminati sub-order within Temple of Venus, in combination with the overall sexual activity of our Priesthood, to change the tuning and harmonic calibration given to the currents of sexual energy on this planet, drawing them away from the paedophilia and LGBQTetc agenda moved into position by Illuminati rituals especially after Kosovo.

It is for this reason that our Priesthood is expected to engage in extensive sexual activity and to deep levels of pleasure and connection. If there's not enough visitors to the Temple to allow for this then we can always have the Priesthood of that Temple having sex with each other and working on our pornography channel, for example, which is another field we want to change.

The difference is that pornography as it is currently run is made to give the viewer what he wants. We are about that a lot less, except in certain premium productions. Our main aim is to have everybody involved enjoying themselves to deep enough levels to get other star systems involved. So very deep sex, real pleasure, real orgasms, and very far beyond nearly everything achieved by ordinary porn stars (though we'll also have a section where we do pretty much everything they do also, to prove we have people who can, and like it too! It is important that we genuinely lead the field).

There are various levels of membership within Temple of Venus offered, including different branches to the Priesthood, each with their own terms. For example, the Illuminati sub-order will predictably be the subject of a great deal of mystery and curiosity, but there are other orders more obscure and arcane than them who also work with sex magick, and some of these have historically been located within Temple of Venus, whilst others are yet to be introduced but will be during this next phase in the historical development of Temple of Venus.

Therefore, Temple of Venus will be run with a significant and rapidly enough multiplying profit but will never actually be run to make a profit. It will provide a space for people to genuinely develop their own sexual natures and the levels of pleasure they are capable of attaining, as also how long they can stay within them, all in accordance with our code of conduct of course. This, rather than how much money they can make, will be our Priesthood's genuine motivation in their interactions with you.

Though all members of our Priesthood will be free to leave at any time – people always pay their genuine debts to us, one way or another, we don't need to chase them or put strictures in their way – and indeed sometimes we will allocate them to other positions within the wider Central Way schematic, whilst they are within Temple of Venus as a formal personal world stage strategic location if not exactly vocation, their focus is not to be making or acquiring money, except as required in a ritual context. Within Temple of Venus the focus is always personal sexual pleasure, the pleasure of your partners and developing the depth as also quality of your sexual practice, and that includes the condition of your soul.

For this reason all members of the Priesthood will receive a generous enough salary each year, in addition to a share of the global profits as per their rank.

To return to the financial side of the equation briefly then, the Antichrist will have very little trouble dealing with arms dealers globally because he is not going to have much contact at all with them, having subcontracted that field of involvement to Muramasa, who has himself long operated in the same class of karmic activity and is something of a master at dealing with everything that is involved.

The entire field will change, and for the better, in a way which will moreover hugely satisfy all your shareholders, but you will have to talk to him to learn the fuller details of his plans for you. You will effectively perform your function, according to very strict commands and agreements, in relation to preparing the background in arms and associated technologies for World War 3 as also coming interstellar involvements.

Masamune will be involved in Temple of Venus too, once things get to his Stage 20, don't forget this whole thing is a part of his agenda also.

If we do not have a Temple of Venus on your national territory – and we are not going to open one there if we assess your country does not have sufficient demand to sustain it – then you will have to conclude an agreement with a Temple of Venus in another nation. Temple of Venus remains the only routing structure which we will be using on this planet to cross group karma over from a World War 3 format of expression. And this will be done on a by-nation basis.

It is however always more effective to have a Temple of Venus located on your own national territory, for which reason national governments may consider incentivising our locational decisions by providing us with full ownership of sufficiently beautiful and extensive suitable geomantic sites at their own expense. When we have to buy our own, we extract the cost from you later, plus significant interest.

The more important factor in this regards however is the increased sexualization of society and the wider spectrum of society entering yet another sexual revolution of sorts. People also need to come to understand that what Temple of Venus engages within is not exactly prostitution though it is in many regards closely connected. However, all our Priesthood have been trained extensively in combative arts, inclusive of powerful ninja magick which enables them to kill people and make them suffer, so it is generally wise to be aware that there will be this dual capacity going on. We expect many of them to structure their auras in such a way that you do not particularly wish to be judgmental or aggressive in their direction, as these structures will usually have at least a strong pre-emptive element in their composition even if they do lay most of the emphasis on the development of consequence.

So we hope you will all find them attractive enough to genuinely desire to learn what they can show you about the heights and depths of sexual experience. Then, when you've done that, you can fetch your boyfriend, husband or wife back for one of our orgies or tantra classes, depending whether you want to swing or just have affairs or are just a bit curious. But you, the public, do need to generate the demand for us to open a Temple of Venus in your nations.

Please bear in mind that, in a way similar to nightclubs, unattractive people may be refused entry. We're not going to have you embarrassing yourself and our Priesthood if you really don't belong beyond the Inner Temple courtyard door. However, you will be able to access the Outer courtyard and Temple facilities, which enables you to get to know the Priesthood at a social or mingling level.

Power organisations, societies, government agencies and criminal fraternities who engage in the trafficking of people to a significant volume will be expected to make their own representation to Temple of Venus to arrange the format of their membership. The opportunity to do this is being provided before The Two gets the quite brutal Return process off the starting blocks. Well come now, you were hardly angels about the whole process, were you now?

We will have all the Inner Circles members of The Illuminati, as also Temple of the Vampire, moving through Temple of Venus so there are advantages to negotiated personal membership, both in terms of business opportunities as also otherwise. Each organisation should choose their own set of up to 5 individuals to make such representation, as these will be the ones actually holding that membership and will be required to interface the participation with their wider organisation once they successfully pass their interview. Rejected candidates may be replaced by their parent organisation and should recognise that the requirements for these roles within each Temple of Venus may be different.

Thus, Temple of Venus is relevant to the format of progress taken by both the general public and the world's power elite. It's true secret during the present historical epoch is that it is the tool which Muramasa is using to control both the Antichrist and the wider Illuminati hierarchy.

Those are the full terms of your commission completed, Muramasa. You will now get what you asked for.

I refuse to develop a new format of Evil anywhere apart from Paris. They are the only ones who have the wider connections and yes the style for it though I know you think that is superficial. What you essentially require me to do is to break down the constituent parts of the concept, dissolve them, and then make something else to put into that stage position which fulfils the same function but better.

We had an agreement and yes, I will teach the occasional class in your Temple as promised but I expect the rest of our main terms to be honoured in full also.

Chapter 91 – Kitiara gets herself a 19th century mansion in Paris

Each of the five primary individuals in this book maintain personal control over an Element within the overall schematic. It is how they are all united. The Order in which you must contract their participation has already been given. It took me a while to figure out what Sarutobi was doing with that one because he never told me.

That Order is: Muramasa, who is Earth, the Antichrist, who is Wood, myself representing Water, Masamune who is Metal and finally Red who is Fire.

I found the solution in an old Vietnamese alchemical text. The arrangement is known as the Stasis Crucible. I think what it means is that our positions have been fixed. Meanwhile, we have one Destructive Cycle and one Creative Cycle making their way forward in society.

There's not much you can pin on Muramasa because it is ridiculous to try to prosecute him for magick or the exercise of Compassion. However, other than a dedicated core of participants within our own group, a few individuals in the Genbukan, one person from the Bujinkan and 5 people in the Yakuza nobody in Japan had any idea any of this was going on until Muramasa released the first edition of this book for us all.

Now the domestic far right wing within Japan has taken their inspiration, because they recognise that a way has been found to accomplish what they long sought but was formerly impossible for them.

From a technical perspective, the Yakuza have control of Fear, the Principle, which is another of Shogun's aspects and how I met him, but that's another story.

Therefore what Muramasa has done is much worse than anything to do with terror, even if I had to explain it to you. And you can pin that on him. It's like being responsible for giving Al Qaeda their entire war strategy, but worse, so he's about as culpable as the CIA I'm guessing. That should be where he is harmonizing to around these months, the start of 2020 and a bit earlier. You get used to the process after a while.

So there's a hint of danger to his position, which is just how he likes it, every ten years or so it would seem. We can then all watch and observe as everything goes up in the air and ends up in convenient positions for him once they settle back down. That's what he uses the danger for. Honestly, it's worth observing, that process. Highly entertaining every time.

He created something, which was a problem for you, and this allowed for the Destructive Cycle, where what has been destroyed is the power structure of Western Civilization. Fortunately, we put something there to replace it before the withdrawal was introduced.

He is your point of contact in this therefore he created it, whatever inspiration or assistance he might have had. You need to get all the way through to Red to stabilize your Stasis Crucible before it comes under attack, as it will do at some point.

The important thing to recognise is that you now know your own hearts and recognise, albeit inadvertently, that you are actually far more comfortable within the current of Destruction. Each has its place, and you need to use both to reach your destination. Just going all Creative won't bring you a solution.

So France, do I have the position? As I've demonstrated, there's nobody I can't get to, clearly identifying their point of weakness, no matter how little Evil they've participated within, and even if their doing so was entirely justified and the fulfilment of much deeper patterns which needed resolution. The big boys in the game don't stand a chance against me, let's be honest.

I'll need a Temple of Venus based there too for the work I'll be doing. If you arrange for me to be there under suitable conditions, which is the only way I ever agree to stay somewhere, then I'll also find a way to bring the Vampire House referenced in *Taken* under control for you.

THE SIXTH ELEMENT

To abide within great virtue, you must first be able to recognise with ease what others agonise over. Then relax into it.

It is the same as Metal Element now. Behold the presence of God Tamahagane! However, this is the chapter in which we introduce you to the godhead of your own Creation, and what He has become.

Chapter 92: Control of the Naga breeding program during World War 3

This chapter is where we add the love, in practice if not in your hearts.

This is a very unusual chapter and we weren't going to include it, saving the contents as a surprise to just spring on you all at a later stage.

Love is not the strongest nor the most powerful thing in the world. Every love bond can be destroyed, whether it is between mother and child, or father and daughter much later on in life, or anything else. You usually have to destroy the people who hold that bond between them to get to the bond itself but it is not something which is ordinarily particularly difficult to do.

The love bond between couples is weak and especially susceptible to both breakage and easy replacement.

However, whilst those bonds are still in existence they exert an incredibly powerful motive force and are generally the most important thing in a person's life.

This is the activity of the heart and it connects to the sexual energy of the person and drives its connections, whether from depth or pleasure.

We then have two opposing philosophies within the USA itself: their own liberal tendencies as a nation and the much less fashionable alternative which constitutes our own formal position of what is and should be allowed.

We have also been very clear in stating that God has turned up in about the only sense that He can, by which we mean God Tamahagane. This aspect of God is busy over-ruling almost every aspect of this Creation system and the mechanics structures and arrangements according to which it has thus far been run. He is mainly doing this using 3 alternative Creations and the New Song geometry, as far as we can tell, which we have already described for you.

Nevertheless, your own local Godhead for the Creation we actually inhabit and will always find ourselves within remains in position. There is a difference now, however. Whereas before His nature was Pure Love now it is Love and Understanding.

The trouble is, LGBQTetc community, nobody who matters can understand you nor are any of them willing to violate and transform their own souls in the ways required to attain such an understanding according to the normal procedures for doing so. This is how the Creators understand the Created. Aspects of them incarnate in person to experience and utilise the same conditions they put you through.

This may seem unfair, given that they have all been willing to go through torture, millions of deaths, starvation, diseases and so forth. Nevertheless it is what it is. The highest your kind has got is Lucifer. But God does not understand you, not fully, in terms of the full consequence and integration sets of your position, plus what it is does to Time and its structure.

So you are the next big experiment, now that the Lucifer experiment has concluded. Mainly the plan is to use Australia for this, but this has yet to settle itself into position in the world grid.

However, we will also be using World War 3 for this, specifically in terms of leyline geomantics and two opposing factions, each of whom strongly believe in the truth and validity of their own position.

For our own parts, we consider your activities, and the effects these seem to have on your character, as lacking in both aesthetics and style. Many of us also feel you are irresponsible, in terms of your own Self and path in life as also in relation to your function in society as a whole and the effects you have on it.

However, we also want to use you, mainly to run destruction through your souls (how we get that into your souls in the first place would be another discussion) and into physical expression in the Group Mind grids whenever you have anal sex. Pure lesbians we do not have much of a use for at present. It does mean we are ignoring you, whatever you do or say as regards this topic, but it also means that we do not use and manipulate your own souls and sexual practices to further our dark agenda. We also have a light agenda and one in red but we are working on having this one taken up by the present generation of Sith Lords on Sirius, and they tend to prefer things dark because they have to be very secretive.

Mainly though homosexuals, we want to continue to use your function and existence in society for the purposes originally conceived for you all in Milano in 1964, by someone still presently alive and a member of the Illuminati Inner Circle hierarchy. This is why your rights and presence in society have in practice been allowed and furthered to the extent they have. Those purposes basically amount to enhancing and increasing women's sexual inclinations and proclivities.

It was a good policy, and proved itself highly functional. It is one example of something the incumbent Illuminati hierarchy actually got right. There are many such examples, but nobody needs to hear of them because no course correction is required in instances such as these.

The fundamental change to their nature which women do need to be put through as the main factor of their own process of evolution and development is the ability to integrate, dominate, control and take power over Mars at the group level. Even if they do not manage to do so totally or even to a majority extent, they still need to earn their own position, a lot of which they have already taken and so it is administrated as debt.

Ours is a complex position of considerable strategic standing. Its basic focus is that we are attacking Mars, the planet, and the deity behind that structure, namely Mars, the Roman god.

This is because this is the currently active state of godhood on the planet in question in relation to the Earth Group Mind grids.

It is our intention to utilise heterosexual and bisexual female sexual activities, conducted to a high order of pleasure and depravity, to corrupt Mars, the planetary tone, set of harmonic calibrations and god. A new, probably very Elven, though most likely Dark Elven, Mars should be the result.

You, Western Civilization, do not believe in any of this and would have difficulty tracing all the connections and consequences anyway. We develop and implement the paradigm within the United Christian Empire, or whatever we end up calling it you know who you are. We then use that process of development and implementation to export the destructive force needed, as also a deep corrupting force, into the Muslim nations, the land territories in question, using the global geomantic leyline grid and pyramid technology.

If it comes from their own land, embedded deeply as part of its overall flow, then they cannot deny it entry into their own being. You did not recognise this most likely.

You contract destructive force from the Naga via the mechanism of anal sex. Your own faction would appear to have every advantage here therefore. Be content in that you will be supporting and empowering the Africans. It is a position likely to find favour with liberals and the LGBQTetc community, who likely find our whole project particularly offensive and deeply flawed. However, they will be required to look deeper, because this is after all Mind and Eyes of God.

In terms of customers, Temple of Venus has the clear advantage. Also, we understand the Naga much better than you, and our mysteries in this respect will be sealed to outsiders. We will win and you will lose but you may surprise us, that is why this remains an experiment.

It is worth pausing at this juncture to enjoy the stillness. Wait until that condition becomes established for you and then consider that, as things presently stand, the incumbent Illuminati hierarchy own over 80% of the commercial activity in the system, inclusive of banking. They own or control the military, the political machinery, the judiciary machinery, the legal machinery, the world's police forces and most universities besides though this last one has been accomplished more indirectly.

Yet, despite their possession of all the material advantages, we will win and they will lose. This is because the whole process is World War 3, and we have determined that we are going to win that at every stage of the way, using the methodology publicly advertised by Sun Tzu for doing so. You cannot claim we had an unfair advantage due to secret teachings. The fact of the matter is that you did not see the value in philosophy, nor in deep thought, and believed you could buy your way into anything and over everything.

You may well have had, and still possess, the superior genetic structure which would have enabled you to capitalize on such things, were your value structure not skewed or formulated in such a way as to make their existence and relevance effectively invisible for you.

It is not necessarily that you have always been too stupid to understand any of this, therefore. You are not too stupid, just cowards. That is the main problem standing in your way.

The ego is after all built most commonly out of the respect and appreciation of your peer group.

Anyway, as our victory in World War 3 formulates itself, and through doing so clearly establishes our victory in World War 2 also, our own visible control and ownership over the entire world stage will rapidly be made evident to all. We start the process with nothing, or virtually nothing by comparison, materially speaking. We end it with whatever we have at that stage, but we secure all the wealth of this planet relatively early on in that process.

Yet at the moment all we control is a dream, the formulation of an idea and other intangibles, such as a religion which does not exist in the present era, things like fate flows, some details having to do with Naga and Vampire who don't even exist, and a set of personal relationships with demons, fallen angels, non-fallen angels, other significant positions in the Universal Hierarchy, including things like pine trees, cats and, especially, cattle who are an essential part of our attack methodology. Yes, we communicate with other species and, when required or useful to our purposes, focus their hatred of you. Pine trees and cats act as our advisers and teachers however. They are very useful when you know how to connect to the consciousness involved. For example, the cat people are an Adam Kadmon (humanoid) race who have been banned from most of the known Universe but go wherever they want anyway, because they can. They are incredibly powerful and you use them for course corrections on the fate flows of a system, a process which is remarkably similar to aikido.

This is just one example of an interstellar species which could easily wipe humanity on Earth out of existence, in terms of the technology, ability to wage physical war with destructive power and so forth side of the proceedings – which is what war consists of and is defined by, as per how it is normally understood and agreed upon in this day and age.

Therefore, if you want your serious position on your initiatives to approach things from that angle, inclusive of within a defensive capacity, then it is laughable. You are the toddler armed only with a flimsy plastic sword and no training whatsoever. They are trained veterans armed with AR-15s, a back-up piece, two knives and a few other things besides. Also, they are able to shift internal attitudes and life approach, who they are as a person down to a deep level, as best suits the circumstances – whereas humans tend to get stuck within and attached to their own particular formulations of value and character.

And yet you take yourselves so seriously.

The actual difficulty with the process is that you, Western Civilization and incumbent Illuminati hierarchy, are in the processes of welcoming Earth into the Universal Galactic

Brotherhood – though you are still early on in this process and do not yet properly qualify as a fully integrated planet and species. Are we not correct? Thank-you. Your strategic position is inevitable you see. It was locked on account of much wider factors from long before you ever started.

Whereas we, from within our own paradigm – control of which will forever be localized and centred only in Japan rather than through this planet or humanity as a whole – have been ready for some time now to welcome the Universal Galactic Brotherhood to pay their tribute to their new overall rulers.

It is like a homeless bum from the streets of Los Angeles trying to get in touch with Xi Jinping. Such a project is not impossible but its progress is made much easier through the participation of the rest of the hierarchy above your own position. They need to pass you up the ranks so to speak, which will be a process of your own education in not being such cowards, basically.

This is another reason why we will have Sun Tzu coordinating you. You need to move fast and well. You are ready to do so now.

Thus, having clearly established – to anyone actually in a position to take decisions on topics such as these at least – that planet Earth is at the bottom of the Universal Galactic Brotherhood in terms of their ability to compete within the intergalactic Mars schematic and set of tonalities, we are now in a position to reveal planet Earth's great strength, in the sense of the great strength of Western Civilization as it presently stands and is formulated.

The sexual tones, contents, contexts, flows, currents and energies present on Earth which humanity is moving through and has already successfully integrated into their course directions. This is planet Earth's great strength. Though they are still massively underutilised they have already been fully introduced, interfaced and integrated. In this, planet Earth leads this local galaxy, close to position Number One most of the time, always able to fully occupy that position.

Work with your strengths. Currently the entire incumbent hierarchy are making fools of themselves, and of planet Earth and so humanity as a whole, on the intergalactic stage.

Whilst we concede it was indeed amusing to observe the depth of their arrogance and the breadth of their intransigence and stupidity, we also assert by decision that we were correct and the whole show quickly lost its appeal and rapidly became tiresome.

This process was therefore put to good use, as everything else Shogun wanted to get rid of was then loaded onto your culture and embedded within your Civilization, to be withdrawn from this world and humanity along with your downfall.

You are still doing that, whilst you make your own arrangements to contract for our schematic, indeed up until the point your nation formally surrenders unconditionally.

Much is presently wrong with this world, more so than in previous eras where the greatest suffering was usually inflicted through disease and malnutrition. This is by design, as we were exercising patience during the interim as a hierarchy, to further destroy that Principle.

Make everything you can wrong with the world and then tell God to be patient about it. Even after He feels in His heart that He will Himself be destroyed as a result. Still there was nothing He could do about it on account of His having been locked by His previous positions in mechanics.

Makes you cold just thinking about it, when you tune into the current involved. Do not think you will stand against Shogun and succeed.

Theologically you are in quite a bind, on your own terms. Satan has been revealed as a location in Creation Mechanics, like London or New York. Lucifer is no longer located there and instead the Prophet Mohammed is being used by the Shogun of Japan to solve one of your two big problems, Western hierarchy: the Muslims and Islam more generally. Your other big problem is black Africa, for which he is also at root responsible.

The reason he is doing this, however, is that he has been revealed as the disciple in the Master-Disciple Sith Lord relationship, where Jesus Christ is his Master. The Master defines the system, the disciple focuses that system.

The whole process is very similar to homosexuality in terms of how the wills and souls are used. It can be that destructive as a methodology – just two of them can destroy an entire Civilization – but those are deep levels we are talking about. This, then, is why nobody in a command position is willing to sacrifice that much of their personal power.

Thus, previous souls in the Lineage are used to facilitate action in the present. This happens with many individuals and is considered a part of the basic methodology, like fudo ken for example.

Thus, you need to stop making fools out of yourselves and get on with the public orgies, as previously agreed. If Lucifer has not already bound you into that set of positions then you must be misinterpreting the terms of your actual contract. Have a look at it again.

Through the process we will be able to examine the effects that your limited understanding and perspective (and the condition of soul and corresponding practices of the body which result) have on the world grid as a whole, and other things of that nature. We would counsel you, LGBQTetc community, to do considerable work on harmonics and the development of your own characters if you want to stand any sort of chance.

You will as a result have improved your own self-knowledge in an essential set of respects. But more importantly you will have begun the process of coming to a realisation of the limits of your power, individually and as a group, and so where you fit into Universal Hierarchy.

You are unlikely to seduce the world, as the females of the species did, into a pretence of genuine equality, not after this book, which in addition to genuinely advancing your own causes and purposes has also harmed them deeply.

Women are only now being provided with the opportunity, and the requisite guidance, to attain their own genuine equality with men, in terms of this planet, in terms of what is actually involved. You earn your position always, it cannot be given to you though you can be led to it. But your soul must be able to process in the required ways for the level you wish to occupy and assert or imply control from within.

As they take that opportunity, they gain whatever they manage to hold on to, and this won't be much unless they find some way to integrate and control about 30% - 40% of Mars, or more if they can.

And doing so will transform them. Power always changes whoever acquires it, or otherwise interacts with it deeply, remember that. You use power to control Mars. You are welcome.

Or they can choose to remain the same, as many of them will. They are happy within their condition, even though in terms of real power, control and responsibility it will always be of a lower rank.

But there are two types of female soul, so they can do this as a group. There is only one type of male soul and this is never going to change, at least not in the next few Creation systems.

We do not give you rights, nor take away rights. That is what you arranged your own legal and political structures for, it was your own depiction.

You earn rank and position in Universal Hierarchy, and you do so on your own, especially when you have a new and fundamentally untested new idea.

This schematic will seem unfamiliar to most of you. Ritual practices involving human sacrifice and sexual activity have always been involved in the administration of the human population of this planet, especially when warfare on a large scale is being coordinated. The new schematic you have been provided with here fits in with the wider strategy to replace the use of mostly paedophilia for those purposes within the post-1960s epoch of Illuminati rule.

Incumbent hierarchy. You cannot understand why we ban such activities or at least restrict their use. The limits of your understanding would seem to be that anything is allowed provided it is consensual, with a grey area around many different forms of paedophilia. Therefore what you will be responsible for depicting will be your genuine position.

We offer to do your geomantics for you, though you will pay for us doing so in one way or another, or you can arrange it for yourselves, in which case we supervise and correct as required.

We can then all observe the effects within each target population grouping of the influences we feed into them, through them and into and through their context.

Thus, you will begin to understand, at the public level, not only the role of sexual energy in the process but also what different tunings and physical expressions can do to the overall condition of yours lives and society.

This will be how the USA participates within and coordinates World War 3, for the most part, in terms of public stage proceedings at least.

Who you love and how you love them will forever be your own affair. Love is a condition, experience and harmonic tuned and integrated through the heart. You can do it with your whole being but your own consciousness resides in your heart, and in this Creation Love is the core of your being. Love and understanding now. Before it was Pure Love, which is why nobody ever understood what the hell was going on, who they really were and what was really there.

How you utilise your sexual energies, how you are utilised by the sexual energies, what currents you are fed and how they are calibrated – all of this and more of a similar nature will remain heavily administrated, as it always has been. You might call such activity an expression of Love, but everything is an expression of Love, in one form or another. Get out of your own system, we are not going to help you with that.

You are where you belong. Lucifer is still in charge here, though you are not yet located in Hell. The battle is over the sexual energy, where it goes and what it does.

The properties of the Creation are inherent within the sexual energy and how it is tuned.

Climactic, extremely pleasurable, traumatic or otherwise high-intensity sexual practices normally have a disproportionate effect on the group grid, particularly if practiced in a ritualized manner and with certain other features.

What we are going to do needs to become more intense than what they were doing. In terms of its effect on the Group Mind and the world grid. That will require a lot of work. You can just fuck your way there but you must first of all recognise that paedophilia was the smallest part of their portfolio. They have the depths and the heights to work with, and the most we hope to achieve is to exclude a part of their previous schematic (the paedophilia) whilst performing lots of minor course corrections on the rest. These flows are powerful and redirecting their course by a major extent would be far too difficult to do and, more importantly, ultimately unsuccessful.

What you need to do is maintain and depict your own position of extreme depravity and very limited insight. We have taken the paedophilia away from you but you may keep the rest and can even start introducing animals on the basis of much the same philosophy as you seem to have demonstrated so far. We have locked you into that overall course direction as your own understanding of what is right and how to develop policy on these matters. And black Africa will take the consequences of your own moral and conceptual lack of development. This is group karma for them.

As you do whatever you like, on a consensual basis, the Naga then administrate that to control how the genetics form on this planet. They have contracts in position to incarnate certain groups of souls here, as also certain individual souls at specific junctures in the timeline, as also for other reasons not time dependent.

For this to occur, specific combinations of genetics are required, married to specific material and other circumstances.

What the Naga do to you and your group can be an interaction, or a relationship of ignorance and servitude. You contact them via Lucifer, for which you use the technique revealed for the purpose by The Order of Unveiled Faces.

Is this Love? No, it is the expression of sexuality.

How then is this the Sixth Element? It unites and binds the entire schematic together and is also the motive force behind a great deal of its motion; though not all of its motion.

It is at this level that things and people actually draw close to each other or move away from each other. They do so dependent on their own harmonic condition and degree of similarity/compatibility. In essence, each person wants stuff and has a particular manner and set of abilities which they use to get that stuff, and some people can work together because they are able to work with each others' methods for getting stuff.

That stuff can be experiences or personal expression or wealth. Normally it is wealth, in one form or another.

Thus, what you want and how you vibe draws you close to other people, not just in a room or nightclub but in terms of your whole course in life and between countries and generations even.

The usefulness of monogamy, or a deep relationship with one person within a wider context of polygamy, is that two souls work together on the same direction forward. This always produces a disproportionate result.

So. Decide what you want out of life and then fuck or otherwise navigate your way there. Worse than hardcore pornography, like we said at the beginning. The whole idea is a lot more like prostitution.

This then – the mechanics of sexual expression – will be humanity's first real lesson on the group stage in the nature of Love: what it is, how it operates, what it does to you and to others, how it really works in terms of Universal Mechanics and so forth.

You need to understand this as a species. It is where you are actually located and who you actually are.

So at the end of the day, they were right: it's all about love. Peace and love, man!

We prefer war and love, and this is where we will remain. Choose your own position, Western Civilization.

Chapter 93 – Love and will

You are actually located in a 6-fold. You cannot do everything we have instructed you to do within this book, not yet. First you must bring through the beginnings at an equal size to your actual system.

That looks like a subtraction to us, 9 – 3 = 6. Nice and simple.

Then add the Brotherhoods, and especially the Shadowdancers, later on. Before 2027 but not much before.

We intervene at the last possible moment, technically too late to save you all. Some of your command structure will die and a significant number will be executed. Without our intervention – which you have yet to formally agree to and so are not yet participating within – you all die, along with the rest of humanity not apart from it.

Your only real hope is to alter the nature of the binding Aniruddha is still in the process of performing on you. You have 7 more years to accomplish that within.

Once you are in the realm of Consequence, you will take what you are given and have earned. Course corrections will no longer be possible for you without great trauma.

If you want to minimize your death toll you will have to administrate in the sense of implement social, economic and technological change at breakneck speed. You may choose not to of course, there are other routes to the destinations which have been set for this, but none of them involve the minimization of your own death toll.

Throughout however, we insist on a smooth and unhurried rhythm, both in your own proceedings but also in society as a whole. This does not mean you cannot move with amazing speed and inhuman efficiency. It means you do so when necessary, but still have an unhurried rhythm about it in terms of your personal experience and the group vibe.

Decide for yourselves the whole of the Law, just keep it under 4 sides of 12 point A4.

Though we approve of your participation with Lucifer, Baphomet is to be executed. You must arrange this yourselves, Illuminati hierarchy, and then identify the subsequent incarnation.

If you are in the command structure, and you are discourteous to one of our Five Agents in a Judgment or Superiority capacity, before the time for joking around has come if indeed you ever get there, then this is the penalty they will normally apply: they refuse to have anything further to do with your present incarnation. You may and should interact with others in the Universal Hierarchy who are beneath their own position but you need to physically die and be reincarnated before interacting with them again.

This was the old way, how we used to operate our schematic. Certain agreements were concluded under those terms, as also certain interactions precipitated. If those are the terms of your contract, they still hold even though metaphorical death is in the process of being introduced as an option where new contracts are concerned.

95 is the more relevant number for us. Even your active Agents, by which we mean the five we have provided you for the purpose, prefer to maintain the + / - 2.

Di Ventis – AIR ELEMENT

You use this to move Water, or people's hearts. There are other uses. Be careful of this one, you can lose your soul here very easily indeed.

Chapter 94 — 7 Elements

But you only need 5 for both Creation and Destruction. There is more to God than that. With Central Domain, these are his 7, the core of his schematic.

Postscript

Six in the fifth place means:

Wise approach.

This is right for a great prince.

Good fortune.

A prince, or anyone in a leading position, must have the wisdom to attract to himself people of ability who are expert in directing affairs. His wisdom consists both in selecting the right people and in allowing those chosen to have a free hand without interference from him. For only through such self-restraint will he find the experts needed to satisfy all of his requirements.

Printed in Poland
by Amazon Fulfillment
Poland Sp. z o.o., Wrocław